Praise for Patricia Potter and her bestselling novels

"A master storyteller."
—Mary Jo Putney

"Pat Potter proves herself a gifted writer as artisan, creating a rich fabric of strong characters whose wit and intellect will enthrall even as their adventures entertain."
—*BookPage*

"Patricia Potter has a special gift for giving an audience a first-class romantic story line."
—*Affaire de Coeur*

"When a historical romance [gets] the Potter treatment, the story line is pure action and excitement, and the characters are wonderful."
—*BookBrowser*

Dancing with a Rogue

"Once again, Potter . . . proves that she's adept at penning both enthralling historicals and captivating contemporary novels."
—*Booklist* (starred review)

"Gabriel and Merry are a delightful pair . . . Patricia Potter has provided a character-driven story that her audience will enjoy."
—*Midwest Book Review*

continued . . .

"An entirely engrossing novel by this talented and versatile author." —*Romance Reviews Today*

"Interesting and fresh." —*Affaire de Coeur*

The Diamond King

"The story line is loaded with action yet enables the audience to understand what drives both lead characters and several key secondary players . . . a robust romantic adventure . . . [a] powerful tale." —*BookBrowser*

The Heart Queen

"This is a book that is difficult to put down for any reason. Simply enjoy." —*Rendezvous*

"Exciting . . . powerful . . . charming . . . [a] pleasant page-turner." —*Midwest Book Review*

"Potter is a very talented author . . . if you are craving excitement, danger, and a hero to die for, you won't want to miss this one." —*All About Romance*

The Perfect Family

"The reader loses all sense of time as they become entangled in a web of mystery Ms. Potter spins in *The Perfect Family* . . . Flawless characterizations . . . You are holding a work of art when you pick up a book by Patricia Potter." —*Rendezvous*

The Black Knave

"Well-drawn, memorable characters, compelling action, and Machiavellian political intrigue add to a story that Potter's many fans will be waiting for." —*Library Journal*

"I couldn't put it down! This one's a keeper! Pat Potter writes romantic adventure like nobody else."
—Joan Johnston

"A fabulous romantic tale of intrigue and daring . . . will keep the reader spellbound through each twist and turn."
—*Rendezvous*

"A rousing tale of intrigue, danger, and forbidden romance that engaged my interest from first to last page . . . a most satisfying read." —*All About Romance*

Starcatcher

"Patricia Potter has created a lively Scottish tale that has just the right amount of intrigue, romance, and conflict."
—*Literary Journal*

"Once again, Pat Potter demonstrates why she is considered one of the best writers of historical novels on the market today . . . Ms. Potter scores big-time with this fabulously fine fiction that will be devoured by fans of this genre." —*BookBrowser*

Beloved
Impostor

PATRICIA POTTER

BERKLEY SENSATION, NEW YORK

THE BERKLEY PUBLISHING GROUP
Published by the Penguin Group
Penguin Group (USA) Inc.
375 Hudson Street, New York, New York 10014, USA
Penguin Group (Canada), 10 Alcorn Avenue, Toronto, Ontario M4V 3B2, Canada
(a division of Pearson Penguin Canada Inc.)
Penguin Books Ltd., 80 Strand, London WC2R 0RL, England
Penguin Group Ireland, 25 St. Stephen's Green, Dublin 2, Ireland (a division of
Penguin Books Ltd.)
Penguin Group (Australia), 250 Camberwell Road, Camberwell, Victoria 3124, Australia
(a division of Pearson Australia Group Pty. Ltd.)
Penguin Books India Pvt. Ltd., 11 Community Centre, Panchsheel Park, New Delhi—110 017,
India
Penguin Group (NZ), Cnr. Airborne and Rosedale Roads, Albany, Auckland 1310, New Zealand
(a division of Pearson New Zealand Ltd.)
Penguin Books (South Africa) (Pty.) Ltd., 24 Sturdee Avenue, Rosebank, Johannesburg 2196,
South Africa

Penguin Books Ltd., Registered Offices: 80 Strand, London WC2R 0RL, England

This is a work of fiction. Names, characters, places, and incidents either are the product of the author's imagination or are used fictitiously, and any resemblance to actual persons, living or dead, business establishments, events, or locales is entirely coincidental.

BELOVED IMPOSTOR

A Berkley Sensation Book / published by arrangement with the author

PRINTING HISTORY
Berkley Sensation edition / September 2004

Copyright © 2004 by Patricia Potter.
Cover art by Gary Blythe.
Cover design by George Long.
Interior text design by Julie Rogers.

ISBN: 0-425-19801-4

BERKLEY® SENSATION
Berkley Sensation Books are published by The Berkley Publishing Group,
a division of Penguin Group (USA) Inc.,
375 Hudson Street, New York, New York 10014.
BERKLEY SENSATION and the "B" design
are trademarks belonging to Penguin Group (USA) Inc.

PRINTED IN THE UNITED STATES OF AMERICA

10 9 8 7 6 5 4 3 2 1

Prologue

Scotland, 1420

As thunder roared and lightning flashed outside the tower room, the old woman keened over the still body lying in the bed.

Her lady's face was as pale as the death hovering about her. She had not died as planned, but she was dying nonetheless.

Siobhan Campbell had raised Lady Mary, had watched her happily marry a Maclean, only to discover her husband was a monster.

Lady Mary was as dear to her as if she were her own child.

The young lass had always been intrigued by her nurse's "second sight" and had often asked Siobhan to tell her fortune. Only last year Siobhan had looked at her lady's hand and seen death. To her bitter regret, she'd said nothing. She had been called witch too many times. Lady Mary had always protected her, but if she foretold a death . . .

She had earlier warned her lady against marrying the Maclean to no avail. Lady Mary had been dazzled by the lord's dark good looks and had laughed at her warnings.

Bitterness and regret flooded Siobhan. She had failed to protect her charge. She looked down at her lady again. Lady Mary had been married five years, and there had been no children. Her husband wanted an heir at any cost, even the life of the lady who loved him.

But he couldn't be seen as at blame. He had not wanted a feud with the Campbells. He had chained her to a rock to drown in the cold sea. He could then claim a tragic accident: his wife wandered on the beach and was caught by a high tide.

It would have happened as planned had not fishermen rescued her at the risk of their own lives. Her head was all that had remained above water. A few more moments and . . .

They had carried her back to the Campbells, to Dunstaffnage. But in the end, it hadn't mattered. Lady Mary's heart was broken, her spirit destroyed by terror and betrayal. She had simply given up. Fever was doing the rest.

Siobhan leaned down. "They will pay, my lady," she whispered. "They will pay for this."

She held Lady Mary's hand until the last breath came. She had said she would call Lady Mary's father when the time came, but he had been as guilty as the Maclean. He, too, had wanted the marriage. He, too, had ignored her warnings.

Siobhan leaned over and touched her lady's cheek. Then she stood, trod slowly to the window, and looked toward the Maclean holdings many miles away. Rain pounded against the glass window. Lightning lit the land below. Still, men were mounting below. There would be retribution this night.

She opened the window and braced herself against the rush of wild wind laced with rain. The room went dark as the wind blew out the candles. She lifted her arm in the direction of the Maclean holdings.

No one would take Lady Mary's place. Not ever.

She closed her eyes and concentrated. She knew her powers. She had kept them hidden for fear of being burned at the stake. But they were strong within her, and never more so than now.

Her fingers clenched into a fist as she shouted the words into a wild night. "No bride of a Maclean will live long or happily, and every Maclean will suffer for it."

The sky exploded with lightning as if to acknowledge the curse. Thunder rocked the castle. The words echoed in the room, then were seized by the wind.

Tears mixed with rain, yet she knew a certain triumph. Her lady would be avenged by centuries of Maclean grief.

Chapter 1

❧

Scotland, 1509 A.D.

"No!"

The cry tore from Felicia Campbell's throat as she stared at the message from her uncle.

He would not do this to her. He could not do this.

Her hands crushed the parchment as if doing so would erase the words.

She never thought her uncle—and guardian—would agree to a marriage for her with a man more than three times her age. She had met this particular earl once. This chosen husband. He was a man of great girth and dirty hair, and an arrogant and cruel manner. She remembered too well how his eyes had rested on her small breasts in a way that made her shudder.

The words in the letter were stamped on her mind. *"The King wishes this marriage. It is a good alliance for the Campbells. You will be escorted to Edinburgh in a fortnight's time for the formal betrothal.*

Dread as well as despair knotted her stomach. She was being sold for expediency.

As a ward, she knew she had little choice in marriage. She was no beauty, but her uncle was one of the most influential men in Scotland. And that made her not only acceptable but highly sought. An alliance with the Campbells was valuable.

Still, she had always believed her uncle would try to choose a good man as well as a wealthy one. Angus Campbell had taken her into the household after the death of his sister, Eloise, and her husband, John Campbell, of the Loudin Campbells.

But Angus Campbell was rarely at Dunstaffnage. He spent most of his time at the Scottish court in Edinburgh. When he was at home, he was indifferent toward her, but never cruel.

Felicia closed her eyes. She wanted to please her uncle. He and Jamie were all the family she had. He had taken her in and provided for her needs. But she would not marry the Earl of Morneith.

She wandered down the chilled corridor of the keep. She had to see Janet, her friend, who had retired to her chamber to read her own letter. But Janet's was from her beloved, while Felicia's had contained a sentence worse than death. The two messages had arrived together, both by special messenger from Edinburgh.

Felicia knocked at Janet's door, then opened it. Janet sat on a chair and held the letter in clenched hands. "Jamie will be a few days longer in London," she said. "We will have to delay the wedding."

"I'm sorry," Felicia said, desperately wishing she had such a problem. To love the man she was to marry. What a wonder that would be.

Janet and her family had been visiting Dunstaffnage to complete the marriage formalities and await the arrival of Jamie, who had been in London on an errand for the king. Then Felicia's uncle had been suddenly summoned to Edinburgh by King James, and Janet's father left as well. Janet had begged to stay another week to work on her wedding gown.

Janet looked up from the letter to meet Felicia's gaze. "What is wrong? What did your uncle say? Is it anything about Jamie?"

Wordlessly, Felicia handed her letter to Janet.

Janet's face clouded as she read it, then asked in her soft, gentle voice, "What are you going to do?"

Felicia shrugged hopelessly.

Janet reached out a hand to her. "I wish . . . I wish you could be as happy as I am."

"I am glad you are. Jamie loves you." She tried to smile, though her heart was breaking into a hundred pieces.

Janet didn't say anything. She had also been at grand events the earl attended. She had seen him as well. And had probably heard tales of his debauchery. "What can you do?"

Felicia shook her head.

"If only Jamie were here—"

"He isn't," Felicia said bleakly. Janet believed Jamie could solve every problem. She herself had, as well. But how could he defy the king?

"The letter said you must be ready in a fortnight."

Two weeks before my life ends. Her mind worked frantically. She had always known that her one worth to her uncle was marriage, an alliance. But she also knew that she was plain at best and not much of an enticement to prospective husbands. She had hoped . . .

She didn't know what she had hoped. But she certainly hadn't expected him to arrange a marriage with someone so . . . appalling. Her uncle said in the letter that the king wanted this marriage, but she also knew the king needed her uncle.

If only Jamie were here. He was more brother than cousin. He had lost two sisters in their infancy and had readily taken to the role of her protector since the first day she came to Dunstaffnage as a heartbroken and confused child of five.

Her uncle had approved. It relieved him of the responsibility. And as long as Jamie performed well in military arts, Angus Campbell paid little attention to his outside activities.

He did not know—at least Felicia did not believe he knew—that his only son had taught Felicia to fight, to use the bow, the sword. Nor did he care that Jamie had taught Felicia to read, when Angus believed women should not bother with such things.

Amazingly, she was very good at the former and even better at the latter, a fact that had amused her cousin, as had her interest in healing. Nairna, the healer, had been her friend and taught her the healing arts.

Jamie had treated her as an equal, or almost as an equal. He hadn't cared that she was plain, that her red hair was untamable and that she had few of the womanly attributes that most men admired in a woman.

Morneith would care little about her unorthodox skills. He would want a wife to serve his needs, to produce more heirs.

Again her mind went to Jamie. But what could he do? She knew neither King James nor her uncle were men to be defied. She would not want Jamie to lose his head for her.

She must help herself. And she had only two weeks to do so.

"Felicia?"

She tried to smile, but knew she failed miserably. She wanted to cry, but Campbell women did not cry. "I will not," she said again. "I will not marry him."

"But the king—"

"He can do nothing if I am not here." Ideas were already forming in her mind. Anything would be better than marriage to the earl. Anything!

She would go to a convent first and ask for sanctuary.

A convent!

That was the answer. She would far prefer that to being wed to a beast.

There was one not twenty-five miles away.

She would pack tonight. Ride out tomorrow. She and Janet often went riding, though there was usually a guard with them. She would have to find a way to distract the guard.

Would Janet help? Her friend was shy, even timid, respectful of duty and authority. Yet she had a sweetness and loyalty that won hearts. Felicia had often puzzled over their friendship because they were so opposite. But mayhap that was also the attraction.

Felicia would lose even *her* friendship then.

She took the letter from Janet.

Janet stared at her, dismay written on her face. "How can you leave?"

Felicia spoke rapidly, spewing words before thinking them through. "You and I go riding with a groom each morning. Perhaps I can trick him and ride toward the closest convent."

"They will not take you without a dowry," Janet said. "I know my father had to pay one for my cousin."

"I have some jewelry from my mother," Felicia said.

"They would not defy the king." Janet tried another tack.

Her friend was right. Few in Scotland would. If she were to escape, she must flee to outside the king's—and Morneith's—reach. If she could reach Jamie in London, he might be able to help her flee to France without anyone finding out.

"Will you help me?" she asked Janet. "You would have to go riding with me. You can take one of the slower mares, then you can say I fled. You could not keep up."

"I wish Jamie were here," Janet said.

"I am glad he is not. He would be risking his life if he defied the king."

"And he would," Janet said. "He would defy both his father and the king for you." She hesitated, then said in a small voice, "Of course, I will help."

Felicia felt terrible. She knew what it took for Janet to utter those words. She wanted to withdraw the request, but she needed Janet's help too badly. She would make sure no blame came to her friend.

"I will have to sew my jewels in my cloak and decide what I can take with me."

"I will help you," Janet said, her voice more sure now that she had made the decision to help.

Still, Felicia saw the apprehension in her friend's eyes. Guilt as sharp as a knife thrust deep inside her.

But she knew she would never be allowed to leave the castle walls alone. She also knew she had to move quickly.

SHE and Janet supped alone with only her maid in attendance. She had no desire to dine in the great hall with the rowdy men at arms. Not tonight.

They usually dined well, and tonight was no exception. Felicia treasured every bite, knowing that she probably would not have such fare again soon. Mutton and capons, salmon, pears and apples, and freshly baked bread and tarts. Her uncle insisted on having a good cook, since he often entertained other Highland families and even the king on occasion. The cook, Sarah, was rightfully proud, even arrogant, and refused to allow anyone in the kitchen other than her chosen helpers.

Felicia had attempted to visit and learn more about the kitchen, but she was always rebuffed. She'd been rebuffed by everyone when she wanted to be helpful. Everyone but the healer and Jamie.

Apprehension whittled away at Felicia's appetite, but

she knew she needed to eat. She would eat well on the morn as well, for she would be running for her life.

Janet darted sympathetic glances at Felicia as she took one bite, then another. After she had eaten all she could, she took the remaining bread and wrapped it in a piece of cloth. She would take it with her tomorrow.

She dismissed her maid for the night, then she and Janet stitched jewels into her cloak.

When they were through, Felicia reached for Janet's hand. "Thank you. I will see that you are not blamed."

They clasped each other, then Janet went to her room.

Felicia went to the window of her room and looked out at the hills she loved. Everything safe in her life had just shattered into small pieces. Should she try to stay and make the best of the proposed marriage? Then she thought of the earl again, the cruelty and lust in his eyes. He'd already had three wives, and rumors abounded as to the fates of each.

Jamie and Nairna had taught her to value herself. And now she was considered no more than an item to be bargained for.

RORY Maclean stood on the cliff, looking out over the sea, his mood as cold and bleak as the waves smashing against the rocks.

He had returned four days earlier, and already the place was sapping his soul. Ten years away, and yet it seemed he had walked these cliffs yesterday, mourning the lass he had loved above all else.

He wished he were anywhere else.

If not for duty, he would be captaining his own merchant vessel in warmer climes. He was a seaman and trader by choice. He'd long wanted to cut the ties that bound him to a legacy of hatred and bloodshed. He wanted to be away from this place that haunted him.

Duty had brought him back. It was the only thing that could.

His clan was in peril. Campbells had been raiding small villages and stealing cattle since his father died two years earlier. His older half brother, Patrick, had disappeared into France. His younger half brother, Lachlan, was no warrior.

Word of his father's death and brother's disappearance had finally reached him in Leith a year after it was sent. Douglas, the family steward, had apparently despaired of finding Patrick and called for him. It was an urgent plea he could not ignore, however much he wished he could.

He had also learned news in France that would have brought him home in any event. It bode ill for the Macleans.

His gaze went to the Sound of Mull. He gazed at the rock that some said caused all the Maclean misfortunes, including the deaths of Rory's two wives.

It was on that rock decades ago that one of his ancestors chained his Campbell wife, hoping that the tide would drown her. She lived for a short time after, but a Campbell curse, and war, had followed the Macleans ever since.

"Rory?"

He whirled around.

Douglas had approached so quietly he hadn't noticed. It was not a good thing. As a lad raiding Campbells, he could hear the rustle of grass. Another memory he would rather forget.

"We are pleased you have returned," Douglas said.

"You did no' give me much choice."

"We have missed you."

Rory didn't say anything. He did not miss this place, though he did miss friends.

"Rory, you have to wed again."

"The devil I do," he snapped back. His gaze went back to that accursed rock.

"It is a myth, Rory."

"Tell Maggie that. And Anne. *If* you can bring them back to life."

Douglas was silent. "I know you loved Maggie."

"I loved both my wives," Rory corrected, though that was not exactly true. Maggie had his heart. Anne had his loyalty and gratitude.

"We need an heir."

"I have two brothers." He had vowed never to marry again. He had lost two wives. He did not want to inflict a similar fate on another woman unwise and unlucky enough to accept him.

Patrick would return. Everyone but Rory thought he was dead. Patrick was too strong, too wise, too loved to die. He had always been their father's favorite. He had been the heir, something that Rory had never regretted. He'd always looked up to Patrick, always followed his lead. Until the day that Maggie died and he decided to carve out his own path. He had always been lured to the sea and the family's source of wealth. Knowing his grief, his father had backed his maiden voyage as a trader. That was ten years ago.

No sense in thinking about that now. He had responsibilities. But they would not include marriage.

"I do not have to do anything I do not wish to do," Rory reminded Douglas.

" 'Tis not a matter of wishes. We need an heir," Douglas insisted.

If he had not saved Rory's life more than once, Rory would have cut him short. But tolerance did not mean compliance. "Then my brothers will have to produce one."

"We canna take that chance. If you die without an heir, the Campbells will smell weakness. We could not stand against them."

Rory silently, reluctantly, agreed. It was the one reason he'd returned. Not to sire an heir but to create a peace between the two clans. His father had been a strong laird who had held the clan together. But there were conflicting interests, disputed property, feuds even within the clan. And that weakness made them prey for predators. He wondered if now was the time to tell Douglas what he had heard, but it was still rumor. He needed proof. And he did *not* want to assume the position of laird.

"I will not usurp Patrick's place," he said.

"He has been gone three years now," Douglas said. "There's been no word, no message, no demand for ransom."

"I will hear no more of weddings and heirs. I am far happier at sea than I am in this cursed place. There are too many ghosts here. I tire of war, cousin. I tire of these feuds that go back centuries. I tire of vengeance creating more vengeance. I tire of politics and the constant shift of loyalties and betrayals. I want no part of them. I returned because you said the situation was desperate. Now I find you want an heir rather than a leader." He couldn't keep the disgust from his voice. He was ready, in truth, to mount a horse and ride back to Leith where his ship and crew awaited his orders.

If he did not return within a month, Sven, his first mate, was to take command and sail to France with a cargo of wool.

Douglas said nothing else, but Rory knew from his expression that he had not given up.

Rory turned the conversation to another matter. "You said there have been frequent raids?"

"Aye. Campbells burned several of our outlying villages and stole the cattle. I told our tenants that they would not be required to pay their rent this year. I hope you feel that is satisfactory. With no one here to guide me . . ."

"No one but Lachlan has been here for two years," Rory interrupted, "and you have managed well. I am not quite sure why it was so urgent that I return."

"The Campbells are getting bolder. I have sent protests to the king, but I do not have your influence. You are the designated heir. Not Lachlan. He would not have the authority, nor the allegiance of the clan. You must apply for recognition. Until you officially become laird, we have no real power."

"We have little power anyway, compared to the Campbells," Rory said wryly.

"That is why you must marry well. There is a lass, Janet Cameron, who would bring a strong alliance to our clan."

"She is to marry James Campbell. All of Edinburgh knows that."

"But young Campbell is in England. There is time—"

"To steal another man's bride? I think not."

"The Camerons have been friends in the past. They would no' resist. If your brother or you had been here, it would have been a natural alliance."

Rory drove his clenched fist into the palm of his other hand. "I said no, and I will hear no more about the matter."

Douglas stilled, evidently realizing he had gone too far.

"Then the Campbells. What should we do about the raids?"

Rory knew what he said next would determine his leadership. If, in truth, he even wanted it. Which he did not. It was being foisted upon him, and on his infernal sense of duty.

"Arrange a truce. Petition the king for peace. Even the Campbells would not defy him."

"They will not agree unless they feel we can bite as well. And our Macleans want vengeance."

"Then they will be disappointed."

"And the destruction of our villages?"

"I am not going to destroy their innocents because they destroyed ours," he said curtly. "Not if we can accomplish peace through negotiations."

"They will see only weakness." Douglas paused. "It means more than that. Our people need those cattle. They will starve without them."

Douglas was right. He would need some threat to bargain with. He finally nodded. "But cattle only. I will have no killing."

Douglas nodded. "It will be done. I will arrange a raiding party tonight. Do you want to go?"

"Aye." It was necessary if he was to take the role of chief. Only then could he lead the Macleans into some accommodation with the Campbells. He had to prove himself. And he would ensure there was no repeat of the horror of years ago, a night that had never left his consciousness. Tonight no woman or child would be harmed.

Perhaps he could make a truce with the Campbells, then retire to sea again. It was a lonely business, the sea, but the challenges took away some of the pain that was always with him. The loneliness. The regret.

He never quite stopped thinking of Margaret—Maggie—his first wife, his love. She had been lovely. Small but capable of great love. She had been so excited about the birth of their first child. She would take his hand and hold it against her stomach, and they would rejoice in feeling its movement in her belly.

But then something had gone terribly wrong.

He had lost both of them. And his heart as well.

He remarried for convenience, only to find an affection he did not expect, and another sorrow. One that turned his already wounded heart to stone.

He had lived here with Maggie. The chamber he had shared with her still seemed to radiate with her presence. The scent of roses lingered even now, or perhaps it was imagination.

He could not bear to stay there. He had moved to another chamber, the stark bedchamber of his youth that held no memories of her.

But the corridors did.

He did not want to stay here.

Yet hundreds of clansmen depended on him. He couldn't run again. He would do what he had to do, then leave again for the sea. He would find a way to have Douglas named laird until his brother returned.

Patrick *would* return.

Or else he would have to turn Lachlan into an accepted laird.

Because he wouldn't, couldn't, stay here. And he most certainly would never wed again.

*W*HEN Felicia and Janet reached the stables the next morning, they were told that they could not ride, that orders had come from the captain of the guard that no one was to leave the castle grounds.

The Campbells had raided the Macleans. There was bound to be retaliation.

Felicia begged. "George, you know I ride every morning."

"Aye, I know, but William told me ye were not to leave the walls. 'Tis far too dangerous, he said."

William was her uncle's steward and no doubt had orders from him. They would have nothing to do with her safety but everything to do with ensuring she would remain at Dunstaffnage.

"Just for an hour. My mare needs exercise."

"Ye can exercise her in the bailey. Or I can gi' her a ride. I can do no better for ye, my lady."

His stubborn expression told Felicia that nothing would move him. He needed the position as head groomsman.

"I will talk to William," she said, lifting her head and trying to keep her dignity. William was not a man to be challenged. He had her uncle's full confidence, was empowered to conduct raids on his own.

"What do we do now?" Janet asked as they walked back to the tower.

"You are leaving in four days," Felicia said. "You will have an escort."

"Aye," Janet said, "but how will that—"

"I will take your place. We have the same height. The weather is cold enough that no one would be surprised if you wore a cloak that covered your hair and a tartan your face."

"But my father's men are very protective."

"I will find a way," Felicia insisted.

"But—"

"I will make sure you are drugged, so no blame will come to you," Felicia said.

Janet stared at her as if she were mad.

She probably was, but she had little choice. The very thought of coupling with the Earl of Morneith spurred her to desperate measures.

"It cannot work, Felicia."

"It must," she replied. "Please help me."

"I cannot bear the thought of you alone without protection."

"You know Jamie taught me how to use a sword and knife, and even a bow. I am not helpless."

"You may not have an opportunity to use any of them."

"Aye, you are right, but a small chance is better than none at all. I know Jamie will assist me when he knows. If only I can avoid marriage until I reach France. I know he will help me once I am away from Scotland."

Janet regarded her with wide eyes. "It is very dangerous," she said. "I could not do that."

"You could, if faced with wedding Morneith."

"You are far braver than I am," Janet said. "I just worry about you. I want you to be my sister. You are my best friend. My only true friend."

"Then will you help me?"

Janet nodded reluctantly.

"If only your escort appears in time. My uncle said he would send soldiers for me in a fortnight's time."

"They will. My father dislikes inefficiency," Janet said. "They will arrive as ordered."

Felicia reached out and took her hand. "I am so pleased Jamie chose you."

Janet smiled, her eyes lighting. "I know I am lucky that my father agreed to the match. He really wanted an alliance with the Macleans. If Patrick Maclean had not disappeared . . ."

"The Macleans are said to be a brutal clan," Felicia said. "Thank God that you and Jamie are pledged."

Janet shivered. "I am. I have heard about the curse your family placed on them. 'No Maclean bride will be happy.' "

Felicia shuddered. She had heard of the curse, too. And knew that disaster had befallen nearly every Maclean bride since it had been spoken. It was deserved, she knew. A Maclean had tried to drown a Campbell. But she never understood why the curse was against the brides and not the men, since it was a man who had been responsible for the villainous deed. It was unfair, but then everything about being a female was unfair.

They both considered the injustice of it for a moment, then Janet took her hand. "I will do whatever needs to be done."

*D*ouglas continued trying to convince his lord he should marry. On the fourth day, he agreed with Archibald that they should take matters into their own hands. "He refuses to consider a bride," Douglas told the Maclean captain of the guard.

Archibald sighed. "I feared that."

"It is important to the clan."

"Ye canna' make a man do your bidding. Particularly a Maclean."

"If he has no choice . . ."

"I do not ken your meaning," Archibald said.

"I hear Janet Cameron is visiting the Campbells. Word is she will be traveling home in four days. We can bring her here for Lord Rory."

"He will have none of it."

"But if she's taken, she would be ruined," Douglas said.

"He would have an obligation. It is said Janet Cameron is a beguiling young lady. Beautiful, well-mannered and obedient. I know Rory. He will want to protect her."

"He will have our heads."

"He yells much, but he is no' a cruel man," Douglas said. "He would know we have the clan's interest at heart. He is still mourning for Maggie. Perhaps he always will. And for the wife in Edinburgh. But we can help him realize he can be content, that the curse is naught but a myth."

"And we will have an heir," Archibald replied.

"We will have an heir, and take a measure of revenge upon the Campbells by taking young Campbell's bride. Pick your men carefully and leave tonight after we depart for a raid across the border. Malcolm and I will keep our lord occupied elsewhere."

Chapter 2

❧

THE night was perfect for a raid, though miserable for Rory and the men accompanying him. Freezing winds blew against their mantles and cloaks. Heavy, rain-swollen clouds shrouded the craggy hills in complete darkness.

Clansmen, familiar with the area and experienced in stealthiness, led the way. Rory was second in the single file of riders. Malcolm, the man second only to Archibald among the Maclean soldiers, led. A scout had gone before them.

Rory had been gone far too long. He knew he did not yet command the confidence of his clan. He would have to do that tonight. He had expected Archibald to accompany them, but the man was ill, and Malcolm had taken the captain of the guard's place. The long ride had prompted too many memories, too much time for thought.

Rory felt none of the anticipation he'd felt as a young lad embarking on his first raid. It had been an adventure then. Little had he known it was to turn into a nightmare.

His stomach constricted at the memory. He'd been leader of what was to be a small, punishing raid of a Campbell village. But someone had seen them and alerted others. His party had been ambushed. Three had been mortally wounded, and in a vengeful rage, his clansmen had burned every croft. One had raped a woman and killed her child for defending her.

Rory would never forget the sight of one of his own clansmen standing triumphantly over the body of a young lad who had tried to protect his mother. Nor would he forget the look of surprise on the man's face when Rory had slain him as he turned on another child.

He'd been but nineteen, a callow youth who thought he owned the world and was a warrior in the truest sense. He had changed that night and over the succeeding weeks, when he had been mocked and derided by his fellow clansmen. It ended only when his father and Patrick had supported his actions. He'd known that some among his clan did not understand, would never understand, his defense of a Campbell. Even a Campbell child.

He remembered every moment now. He felt the sickness in his gut as he had then.

He would have left Inverleith, his clan's seat, had he not met and married Maggie. She'd brought magic into his world, as well as solace. She had understood his pain over that night and had told him that was why she loved him.

That magic and happiness had lasted exactly fifteen months.

He did leave then, and had gone to sea, finally marrying the daughter of the shipping master and becoming captain. It had been a marriage of convenience for both of them, and yet he had come to care deeply for Anne. It was not the magic that he'd had with Maggie, but he did care for her and tried to make her happy the few months he was in port.

He had not brought Anne back to where Maggie had died. If he stayed away, mayhap the curse would not touch him again.

But it had found him . . . and Anne.

He'd still not returned, not until twelve days earlier, ten years to the day he had left. He had found a keep falling into ruin, a dispirited clan decimated by the feud with the Campbells and a household with few women. Many apparently had come to believe that the Campbell curse affected not only the chiefs of the clan but all the Macleans.

His brother Lachlan seemed to care more about his lute than management of the keep. And while an aging Douglas served as steward, a woman named Moira was responsible for housekeeping duties. She was a healer who had been forced into a position for which she had no aptitude or training. The few women servants she instructed were no more trained than she. Some were timid wives of his soldiers; some were daughters. Some cared, but most did not.

Rory had kept his ship spotless. He knew discipline was vital to the well-being of his crew, and discipline began with keeping some measure of order.

There was no order at home.

Lachlan deserved some blame but not all. He was not a soldier, had no inclination to be one, nor was he meant to be a steward. He was too soft, too forgiving of the unforgivable. He had planned to be a priest and was well suited by temperament to be one. Rory hadn't discovered yet why he had not pursued his vocation. Lachlan had avoided questions thus far.

Rory only knew that once his father had died and his oldest brother disappeared, the clan had lost heart.

The scout returned. Malcolm held up his arm. They stopped, dismounted, and spoke quietly.

Rory was excluded. Though all appeared to respect and

look up to him, it was obvious that they trusted one another more than their newly arrived chief.

He turned to the scout. "You have found the cattle."

"Aye," the man said cautiously.

"How many guarding them?"

"Four."

Rory turned to Malcolm. "I do not want anyone killed. It will only bring more attacks. I will take one man—the scout—and silence the guards. You stay here until you hear a whistle, then approach and take the cattle.

"But my lord . . ."

"There is no but, Malcolm. Those are my orders."

The other eight men stared at him in disbelief. And unhappiness. Blood lust was apparent. They all looked at Malcolm, who nodded. Reluctantly.

He turned to the scout, "Nab. You lead." The man seemed to have eyes that penetrated the dark, but then so did Rory. He had perfected that ability during his years at sea and the need to adjust his eyes to absolute blackness.

The man turned, gave him a wary look, then moved ahead. They walked for a long while, then the man stopped. Nab climbed a hill and signaled Rory to move next to him.

He looked down. Shadows materialized beneath them. Cattle. Many of them. A fire was barely visible under a shelter of some kind.

"Maclean cattle," the man next to him muttered. "There were none here three days ago."

Rory did not ask how he knew. Apparently his kinsmen kept an eye on Campbell properties.

He peered through the mist that had started to fall. He could barely make out three shapes. "You said there were four men. I see only three."

"Two near at the shelter. One straight across. Another to the left of us."

"I will take the one closest to us," Rory said, "then the one to the far side. Move close to the two near the fire but do not act unless they see one of us. Wait until you hear the hoot of an owl. That means I have taken down the two." He paused, then added, "I do not want anyone killed unless you have no choice."

He did not give Nab an opportunity to protest, though Rory sensed the man intended to do just that.

Rory moved swiftly ahead, his shoes making no noise in the gentle but incessant patter of rain. He skirted around until he was in back of the first man, then he stepped forward and put his left arm around the man's neck, the other hand over the man's mouth and dragged him down. Before the Campbell had time to react, Rory hit him sharply with the heavy hilt of his dirk, then bound his captive with strips from his own clothes.

Then he moved stealthily behind the second man, who sat on a rock.

He threw a stone, and when the guard turned, Rory struck him on the head and caught his body as he fell. He quickly bound him as he had bound the first man.

He glanced toward the flickering light of a fire, which just barely flamed. He saw Nab's large figure in the shadow.

Rory moved swiftly between trees until he was near the shelter, made a soft sound, like the hoot of an owl. As he threw another stone in the opposite direction, two men moved from the makeshift shelter of limbs and brush. Nab took one, and Rory lunged toward the other. Stealth no longer mattered.

In seconds, Rory had his man bound. Nab was still struggling with his. Both men—his and the Campbell— had daggers. Rory stepped behind the Campbell and grabbed him behind the neck. In a moment, he, too, was bound.

Nab looked at him indignantly. "I could have taken him."

"Aye, and blood would have been shed."

" 'Tis a natural thing to shed Campbell blood."

"If we want them to exchange the favor," Rory said
dryly. "There has been enough bloodshed. We take back
that which belongs to us. We need do no more."

"Except to avenge our people."

"Do you want more to die?" Rory asked.

The man stared at him through the rain. Faces were
barely visible.

Nab finally nodded. "I will fetch the others to take the
cattle."

"I will wait with these guards in case anyone comes."

Rory watched his companion disappear into the rain,
then he checked the bonds of the Campbell prisoners before squatting before the fire. He'd barely warmed himself
when Malcolm and the others appeared, herded the cattle
in front of them, and started back to their own property.

Rory watched them leave, then loosened the bonds of
one of the prisoners. It would still take the man hours to
free himself but it was no longer impossible. No Campbell
would die this night from exposure.

FELICIA waited until well past midnight.

The Cameron escort had arrived late that afternoon. They planned to leave with Janet at daybreak. Felicia's escort to Edinburgh was to arrive in ten days.

Felicia instructed the staff to serve their best wine to
their visitors, while she avoided as much contact with them
as possible.

As she had hoped, most retired early, having drunk co-
piously of wine usually reserved only for their chiefs. Felicia had been uncommonly generous.

She hadn't told Janet what she planned for later in the
evening.

Instead, she told Janet she needed sleep, went to her
own chamber, and stayed awake until the castle had stilled.

When she felt confident that most were abed, she took the candle from her bedside and crept down the corridor and the stone steps to the great hall where the Camerons slept.

No one stirred. She opened the great door and slipped outside, hurrying to the stables. The grooms, knowing the castle gate had been closed, should be abed as well.

The night was very dark. Clouds eclipsed any light from stars and moon. Moisture was in the air. Rain would fall the next day, possibly in the next few hours. A cold wind blew, molding her cloak against her body and blowing her hair free of the bonnet she wore. Her hand shielded the flame from the candle to keep it from going out.

She relished the feel of the sharp, cold, wet chill. Her prayers had been answered. Almost.

She could assist those prayers.

She went into the tack room. The candle flickered from a breeze blowing through the barn doors. Her heart nearly stopped. It couldn't go out. Not now.

The flame stabilized. She carefully placed the candle-holder on a ledge, then went to the saddles belonging to the Cameron clansmen. She slipped a dagger from her boot and quickly sawed halfway through a dozen girths from underneath. Hopefully, no one would detect the cuts until it was too late. Falls. Confusion. A chance for her to escape those protecting her.

She worked with quiet efficiency and buried her guilt. They were good horsemen. A simple fall would not hurt them.

And she would need all the diversion she could contrive.

Finished, she crept back to her big feather bed. Tonight would be the last time she would sink into its comfort.

FELICIA slept restlessly for only a few hours and woke before dawn. She went to the window and thanked God when she saw heavy rain falling.

Janet would be expected to wear protective clothing.

In an hour or less, the Cameron escort would be prepared to leave.

She lit a candle from the huge fireplace where a few embers still burned from the great pieces of wood that had filled it last eve. She placed several additional pieces of wood inside, then waited until the chamber warmed.

She dressed hastily before her maid came in. A boy's clothes first, clothes filched from the trunks of her cousin's younger days. Then a chemise and a plain underdress and overdress of her own. She tucked her hair beneath a dark cap and stared at herself in the mirror.

She and Janet both had blue eyes, although hers were darker; hopefully the difference would not be noticed in the gloom of dawn. Most of her face was shielded by one of Janet's wool plaids. The cap and cloak would cover her unruly red curls.

She planned to be late, to join the departing riders after most were already mounted.

Janet knocked and entered, a tray in hand. "I told your maid that you were ill and I would bring you something to eat," she said.

Felicia went to her friend and took the tray, put it down on a table, then clasped Janet's hands. "Thank you. I will see that no one blames you. A sleeping potion. Take it when I leave. Everyone will believe I gave it to you."

Janet's eyes met hers.

"Felicia, are you quite determined to do this?" Janet's voice broke with worry.

"I am," Felicia said.

"If they discover who you are, they will bring you back. Your uncle will be very angry."

"He cannot do anything more to me than what he has already done," Felicia said. "If only I can get to London . . ."

"But how?"

"I'll travel as a boy to London. I have my mother's jewels. I can sell them if necessary. If I can find Jamie, I think he will help me."

"But you are a woman."

And gently born women did not travel alone. Many terrible things could happen, which was why she intended to pose as a lad. But she knew her fate if she remained in Scotland.

Her silence prompted another question from Janet. "How will you lose the escorts?"

"I have an idea or two," Felicia replied, once more feeling a stab of guilt at not telling her friend that she had already taken some action to make escape easier. The less Janet knew, the safer she would be. Her friend did not lie well.

Neither did she. But now her life and future were at risk, and desperation made possible actions that had been unthinkable before.

"Then what?" Janet asked.

"There are many caves in the area," Felicia replied. "Jamie used to take me exploring. He said I should know where to hide if I were ever caught outside the gates." If she could reach them, she could hide for several days, then travel as a lad to London, to Jamie. He would find a way to assist her, and in London he could do it without anyone knowing.

She realized it was not a particularly clever plan. In fact, it was not even a plan, just a desperate, headlong escape.

"Jamie *will* help you," Janet assured her. Her face softened as she mentioned Jamie's name. "He cares for you," she said. "He feels you are the only one in this family who has truly loved him."

Felicia was startled by the observation. Jamie seldom expressed his feelings. She knew that there was little affection between him and his father.

In the back of her mind were many questions and fears

she would not admit to Janet. Could she ask Jamie to risk his future, even his life to help her? The only possible way she could ask for his assistance was if she could do it in a way that no one would ever know his connection with her disappearance.

Janet helped her pull her long red hair into a cap so that not a single tendril escaped. Then she assisted her with the cloak and plaid that wrapped around most of her face.

Felicia went to the window. "They are mounted and waiting." She went over to Janet and put her arms around her in a hug. "I will never forget you for this. Thank you."

"Just be safe. Find a way to let me know you are."

"I will. God keep you."

"And you."

Felicia tried to still the trembling in her hands. She was leaving everything she knew for an uncertain future. If she were discovered, her uncle would keep her captive until the wedding. He most probably would do more.

She swallowed the bile in her throat.

She was alone. So very alone.

She hurried down the stone steps to the great hall, then out the door. Ten mounted men waited for her.

The rain had slowed to a fine drizzle, but a light fog enveloped the distant hills. The cold temperatures would make the day miserable for all of them. The men were obviously anxious to get under way.

One soldier, obviously the leader, gave his reins to a mounted man and helped her mount. She nodded her thanks as she swung up on the saddle. Thank God both she and Janet were good riders. And she knew Janet's white mare. Somehow, she vowed silently, she would get the well-mannered horse back to her friend.

"My lady," the soldier said. "We will make the journey as comfortable as possible."

She nodded again.

The first deception had succeeded. Perhaps the mist and fog would assist her escape. She prayed that both held.

She held her breath as they departed through the gates. Another small success.

As if in answer to her prayer, the fog deepened, obscuring everything but the rider directly ahead and directly behind. If it would last only a few more hours.

She prayed harder.

Janet's maid rode just behind her, bouncing up and down like a sack of potatoes, and close behind her rode two men. The others rode in front, the leader often looking back to see whether she was still with them.

Despite the slice in the girths, she knew they would not part without strain. She needed to increase the pace and the pressure on the girths. She looked around. No one was looking at her.

The trail widened. The fog was still thick. This was her chance!

She dug her heels into the sides of the mare. The mare bolted, running past the forward member of the guard. She screamed for help, then held on for dear life. She heard the shouts of her escort, the pound of hooves behind her. The mare was frantic now, and Felicia did nothing to curb her. A horseman approached close to her side, reaching for her reins when he cried out and she saw him tumble from the saddle.

Another horseman drew close. She glanced back, screamed as if in terror, then he, too, fell. Shouts and curses followed her as her mare ran into another thick patch of fog.

She worked the reins, managed to regain control but slowed the pace only slightly. The shouts continued behind her. She noticed an opening to the left and abruptly guided the mare into it and dismounted. The mare shuddered, and she ran her hand down her neck to calm her.

The human noises faded as she walked swiftly. She was not sure where she was. She would worry about that later. She wanted to put distance between the escort and herself. But first she had to calm the horse and make sure the mare did not stumble into some hole.

She left the faint trail and moved into the forest. The going was much slower now. The fog confused her sense of direction. She stopped frequently to listen for voices or the sound of horses.

Minutes passed. She hurried her steps, praying she was going in the right direction.

Her feet sank into wet ground. Her skirts were heavy and laden with moisture. Still, her only concern was reaching the hills and caves. She could hide there until they stopped searching the area.

A hand suddenly clasped her arm, another stifling the scream that rose in her throat. A piece of cloth was expertly tied around her mouth, and she felt herself being hoisted onto a horse.

Fear spiked inside her as a body rose behind her. Thick arms imprisoned her and grasped the reins of a horse far larger than the mare she'd been leading.

The Camerons?

But they wouldn't treat their lady in such a way. Nor would they gag her if they had discovered her deceit. Her body necessarily leaned against what seemed an enormous man.

"Ye will no' be harmed," came a whisper in her ear.

Then without any additional words from the man, the horse plunged back onto a trail, and she was aware only of speed and strength.

She had escaped.

But to what?

Chapter 3

❦

"*W*HERE in the devil is Archibald?"

Rory faced Douglas in the room that served them both as an office.

Douglas raised his eyes upward, as if appealing to a higher being. "I canna say, my lord."

"Can not or will not?"

"Archibald goes his own way." Douglas avoided answering the question.

"Aye, and so do too many on this property," Rory said without trying to disguise his displeasure. "I do not think my father tolerated such disrespect."

"I do no' think Archibald meant any disrespect," Douglas said. "He has always had the clan's interest at heart."

His gaze didn't meet Rory's, and that was rare. Douglas was the most forthright man Rory knew, particularly in the

Scottish highlands, which too often bred duplicitous scoundrels.

Rory was getting a very bad feeling.

"I want to make peace with the Campbells," he warned.

"You made that clear," Douglas said. "But they burned some of our crofts to the north. If we do not retaliate beyond reclaiming our cattle, they will continue their burning and stealing."

"I plan to meet with the Campbell in Edinburgh. A truce would help both clans."

"'Tis a fine dream, but I fear an impossible one. We have been fighting near a hundred years, ever since—"

"Then it is time to end it. There has been enough pain and death. Both the Campbells and Macleans are losing cattle and men. Even power. An alliance would gain us both."

"And put the curse to rest," Douglas added.

Rory glared at him. God's blood, he hated the very mention of that damned curse.

He told himself he was a modern man. He did not believe in curses. Many women died in childbirth. Many lost their child as well. And his second wife? Fever had swept through Leith, the seaport near Edinburgh. His wife was one of many who died.

Bloody bad luck. Nothing more.

Still, the pain was always in him like the tip of a poisoned spear. He lived with loneliness. With fear. With memories.

Maggie walking among the heather, her eyes lit with laughter and love and the pure joy of living.

Maggie giggling as she told him they would have a child. A son. She was quite convinced of it.

Maggie as she clutched his hand and tried gallantly to stifle screams when the baby wouldn't come and she bled to death.

Maggie who had been his first love, who had stolen his heart and never disappointed. She had thought otherwise. Her last words were, "I am sorry, so sorry . . . your son . . ."

And then she stopped breathing.

The agony was as fresh now as it had been then. Just as it was for Anne who had been an innocent, who had loved him even as he had not been able to return that love until it was too late.

"Rory?"

He looked back at Douglas.

"You canna mourn forever. You have a duty to the clan."

"I will hear no more of it. Patrick will return. He will provide an heir. I will not."

He strode away, his heart like a rock inside him. He would not marry. He could not. He did not believe in a curse, but he did believe he was a Jonah to anyone who loved him. It had been the sins of his past, not a century-old curse that haunted him.

Damn this place. Tragedy and death stalked every corridor. He hated every foot of it. He hated the endless and futile feuds. The victims were never the men who instigated the violence, but the crofters who wanted only to grow enough crops to see them through the next year.

How many had been burned out, their homes destroyed, their crops spoiled, their animals taken? How many babies would die this year?

He knew overtures to the Campbells and the Scottish king would dismay his clan, perhaps alienate them. He was chief by consent. He could well be displaced.

But by whom?

As if summoned by his thoughts, his younger brother approached him. Rory stopped and glared, his anger—and despair—finding a new target.

"No need to glower at me, brother," Lachlan said with his easy grin.

Lachlan had always been able to charm, even though he was unaware of the impact he had. Perhaps his charm came from a refreshing lack of guile and ambition.

Rory relaxed. He always did in his younger brother's presence.

He had always competed with Patrick. It had been expected, and he'd usually been bested by his older brother. Patrick was a natural warrior. Rory always had to work at it. But Lachlan had avoided competition and physical tests. He'd always preferred music and books.

"Are you here to tell me I should wed again?"

"You should know me better, brother. I dislike interfering in the lives of others for fear they might try to interfere with mine."

"Patrick does that anyway."

"Aye, he does. He wants to make me into himself. But you never have."

"I like you as you are."

"My lack of ambition appeals to you?"

"Nay. Your music does. Your good nature does."

"You once played the lute. You were very good."

"It was a boyish pasttime."

"Was it?" Lachlan said. "Then I hope I am always a lad."

"You want me to sing of lost loves, Lachlan. Unlike you, I've tasted the pain. I have no desire to sing of it."

Lachlan's handsome face clouded. "I am sorry. You know I loved Maggie. We all did."

"I know."

Maggie had loved Lachlan more than any other member of the family. They sang together, walked together, told stories to each other. Rory would have been jealous if he had not loved them both so much and known that they loved him as well. Maggie had made him appreciate Lachlan's gentleness, something Patrick constantly belittled.

They—Maggie and Lachlan—had a connection he'd never quite understood.

"She would want—"

"Lachlan, you cannot know what she would want. You were not her husband."

He turned and strode away from his brother, not understanding the sudden, overwhelming anger he felt. Why for God's nails wouldn't everyone leave him alone? He did not even want to be here.

The sea was solace. Scotland was pain.

FELICIA tried not to touch the body of her abductor. The cloth was taken from her mouth after several miles. She was warned, though, that any cry would mean that the gag would be returned.

She had no intention of screaming. She was frightened. Beyond frightened. But she was equally terrified of being returned to her home. And to her prospective groom.

They stopped after several hours. She was gently dropped to the ground, and food was offered. It was naught but rough bread and cheese, but she was hungry.

She glanced around as she ate. The mist had lifted, but clouds kept the sun at bay, and it was cold and dreary. There were no more than five men. 'Twas odd, but she felt no threat from them. She should. She knew that. She had been abducted by men unknown to her.

She only knew that they had been respectful. That boded well.

"My lady?"

The speaker was the same large man who had lifted her onto the horse. He looked even more fearsome as she sat on a fallen log, staring up at him. His beard was red and long, and he had but one visible eye. The other was covered by a patch.

Despite his wicked appearance, there was a soft courtesy in his voice.

"Why have you taken me?" she asked.

"For yer good and the good of my lord," he said.

"My good?" she asked incredulously. "I do not understand."

"An alliance between the Camerons and Macleans

would be good for both," he said. "My lord is a handsome man, a man of strength and wealth, and he be needing a bride."

Maclean.

Dear Mother in Heaven. *The Maclean.* Everyone knew the Macleans and Campbells were mortal enemies.

Suddenly she realized what had happened. They thought they had Janet.

What would happen to the courtesy when they realized they had abducted a Campbell as bride for their lord? Their courtesy would unquestionably vanish.

Her blood turned to ice. If he discovered who she was, the Maclean would hold her hostage, if not slay her. She had to continue the masquerade. Only now it was even more important. If the Camerons had discovered her identity, they would merely have returned her home. But the Macleans were known for their ferocity. One had even chained one of her ancestors to a rock in hopes she would drown. Others had raided Campbell properties. Only fifteen years ago, a Maclean had led a party that had raped women and killed children.

Could it be this Maclean?

She tried to contain the new terror. Maclean was worse even than Morneith.

She would have to pretend to be amenable to the match, then escape before they discovered her true identity.

How soon would an alarm be raised? How quickly would her uncle discover that she had been abducted? And what would they do to the Macleans? And the Macleans, in turn, do the Campbells? To her cousin Jamie?

Dear Mary in Heaven, what have I done?

The food she'd just consumed rose in her throat.

"My lady," the man, obviously alarmed at her distress, tried again. "My lord is a fair and true mon."

She would be expected to protest.

"How dare you?" she said. "My family—"

"Your family canna but be pleased. We have had long alliances."

"Is that why you felt free to abduct me?" she asked with the indignation he would expect.

"My lord. He . . . he . . ."

The man was stammering. His large face flushed red. It was such a strange reaction that apprehension ran rampant inside her.

"Is he a monster that he needs to abduct a wife?"

"Nay, lady. You will find him well favored and of mild temperament. It is only—"

"Only what?"

"He does not wish to wed again. But men speak of your beauty. He will surely be . . ."

Just then his gaze met her eyes. The cloak had fallen from her head, and her hair had come out from under the cap. She knew it was plastered to her head. Even at the best of times, she was certainly no beauty. Now she must look like a drowned rat.

Janet was the beauty, not her.

When would they discover their mistake?

She realized now they must have heard that Janet was to return home. The Macleans must have followed the escort, and when she had veered away they had followed. They probably couldn't believe their luck. No battle. No casualties. And they had their heiress.

What if Janet had accompanied the escort?

Well, she had much less to lose than Janet.

Felicia had no man she loved. And Janet was not being forced into a marriage with a man she detested.

The big man tried to reassure her. "I am Archibald," he said. "Know that no harm will come to ye while under our protection. We will reach Inverleith tonight, and you will be made most comfortable."

"My family will not be pleased," she said haughtily.

"They would no' be displeased at the match."

"I am betrothed to Jamie Campbell."

The man spat on the ground. "A Campbell. Ye can do far better than that."

"I love him."

"Ye have not yet met our lord."

"The king will be most displeased."

Archibald shrugged as if King James was of no matter. " 'Tis time to continue."

"You said your lord does not wish to be wed," she said desperately. "You can let me go now, and I will say naught."

"I must admit ye are no' what I thought to be bringing to my laird," he said, his gaze wandering over her face and her rather large size caused by her several layers of clothes.

The observation wounded. To be disparaged by a criminal Maclean was adding insult to injury.

"You, sir, are a brigand and thief and have no right to judge me."

Archibald grimaced. "Ye should be grateful to avoid a wedding with a Campbell," he said. "Any good Scot would say so."

The words confirmed the seriousness of her situation. What would happen when they learned who she was?

They could not. They simply could not discover she was not Janet Cameron.

Not until she escaped again.

But she realized it would not be as easy as it had been when she'd had Janet's help.

The Camerons had not known what she intended. They had trusted her.

This man would not do that. He had taken her captive and meant to keep her one until she did their bidding.

If she succumbed too easily, would she be suspected?

Or should she fight them?

Humility and fear would disarm them. Would allow her to escape again.

She forced tears, hiding the hurt and rage within her.

She really wanted to stab the bloody man with a sword. *No' what I thought, indeed.*

Mayhap she would get the chance.

That thought produced a momentary satisfaction. The Macleans would discover this Campbell had a sting.

Chapter 4

❦

THE sound of the horn echoed through the keep.

It was followed by a shout, "Riders approaching!"

The alarm came from the rampart, then echoed as other Macleans took up the call.

Rory left his supper and took the stone steps quickly to join the sentry.

Rain had fallen most of the day, but the sun had peeked between the clouds in the past hour. It was setting now, coloring the sky with scarlet and golden hues. Shadows made it difficult to identify the riders approaching the gate, but one was obviously Archibald. No one could mistake his size.

Rory signaled his men to open the gate and watched his riders file inside. Archibald led a white mare that was carrying a small but bulky figure.

A woman!

Rory suddenly understood the sly looks, the evasive answers.

His men had stolen a bride for him.

Such actions were not that unusual in Scotland, he knew. Brides had been stolen before. But he had made his feelings about marriage very clear.

His hands clenched into fists.

His clansmen would not have dared disobey his father, or Patrick. Rory was an unproven leader to them, but by God, they would learn now.

"Find Douglas," he told the man standing next to him. "Tell him to meet me in the courtyard."

He strode toward the stairs, took them quickly, and reached the riders as they dismounted.

Archibald stood in front of him and removed his helmet.

"What is the lady doing here?" Rory demanded, his anger barely contained.

"I . . ."

Douglas appeared at his side. "Rory?"

Rory turned on him. "What have you done?"

"Milord," Archibald said in a low voice. "Douglas did nothing. It was my doing alone. We brought you Janet Cameron to be your bride. She is said to be pleasing and gentle."

Only then did Rory look up at the rider on the white mare. Her back was ramrod straight, and she was covered head to toe by a fur cloak and hood that protected her face from the cold. He wondered if she had heard Archibald's words.

He went to her side and offered his hand to her. She ignored it and started to dismount on her own. He caught her by her waist and eased her down, surprised at how much lighter she was than she looked. "My apologies, my lady," he said.

She looked at him with dark blue eyes that were quite

remarkable. They roiled with emotion, but he could not decipher it. Fear? Anger? A combination?

He tried to reassure her. "My men acted without my approval. I will be sending you home as soon as you are well rested."

She shivered, and he was not sure whether it was from fear or the cold Highland wind that blew through the bailey. All her clothes were damp. Her eyes regarded him warily.

He had heard of Janet Cameron. There had even been talk of an alliance between her and Patrick. He also knew that she was pledged to Jamie Campbell. He tried to tamp the fury bubbling inside. The Campbells most assuredly would retaliate. That meant more Maclean deaths.

The lady did not reply. He could not blame her. She had been stolen by men she did not know, forced to ride long and hard in wet, cold weather.

Any gentle maiden would be stunned with fear.

He turned to Archibald. "She will be returning. Rest your horses and prepare to ride on the morrow." He turned back to the woman. "My cook will make you comfortable and find you warm clothing. We have no lady's maids, but there are scullery maids that can assist you." He did not like feeling awkward and in the wrong. It didn't matter that others had put him there. He was responsible, God help him.

She still didn't speak. Why did she not rage at him? The silence made him feel even worse.

Even in Edinburgh, he had heard of Lady Janet Cameron's beauty. He searched for a hint of it, but it eluded him.

He told himself that if he had been hauled across many miles in a cold Scotland mist, he, too, might look worse than he would like.

He bowed. "I am Rory Maclean, Lady Janet. I assure you this is a mistake," he said, afraid she hadn't understood his earlier attempt to explain. "You will not be harmed in any way, and I will see you returned immediately."

Her gaze did not waver as she regarded him, but he could read little in it.

"Your men were considerate," she said. She spoke in a low mellow voice. Only the slightest tremor was audible.

"As well they should have been," he said abruptly, his anger barely under control. But he did not wish to frighten her. "I will see to your comfort and send word to the Camerons," he said.

She swayed slightly at that. She was obviously exhausted.

He took her arm and guided her toward the great hall, but her foot slipped in the mud. He caught her as she started to fall, and her body leaned into his as she struggled to remain upright. She looked up at him as the hood slipped from her head.

Despite her reputation as a beauty, her face was plain except for her eyes. Her face was more square than oval, her mouth too wide, and her nose small, like a button. He could tell little about her hair, but a dark red ringlet curled tightly against her face. Although it wasn't beautiful, it was an intriguing face, an appealing one.

What was extraordinary was her controlled expression. There was no hysteria, nor apparent anger, and that stunned him.

She should be angry. Fearful. Indignant at the very least.

He picked her up to avoid getting her skirts muddier than they already were and confirmed his earlier impression that the bulk was more cloth than body. Her clothes smelled of damp wool, but there was another scent as well. Light and flowery.

It reminded him of another woman. Too much. A jolt of heat struck him.

He saw a satisfied smile on Archibald's face and knew it was long past time to have a discussion with his captain of the guard.

A clansman ran ahead and opened the door.

Rory entered and set the lady back on her feet, ignoring the stunned look on her face. He wondered whether she had felt the same jolt that he had. But no, that was ridiculous. He had been long without a woman. 'Twas only natural urges.

"Moira," he bellowed and noticed that Janet Cameron flinched slightly.

"She will see to your comfort," he said, anxious that his reluctant guest feel safe until he could send her home without bringing harm to her reputation or his rebellious clan.

He would send word ahead to the Camerons.

Then he caught himself. He needed to know the exact circumstances of the abduction. Had anyone been wounded? Killed?

He would like to wound Archibald at this very moment.

Moira appeared, her size testament to her love of sweets.

"Moira, this is Lady Janet Cameron. She will be a guest this eve. See her to my mother's chamber and fetch her anything she might need. He looked back at the captive. "Do you have any dry clothes?"

She shook her head.

"She is to have whatever she needs from my mother's wardrobe."

"Aye," Moira said, her lips pursed with disapproval. "Puir child," she said, clucking like a mother hen. "Ye come wi' me."

Rory suddenly realized that Moira knew exactly what had happened. Bloody hell, had everyone known about Archibald's plan but him?

He watched as they mounted the steps together. Midway, Moira looked back to order hot water for a bath. He noted at the same time that the Cameron woman moved with uncommon grace despite the bulk of her clothes.

Rory strode back outside to where Archibald, his bearded face apprehensive, remained standing.

Rory glared at him. "I would have a word with you." He

turned and strode into the great hall where a log blazed. He whirled around to confront Archibald. "Who is lord here?"

Archibald's pale blue gaze met his. "Ye are."

"I had no wish to return," Rory said. "Now that I have, I am laird. I will no' have anyone doubting that."

"We need an heir," Archibald insisted stubbornly.

"You will not be getting one from me. If that was all you wanted, you should have looked elsewhere. I have made my wishes clear. They will be respected. Dammit, man, Lady Janet is betrothed to a Campbell."

"All the better," Archibald muttered.

"I will not continue warring with the Campbells. It may please you, but it does nothing to help our clan. 'Twas not your crofts burned out, but theirs."

"Ye canna' make bargains with the devil."

"My ancestor was at fault. I will not have it said that the Macleans continue to mistreats ladies."

"Ye would be a fine husband. Far better than a Campbell. She was not mistreated. She dinna say she was."

"Of course not. She was probably frightened half to death."

"No' that one," Archibald said in a barely audible voice.

Rory narrowed his eyes. "I do not ken your meaning."

"Not a cry. Not a protest. 'Twas almost as if she were . . . relieved."

Rory thought that only an excuse, though he also thought the woman far too calm under the circumstances. "How many men were killed?"

"No' even one."

Rory stared at his captain of the guards with disbelief. "Are you saying her escort did nothing to protect her?"

"She was no' with them. We were following. We heard noise. Curses. Little Willie snuck up and said some had lost their saddles, then he saw the lady turning away. Confused or frightened in the mist, mayhap. Ye could say we found her."

"Then no one knows she is here?"

"Nay. She disappeared in the mist."

"She did not scream?"

"Well . . ."

"Well what?"

"I might have had my hand over her mouth."

Rory sighed. "I will talk to her. If she will say we rescued her, then no harm done. If she does not . . ."

"A Cameron alliance would help us against the Campbells," Archibald said hopefully. "She would not say nay to
you. Any lady—"

Rory's temper was near explosion. "I will hear no more
about marriage. She returns tomorrow. Let us hope that she
is agreeable. King James has made it clear he does not
want the clans feuding. It is my neck you are risking,
Archibald. And those of the crofters. If you had not helped
raise me, I would see you gone this day."

He strode off before he said more. Archibald and Douglas had been a part of his life since he had been a wee lad.
Archibald had instructed him in warrior arts, and Douglas
had taught him to read and write. Both had been more father to him than his own sire.

Mayhap that was the problem. They both saw him as a
lad, not as a man of three and thirty years, a man who had
commanded a ship for the last six of those years.

He was hesitant to exert authority for that same reason.
He had never wanted to be laird. He held this place for his
older brother, nothing more.

Rory retreated to his room and poured himself a tankard
of wine from a jug on the table, then went to the window
that overlooked the sea. It was low tide, and the rock where
his ancestor chained his wife jutted upward from the
beach. Waves washed around it, splashing water high into
the air.

He could only imagine the lady's terror as she watched
the waves rise slowly, as her body was buffeted and frozen
by wind and icy spray.

He brushed the images from his mind and thought about

the woman in the chamber below him. It was the room his mother had used years ago before her death, the same room that Patrick's and Lachlan's mothers had inhabited.

He had not taken the chamber next to it, the one which belonged to the laird. Although it had been prepared for him upon his arrival. He felt the chamber belonged to Patrick. Rory preferred the plain, stark chamber of his youth.

He turned away from the window and took another sip of wine as he considered how to approach the lady, how to convince her that she had not been abducted at all.

FELICIA followed Moira. She tried to control the small tremors that racked her. They did not all come from the cold winds that had buffeted her all day.

She had never been a timid person, but she was in the enemy's lair, and she knew she had to keep her wits about her.

She had expected a villain. According to her Campbell clansmen, every Maclean was a fearsome being. Corrupt, brutal, and untrustworthy. She had expected someone like Morneith, only younger.

Instead, the Maclean had been courteous, apologetic, and solicitous. Even charming with his unexpected apologies. He'd appeared to be as confused by her kidnapping as she had been. Mary help her, but he was also as handsome a man as any she had seen.

She kept telling herself he was an enemy, yet he had been nothing but kind. He was tall and well formed. His eyes were steel gray and his hair a dark brown, almost black. His face was hard, and his lips unsmiling, but he had a face that attracted attention. In that, he reminded her of Jamie.

But while Jamie was open and frank, Rory Maclean seemed surrounded by shadows despite his outward courtesy. His eyes were guarded, and despite polite words, there had been no smile. His touch had been electric, and when he'd so unexpectedly lifted her, she'd felt a brief impression of confidence and strength. She'd even felt safe.

She knew that for the falsity it was. He believed she was Janet Cameron, and it was to his advantage to be charming and protective. His charm would vanish quickly enough if he discovered he had a hated Campbell in his keep.

Still, her skin remained warm where he had touched her, and an unfamiliar ache plagued her.

Moira opened the door to a large chamber. The furnishings were magnificent, though covered with a film of dust. The bed was finer than hers at home, but it looked neglected, the covering slightly stained.

Moira's face fell. "I know it must no' be as grand as that you know."

"It is fine," Felicia assured her.

Moira's anxious face creased into a smile. " 'Tis a long time since we have had a lady here. We have needed a lady's presence." Her face fell as her gaze moved around the room. "We have had no lady or lord for too long."

Felicia looked at her. "But I just met . . ."

"Lord Rory returned just a few days ago from years at sea. The old lord died nearly three years ago, and Lord Rory's older brother, the heir . . ." Her voice trailed off.

"His older brother?" Felicia prompted. She knew some of the story. And a Cameron that had maintained relations with both clans should know more. Yet her life might well depend on information tossed like crumbs to a hungry bird.

"He went to fight with the French three years ago. He was an adventurer, that one. He has no' returned. No one knows what happened to him."

They were interrupted by a succession of men who filled the fireplace with wood and lit it. Others brought a tub and steaming pails of water. The old woman quickly shooed the men out and offered to help Felicia undress.

She could not allow that to happen. "Nay," she said. "I would prefer privacy."

The woman looked crestfallen, as if she had failed in some way, but she backed out the door. "I will bring ye a nightrobe and some food," she said.

Felicia remained standing until Moira left, then she went to the steel mirror on the wall and looked at herself. She did not know when she had looked worse. Her hair clung to her head in tight curls, and her eyes were tired and dull-looking. No beauty here. How long could her masquerade last?

She turned away from the condemning object in front of her and hurriedly undressed, discarding one layer after the other. She laid her cloak with its jewels sewn inside in the empty wardrobe and removed her gown, then the one underneath it. She finally reached the lad's clothes, took them off, and tucked them under the mattress. She had little doubt she would need them later.

Wearing only the chemise, and many pounds lighter, she stood in front of the first flickers of flame in the fireplace and tried to control the shivers that ran down her body. She removed that last garment and slipped into the tub, relishing the hot water. She closed her eyes, wondering what she should do next.

She was tired, so very tired, yet she knew she needed all her wits about her. Still, her thoughts kept returning to the tall lord who had carried her with so little effort and whose gaze had been so direct.

A knock came at the door, and before she could say anything Moira entered with a tray of food. A young lass behind her carried a luxurious robe trimmed with fur, along with warmed thick towels.

"This is Robina," Moira said. "She will be attending ye. She is no' a lady's maid, but she is a fine worker and wishes to please."

The lass bobbed her head, then stood ready to towel off her new charge.

With a sigh, Felicia stood. The water was cooling all too quickly, but she hated to leave it just the same. Robina quickly wrapped her in towels, rubbing her until she thought she would have no skin left.

"Ye have bonny red hair," the girl said shyly.

Felicia had always hated it. It was the color of rust and crinkled in hundreds of curls rather than running smoothly down her back as did Janet's dark hair.

"Thank you," Felicia said and reached for her chemise, slipping it over her shoulders.

Robina bobbed again and fetched the robe, helping Felicia into it and nearly knocked her back into the tub with her eager ministrations. "Milady . . . I . . . I mean . . ." the girl stuttered.

Moira scowled at her.

Felicia's heart melted. The maid was no more than a child, probably no more then ten and three years. Felicia knew being a lady's maid was a much valued position, and the young lass was a combination of inexperience and hope.

Felicia knew much about both. "It was my fault," she said, and the child beamed with gratitude.

"Ye must be hungry," Moira said. "I am not the best of cooks, but there is fruit and cheese, bread and mutton."

She waited, apparently expecting Felicia to crawl into the bed, and she did so. Gratefully. Despite the faded tapestries and layers of dust, the bed was warm and comfortable.

The tray was placed in front of her, and she suddenly realized how hungry she was. She took a bite of cheese and struggled not to wince. It was undoubtedly the worst cheese she had ever tasted. She tried a piece of fruit, only to find it spoiled. She could not cut through the mutton. The ale in the tankard was sour.

"I am very tired," she said, pushing the tray away. Moira's face fell.

"It is not your food, Moira," Felicia said hurriedly. "I am just too weary to eat."

The woman looked unconvinced. She curtsied and took the tray. "Robina will stay here and see to yer every need," she said.

That would not do at all. As tired as she was, Felicia had scouting to do this night.

"I would prefer to be alone," she said with a touch of haughtiness. Haughtiness, she thought, would probably be expected when a high-born lady was spirited away from home and clan. She was not quite sure, since she did not feel high born at all.

Robina looked as if she were about to cry.

Felicia was being put in the very strange position of trying to comfort her captors. The lass obviously, desperately, wanted to succeed in this duty.

"I would like my garments laundered," Felicia said.

"Aye, milady," the lass said hopefully as she gathered up the clothing and fled.

Felicia wondered for a fleeting second whether the girl had any idea as to how to launder. But of course she would.

Moira took the tray. "I wish ye a good night, milady."

The door closed behind the serving woman. Felicia waited to hear a latch fall. It did not.

So she was not to be locked inside.

By orders of the lord?

She'd felt fear when she'd learned where she was going. The stories of the Macleans were told repeatedly in the Campbell keep. Then she had come face-to-face with the man she had been taught to hate. Not only was he a striking looking man, but there had been no cruelty in his face. To the contrary, there had been only concern for her. There was no sign of the demon she'd been taught to fear, the Maclean who had butchered women and children years ago.

But then he had mistaken her for Janet Cameron, and he had reason to be conciliatory. And charming.

For a fleeting traitorous moment, she had thought that prospect not an unwelcome one.

He *was*, as his man had said, well favored. He wore his dark hair short, like a soldier, and he had cool, gray eyes. His body—when she had stumbled into it—was hard and muscled, and he had lifted her as easily as she might lift a feather.

That had shocked her beyond reaction. So had the heat that had rushed through her. When he had put her back on her feet, her legs barely held her, and she'd been mesmerized by his flinty eyes.

She knew then she had leaped from the pot into the fire. If the Macleans learned who she really was, she would be returned immediately or held for ransom. The latter did not concern her as much as the former, though she doubted the same amount of cordiality would be accorded her, under those circumstances.

And when would her uncle discover she was missing? No doubt, there would be a hue and cry, and the Macleans would realize who they had.

Certainly they must already understand they didn't have the beauty that Janet was known to be. How much time did she have? She would have to escape again, before her true identity was discovered.

She probably should have wailed and trembled and cried many tears. Yet she hadn't been able to force them. She never cried. She couldn't feign outrage when she was at fault. She truly regretted that honest streak.

There was no choice but to continue the masquerade until she could run once more. The lad's clothes hidden beneath the mattress, and the jewels sewn into the cloak were her tools of escape. She had to believe it and to make it so.

A knock came at the door. From the impatient sound, she knew exactly who stood outside. She did not answer. After a few seconds, the door opened, and Rory Maclean strode in.

He filled the room with his presence. He paced back and forth before saying anything, then looking as if he had steeled himself, he confronted her. "You are not frightened," he said. "Why?"

"Mayhap I am," she challenged him. "Mayhap I just choose not to display it to my captors."

His gaze speared her, then a small mirthless smile played on his lips. "I am not sure you are afraid of anything, milady."

But she *was* frightened and for very different reasons than he could possibly imagine. Feeling very much at a disadvantage in the bed, she attacked. "Is it your custom to invade a lady's bedchamber?"

He looked startled at being challenged. "You have not demanded to be taken home."

"You already told me you were sending me there. Did you lie?"

He scowled. "I do not lie."

"You just kidnap brides."

"A mistake was made. My men believed you were in trouble. You were alone."

"Archibald said you needed a bride."

His expression did not change as the lie was exposed.

He shrugged. "Archibald has fantasies. I hope Moira has made you comfortable. I will personally escort you to your father tomorrow. We will leave at dawn."

She merely nodded.

"If there is nothing else I can do, I would leave you to your rest," he said stiffly.

"There is nothing."

He did not leave immediately. Instead, his eyes studied hers even as she did the same. She found it difficult to tear her gaze from his compelling face, his watchful eyes. She doubted he missed much.

It did not make sense. None of it did. Why did his clansmen feel they had to go to such extraordinary measures? Their lord was not ill-favored, though there was a sense of aloneness about him. Most women, she was sure, would find him appealing.

She flushed as warmth washed through her. Blithely ignoring reason, she did not want him to go. She wanted to know about this Maclean. It was madness, she knew.

He was an enemy. And she was plain Felicia Campbell. Pledged to a monster.

He hesitated at the door as if he wished to say more. Again their gazes met, held, and she felt a rush of her heartbeat. She had a wild desire to feel his arms around her again. For that brief moment in the courtyard, she had felt safe. More than safe.

She didn't understand her conflicting feelings. She had the desire to linger, to learn more of him, while he expressed nothing but an urgency to rid himself of her. Reason told her he had likely known of the abduction and simply had been disappointed in her.

In spite of reason and his insistence that she leave on the morrow, she thought she saw a flash of awareness in those wary eyes, a glint of masculine interest.

Impossible.

She only wanted it to be true. More the fool, she.

"I wish you a restful night, my lady," he said again.

She closed her eyes as he left the room, but his presence lingered, a strong masculine power that made her wish she were not a Campbell and that she had Janet's fair countenance.

Wishing would not make it so. She could not change the facts. She must have mistaken the sudden glint in his eyes.

She had to think of a way to prevent her departure in the morning. She could not be taken to the Camerons and exposed, and ultimately returned to her uncle.

She had to find a way to leave the keep alone. Undetected. There must be a private exit somewhere.

She would find it. She had to.

Chapter 5

JANET Cameron was the most puzzling female he'd ever met.

Rory went down to the great hall to sup, even as the lass remained in his thoughts. It was the first time in several years that a woman had raised more than a fleeting physical reaction in him.

He didn't understand why. Though she had been hailed as a beauty, she was more intriguing than lovely. No quaking lass, she.

Her face was interesting, if not beautiful. None of the parts went together—the wide eyes, the button nose, the square chin—and yet they were appealing to him. The bulk of her clothes had been deceptive. The robe had swayed when she moved and could not conceal the graceful outlines of her slender body.

God's breath, but those eyes held challenge.

She was as unlike Maggie as any woman could be. Maggie had been gently rounded and her nature had been kind. She had been a dreamer who saw the best in everyone. She liked everyone and expected everyone to like her. They always had.

She'd loved flowers and sun-filled May days. She rejoiced in the moon and stars and even the cold Highlands rain. And when she was carrying his child, she would sing to it and tempt him into playing the lute.

The world had been enchanted then.

Loneliness pierced him. He thought he had conquered it. Now he realized he had not.

The woman revived memories he did not want, that he had held at bay for years. Why had they flooded back now?

By all that was holy, the sooner the Cameron woman left this hall, the better.

Douglas met him at the entrance of the hall and walked in with him. "Should I put a guard on her door?" asked his steward.

"No," Rory said as he stretched his long legs out at the table. "She is not to think she is a prisoner. She will be gone tomorrow. Why should she try to escape?"

"She may not believe you."

"I think she did. She appeared to accept my explanation."

"Will you not reconsider, my lord? I saw her expression. She was not displeased with you."

Rory stared at his steward. "Do you not remember how my mother died, and Lachlan's? My Maggie and, God help me, Anne.

"Maggie died in childbirth," Douglas said, "and Anne of a fever. Half of Leith died."

"Anne was there because of me. Waiting for me to come home."

"It was her choice, my lord," Douglas said. "Not yours."

"It does not matter. The Cameron lass goes back," Rory said firmly, weary of the subject.

"Aye, my lord."

"In the morning."

"Aye."

"No more tricks."

"Nay, my lord."

Rory did not like Douglas's agreeability. He never gave up that easily. Still, what could he do? Rory planned to escort the lady himself. He drained the tankard in front of him. He would take his rest and prepare to leave early.

FELICIA waited until all sounds ceased.

Judging the hour to be well past midnight, she took the candle and tried the door. *Unlocked.* She said a brief prayer of thanks.

The candle flickered from the air in the hallway. She shivered in the cold air, but then stiffened her resolve. She needed to know more about this place.

The adjacent chamber to hers was much like her own, more dusty, but truly grand. When she stepped on the elaborate carpet, a cloud of dust rose.

Rory Maclean was laird. All those she'd encountered acknowledged him as such. Why did he not use the chamber obviously intended for the chief?

She studied the interior, wondering if it, like some in the Campbell home, had secret chambers and passages.

But she found nothing that would indicate such. It was richly furnished with tapestries and exotic floor covering, unlike the rushes used throughout her home.

She wondered again why the laird did not use the chamber, though she was grateful he did not. The thought of his proximity sent a new shiver down her back. The fact that it was not one of fear frightened her in an entirely different way.

She found nothing and left the room, following the stairs up to the next floor. She continued up as she heard voices. On the fourth level there were more chambers, all of them had obviously been unoccupied for a long time. They had minimal furnishings: bed, table.

Then she found a chamber that appeared to have been sealed off. Shrouds covered the furnishings. She lifted one and saw an intricately carved cradle. A nursery. Another shroud covered a large box half filled with both new and worn toys. She regarded the box thoughtfully. It was large enough to secret a body her size, if need be.

Her gaze went back to the cradle, and she felt a sudden pang. She adored children. Now it was unlikely she would ever have any of her own. She banished the thought as she inspected a connecting chamber, plainer than any of the others. It would have been for a child's nurse.

Melancholy seemed to linger here. It shouldn't. This should be a happy place. She shivered and went to the window. It faced the sea, much like her own room at home, and she glimpsed a rock far from shore. Was this where the Maclean had attempted to murder his Campbell wife in the sea? Had he watched her struggle?

The light from a half moon bounced off the wild waves. Felicia wondered whether that woman had looked at the sea from here. Had she dreamed of having a child? Had she loved the man who had ultimately caused her death?

Fate had played a strange trick bringing Felicia here. Yet she had an odd feeling of belonging, of familiarity. A shudder ran through her. She had not come here to indulge in fantasy. She needed to find places to hide.

She could not go to the Camerons tomorrow and have her identity revealed. She would be returned quickly to her uncle. She needed time to find a way safely out.

She left the room, oddly reluctant to do so, and continued her exploration. Everyone in the tower seemed to be asleep, though she knew there were guards on the ramparts.

Felicia combed the rest of the rooms, stopping only when she reached the steps leading to the ramparts and the guards.

She started back to her chamber, her slippers making only a whisper of sound.

She passed her room. Hesitated. The lower floors would have more activity. Yet she needed to know more. If she met someone, she could always say she was still hungry.

She stopped when she heard voices in the passageway below her.

One belonged to the tall laird. She recognized the deep, authoritative tone.

"Have twenty men ready at daybreak."

"I think you should take more. There will be parties looking for her. They may act before you can explain."

"Explain what? That we took their heiress? Damn it, Douglas, you should have stopped this. But now I will no' have killing over it."

"If you would but consider wedding her . . . even hand-fast. They would be bound then to help us against the Campbells."

A silence. Then the man called Douglas said, "Perhaps the Camerons will be grateful."

"I doubt it," the Maclean said. "You will have the men saddled and ready to go. I will not use a woman in that way."

"Aye, my lord."

She moved swiftly back to her room. *Help us against the Campbells.* Against Jamie. Her blood curdled at the thought of a combined force of Macleans and Camerons.

It wouldn't happen. Janet loved Jamie. And Felicia was not a Cameron. They would not fight for her.

She'd heard her Campbell kinsmen talk about the raids on Maclean properties. The old laird had died, and the heir had disappeared in foreign lands. The middle son had been at sea. A good opportunity to grab Maclean land and cattle and crops.

The hatred was obviously reciprocated. She heard it in Maclean voices every time her clan was mentioned.

She would be safe if they took her to the Camerons. The Camerons would protect her, but then they would see her delivered to Edinburgh.

No, she had to continue with her original plan. Reach

Jamie. Or a nunnery where no one knew her family. Either would be preferable to the marriage planned for her.

But she had to delay tomorrow's departure. She needed time to find a way to leave on her own and travel to Edinburgh—and Jamie.

She opened the door to her chamber again. No sounds. She had another mission now. She found her way down the steps and moved silently across the great hall to the kitchen. No one had stirred yet, though a great log was burning in the giant fireplace.

Using the candle for light, she found what she needed, then swiftly returned to her chamber. She closed the door and leaned against it for a moment. She had a plan and it was every bit as desperate as her last one.

"MILADY is ill!"

Rory had risen long before dawn. He had shaved and bathed in ice-cold water, then dressed in his white shirt and the plaid. He wore more constrictive—and fashionable—clothes when he sailed and visited foreign ports, and he appreciated the freedom of the plaid.

He'd been ready to leave his room when Moira had knocked.

Moira was more family than servant. She had helped raise him, along with Douglas. His father, like himself, had not wanted to take and lose another wife. Alexander Maclean had married for love three times and had watched each bride die.

As Rory had twice.

He followed Moira along the passageway, his soft shoes barely making a sound on the stone floors.

The door was open. He entered, Moira trailing behind him. A servant was beside the slight figure in the large bed.

Her cheeks were flushed with fever, her eyes hollow, and she sneezed.

"My lady," he said with a frown.

She looked up at him with clouded eyes.

God's blood. If the Cameron lass were to sicken in his care . . .

He looked helplessly at Moira.

"The poor lass canna be traveling today," she said. "I will be making a potion for her."

"When will she be able to travel?"

"I do not know," Moira said.

"I should send word to the Camerons," he said.

Janet Cameron began to cough.

" 'Tis no' a good idea," came Douglas's voice from the doorway.

Rory whirled around, saw Douglas's concerned face.

"I will be back," Rory told Moira and stepped outside with Douglas, closing the door behind him. "Why is it not a good idea?"

"Archibald claims that no one knows we took her. No one knows she is here. I think it best if we return her in good health."

Rory knew instantly that Douglas was right. If anything happened to the lass, the blame would fall on Maclean heads.

She would not worsen. She could not.

A cold knot formed in his stomach. He did not know if he could bear to see another woman die. Especially by his hand, or that of his clan. They were the same, he knew, and would be judged so. Intentions did not matter.

He could not allow it to happen.

He turned to Douglas. "Is there a physician?"

"Not in fifty miles."

"Send someone for him. Take two horses and change them on the way."

"Moira—"

"Moira is a fine healer, but I will not take any chances with the lass's life.

Douglas nodded. "I will send one man and tell the others to dismount."

"Nay. I want them to scout the area. And I want more

sentries on the walls. There is always the chance that someone did see her taken."

Rory watched him go down the steps, then stared at the closed door of the chamber again.

He hated indecision. He did not like feeling helpless. Nor did he like the feeling that he had been here before. He had watched two wives die. Pain rushed through him at both memories.

He vowed that if the fever worsened, he would send a rider to the Cameron keep. She should have those who cared for her nearby.

He went back into the room.

Moira was washing the lady's face with cool water, and some of the fever flush was fading.

Mayhap God was with him this time.

He knelt at her side. "I can send word to your clan that you are ill."

"Nay," she said with a soft sigh. "I would no' wish to be the cause of war."

"They must know you are missing now. They will be worried."

"My father is in Edinburgh."

"Your mother then."

A cloud passed across her face, and she turned away.

Was there some reason then that she would not want her family to know where she was?

By all that was holy, he had been responsible for enough misery. And now he was responsible for her. He would do as she wished. For now. But he felt bloody uncomfortable doing it. The longer he waited, the more blame could come to the clan.

He had returned home to try to bring peace after years of war. As a youth, he had taken part in the bitter warfare with the Campbells. It wasn't until he heard a woman's tortured cries and realized a child had died that his blood had cooled. He would never forget that day. Though he had not dealt the death blow, the cries of the mother still haunted him.

And then he had wed Maggie, though he had never felt worthy of her. She had brought gentleness to his life. Now he was facing conflict with still another clan, one nearly as powerful as the Campbells.

He rose to his feet and turned to Moira. "Let me know of any change. Even the smallest one."

ELICIA had always taken pride in being forthright and honest. Now lies were tumbling from her mouth quicker than fleas jumped onto a dog.

She had not expected the stricken look on the lord's face, nor Moira's deep concern. She had expected that everyone would leave her in peace just as they did when she was ill at Dunstaffnage. She was naught to the Macleans. The lord only wanted rid of her.

A few hot stones wrapped in cloth and placed next to her cheeks, pepper to make her sneeze, and no sleep to make her eyes red-rimmed made her look ill. Enough, she'd thought, to delay the journey.

She thought she might have four days to make her escape. Not much more. Janet would have returned to the Camerons, and there would be no outcry there. The steward at Dunstaffnage was not a timid man, but he did fear her uncle. He would not report her escape to his lord until he felt certain he could not find her. He would comb the entire area for her before admitting failure.

But rather than being left to herself to recover, she was being smothered by care, by worry, by concern. It was new to her; no one other than Jamie had ever shown such bother over her before. Even the cold, angry lord had seemed uncertain. She'd felt warmed by the concern in his eyes. For the first time, they had reflected something other than the fact that he felt her to be a monumental nuisance.

He had looked intensely masculine and appealing. He

entered a room like a storm, directing all attention to himself just by his presence.

He is a Maclean, her family's greatest enemy. And hers was his.

And now he was thinking about sending someone to notify Janet's family. Her family.

Dear mother of God. She had become enmeshed in a web of her own creation. This was why she so rarely lied.

"Milady, do you feel ye could eat something?"

She nodded. "Mayhap a little."

"I will return in a wee moment."

Moira left, and Felicia rose from the bed, and looked under the bed where she had hidden the rocks. She had only a few moments, if that many, before someone else came to inquire about her health.

Using the fireplace tools, she placed the rocks in the fire, waited until they heated, then very carefully wrapped them back in pieces of cloth and scampered back to the bed. She placed the wrapped stones against her cheeks, forcing herself to bear the heat. When she felt sufficiently fevered, she again placed them under the bed, then snuggled down under the covers.

Moira arrived several minutes later, a tray in her arms. Unfortunately there seemed to be naught but a tankard and a bowl of porridge.

Moira's face darkened as she saw the newly produced flush in Felicia's cheeks. "Here, milady," she said, presenting the tankard filled with a foul-smelling brew. Felicia sniffed, then sneezed.

"'Tis good for ye, milady," Moira said.

Since she had an interest in seeming to try to make herself well, Felicia forced herself to drink the mixture, which truly was quite terrible. The porridge was not much better.

"The fever seems worse," Moira said, her brow crinkling with worry.

"I think I just need rest," Felicia said.

"I will stay with ye."

"Nay," Felicia said. "I know you have duties, and I have taken you away from them. 'Tis nothing but weariness, and I canna sleep with someone worrying over me." She said the last with a smile to indicate it was her own foible and not Moira's presence that was the problem.

"The lord—"

"The lord would like to see me better," she said.

The woman clucked, but gave her one more worried look and backed out of the room. She hesitated before closing the door, obviously loath to leave her charge. "Ye let us know if ye need anything?"

"Aye," she said.

"I will have someone outside the door."

"There is no need," Felicia protested.

"The lord will have my head if aught happened to ye." She hesitated. "He is a good mon. He should have no blame on this."

"He will not," Felicia said, hoping that it was true. She truly did not wish to be responsible for any violence.

Moira gave her a rare smile. "He would make a good husband."

Did everyone wish to marry them off? "He obviously has no wish to wed," she said.

"He has had much sadness," Moira said. But then she quickly disappeared out the door and closed it quietly behind her.

What sadness?

She tried to remember everything she had heard about the Macleans. There had been the curse. And since then constant war. In her mind, the Macleans had been frightening and evil. But in truth, she had seen little that was frightening and even less that was evil.

The man called Archibald had been uncommonly thoughtful after their initial encounter, and the Maclean laird had not fit her image of a monster. He was, in fact, the opposite.

The sea was alluring too, beautiful, but there was also

deception and danger in the tides, in the rush of water against rocks.

It was foolish even thinking such things. She should be thinking about escaping from the keep and making her way to her cousin.

She found herself yawning. Mayhap something in the foul potion she'd just consumed made her drowsy, or the fact she had stayed awake last night and had had little sleep the nights preceding that.

She fought it. The fever would leave without her trickery. So would the sneeze.

Mayhap a short nap. No more.

Her eyes closed.

*R*ORY stabled his horse.

The quiet had worried him. He'd expected Camerons at the gate, and he didn't understand why they were not.

Surely the disappearance of the daughter of the house would have aroused men to search all the lands around the area where she disappeared. The fact that this was not happening caused him concern.

He had ridden out with several of his men. They had spied no Camerons, only a band of Campbells. He had ordered his men to disappear into the wooded countryside. He wanted no confrontation even as he saw the disappointment in the faces of his men.

Rory knew they were not pleased. Their grumbling was meant to be heard. Patrick would have fought.

None called him coward. They had seen him fight in the past. But he had heard their whispers that Maggie had softened him, had changed him. He had been gone too long.

They wanted Patrick.

Bloody hell, he wanted Patrick back as well.

When he returned to the keep, he strode up to the chamber the Cameron lass occupied.

He knocked lightly.

No answer.

Moira should be there.

He opened the heavy door and stepped inside. The fire warmed the chamber and cast flickering shadows across the bed.

The lass was asleep. Long black lashes sheltered those striking eyes. The red of fever had left her cheeks. She breathed naturally.

His prayers had been answered. Apparently, Moira had left her because the danger was over.

He wanted to lean over and touch her cheek, to feel that the fever was indeed gone. But he knew that was an excuse. It had been a long time since he had touched a woman.

Rory could have bought women in the ports he visited. He probably wouldn't have to buy favors at all. Women often looked at him with invitation in their eyes.

But when Anne had followed Maggie in death, he had forsworn casual dalliances, which seemed disloyal to him.

He found himself staring down at the lass. He did not know why she intrigued him. Nor did he understand the brief tenderness that made him want to reach out.

She seemed so alone. She had, in truth, seemed that way when she entered his courtyard and met him with a quiet dignity that affected him far more than tears would have.

He stared at her for several more minutes, at the wild red hair flowing over the pillow, the stubborn jaw. He thought of the fire that had been in her eyes earlier.

Before he realized what he was doing, he leaned down and tucked an errant curl behind her ear. Her skin was smooth. Cool.

Thank the saints.

He should take her to the Camerons on the morn, but mayhap it would be best to give her another day of rest, time to gain her strength.

It was not because he wanted her to stay another day.

He carefully opened the door, left the room, and closed the door behind him. He despaired at his reluctance in doing so.

Chapter 6

❦

$\mathscr{S}$TREAMS of light woke Felicia. She burrowed deeper into the feather bed and stretched like a lazy cat even as she realized her situation was precarious.

She knew she should feel urgency. Fear. She should feel terror.

Yet she should be safe enough today. She would talk to servants. She would explore. She would find a way out.

She must!

She touched her cheek. She'd dreamt that someone had touched it last night. Not just any man. Lord Rory Maclean.

He should be the last man in Scotland to haunt her dreams. Her uncle had proclaimed all Macleans to be devils. But she had not seen that in him. Instead, he appeared a man very much alone, but not unkind. And certainly not a monster.

Her cheek still felt warm from that brief impression, or dream, or whatever it was. It was far warmer than the hot rocks she'd held against her cheeks. Rocks didn't convey tenderness, nor did they send rivers of heat throughout her body.

Had it really happened?

And if it had? He was the enemy.

She sank deeper into the bed, trying to avoid the image of the Maclean standing above her, his hand touching her. She should shrink from the thought. Instead, she was drawn to it like a moth to light, and it remained a small treasure stored in her mind.

Memories. The touch awakened memories. She had known tenderness before, but it had been so long ago . . .

She turned over, trying to reject the clanging thoughts and memories. They were too painful. Instead, she concentrated on the warmth and comfort of the bed.

Another image struck her. *A bare cot in a tiny room in a nunnery.*

One of the options she'd considered. Still considered, as a last resort, if she could not find Jamie. Or, if she did, but he could do nothing.

She had always considered herself devout. Perhaps not as much as she should be, but she tried. A life of prayer and peace had seemed a bearable compromise to marriage.

But as her body remembered and reacted to that dream-like sensation, she realized she was probably not very suited for a religious life.

That frightened her far more than any of her previous thoughts. She *had* to find a way to leave the walls of this keep for London. And before those beguiling feelings deviling her caused her to make mistakes. She could *not* be attracted to Rory Maclean.

The door opened, and Moira entered, carrying a tray. She glowed as she looked at Felicia.

"My herbs did well. Ye look much better."

"I feel much improved," Felicia said. "Thank you for all your care. I know I am added trouble."

"Nay, it is good to have a lass here again. My lord has been—" She suddenly stopped, obviously afraid she was speaking out of turn.

"My lord has been what?" Felicia asked.

"'Tis not my place to say," Moira said. "I will return with yer clothes. They be washed and mended. My lord said ye should also have anything else you need. We still have clothes that belonged to his or Lachlan's mither."

"Lachlan?" She immediately identified the name as the one belonging to the Maclean who had chained his Campbell wife to a rock.

"He is Lord Rory's brother."

"Tell me more about your lord," she said. "Does he ever smile?"

Moira looked wistful. "He once smiled all the time."

"But no more?"

"He ha' much sorrow."

Felicia knew there were three Maclean sons. She also knew each had different mothers and each mother had died young. She knew all that because it was part of the legend and smug gossip among Campbells. Deserving, they all said.

She also knew that one of the Macleans was said to have destroyed a Campbell village years earlier. It was said that women and children had been killed then. She found it difficult to believe the man responsible for that was Rory Maclean. He had not been welcoming, but he had treated her with every courtesy. Would he do the same if he knew she was a Campbell?

She couldn't stay here in his keep to find out, yet she wondered at Moira's words.

"What sorrow?"

Moira searched her face as if trying to decide whether she was worthy to hear more. Then she nodded as if making a decision.

"He lost two wives. Inverleith is a sad place fer him."

"He loved them?" She had heard of too few love matches.

"Oh yes, particularly his Maggie. The other I did no' know, but his Maggie was a love."

His Maggie.

The way Moira said the words told her much. "I heard . . . there was a curse."

Moira scowled. "I donna believe in curses." She set the tray down on a chair with a bang that belied her words. "'Tis naught but foolishness," she said though her voice quivered slightly. "Women die giving birth."

Felicia couldn't help herself. "Is that what happened to Maggie?"

"Aye. Both she and the wee lad were lost."

A wave of sadness swept over Felicia. She remembered her own mother and father. They had both been taken by the same fever that had swept the nearby village.

But now she understood the aloofness of Rory Maclean. Did he worry another woman would die? Or did he fear the Camerons' wrath if she were to die?

"And Lachlan?" she asked.

Moira smiled, her eyes crinkling with affection. "He be a gentle soul."

A Maclean a gentle soul?

"I will be leaving ye to eat. My lord will want to hear the fever is gone."

But Felicia did not want her to go. She wanted to hear more about Rory Maclean and his brother. The more she knew, the more likely she could escape before anyone discovered she wasn't Janet Cameron.

"Will you keep me company?" she pleaded.

Moira looked pleased. "Aye."

"Is the laird here?"

"He left to see if there are parties searching fer ye."

Stark terror struck her. What if he encountered Campbells looking for her? Her web of lies would be discovered.

Moira regarded her with an odd look.

Felicia tried to act as if she'd nearly swooned. "I am still light-headed."

"Of course ye are," Moira replied sympathetically. "Men," she muttered then in a barely audible voice.

She stepped aside. "Ye eat, milady. Lord Rory will have my head if ye are not better."

"So he can send me away?"

"Aye, I fear so. I thought it a foul scheme in the beginning, but I would like to see him wed again." Again, blue eyes weighed her.

"You knew about it."

"Aye."

"And Lord Rory?"

"Nay. Archibald knew he would forbid it."

"He said it was a 'mistake.'" She did not add that she thought it might have been because she was plain and not at all what he expected. Nor did she add the hurt that the thought caused. She had not wished to be kidnapped, but neither did she wish to be a rejected prisoner. That was humiliating beyond tolerance.

"Our laird just returned from the sea. He were summoned when Patrick did not return from France, but Archibald fears he will no' stay, that he will return to the sea. He canna do that as long as there is war between the Campbells and our clan. He wishes to make a truce so he can leave again."

"He does not wish a wife? Archibald said . . ."

"Archibald did not consult him."

"Then why can he not give me a horse, and I will return on my own? No one will know Macleans had aught to do with it. I will say I became lost in the fog."

Moira shook her head. "He will want to see ye safely back."

Felicia was tempted to bargain. But bargaining with Moira would do no good. She would have to make her devil's bargain with the laird himself.

"I will leave ye to eat," Moira said and left before Felicia could ask any more questions.

Famished, Felicia sat up in bed and started to eat from

the tray. There were pastries and fruit and bread. Despite her hunger, the pastries were not very good. In truth, they were dreadful.

She started on the bread and that, too, was nearly leaden, not light and tasty like that made at Dunstaffnage. Even the fruit was poor, overripe and overly sweetened.

She managed only a few bites when the door opened again, and a young man with cropped auburn hair peered inside.

"May I come in?" he asked cautiously.

"Since you are the only one to ask permission, aye," she said.

He stepped inside and bowed extravagantly, despite one hand carrying a lute. "I am Lachlan, the youngest of the Macleans." He grinned. "And the most personable. Moira said you were eating. I thought to entertain you and try to counter my brother's more surly manner."

His grin and teasing words were infectious. She found herself smiling. Perhaps she could find out more about Lord Rory and how he might react if he discovered who she really was.

"Thank you, I would like that."

"Moira said you were ill."

"I was. Her good herbs and a night's rest were miraculous."

"I am glad," he said simply, and she knew he truly was. He glanced at the tray. "I but wish she was as good with food as she is with healing herbs. But I imagine you have already discovered that." He spoke the words with true amusement.

She studied him. He was slighter in build than his brother, tall and lean. His face had not Rory Maclean's striking handsomeness, but in an odd way was more attractive, since it had none of the dark wariness. His mouth was wide and expressive. He smiled easily, and when he did, his entire face lit up, and the area around his eyes crinkled. It was a face that one instinctively trusted.

"You are Lady Janet Cameron. Now that the formalities are over, I want to welcome you and wish most sincerely you suffered no ill effects as a result of a too enthusiastic quest to find my brother a wife."

"You did not approve?"

"I neither approved nor disapproved. I am rarely consulted."

"Why?"

"I am not sufficiently warlike."

"And your brother is?"

"Both of my brothers are. I am the only embarrassment. I prefer books and music to swords. I keep the estate records," he offered without rancor, as if he happily accepted the role of misfit.

She never had. Her uncle had never understood why she wanted to learn to read, but he had readily accepted Jamie's reasoning that it would enable her to better run a household. Jamie had never told him she knew little else about running a household.

Still, despite the younger Maclean's words, she recognized strength in him. Perhaps because it took strength to realize what one was and to be true to oneself. Lachlan Maclean appeared to do just that.

He sat down and started strumming the lute. He was good, very good.

"Do not let me stop you from eating, my lady," he said, looking up.

She did as he asked, despite the unappealing fare. She wanted him to stay. She wanted to learn more about the Macleans. "I have heard of a Lachlan Maclean."

"No doubt my infamous ancestor who tried to kill his wife in a most unpleasant manner."

"I pray it's not a family trait."

"Nay," he said with the grin that made her want to smile, too. "My brothers like the ladies too much."

"Lord Rory does not seem to like me." *Why did it even matter?*

His grin faded. "'Tis not you, my lady. He wants to make peace, and your . . . misadventure could spoil his plans. Once he decides on a course, he rarely moves away from it."

"I thought the Campbells and Macleans have fought for years."

"They have. Some of us would like to end it. It hurts both clans and benefits no one."

"And others?"

He shrugged. "They know nothing else. Hatred has existed between our clans for years. The Campbells kill Macleans, and Macleans kill Campbells."

"But your brother seeks to end it?"

"Aye." He started to finger the lute again, and she listened to the plaintive melody. Then he started to sing in a soft, true voice. It was her story, a tale of a beautiful lady who was spirited away to be the wife of a handsome lord.

"I am not beautiful," she said when he finished. "But it is a fine song."

He eyed her critically. "Why do you think you are not beautiful? Songs are written about you."

About Janet Cameron. Not about Felicia Campbell. Everyone here must wonder about that.

She did not answer. Instead, her mind worked furiously. Perhaps he could help her escape the walls of the keep.

But that was only if she could avoid being returned to the Camerons today or tomorrow.

"Archibald said he wanted me to wed Lord Rory, but Moira said the lord did not want to wed. I thought it might be because I am . . . not as he thought."

He looked at her with renewed interest. "It has nothing to do with you, Lady Janet. It's just that his . . . Maggie, died here in childbirth. He lost his wee son as well. He would have gladly given his life for hers. She made him forget—"

He stopped suddenly as if he realized he had said too much.

"Forget?"

Instead, he started playing again, his head bent in concentration.

When he finished, he stood and walked toward the door. "All my songs are true," he said as he opened the door and left.

"*T*HE lass ate well," Moira reported when Rory returned and summoned her.

"The fever?"

" 'Tis gone."

"We can leave then." He did not like the unexpected reluctance he felt. It was only because he had been too long without a woman. Since Anne's death, he had not made love to a woman.

His own private penance.

In any event, Janet Cameron was not the sort of woman who appealed to him. He liked gentleness. Compatibility. Her eyes were too challenging, her chin too stubborn. Even that unruly hair spoke of wildness.

Moira hesitated. "She offered to take a horse and return alone, to say she was lost. Then no blame would visit here."

"I cannot do that. What if brigands attacked her?" He stopped, then said ironically, "I guess they already have."

"Archibald is no' a brigand."

"I wonder if she thought so when he grabbed her. But I will not have her riding alone. The borders are too dangerous."

Moira sighed. "I do not think she should leave today even if it were safe. She is still weak. Ye would no' wish to see the fever return."

"Every day adds danger. She is pledged to the Campbell heir. We could not withstand a siege by both Campbells and Camerons, especially when they both have the ear of King James."

"Mayhap she is no' so happy with the event," Moira said slowly. "She does no' appear to be so anxious to return."

He had received the same impression, and it had puzzled him. She had not demanded an immediate return to her family or to the Campbell keep. He had believed it fear, fear of him and the Macleans, but mayhap Moira was right.

It did not matter, he told himself. He could not risk his clan's future for a reluctant lass.

"I will judge her fitness for travel myself," he said, leaving Moira and taking the stone steps two at a time. The sooner he returned the lass, the better.

He reached her door and heard the sound of the lute inside, then his brother's voice. He was singing a song.

Lachlan used to do that for Maggie. His brother had been but a lad but half in love with Maggie himself. But then every man had been. Rory leaned against the stone wall and listened. It had been a long time since he'd heard his brother play. Not since Maggie died. He wondered what had prompted it.

And then he heard Lachlan's words about Maggie, and his heart seemed to stop.

Lachlan saw him as he left Felicia's room, and he closed the door behind him.

"It has been a long time since I heard you sing."

"You have been gone a long time."

"Not long enough." He changed the subject. "How is our guest? Do you think she is ready to ride?"

"No," Lachlan said. "She barely ate. She is pale. You do not want to deliver a sick hostage."

"She is not a hostage."

Lachlan shrugged. "Why not send a message to the Camerons? Tell them that our men found her wandering and lost."

"I considered that. But I did not want to invite Camerons inside the walls until I was sure what she would say. And to deny hospitality would be to admit guilt. On the other hand, an escort of Macleans would signal our goodwill."

"You will have to charm her," Lachlan said lightly.

Rory looked at him suspiciously. "Not you, too?"

"Oh I have no intention of asking you to seduce her. Merely to make her sympathetic to the misguided efforts of our kinsmen. That might take a few days."

"We cannot wait that long."

"They probably think she is lost. They will be hunting her in the hills and caves. In the meantime, you can be pleasant to her."

"A day," Rory said. "No more."

"I have no doubt you can accomplish much in that time," Lachlan said before turning toward the stone steps.

Rory took a deep breath. Unfortunately, Lachlan was right. If he wished to keep peace with the neighboring clans, he would have to enlist his prisoner's assistance.

He opened the door.

Janet Cameron was sitting on the bed, brushing her long, unruly, red hair. Her eyes widened when she saw him.

He bowed. "My lady. You look far better than you did when you arrived."

He suddenly realized how that sounded. So much for charm. "I mean your health appears much improved."

She smiled suddenly, and he was surprised at its power. Her entire face lit. "I was wet, my lord. I must admit I felt like a drowning rat."

His gaze met hers. "Would you like us to take you home today?"

"I am very weary from the journey. Your men ride hard."

"We can send word to the Camerons."

"I would prefer to borrow a horse tomorrow and travel on my own. That way, no blame will come to you."

"You care about that?" He did not tell her Moira had already conveyed the offer.

"I like your brother. I would not wish harm to come to him. My family is offended easily. But if I were just lost . . ."

Not that she did not wish harm to him. She had specified his brother. An inexplicable jealousy struck him.

He realized that she was holding her breath while awaiting his answer. Did she truly care that no violence came as a result of Archibald's actions?

"You cannot travel alone. The Campbells . . ."

"I am betrothed to a Campbell," she said. "They will do naught to harm me."

He shook his head. "I will accompany you."

The light in her sapphire blue eyes dimmed. The room seemed to grow darker with it gone.

He wanted to ask whether there was a reason she did not rush to the keep of her family. But he didn't. It was best he did not know. He could allow nothing to affect his decisions. Nothing but the welfare of his clan.

Charm her, Lachlan had instructed.

That from his brother who seldom indulged in guile.

Perhaps he, too, realized the stakes this time.

"Will you have supper with us tonight?"

"I have naught to wear."

"Moira will find something."

"Then aye."

"I must warn you. Moira is the cook and—"

"I know," she replied and the light was back in her eyes. Her lips twitched.

"Since my father died, there has been little order. Moira is Archibald's aunt, and she needed the position. We needed a cook. I have decent wine, though," he added quickly. A little too quickly, he thought.

Charm, Lachlan had insisted.

She nodded slowly.

"Moira will check on you during the day and bring several gowns. Select whatever you like."

"Thank you, my lord."

He looked at her as her hands continued to plait her hair in one long braid. Wisps of red hair escaped and curled around her face. She looked young and innocent and uncertain.

And fetching.

Not beautiful, but appealing.

Too appealing.

He stepped outside without another word and closed the door behind him. It was only then that he wondered whether his guileless younger brother had been in on the scheme to see him wed again?

If so, he would be disappointed.

Sorely so.

Chapter 7

ELICIA knew she had to be careful. She could not
appear to have recovered too quickly, and she had to
evade Moira's overprotective mothering as well.

She had to do more exploration. She had to find a way
to escape. But every time she stood, Moira seemed to appear and suggest she return to bed.

Toward late afternoon, Moira disappeared. Felicia managed to dress herself in her own garments, which had been
washed and returned.

She put on the sorely used pair of slippers and quickly
snuck out before Moira returned. She moved quickly down
the stone steps, darting into a corridor when she heard the
sound of boots coming from above. When it felt safe
enough, she managed to open the heavy door.

She found herself in a large bailey. She had been here only at night before, and her room looked out over the sea. Now she studied the interior of the keep.

Heavy gates were open, and riders galloped in. The great doors groaned as they closed behind them. She darted into the afternoon shadows, hoping no one would notice her, and watched as they dismounted and went through the same door she'd just departed from.

Her gaze skipped to a door in the wall. A guard stood immediately above it. She turned toward the stable and walked inside. Grooms were busy with the newcomers' horses, taking off saddles and halters. She went down the long line of stalls, finally finding Janet's little mare. She wished she had something from the kitchen to offer when the mare nuzzled her hand for a treat.

"Later," she assured her. Such an errand would provide another opportunity to visit the stable.

In the meantime, she studied the interior. Four boys were working the horses. Were they always here?

One of them caught her eye and came over to her. "Milady, can I help ye?"

"I was just thinking my mare needed some exercise, but you seem very busy."

He looked regretful. "Ye canna leave the bailey, milady. Archibald, he said nay."

"I do not care about leaving the bailey. I just wish to exercise the mare. I will stay within the walls."

The boy looked skeptical. "I will ask Archibald, but first I must help cool down the horses. Lord Rory feels strongly about his beasts."

That said something about Rory Maclean. She turned away and let him get back to work. She walked down the line of stalls until she reached the end. There was an extra large stall in which a black mare moved restlessly. She was obviously close to foaling.

Felicia held her hand out, and the mare nipped at it. One of her fingers bled, but Felicia held no malice. Ordinarily she would have disciplined the mare, but had she been as swollen and as uncomfortable, she probably would nip, too.

She watched as the grooms started bringing in water from the well for the watering buckets, wondering if she could befriend one of them. She feared not. The lad she had spoken with seemed to have a healthy respect for authority. She supposed the others did as well.

Still, there might be one . . .

She *had* to find some way to leave.

The groom returned and regarded her curiously. "Archibald said you were no' feeling well."

"I am improved," she said, "and needed some fresh air. I feel like a prisoner."

"I canna help that, milady. But someone might accompany you on a ride tomorrow."

"I would be most grateful." She hesitated, then continued. She wanted to form a bond with the lad. "The black mare is ready to foal?"

"Aye. Tonight, Lachlan says."

"I would like to watch," she said wistfully. She had always loved the sight of a foal taking its first few uncertain steps. It had always seemed a miracle to her.

The lad looked at her in shock. " 'Tis no sight for a lady," he said.

She had seen more than a few foals born. Neither Jamie nor the grooms at Dunstaffnage had this quaint idea of what a lady should do.

But would Janet have made such a comment? She had to remind herself that as of two days ago she *was* Janet. Fair and modest. Certainly not someone mucking in straw and blood. She had to stop making mistakes.

She changed the subject. "What is your name?"

"Mine, milady?" He looked startled to be asked.

"Aye."

"'Tis Hector, milady," he replied, his face growing bright pink.

"I will not forget it," she said. Nor would she. She needed every ally she could find.

She had to delay tomorrow's journey to the Cameron property and find an opportunity to get outside the walls. Every moment she stayed here, she risked her freedom. Perhaps, even, her life.

Reluctantly, she left the stable and returned to her room. She had not accomplished all she wished, but at least she knew more about the bailey and the walls.

She only wished she'd discovered more about the laird. Despite his courtesy, his eyes appeared to miss little. They were always watchful, always cautious. He would not be as easy to trick as the unsuspecting Camerons had been.

*W*HEN she returned to her room, a fretful Moira was waiting for her. Several dresses lay on the bed. Robina was with her.

"Milady, ye should not be wandering in these drafty halls," Moira scolded with the authority of someone who knew her position was safe. "Robina will help ye dress. I must go and see about supper." She turned and left the chamber.

Felicia's gaze went immediately to an underdress of pale green and a surcoat of a darker green trimmed with fur. 'Twas out of fashion but the color suited her.

"These are for me?"

"Aye, milady," Robina said. "Moira chose them."

Felicia tried on the garments, and they fit perfectly.

"Oh, milady, 'tis perfect with yer coloring," Robina exclaimed as she stood back. "Now yer hair."

Unfortunately Robina knew nothing about taming Felicia's wild curls. Felicia brushed it, and Robina attempted to confine it with pins, but nothing worked. Felicia finally plaited it into her usual long braid even as she wished she had Janet's hair that fell in silky waves to her waist.

Why did she care? The Maclean was an enemy, an impediment to her escape.

She *did* care. She'd once overheard her uncle telling Jamie that it was unfortunate she had not inherited her mother's beauty instead of the plain features of Felicia's father. It had wounded her deeply, and even Jamie's reply had not helped. He had praised her intelligence and spirit.

Jamie never knew she had overheard the conversation. He had, in truth, often told her she was bonny. But she'd known he lied.

So how, she wondered, had the Macleans accepted the tale that she was a famed beauty?

When she rose from the chair, Robina beamed as if she was indeed a beauty.

No one else would believe it, though. She only prayed that no one at the table had seen Janet.

A knock came at the door. Felicia stiffened as Moira opened it.

She did not want to see the disappointment in Rory Maclean's face when he saw her, but not to look would be cowardly, and she prided herself on being brave.

To her surprise, she did not see disappointment or disapproval, but a certain glint that warmed his eyes considerably. It disappeared quickly enough that she wondered whether she had actually seen it.

"My lady," he acknowledged, respect in his voice.

Startled, she found herself speechless. She felt totally inadequate standing there.

"Am I that frightening?" Lord Maclean queried, apparently taking her silence for fear.

"Nay, my lord," she said, "though your reputation and that of your clan is fierce."

"Only toward our enemies," he said.

That did not comfort her.

She did not move away as he offered his arm and approached the stairs. She needed his steadiness. Her legs felt suddenly weak, and her skin unexpectedly warm.

She mused for a moment that perhaps she really was ill, then his hand steadied her. As his strength and warmth surrounded her, she realized the flutter in her heart was not from any illness. Far too aware of his impact on her, she stumbled and was suddenly in his arms. The warmth turned to white-hot heat.

"The steps are rough, my lady."

She did not reply. She feared she would babble.

She was relieved when they reached the foot of the stairs and his hand relaxed on her arm. He did not release her immediately. Nor did she wish him to. She felt safe. Safe and protected and wanted.

Illusion. He thought her an heiress of a friendly clan. That was all. His interest would fade quickly enough if he knew the truth. Most likely it would turn to hatred, just as her uncle and cousin hated the Macleans.

As she should. The Macleans had been responsible for the spilling of Campbell blood, even that of women and children.

For now, though, she was aware only of the tingling of her blood, the heat crawling up her spine, the exhilaration of being in his presence, the unexpected pleasure of seeing his rare smile.

The Maclean accompanied her to the great hall, which was filled with male voices. There were no women in attendance except for the servants.

She thought that most odd. Except for Moira, she had seen few other women and certainly no well-dressed gentlewomen.

The keep itself also looked as if it had had no mistress for a long while. Dust was everywhere. Fireplaces looked as if they had not been cleaned in months, windows were dark with grime, and there was a general feeling of neglect.

Well, the former laird had been dead these past three years, and apparently there had been no one in charge until Rory appeared. Was he indifferent to it? Or did he not care because he intended to leave soon for the sea?

How she wished to hear of his adventures. How she longed to sail the world herself.

Not for the first time she wished she had been born a man. But for the first time, she felt the thrill of being a woman.

It was perverse, the devil playing a nasty trick.

Nonetheless, all eyes were on her as the Maclean led her to the head table and seated her next to him. Avid eyes studied her.

Among the men were those who had abducted her for their lord. Their faces beamed as they watched their lord treat her with courtesy. It was obvious they had not surrendered hope. Perhaps she could play on that as well.

She noticed an empty seat to her left, and before she could wonder about it, Lachlan appeared. His dress was disheveled, but he sported a wide grin. It seemed to be aimed directly at her.

"You are late," Rory Maclean said.

"Aye, a foal," he said. "It came faster than I expected. Perhaps Lady Janet would like to see her later."

Janet's heart jumped. "The black mare?"

Lachlan looked at her with surprise.

"I saw her earlier."

"Aye, it was a quick birth."

"And the foal?"

"A filly. Would you like to visit her?"

"Thank you, I would like that."

"Tonight?"

"Aye," she agreed and turned toward the platters of food being displayed. Rory Maclean poured her wine from a pitcher, and she sipped it. In contrast to the food, it was a very good wine.

"It comes from France," he said as he watched her.

She took another sip. Mayhap she could act as if she had drunk too much.

She tasted the partridge. It was underdone. She tried a piece of meat, and it was charred, too hard to eat. She took some bread and nibbled at it, knowing she needed the strength.

He said in a low voice, "I have no' had the time to find a new cook, and Moira tries hard."

She admired the loyalty. Her uncle had little loyalty to any of his servants.

She bent her head and tried to eat again. She would need food in her stomach if she were to escape tomorrow. Perhaps after viewing the foal, she would ask Lachlan to accompany her on a ride at dawn. She would try to lose him. Or bargain with him.

"I hope you are comfortable," the older Maclean said.

"Moira and Robina have been very attentive," she said. She sipped the wine. "I heard you have been at sea and have just returned."

His gray eyes impaled hers. "Aye."

"How long?"

"Ten years."

He had been here, then, when his clan had raped women and killed a child. She had hoped otherwise. She tried to keep her voice even. "Where have you been?"

"France and Portugal, mostly. Depends on who is at war with which country," he added wryly.

Felicia played with her goblet of wine. "I would like to sail. At times I wish . . ." She stopped.

"Wish what?" he prompted.

"That I had the freedom to do as I wish."

"The sea is a dangerous place."

"So is Scotland," she said. "People are abducted."

He had the grace to flinch, and the corner of his mouth twisted up in a half smile. "Aye, it can be."

Their gazes met, and again she thought she saw shadows in those gray eyes that were so watchful. There was fleeting amusement, even a flicker of appreciation, but then both disappeared. The shadows returned, and something more, an anguish that tore at her heart, and a loneliness that was stark.

Remarkably, she wanted to ease the lines of pain bracketing his mouth. She wanted to touch the dark hair that framed the hard face.

She struggled to return to their conversation. "Have you been in storms at sea?"

"Every sailor has been."

"I like storms."

She saw the surprise in his eyes.

"I doubt whether you would like one at sea," he said. "It's sheer terror when you are at the mercy of the sea and wind."

"I cannot imagine you ever feeling terror."

"Every man knows terror."

She took another sip of wine. Most men did, of course, but few would ever admit it.

She felt the warmth from the wine, from his presence. Why was she drawn to him? He was her family's enemy. Yet she was drawn to him as she had never been drawn to another person.

"Tell me about France."

He shrugged. "They have fine silks and even better wine."

"They are allies of Scotland."

"Only when it suits them," he said.

"And women? I have heard they are beautiful."

"I prefer ours," he said. "There are few pretenses."

She felt her cheeks warm. She hoped it did not show, and she turned her attention back to the food. No traps here.

The supper seemed to last for hours as Maclean clansmen drank and grew loud and bawdy.

"We brought you a bonny wife," one large man said, sloshing wine over his plate.

"And she has a worthy man," another chimed in.

The Maclean finally banged down his goblet of wine, some spilling over the table.

"I will hear no more of this," he said in a low voice that nonetheless carried across the room. "The lady is already bespoken. She will be returning home."

A choir of nays echoed in the great hall.

Rory looked rueful as he turned to her. "I apologize again for the behavior of my clansmen."

"They care about you."

"They care about the clan," he corrected.

"That is you, is it not?" she asked.

"It cannot be." His gray eyes turned cool. Distant. "You will be returned home safely for your own wedding."

"I have been here overnight without chaperones," she said quietly. "If it becomes known, I will be ruined. Jamie Campbell will not be wanting me."

"Then he would be a fool," he said, his hand touching hers and sending unexpected jolts of lightning through her.

She gazed up into his eyes. In her experience, wine usually dulled eyes, but his were clear and probing.

"Still, it would be far better if no one knew I had been here."

"I take responsibility for what my clan does," he said stiffly.

"A compromise," she offered. "You can take me almost home and watch as I enter the walls."

"A noble offer," he said, but there was a hint of amusement in the words.

Holy Mary in heaven, he seemed to read her mind.

She took a piece of fruit and was barely able to swallow it.

She looked down the table and noted that the wine was being consumed at a much more rapid rate than the food. There were needs here.

No. Do not think about it.

And she would be the last person to make any change. She could not cook or run a household. She *could* engage in swordplay. She doubted anyone at this table would appreciate that particular talent. It most likely would not go with the image of a fair and modest lady such as his kinsmen apparently believed they had captured.

She tried to eat again, but it was more than a little difficult with so many eyes on her. They all weighed, judged, speculated. Apparently they still had not given up on their fervent wish that their lord marry again.

She could not help but wonder about his wives.

"My lady?"

She started. She had been too engrossed in her own thoughts. She looked up at Lachlan.

"Perhaps you would like to name the foal. Hector said you seemed taken with the mare."

She looked at Lord Rory. She was only a guest here. Or to be more exact, a captive of sorts.

"I am sure you can think of something better than I," he said with that rare smile. "Lachlan is afraid I will call it 'horse.'"

"My brother has a practical nature," Lachlan said.

"What is the name of your ship?"

Silence. Lachlan raised an eyebrow and looked at his brother.

Rory shrugged. *The Lady.*

"I can see why Lachlan is concerned," Felicia said, even as she wondered why it did not carry the name of his first love. Was it simply because he could not bear being reminded of her? Did people really love that much?

She had really not believed that they did, though she thought Janet and her cousin a good match. They obviously cared about one another.

Had Lord Rory Maclean had a wild passion?

And had her cheeks just flamed at the forbidden thought? It was none of her concern whether or not a Maclean was passionate. Particularly when it was quite evident that his only wish was for her departure.

Still, she wanted to know more about his Maggie.

Even surrounded by clansmen, he seemed very much a man alone. Though he had an easy manner with his clansmen, there was not the jocular familiarity that Jamie had with the Campbells. She wondered if it were a cloak of grief that separated him from others, though he did not wear it openly.

She used to think that the legend regarding the Macleans was cruel and directed toward the wrong party—the wife. But she had been wrong. It must be terrible to be left behind.

Rory Maclean stood then, as did the others.

Lachlan grinned at her. "Do you want to see the foal?"

"Oh yes. But I will be leaving. It is not fair for me to name her."

"You can tell this is a masculine household," Lachlan said. "There is not a man here who can name a filly. You would be doing us a kindness."

She turned to Rory, but he merely shrugged. "Do as you wish."

His indifference stung. But Lachlan touched her arm lightly, and she curtsied her farewell to Rory. She accompanied Lachlan to the stable and to the back of the barn. She heard a soft whinny as they approached and watched the mare nuzzle her baby.

"Oh," Felicia exclaimed as she saw the foal wobble on thin legs, seeking her meal. She was as black as her mother with a head that looked too large, but Felicia knew she would quickly grow into it.

Her heart skipped a beat and tenderness filled her soul. She never tired of seeing a newborn, particularly foals. They always seemed so ready to take their place in the world.

"She's greedy," she said.

"Aye, she will be strong and swift."

"How do you know that?"

"Her bloodlines, my lady. They are very fine. My father prided himself on his horses."

"And your brother?"

"He is a fine horseman. But now he has no special mount. Instead, he rides them all. He hesitates to keep one horse for his own use.

"Because he might lose it?"

He looked at her with surprise, and a new warmth. "He does not say as much but aye, I think that is the reason."

The foal stumbled, then regained her footing as her mother nuzzled her.

"I always think it a miracle when a foal is born. Or any birth," she added.

"We will call her Miracle then," he said.

"And I will send her to you once she can leave her mother," came a familiar voice from behind them.

She whirled around, wondering how long he had been there. Had he heard her ask questions about him?

Rory leaned against the wall. His expression enigmatic, he took a few steps forward and looked inside the stall. He did not smile, yet he seemed to relax as he watched the mare with her foal. Then she understood what he was saying. He was giving this magnificent filly to her.

Except she wouldn't be where she should be. She could imagine the surprise if the animal went to the Camerons.

"Thank you, but it is too generous an offer." Her heart cracked as she said the words. How she longed to accept his offer. She had never had a horse of her own.

"We have delayed your journey and possibly your marriage. I would feel far better if you accepted this small token as an apology."

That wasn't what she wanted at all, but more refusals might well spur questions she could not answer.

"My thanks then," she said simply, knowing she would never see the animal in a Campbell stable, not unless it was stolen. But dear Mary, how she did want the foal.

"It is becoming cold, my lady," he said. "You should go inside."

"I would prefer to stay out here and watch Miracle."

"You were ill hours ago, Lady Janet. I do not wish to return you in poor health."

His words were like hammer strokes, hard and sharp. Not to be disobeyed. She had witnessed his displeasure when she had first been brought into the bailey. His frown could quell a rebellion.

And yet his clansmen had obviously disobeyed him to bring her here, and she had witnessed no punishment. Her uncle would have taken harsh steps had he been so disobeyed.

She reluctantly acquiesced. Perhaps she would steal back down later tonight.

He offered his arm, and she wondered whether it was courtesy or simply a way to ensure he was obeyed.

She took it and felt a now familiar jolt of heat. She looked up at him and saw a startled look in his eyes as if he, too, felt a certain recognition between them, a mutual acknowledgment of attraction.

She tried to tamp the sudden excitement she felt. He made her feel more alive than she ever had before. She found herself longing for a more intimate touch. A kiss . . .

She had never been kissed.

But he was a Maclean, and she was a Campbell.

And if that was not bad enough, Maclean brides did not survive. This keep and its disarray was a constant reminder.

Walk. Do not stumble on legs that always seemed to weaken in his presence.

I am a Campbell. I can never forget that.

DESPITE his best intentions, Rory was intrigued, fascinated, and, God help him, attracted to the Cameron lass.

He had been surprised when he had first met her, wet and in dishabille, and not at all bonny. In truth, his first impression was plainness, though she had a certain dignity that he respected. But now he understood why rumors abounded. She was not a beautiful woman, but she was a striking one with that flaming red hair and sapphire eyes. More importantly, she had a spirit that challenged, and a curiosity that intrigued him.

Although she appeared compliant and calm, he saw occasional flashes of rebellion in those striking eyes. This was no shrinking lass but one that stood straight and bold, though she was pretending to be otherwise.

She was as unlike Maggie as any woman he'd met. Maggie had the same surface calm about her, but there had not been the fire he sensed in the Cameron lass. Maggie had been as gentle as a butterfly and as complete in herself as a woman could be. She had longed for nothing other than her husband and children.

He suspected Janet Cameron longed for a great deal more. There was a restlessness in her that echoed his own, and her questions about the sea had not been idle conversation. Perhaps that was where the attraction lay, a shared sense of adventure.

But it was a moot thought. She was already pledged, and to a clan with which he sought peace after decades of warfare. He had resigned himself to a life without a wife, and meant to keep that vow.

He'd overheard her comment to Lachlan, and had been struck at how perceptive it had been. He did not want more losses. They were too painful, particularly when he felt partly to blame.

How had she known that?

Why did his heart beat a little faster in her presence? He thought he had it well under control until he heard her talk about the foal and saw the light in her eyes when she had turned to look at him. He'd been caught in the magic, in her delight of new life.

He had forgotten that magic like that existed.

They reached her chamber. He opened the door, guided her in, and intended to turn and leave. He would have done exactly that had not his hand touched hers, sparked a burning sensation that ran through his veins.

He looked down at her, at the face tilted up toward his. His eyes searched hers and found mysteries.

Go . . . step back . . . leave her.

Instead, he did the worst thing possible. He put a finger to her cheek and ran it along the side of her face.

She trembled slightly. Desire flamed between them.

Go. Now!

He leaned down and his lips touched hers in gentle exploration. She stiffened even as her lips responded to his. Her body trembled slightly, and, closing the door behind him, he wrapped his arms around her, drawing her near.

He caressed her mouth, tasting the sweetness of her lips. Her body leaned into his, and his kiss deepened.

He expected her to jerk away, but instead her lips became as demanding as his own.

And the devil himself could not stop him.

Chapter 8

⹂⹂⹂⹂

$\mathcal{I}$T was a soft, searching kiss.

Felicia had always wondered how a kiss would taste, would feel. Now she knew.

It was pure wonder.

Her body trembled, even as she felt his body tense. Though his lips were gentle as they explored and tested, she sensed he was fighting against the attraction that bounced like lightning strikes between them.

His mouth opened. His tongue darted along her lips, inviting them to part. She yielded, caught in the moment, in a special enchantment that made her forget all her misgivings, all her warnings to herself.

She hadn't expected the fire that erupted deep inside, the blaze that enveloped both of them. Or the odd yearning that seized her as she moved closer to him.

She touched his face, the stark angles, just as he had touched hers. A shudder ran through his body, making her aware that he was as affected as she. His right arm pulled her closer against his body as he released her lips and gave her an almost bewildered look.

His eyes closed, and then with a heavy sigh, he leaned back down and touched her lips again, this time with a sweet, lost wistfulness that held her in its spell. There was both surrender and poignancy in his touch. The longing inside her deepened, became a fiery craving throughout her body.

His kiss became harder, more demanding, almost ruthless. His tongue invaded her mouth, just as his body blatantly sought hers, and she responded shamelessly, fitting her body into his, feeling the change of his.

She reacted instinctively. Surprised, even shocked, by a knowledge she never knew she had, she wound her hands around his neck and played with the thick hair along his nape. A moan ripped from his throat, and she leaned back. His eyes were dark with passion. And pain.

Her heart ached for him, even as her body burned. He must have seen those feelings in her eyes, because he suddenly tore himself away with such violence that she stumbled back and nearly fell.

His hand caught her, holding her steady with an easy strength. The muscles in his shoulders bunched, and his breathing was labored as he obviously battled himself for control.

She did not want that.

"I apologize, my lady," he said in a harsh voice. "I had no right."

He had every right. She had invited it.

"You are promised to someone else," he continued. "You are here against your will. You are vulnerable. I acted dishonorably."

She stiffened her back. "I wanted you to kiss me," she said in the direct manner that usually got her in trouble.

His eyes were agonized. "You do not know what you want," he said, "and I took advantage of that."

She had always been told the Macleans were dishonorable. She'd had no reason to disbelieve it. But now she knew that description did not include at least one Maclean.

For a moment, she wished he lived up to that abominable reputation. Her body ached, her heart pounded, and her blood sizzled. If she could not reach Jamie and safety, could she truly accept life as a consort to Lord Morneith? Or spend her life in a convent if so decreed by her uncle, because her reputation would be destroyed? She had welcomed the thought days ago. It was unbearable now. How could she never know the reality of the promise she'd just tasted?

The desire? The anticipation? The tingling in every part of her body? She'd never felt so alive.

She wanted to tell him she was not Janet Cameron, that she was not promised to Jamie Campbell. But she *was* promised to a monster whose kisses, she knew, would be nothing like the one she'd just experienced.

Would the admission make a difference?

She could not risk it. However attracted he might be to her—and that itself was a miracle—she was but a woman to be bartered or sold. Most likely he agreed. Most men did.

She could have today, though. These few days. And perhaps if her reputation was sullied, Morneith would not want her.

She could seduce the Maclean! Once that fact became known, surely she would be tarnished goods. Not even Morneith would want her if all of Scotland knew she preferred the Campbell's most hated enemy to him.

How did one go about seducing someone determined to be honorable? She had never been seductive in her life. And yet there was certainly something between them, a connection that caused sparks whenever they were together. She did not understand it, or even trust it.

But mayhap she could use it.

Unless it used her, she warned herself.

She gazed up at him.

A muscle throbbed in his throat. She sensed he was having as much difficulty as she in turning away.

He stepped back, obviously more successful than she in making that first move apart. She could not let him go now. If she did, he would send her to the Camerons in the morning, and all her efforts would have been for naught.

She decided to swoon. She had never swooned before in her life. Still, she tried. She swayed and started to fall.

He instinctively put his arms around her again. Her body pressed against his, and she felt its hardness.

He cursed in a low voice.

But he did not move away this time.

She looked up and fluttered her eyelashes as she had seen Janet do with Jamie.

It was surprisingly easy since the air was suddenly still with a thrumming tension.

His face changed, his eyes becoming dark, and brooding, and wanting. Her body instinctively moved into his, and she was swept into a whirlpool of feelings that were uncontrollable. Her face turned upward, inches from his.

Then his lips were on hers again, and the kiss became more demanding, even desperate.

His tongue searched, teased, seduced until she felt her legs might collapse under her. She'd never felt anything like this, not this wild, mindless elation. Tremors of pleasure ran through her, as his tongue and hands created a flood of heady sensations.

She did not care about seducing him to avoid marriage now. She was too filled with new needs. She knew desire now for what it was. She knew its depth and intensity. It smothered every caution and thought.

He took his mouth from hers, and his lips burned a trail down the side of her face with unrestrained passion.

A knock. Another. For a fleeting second it was muted by the intensity between them. Then it came again, louder and insistent.

The Maclean stepped back, shaking his head as if to bring himself back to reality, then looked at her with an expression of chagrin and disbelief. As if he could not believe he had kissed her.

Neither could she. She knew her face must be flushed with color.

Another knock.

The Maclean mumbled what sounded like an oath to her, then opened the door.

She heard the steward's voice.

"Rory, a runner just came in. The Campbells have attacked the village near their border. Took cattle. Burned crofts. Trampled fields. Two crofters were killed. Many wounded."

Felicia's blood cooled as Rory Maclean stiffened. "Have a horse saddled for me. Pick fifteen men. We will leave within the hour."

The door closed. Douglas had not seen her, and she was glad. But Rory would see her stricken expression.

Her clan had attacked his. Douglas's words kept echoing over and over in her head.

Because they were searching for her?

She leaned against a wall. Had she been responsible—in some way—for the deaths of innocents? Had her disappearance sparked unreasoning retribution?

Rory turned to her. Hot anger had replaced the desire that had been there just seconds earlier. Anger and resolve.

"I am sorry," she said.

"It is not your doing, lass," he said. He touched her cheek for a moment with a wistful finality. "I should not have been here when my clansmen are in danger. I can only ask that you forgive me."

She heard the guilt in his voice, but she had no chance to say more.

"Lachlan will accompany you home. Again, my apologies for your misadventure." The wistfulness had left his voice. It was impersonal now, all his vital intensity—

everything that so attracted her—turned to protecting his people.

What if he knew she might be the cause?

Guilt and a terrible sense of loss filled her as he gave her one last look, then disappeared out the door.

*D*AMN *these cold, damp Highlands.*

Rory and his men wended their way to the outlying village. The night was as cold as it had been several nights earlier when they'd stolen Campbell cattle. Had the destruction of a Maclean village been in kind?

When would it ever stop?

At least the bitter wind brought him back to reality.

Rory needed that cold. It reminded him of duty. It took his mind away from the Cameron lass.

Why did she so bedevil his thoughts? She was no beauty.

Yet deep inside he knew. She had a passion for life that had been missing in his all too long. It glowed in her eyes even as she tried to hide her emotions. It was in the kiss, in her response, even in the way she'd engaged him rather than cower in fear or strike out in anger.

The devil take it. He could not afford the distraction. He looked around. Archibald rode on one side, Douglas on the other.

He was grateful for their silence. He nursed his thoughts, tried to quench the fires that still raged inside him.

By all the saints, what had he almost done?

He had nearly broken a vow. He had allowed himself to become distracted when he should be attending to the business of the clan.

God's eyes. She was nothing like Maggie. Or Anne. Both had been physically lovely and sweet and caring in disposition.

Janet's eyes flamed like an out-of-control fire. He suspected that she had as many thorns as petals. But a man

wanted to smile when Janet did. Her eyes lit, and a small
dimple appeared in her cheek. And in the sun or candle-
light, her hair took on the shine of copper.

She was both calm and peace, and fire and storm.

The combination was irresistible to him.

And a challenge.

A challenge he had to refuse. He was a trader, and a
trader spent months, even years at sea.

Worse, he was a Jonah.

Even had that not been true, she was pledged to another.
He'd reacted as he had because it had been years since he'd
been with a woman.

But he was not a man to lie, even to himself, and he
knew that was not entirely true. Aye, he'd wanted to touch
that flaming hair, rub his hand down her flushed cheeks,
lock his arms around her body. He wanted to feel her and
taste her. The devil take it, he wanted to bury himself in her.

Even now, his loins tightened at the thought of her
standing there, looking up at him with something like wonder in her eyes.

He'd felt the desire in her. He also recognized the awakening. There was an innocence mixed with passion that had
been intoxicating. More than intoxicating. For a moment,
the aching loneliness had left him.

And that was dangerous. He had come home to solve
problems. Not to create them. A liaison with a woman
pledged to the son of the enemy he hoped to lead into a
truce was pure madness.

She would be gone when he returned. He had made
Lachlan pledge to take her back to the Camerons on the
morn. They would probably never meet again.

He spurred his horse on. The others increased their pace
to match his. He wanted to be at their destination by dawn.
Perhaps by riding hard, he could ignore the hole opening in
his heart.

* * *

*H*E smelled the destruction even before they arrived.

Then he heard the keening. The sound of death.

Archibald blew on his horn to tell the village that friends were approaching.

Silently, clansmen crowded around them as they approached the smoldering ashes of the crofts.

Some knew him from years earlier when he rode and raided the Campbell properties. Others looked at him with curiosity, still others with anger.

"We ha' wounded," said one man. "Our healer was killed when she tried to stop them."

"How many dead?" he asked. "How many wounded?"

"Three dead now," another man stepped forward. His tone was belligerent. "Eight wounded, including a mere lass who was trampled. We ha' no protection. Now we ha' no homes, no cattle. Our fields were destroyed."

"What is your name?" he asked.

"Ramsey," said the man. He looked at the man next to him. "Sim lost his brother."

Sorrow filled Rory. And memories.

"I cannot bring back the dead," he said, "but we will replace your cattle. There will be no rent due this year. I will see that you have enough food for the winter." *So much for the cattle he had taken just days ago.*

"If ye are still here," Sim muttered.

Another man moved toward him in an obvious attempt to silence him.

Rory held up his hand to stop him. "He has the right," he said.

"We ha' been asking for help," Ramsey said angrily. "We are herders here. And farmers. We are no' warriors."

"You are certain the raiders were Campbells?"

"Aye. One wore the Campbell crest. They said they were looking for someone. They did not say who."

"A woman?"

The man shrugged. "They did not say."

It had to be the Cameron lass. She was, after all, the betrothed of the young Campbell. The enthusiasm of his men on his behalf had caused this. He'd never had these problems with his crew aboard ship. They had known discipline, had realized what he wanted and obeyed instantly.

He had been away too long. They all remembered the lad he had been, the young man who had been so in love with his wife that he had neglected all else. And because the man he was now was a stranger to them, he had not yet earned their respect.

He must do that before they would follow his lead.

He had been convinced that the future of the Macleans lay with forging a truce with the Campbells. But now looking at the ruined village and the despairing villagers, he wondered whether that was possible. They and other Maclean clansmen would expect retribution.

More bloodshed. More widows and orphaned children.

He hadn't wanted this. God in heaven, he did not want this.

"Our wounded?" Ramsey asked.

"I will send them back with my men. We have a healer at the keep."

"Two of our lads are missing. They were tending some sheep."

"I and one other man will stay and search. We can cover more ground on horseback," Rory said.

The crofter looked disbelieving, then he touched his forehead. "Thank ye, my lord."

"You will not be left to fend for yourself again," Rory vowed. "From this day, you will have protection."

Skepticism showed in some faces. He could not blame them. They had every right to feel abandoned.

Rory would have a word with Douglas on his return. The man should have taken more responsibility. Then he sighed. That assessment was unfair. He and Patrick had left the clan of their own free will. Neither could have foreseen their father's death, but they had left a void in leadership. Douglas, a distant cousin and steward, had no real authority, and Lachlan apparently had chosen not to take it.

He had to set things right before he left again. A flicker of apprehension swept through him. How could he leave now? Or even in the near future? Too many people depended on him. Yet how could he stay where grief shadowed every step?

How could he be of any use when he doubted himself, when he was haunted by ghosts and curses?

For a few moments he had forgotten . . .

He saw to it that litters were prepared and attached to the horses. Those not badly wounded were assigned to ride with some of his men. He watched as they departed.

"Let us find your missing lads," he told Ramsey.

FELICIA rose with the sun and went to the window. The dawn was cloudless. It would be a glorious day. She did not want a glorious day.

Lachlan had told her last night they would leave at early morn. She would have to pretend an illness she did not feel. A relapse.

Back to the fireplace.

But how many times would that sham work? Still, she pushed several stones in the embers and waited impatiently for them to warm again.

When she dared wait no longer, she wrapped them in cloth and crept back to the bed. She put them to her cheeks. When she heard a knock, she quickly moved the rocks near her feet, replaced the covering, and huddled in the bed, hoping to look ill.

Another knock. She tensed as the door opened.

Moira entered with a breakfast tray and stopped suddenly as she saw Felicia. "Oh milady. The fever is back."

Felicia tried to look ill. Very, very ill. "My fault," she said. "I did over much yesterday."

"Lachlan has already broke fast. He and an escort are waiting."

"I do not think I can travel today. I feel light-headed."

Moira looked quite pleased at the news. "I will tell him and bring ye some porridge."

Moira's porridge was quite terrible, but a price well worth paying if she could earn herself a few more hours. Perhaps without the lord in residence, it would be easier to escape the keep.

The lord. Rory. Rory Maclean.

She had to stop thinking of him.

Nothing was more impossible. There was no future with him. But he remained in her thoughts, as welcome—and as impossible to dismiss—as an enemy army at the gates.

She still remembered how her body felt next to his, the heady exchange of kisses, both gentle and demanding.

God's love. He was a Maclean. She was a Campbell. He had raided her people. Her people had just raided his, and he had gone to do only God knew what.

He said he wanted peace, but how could there be peace after the latest raid and what was sure to be retaliation? Was he killing Campbells now? Men that she knew? Men who had watched her spar with Jamie? She could still hear their shouts of encouragement as she'd lifted the heavy sword.

Moira still regarded her with a worried look. "I will tell Lachlan."

She disappeared out the door, and Felicia quickly placed the stones close to her cheeks again. The stones were cooling, but she hoped they were hot enough to redden her cheeks. Then she shoved them back under the covering as the door opened.

Lachlan strolled in. He was dressed for riding with a warm fur mantle covering most of body. He wore long hose and soft boots.

"Lady Janet," he said. "Moira told me the distressing news. He leaned down and touched one of her cheeks.

Something like amusement flickered in his eyes, and she wondered if he sensed her deception.

"I am sorry to ruin your plans," she said in as weak a voice as she could feign.

"Ah but it is your welfare that concerns me," he said. "I know you must be anxious to return home. Your family must be most distressed. In truth, I thought we might have visitors by now."

Could he possibly know what she was about? But no. How could he?

"My mother and father are not at home. They are at the court in Edinburgh," she said.

"Still there must be someone concerned about your absence," he said with annoying persistence. "We should send a rider to your home and tell them you are safe."

"Nay!" she said before she could stop herself.

"And why not?"

She frantically searched for a reason and finally came up with one. She finally came up with a half truth. "They wish me to marry someone I do not wish to marry."

"The Campbell?"

"Aye," she said reluctantly, mentally asking God to forgive the lie. A day. Mayhap two. That was all she needed.

He looked thoughtful. "You cannot remain missing forever."

"Nay, but if he thought I had been abducted—"

"Your reputation would be ruined, and he would not want you," he completed.

"Aye," she said as she watched him carefully.

"You wish to use my brother?"

"I was the one who was taken," she reminded him.

"And you wish to take advantage of it. Have you thought what the Campbells might do if they thought we abducted you? The Campbells and Camerons together?"

"You *did* abduct me," she said reasonably.

"Aye. Unfortunately, my brother refuses to make it right. He could marry you, and all would be solved."

"Would I have naught to say in this?"

She saw a gleam in his eyes.

"I have seen how you look at him and how he looks at you."

"He looks at me in no special way. He had made it clear he wants no marriage. He certainly does not want me."

"Then you are blind, my lady."

"I believe what he says."

"And if you did not?"

"I am but a pawn," she said. "My desires have no value. But I do not wish to marry anyone. I want . . ."

He waited.

She had almost blurted out the words. She wanted to get to London to see what help Jamie could offer. She could not be the bride of a Maclean even if he did want her. He most certainly would not if he knew who she was. He would despise her. He no doubt felt her family was responsible for every tragedy that had beset him.

"A woman seldom has the choice of loving. Decisions are made for her."

He searched her face. "I want my brother to love again. He was a different man then."

"And you. Have you ever loved?" she asked, suddenly curious.

"I am of no matter," he said.

He was avoiding the subject, and that made her wonder. She wanted to learn more about all the Macleans.

They were not the barbarians she had been told, and had believed. Of course, they might well turn into such if they learned her true identity.

"You were a lad when Lord Rory left?"

"Aye."

"And the older son?"

"Patrick?"

"Aye. How long has he been gone?"

"More than three years."

"You do not believe he will return?"

"Rory does."

"But you do not?"

"If he were a prisoner somewhere, ransom would be asked," he said. His expression changed, his brown eyes darkening. "Are you concerned that Rory will not inherit?"

"I care nothing about rank or power," she said.

"Then we are two of a kind."

"Are we?" she asked suddenly. Was it possible that Lachlan would, could, help her?

"I must leave," she said urgently. "Will you help me?"

"I thought you were reluctant to return."

"I do not wish to go home. I wish to go to London."

His eyes widened with surprise. "London?"

"I have friends there. They will help me."

"Do you hate James Campbell that much?"

"Would *you* like to be traded like a horse?"

"Nay, no more than I like expectations of what I should be."

"Will you help me then?"

"You cannot travel alone safely."

"I can travel as a lad."

He studied her for a long time. "Aye," he said softly.

"No more questions?"

"Nay."

She knew what she was asking of him. He would be going against the orders of his chief. His brother.

For her? For reasons of his own?

Or could he be trusted at all? She did not know him that well, nor did she have much experience at judging the motives of others.

"Why?" she asked bluntly.

"Because you are desperate," he said simply. "And I have been, as well." He did not elaborate, and his tone warned her not to pry further.

"I do not wish any harm to come to you."

"I know," he said. "My brother no longer knows how to love. Or laugh. Or be happy. But he would not punish me for doing what I think is right."

She prayed it was so.

"When?" She wanted to leave now. Before Rory Maclean returned and she lost her resolve.

"On the morn. Moira has already announced that you are ill. You should stay in today." He gave her a crooked smile. "And you can take the stones from the bed. They are no longer needed."

His smile widened slightly as he regarded her, and she knew guilt must be evident on her face.

"You are not the first to think of such tactics," he said.

She wondered why he—the son of a powerful earl— had also resorted to trickery, but while he usually wore an amused smile, she was quickly learning there were depths to him and as many shadows as followed his older brother.

"We will leave for your home with a small escort," he said. "No one will wonder that I would lose you."

His expression went straight to her heart. As she had always felt out of place, so, apparently, had he.

"Thank you."

"I think this afternoon you can go down and see your foal, though."

"She is not mine," she said.

"Rory gave her to you."

"He will not be so generous when I do not do his bidding."

"He keeps his word. He will send her to you when she is old enough."

"You admire him."

"Aye, I do. He follows his own star."

"So, I think, do you."

He shrugged. "I am nothing."

Before she could reply, he left her, the words leaving a sad echo in the room.

Chapter 9

❦

FELICIA stayed away from the foal as long as she could. She did not want to say good-bye.

She coveted the foal with all her soul. She had never had a horse of her own. Everything at Dunstaffnage belonged to her uncle.

But it was not her foal. And never could be.

Not wanting appraising eyes on her at the table in the great hall, she took supper in her room. She asked Moira for only bread, cheese, and soup, saying the fever had sapped her appetite. She had learned that these items were the least offensive of all the food.

How she would like to help Moira improve the life here. She liked Archibald, and even the tight-lipped Douglas. Every man and lad had been kind to her.

And the household was in deep need of care.

She ate, then put on her cloak and went down the steps. She passed by the kitchen. Several servants were darting in and out. She found two apples and a knife. She cut the apple in quarters, then passed the great hall where some Macleans were eating. Their number was much fewer than it had been the previous night, and, unlike other meals, there was none of the customary hum of conversation or boasting. Macleans were dead this day.

A shudder ran through her. She had always believed there was only one side to the feud. No more. An innocent village had been attacked. Rory Maclean might well be engaged in a battle with troops from Dunstaffnage. Thank God that Jamie wouldn't be with them.

She could not bear the thought of the Maclean and Jamie crossing swords.

The Maclean does not mean anything to me.

She repeated the words over and over, but she soon realized saying them did not make them so. She did care. A suffocating sensation tightened her throat as she realized how much.

How could that happen so quickly?

Jamie and Janet had known each other for years, but it was not until Jamie's father pressed him to take Janet for a wife that he offered for her. She had no doubt that he cared deeply for Janet now, but it had not been immediate.

Was it the appeal of forbidden fruit? Of all the men in the world, a Maclean would be the most impossible match for her. She sighed. It could also be, she admitted, that no one had ever before displayed any interest in her. Perhaps any man's kiss might have had the same effect.

She reached the stables and stopped first to feed Janet's mare the quarters of one apple, then she continued on to the stall where the new mother and baby were stabled.

The mare smelled the treat and nickered softly, then moved to take the apple from Felicia's hand. The baby followed on long, awkward legs.

Felicia reached over and stroked the foal's long, silky

neck. She truly was beautiful. Her eyes were huge. "You are going to be a fine mare," Felicia said. "I wish . . ."

The loud piercing sound of the alarm horn cut through the night. Riders approached!

Felicia's heart pounded against her rib cage.

Rory Maclean had returned. Or was it a party searching for her? Would the Campbells send a party here? Certainly not after raiding a Maclean village?

It had to be Rory. Her heart tripped at the thought of seeing him once more, even though she knew it would make escape even more difficult. Would he still entrust her to his brother?

She left the stables and entered the great hall, taking the steps up to the ramparts. There she joined the sentry and looked down.

She counted ten horses, each carrying two people. Several horses dragged litters behind them. Men and women walked beside them.

The order was given to open the gates. She quickly descended and ran out into the bailey as tired horses and exhausted Macleans—men and women, several carrying bairns—entered. Macleans poured from the great hall and other buildings.

Moira and Robina joined her, as Archibald approached them. He was walking, holding the reins of a horse following behind him. He stopped, wearily, walked around to the saddle, and assisted a woman and young girl in dismounting.

"We have wounded," he said to Moira who quickly moved to check each litter.

"My brother?" Lachlan asked Archibald as they helped villagers dismount.

"He stayed behind to search for several villagers who ran when the Campbells raided the village," Archibald said. "The healer was killed, and crofts burned. There was no shelter left for these people."

"Take them into the great hall," Lachlan said.

"I can help Moira," Felicia said. "I learned much from the healer at . . ." She stopped herself before she said Dunstaffnage.

Moira obviously heard and looked up. "God save ye, milady," she said gratefully.

Lachlan's startled expression gave her pause. Was it because she had stopped in mid-sentence, or because she had claimed to know healing?

But Lachlan said nothing. Instead, he picked up a young girl from a litter and carried her inside. Moira was occupied with a villager who had a huge gash in his shoulder.

Felicia followed Lachlan into the great hall. Lachlan gently lowered the girl onto a table, and Felicia leaned over to look at her.

The child could have been no more than eight years old. Her leg was bloody and crooked. She regarded Felicia with pain-filled eyes, yet did not utter a word.

"Her name is Alina," a woman who had followed them inside said. A small dog whined and tried to jump up on the table.

"How was she injured?" Felicia asked.

"A Campbell on horseback ran 'er down when she ran out to get the dog. Did it on purpose, he did. I would have left the cur, but Alina would no' hear of it."

A Campbell deliberately ran her down.

Pain twisted inside Felicia. Was it a man she knew?

She looked at the ugly wound. The bone had obviously been broken.

Moira joined her and stooped down to look as well. "Ye are a brave lass," she told the child softly.

"Will I lose . . . my leg?" Alina asked in a quavering voice.

Felicia looked at Moira. If there was no infection, there was a chance the leg could be saved, but that was unlikely. At the very least, she doubted the lass would ever walk properly again.

"I do not know," she said honestly.

Approval flickered on Moira's face. "There are herbs for poultices in the kitchen," she said.

"I can mix poultices, if Robina will show me where they are."

Moira looked unsure. "Why do you no' stay with the young lass while I go and show Robina what to do?" Before Felicia could protest, Moira was out the door, pushing Robina ahead of her.

The dog whined and tried to move closer to his young mistress.

"What is your dog's name?" Felicia asked, trying to divert the lass from her pain.

"Baron."

"A noble name."

Alina's mother snorted. "He is nothing but trouble, that one."

"Nay, he is the best dog in the world," the child said.

"Then we must take good care of him," Felicia said. "I will see that he is fed."

The child's face brightened despite her pain. "Mither blames him, but it was no' his fault."

"I will get him some food and take him to my chamber so he will not be underfoot," she said. "Is that acceptable?"

"Aye, milady," Alina said uncertainly.

"You will have him back. I swear." Felicia looked at the mother.

She picked up the dog and went into the kitchen. Moira had put Robina to boiling water on the fire. Several knives lay in the fire as well, the steel glowing red. Felicia shuddered, knowing what was coming.

"I thought I should get the dog out of the way," she said. "I will take him to my chamber and be back down to help."

"We will have to seal the wounds," Moira said.

Felicia struggled to keep the bile from rising into her throat. She had performed the task once before when the healer was elsewhere, attending a birth. It was a task she had hoped never to repeat.

"I know," she said. "She can use my chamber," she said. "She will be more comfortable, and I would like to look after her."

Moira's lips spread into a smile. "Nay, milady," she said. "She can have the chamber next to yours. No one is there."

"Lord Rory?"

"I dinna think he will object," Moira replied. "I dinna know what to think when he returned, but he is a mon who cares about his clan, I think."

Felicia grabbed several large chunks of bread and filled a bowl with water from a pitcher and took the dog upstairs to her chamber. He attacked the bread as if he'd had no food in days.

Felicia closed the door and hurried back to the great hall. Lachlan stood next to Alina, murmuring something to her and getting a pained smile in return. The hall was filling with the injured. One man was moaning, but the other injured crofters were stoic as fellow clansmen tended to their injuries. Moira moved from one to another, with a pail of poultices.

"Your Baron is fed and happy," Felicia told Alina, who tried to smile. Her face twisted in agony when she moved her leg. Felicia found a clean piece of linen, dampened it, and cleaned around the wound. When she finished, Moira had returned.

"I must try to set the leg," she said. "Lachlan, carry the child up to the laird's chamber next to milady's."

Lachlan looked startled but nodded. He picked the child up with obvious tenderness, wincing as he heard a small smothered moan. Felicia, Moira, and the child's mother followed him up to the laird's chamber.

The spacious chamber was still covered with dust but it had a great bed, which was certainly far superior than using the floor in the great hall.

Lachlan put the lass on the bed, then stepped aside.

"Lord Rory said he had something to help dull pain,"

Moira said, "but we canna wait. We donna know when he will be back, and I must try to set the leg." She leaned down. "'Tis going to hurt, lass."

Alina tried to look brave.

Moira gave her a piece of wood to bite down on and knelt beside her. "Hold her tight," she said to Lachlan.

Felicia clamped her lips together, as Lachlan held the child's slight body down, and she took Alina's right hand. "Squeeze," she said. "As hard as you can." Alina's mother hovered at the other end of the bed, obviously intimidated by the room and those working to save her daughter.

Moira pulled on the leg, and Alina bit down hard on the piece of wood, but Felicia saw the silent scream in her eyes, then the child went limp.

"She is unconscious," she said.

"Thank God for small mercies," Moira said. "Hurry and get me a knife. Mayhap we can finish this before she wakes up."

Felicia ran back to the kitchen and took one of the knives from the coals in the fireplace. There had been six. Now there were three. Others were performing the same task.

When she returned, the child was still unconscious. Moira took the knife while Lachlan pressed down on the shoulders again in the event Alina regained consciousness. After the slightest pause, Moira touched the knife against the child's wound. The skin sizzled. Felicia held her grip on Alina's hand until Moira finished the grim duty, then tied the leg to a length of wood.

"I have others to attend to," Moira said, her usually pleasant face drawn and angry. "The demmed Campbells," she hissed. "May they all rot in hell."

Felicia saw the same rage in Lachlan's face.

She swallowed hard, not wanting them to see her own outrage and despair. "I will stay with her," she said. "Alina's mother and I." She motioned to the woman to sit beside the bed.

"She can stay here," Lachlan said. "I will arrange for pallets for the others." Lachlan stood. His face was pale. His hands trembled slightly.

He left the room and Felicia sat on the side of the bed next to Alina. She wanted to be there when she woke. She wanted to reassure her. Alina had been so afraid. And so brave.

"Your husband?" she asked the woman sitting on the other side of the lad.

"He stayed back at the village with my lord," she said. "My son . . . we have not seen him since the raid. He was watching the cattle."

"I am sorry," Felicia said. More than sorry. She was ravaged by guilt that her own people would do this. These people were not warriors. They were simple farmers, trying only to survive. Then she remembered the raid many years ago when the Macleans had done the same. How many times since had this been done to one or the other of the clans?

Would it never stop?

She sat next to the lass, uncaring that her gown was stained with blood. She reached over and took the mother's hand, clasped it tightly as the two women united in their vigil.

RORY blessed the sun. The rain had stopped, and dawn came with few clouds. The sun followed, a glorious golden ball that dried the hills.

He and ten men from the village had searched during the rain-drenched night for the missing lads, though it had been a fool's effort. He could not see anything much farther than the tip of his horse's head. Still they had tried, covering the common area where the cattle had grazed just before the raid.

That they had found no bodies had been a hopeful sign. Once the rain stopped and dawn broke, Rory and the others expanded their search. The boys had been missing a day and a half now. His heart ached. He should have returned home earlier. He should have known this could happen when he raided the Campbell cattle days earlier.

There were four small villages in the countryside around the main Maclean keep. Why had he not sent out forces to protect them?

He knew the reasons, but they did not comfort him. He had wanted to make peace in order to leave again. He had placed his needs above those of the Macleans, and others had suffered for it.

It did not help to know that Douglas bore blame, as did Lachlan. Neither were suited to lead the clan. Douglas's job was to ensure that crofters paid their rents. And Lachlan? Lachlan had no faith in himself, nor did the clan have faith in him. No one had said anything to him, but he sensed something had happened while he was gone, something that had tainted the clan even more than the Campbell curse.

He had not been home long enough to extract that piece of information. There had been too many other problems.

Home. It was the first time he had acknowledged Inverleith as home in many years.

Rory and Ian, the rider who had accompanied him from the keep, searched in a pattern of ever-widening circles. The villagers, armed with bows and arrows and several pikes, followed on foot, combing each dip in the land, discouraged yet not giving up.

He stood up in his stirrups and looked around. To the left was a steep, wooded hill and a waterfall tumbling over rocks, making its way between clumps of gorse.

He thought he saw movement in the gorse. When he looked again, all was still.

A tingle ran down his spine.

His legs signaled his horse into a trot. Ian, some distance away, followed.

Another movement ahead.

He shouted out, "Macleans."

A small movement again.

Rory tightened his knees around his mount, and the horse went into full gallop. He looked back. Villagers, armed with pikes and bows, followed at a full run.

He approached the gorse carefully. He did not want to frighten whomever was there.

A stone hit him, making a gouge in his arm. Another hit the horse. The startled gelding shied, but Rory quickly regained control. "A Maclean," he shouted again.

"Donna come closer," a youthful voice shouted back.

"I am a Maclean. I am here to help. Your father is behind me."

Slowly, a slender lad stood, a slingshot ready in his hand. He was obviously not going to go down without a fight, even with such an inadequate weapon.

Rory dismounted and walked toward the lad, his hands in plain sight. "You are John . . . or Alex?"

"Alex," the lad said, his pale blue eyes suspicious.

"I am Rory Maclean. What of the other lad?"

"My lord?" The boy looked suddenly frightened as he saw blood drip from Rory's arm.

" 'Tis nothing, lad," he said. "Where is the other lad?"

"He is hidden above," Alex said. "He was wounded. A pike through his shoulder. He tried to stop them. I hid." Self-contempt was in his voice.

"You brought him here?"

"Aye," the lad said, his eyes downcast. "I saw the fires. I feared they would slay everyone, so I carried him here. Then I could no' leave him alone."

"You did the right thing."

"The village. My fa? My mither?"

"Your father has been looking for you. He should be with us soon. Your mother and sister went to Inverleith with my men." He did not say the lad's younger sister was sorely wounded.

The boy's eyes filled with tears. Angrily, he wiped them away. "Are the Campbells gone?"

"Aye?"

"Did ye kill them?"

"They were gone when we arrived here," Rory said.

Shouts of joy interrupted them, as three of the villagers, one of them Alex's father, reached him. The villager stood in front of his son, stunned at his good fortune. He reached out a hand and placed it on his son's shoulder.

The boy did not look at him. "I hid," he said with shame.

"Thank God, ye did," his father said. "John?"

"He is above."

Minutes later, Rory examined John's shoulder. The boy was weak from loss of blood, but Alex had bound it tightly enough to stanch the flow.

John tried to struggle to his feet, but fell back. Rory prayed the wound would not become infected. It needed to be stitched, but he had nothing with which to do it, nor was any needle or thread left in the village. Everything was gone.

He would help make a temporary shelter for those few villagers who refused to leave, then return to Inverleith with those who wanted the safety of the Maclean keep. He would send men back with them later, along with carpenters and a blacksmith. He leaned down and took John in his arms, then looked at Alex. "You saved his life," Rory said. "You used your head. Be proud."

He looked at his father, who gave him the slightest of nods.

Rory knew it would be a long ride for tired horses, but he was anxious to get back.

He had reason to live again, and that reason was the lives and fortunes of the clan, which had been entrusted to him. He hadn't wanted war with the Campbells. He had meant to do everything to avoid it.

But if war was what they wanted, he was prepared to meet them.

He only hoped that Janet Cameron, as the intended bride of a Campbell, would not be caught in the middle.

She would be on her way home now, if she had not already arrived back at the Camerons' keep.

It was best for everyone.

He wished he really believed that.

JAMIE Campbell neared Dunstaffnage. He had finished his errand in London far quicker than he'd thought. He had gone to reassure King Henry's court that James had no hostile intent toward England and hoped the two countries could live in peace.

At the same time, he knew James had no intention of keeping a peace with England, not with the constant raids between the borders. But that was not his concern. He had relayed the message.

Janet would be pleased. So, he admitted, was he. He had enjoyed the freedom of being his own man. He had resisted the notion of marriage because he was determined that when he did wed, he would be faithful. He felt that honor demanded it.

His mother had turned into an embittered, unhappy woman because his father had no such inhibitions. He openly kept a mistress in Edinburgh and was a well-known lecher.

But Jamie had grown close to Janet these past few months as he had advanced his suit. He had always been attracted to her, and the alliance was good for both clans. He had agreed because he wanted to please his father, and then he had found himself looking forward to the marriage.

His intended wife was gentle and well bred. Yet she had the capacity to surprise him. That she and his wayward cousin had become fast friends fascinated him. He could not imagine two women more unalike.

Felicia should have been a lad. She was stubborn and adventurous and had endless curiosity about all things. She had a special love for astronomy, which had amused him. So had her competitive spirit. In a rare moment of whimsy, he had agreed to teach her sword-play. He had not expected her to practice for hours, and days, and even months. If she had more strength in her arms, she would be formidable. As it was, she could give an average swordsman a contest in the short run.

He did worry about her. She would make a poor wife for most men. She disliked womanly activities. She challenged ideas and thoughts and perceptions. It would take a rare man indeed to appreciate her.

He smiled as his thoughts shifted back to Janet. She, too, surprised him endlessly. She listened and absorbed far more than anyone thought, even as she was gracious and knowledgeable about running households. He was amazed at how much he wanted to see her again. How he had ridden so hard to return to her.

His body hardened as he thought of their wedding night. They had exchanged stolen kisses, nothing more. But she had never shied away. She was eager and receptive, and he yearned to teach her the depths of passion.

A furlong or more and he would be home. He wondered if Janet was still there. He knew she had planned to stay only a few weeks, and he'd been riding night and day to get home.

He heard the sound of hoofbeats ahead.

He guided his horse off the road and into the woods, then stepped back out when he recognized Campbell colors.

"Lord James," said the leader as he pulled up his horse. "We did not expect you."

"You seem in a hurry?"

The leader looked uncomfortable.

Apprehension filled him. "You have bad news?"

The leader looked at the man beside him, then shifted in his saddle. "Lady Felicia has disappeared."

"What do you mean, disappeared?"

"She seems to have spirited herself away."

"Why would she do that?"

The man swallowed hard. "I am not sure, my lord. I

know only that she apparently took Lady Janet's place in the escort to take her home. The escort . . . ah . . . lost her."

"Why would she take Janet's place?"

The man shrugged helplessly.

"Come man, tell me."

"I only heard the rumors."

"What are the rumors then?"

"Her uncle pledged her hand in wedlock to the Earl of Morneith."

"Morneith?" God's teeth, but he understood his cousin's flight. He knew Morneith. How could his father have condemned Felicia to a man like that?

"And there has been no sign of my cousin?"

"Nay."

"For how long?"

"Eight days now."

"God's blood," he said. "You have no idea where she might have gone?"

"Nay."

"And did Lady Janet aid Lady Felicia's flight?

The guard shrugged. "Lady Felicia drugged her and took her place."

"They look nothing alike."

"It was a cold, rainy morning."

And he knew his cousin. She would venture anything.

"Has Lady Janet returned home?"

"Aye."

"And my father does not know about my cousin?"

Again silence.

They were obviously afraid to deliver the bad news to his father. That came as no surprise. His father did not like incompetence.

"And William?"

William was his father's steward. He might not be much longer if Felicia was not found. William would be very aware of that. He apparently was praying that he would find Felicia before he had to report her disappearance.

"We have searched the countryside," the soldier said. "We have scoured the forests, sent messengers to the Camerons and other clans. We even searched Maclean lands since they are near Camerons. She has just . . . disappeared."

"You think the Macleans could be responsible?"

"There has been no demand for ransom, but it is possible."

Fear spiked in his chest. Felicia had been more than a cousin to him. She had been sister and friend. He had vowed as a lad to always protect her. God help anyone who tried to harm her.

"I am returning to Dunstaffnage to have a word with William," he said.

"We will continue to search the caves south of here."

"Maclean properties?"

The man spat on the ground. "We already visited them."

Jamie stiffened. "And found nothing?"

"Nay, naught but cattle."

"I would not like anything to happen to my cousin because of something Campbells did."

"Macleans are nothing. They would no' dare to take a Campbell."

Jamie did not think so, either. The Macleans had weakened over the past years, but neither did he want to revive a feud. King James wanted the clans united to prevent any aggression by the English. He had made it clear that he would not tolerate private feuds.

"Continue your search," he said. He went around them and, with a slight flick of the reins, urged his horse into a trot, then a canter toward Dunstaffnage. He wanted to learn more from William.

He had to find Felicia.

·

Chapter 10

❧

TOTALLY exhausted by three days with little sleep and most of that caught while riding, Rory reached the walls of Inverleith in mid-afternoon.

After finding the lads yesterday morning, he'd helped build a temporary shelter for the few remaining villagers before leaving with the boy at sunset. He then rode most of the night.

The horn announced his arrival. He was surprised—but grateful—when he saw grooms awaiting them. It was the first time he had seen any efficiency.

John, his arm in a sling to keep pressure off his shoulder, rested against him. Rory knew from his own past injuries that the lad was probably in agony with every movement, but John had not complained.

The boy's father had remained behind. He did not know

how to ride, and Rory wanted to get John to the keep as quickly as possible. Alex stayed behind as well, as did Ian, who was to stay with the villagers until Rory could send additional men.

Rory slid down from his mount. Ignoring the growing pain in his arm from the slingshot, he lowered John who stood unsteadily for a moment.

Douglas appeared, and his gaze moved from Rory to the lad. "You found them then?"

"Aye, both boys are alive, though John here needs Moira's skills."

"The other wounded are in the great hall," Douglas said. "I will fetch Moira, or the Cameron lass."

"The Cameron lass?" Rory had tried not to think about Janet Cameron these last hours. He'd thought he would not see her again. Lachlan had been told to return her home.

"Aye, she has been helping with the wounded."

"Lachlan was to take her back," he said, his voice harsh, even as he found himself unexpectedly eager to see her again.

Douglas shrugged. "The fever returned, and then the wounded came. She has healing skills, and we needed her."

"God's eyes, does no one heed my orders?"

"I did not feel we should endanger her," Douglas said, "no' with Campbell raiding parties roving about. They might well attack before they knew who she was. And we canna lose any more men, not if you want the villages guarded."

Douglas paused, then added, "And we needed Lady Janet. She was helpful in treating the wounded. The wee lass might lose her leg, and she clings to Lady Janet. I could not send her away, even if we could spare the escort."

"We will need far more men than we have if the Camerons join the Campbells to attack us."

"Just another day," Douglas insisted. "Alina needs her."

"God's blood, a soft spot, Douglas?"

"She's but a wee lass," Douglas defended himself. "And there have been no alarms about a missing Cameron lass.

They are perhaps still searching for her somewhere in the hills."

"She leaves tomorrow," Rory said. "I will take her myself. I would today but . . ."

"You look as if you need rest." Douglas's gaze went to the bloodied sleeve of his shirt. " 'Tis your blood and not the lad's?"

" 'Tis nothing. One of the lads thought I was a Campbell."

"I will have Moira look at it."

"Nay, the lad comes first. I will see Lady Janet."

"Aye, my lord."

Rory was suspicious when Douglas used the title. He did not care to be manipulated, and he had discovered in the weeks he'd been back that when Douglas used the title, he usually had a purpose in mind, one that Rory would not like.

But he was too weary at the moment to question him further.

He put his hand on John's shoulder and led him toward the door.

Already alerted, Moira was waiting as he and the lad entered. She quickly undid the wrapping around the lad's wound and looked at it. "I think I can sew it together," she said. "We have no need to burn it."

She had a clansman fetch another pallet to join those of a half-dozen other men on the floor.

She turned to Rory, her gaze resting on his sleeve, which was now rust-colored with dried blood. "Now yer turn, milord." She rolled up the flowing sleeve of Rory's shirt and looked at his arm. His gaze followed hers. The small wound was ugly-looking, the skin around it red and angry.

"What happened, milord?"

"A slingshot," he replied wryly. "Finish with the lad first. You can tend mine later."

Her eyes narrowed, but she merely shrugged. "As you wish, my lord."

"Is Lady Janet in her chamber?"

"Aye, or in the chamber next to hers. Milady insisted that the young lass and her mother stay there. More comfortable, she said."

Insisted. He smothered a smile. His father was probably turning over in his grave at the thought of crofters occupying his bed.

He thought about bathing first, but some unwanted urge directed him to her chamber. He knew he looked like a brigand. His cheeks were rough with new beard, and his hair was uncombed. He smelled of horse sweat and blood.

He knocked at the door, opened it slightly, and saw nothing. Then he heard the melody of a lullaby in the next chamber. He knew without seeing that it was Janet Cameron. Her voice was pure and strong and sweet. Some of his tension began to fade.

When the song ended, he knocked lightly on the door. He heard a sharp bark and took it as an invitation, and entered. A small dog at Janet Cameron's feet growled at him. His eyes went to her face.

He had thought her appealing but not beautiful. But looking at her now, he changed his mind.

Her sapphire-blue eyes were filled with compassion, and her lips curved in a gentle smile as she looked up from the child. Her eyes widened, and she started to rise, but he gestured her to sit back down.

The woman seated on the other side of the bed also started to stand. "Milord," she said.

"Do not stand," he commanded.

She sat back down, consternation on her face, as if she worried that he would not approve of her and her daughter occupying such a fine room. He wondered whether he was really that forbidding.

He knelt next to the small figure in the big bed. He ignored the small dog that growled at him.

"Alina," he said softly.

The child's wide brown eyes stared back at him. She

tried to move, and he shook his head. "Stay as you are, lass. I just thought you and your mother would like to know we found your brother, Alex. He is well, and decided to stay with his fa to rebuild your croft. He is a brave lad."

"He is no' hurt?" the mother asked anxiously.

"Nay. His friend, John, was hurt, and Alex got him up a mountain to a place of safety. He was afraid to leave his friend alone."

"Is John . . . will he . . . ?" The question came from Alicia.

"I suspect he will recover. The lad apparently took on a troop of Campbells all on his own." He looked down at the child. "But I want to know how you fare."

Alina's thin face was drawn with pain. She looked at Janet for reassurance. Even protection. *Against him.*

The child's frightened look reminded him how long he had been away, how little they knew of him. When he was a lad, he had earned a reputation as a fierce fighter. It was a reputation he deeply regretted. He hoped that Janet would never learn of it.

His gaze moved to Janet. She had been silent since he'd entered, but her eyes, which had been soft as she looked at the child, turned wary as she returned his glance.

That hurt more than the throb in his shoulder. He remembered the kiss they'd shared, the soft touches, the passionate response. He thought he saw a flash of memory in her eyes as well.

"I thought that you would be home," he said. "Another apology is owed."

"Nay, I was ill. Then I was needed."

"Your family . . ."

"My family is in Edinburgh, and the retainers are probably too frightened to inform them of my absence."

He had puzzled over the lack of any outcry. Perhaps her explanation answered that question.

He swayed. God's eyes, but he was weary.

Lady Janet quickly stood. Her gaze went to his sleeve for the first time. "My lord, you are hurt."

"I only need a little rest."

"More than a little, I think," she said.

She smelled of flowers, and he was aware again of his appearance. "I should bathe," he said. "But I wanted to see how the lass fared." He told himself that was his purpose for coming here, but he'd not lied to himself in a very long time, and he did not wish to start now.

The fact was that he had wanted to see Janet, that the past few days had done nothing to diminish his desire for her.

She approached him and pulled up his sleeve. She breathed deeply when she saw his arm. "You have infection, my lord." Her brow knitted as a tremor rocked his body.

He took a step and realized his legs were weak. Janet caught him and wrapped one of his arms around her shoulders.

"Where is your chamber?" she asked.

"Above," he said. "I can walk alone."

"You cannot," she said. "We can stand here and discuss it, or I can help you there."

He realized he might need her steadying presence. He did not particularly wish to fall on the floor in front of her. Or anyone else for that matter. And he was growing more light-headed by the minute.

She took a step, and he moved with her. He tried to use her only to balance, but each step was becoming more and more difficult.

She was surprisingly strong and steady. They reached the curving stone steps. They looked endless.

A mere slingshot! It was humbling.

One step at a time. He found himself leaning more and more on Janet.

When they reached the top of the stairs and his chamber, he slipped his arm from her and fell rather than sat on his bed. Unlike those in her room and the laird's chamber, his bed was narrow and hard, much like that on his ship.

The room was cold. The fireplace held only ashes.

He saw her surprise.

But he saw no reason to explain that he did not intend to stay here, that he merely wanted to hold the clan together until Patrick returned.

She poured water from a pitcher on the table into a tankard and handed it to him.

He took a sip, then drank it thirstily.

"You need tending," she said.

"Nay, it is but a scratch."

"Why do men always believe they are indestructible?"

He could not stop a small smile. "Oh, I do not believe I am indestructible, but a slingshot?"

She raised an eyebrow. "A slingshot?"

"From a lad."

She sighed. "And what did you do?"

"He was trying to protect his friend against Campbells. 'Tis difficult to be angry."

Something flickered in her eyes, but he was too tired to try to define it.

"I will make one of Moira's poultices," she said. "They seem to work wonders."

"The lass needs you more than I."

"Her mother is there."

"I only need sleep."

"You need a bath as well."

He was only too aware of that.

"Do you not have a manservant?"

"Nay. I am accustomed to caring for myself. And I have been home only a short while." The heat was intensifying in his arm, as was the insistent throbbing.

Janet poured water into a washbowl, and found a folded towel. She dipped it into the water and returned to his side.

She felt his face, and her hands felt cool and comforting against his hot skin.

He saw her worried frown above him, then she said something and left the room.

Rory did not want her to leave. Her hands had been gentle. So gentle. For a moment, he no longer felt alone.

He tried to sit up, but he could not quite manage it. Tired. He was so tired.

FEAR pulsed through Felicia.

She had seen fast-moving infections before. He had been injured slightly, and like most men had not the sense to do anything about it. Instead he had pushed himself until he could barely stand.

He'd looked terrible when he'd entered the room, yet he had been gentle with Alina and more than kind. It was obvious that he had true concern about his crofters.

She had never seen her uncle treat his tenants kindly. He cared about their production, no more. If they did not produce, he forced them off the land. Jamie hadn't liked it, but there had been little he could do, other than vow he would not do the same when he became the Campbell chief.

She prayed Jamie would never change.

But now her worry was all for her enemy. Her uncle's enemy. Jamie's enemy.

Felicia hated leaving him but knew the infection required immediate attention. She hurried down to the kitchen. She knew now where to find Moira's herbs.

Together, she and Robina boiled water with the herbs, then soaked linen cloths in the earthy smelling mixture. Before long she was back in Rory's bed chamber with a hot poultice.

"Maggie," he mumbled when she leaned over him. "Maggie." His voice sounded as if it was coming straight from hell.

She uncovered the wound. It had been small, but now an angry red covered much of the arm. She placed the poultice on his arm, and he threw it off.

She tried to wake him, but she could not.

Felicia replaced it and lay down on the bed next to him, holding it firm. She listened to his labored breathing, heard the beating of his heart, felt the heat from his skin.

She knew how quickly infection could kill.

She prayed for a Maclean.

JAMIE listened to William, the Dunstaffnage steward, with outrage.

"My father intended Felicia to marry Morneith?"

"Aye."

"And she knew it?"

"She knew there would be an escort to take her to Edinburgh late next week."

"I know Morneith," he said, his stomach roiling at the thought of his cousin marrying the man.

"Your father said the king wished the alliance. He could no' say no."

Jamie knew now why he had been sent to London on an errand that meant little. His father knew he would oppose the match, though he could probably do naught about it.

"Where did she disappear?"

"Near the Cameron property."

"It is also near the Macleans."

A muscle twitched in William's face. It was obvious that he'd also considered the possibility that the lass had encountered Macleans. It would be his head if anything happened to her.

Where would she have gone?

To find him? If he knew his cousin, she'd probably headed to London. She would know he would do anything he could to help her, even see her out of the country. What would she do if she could not find him? But if she had tried to reach London, he should have encountered her along the way. There was but one road.

His gut tightened. Macleans were not above abduction and ransom. Or murder. If they happened to run into a Campbell . . .

He would find out whether a woman was being held at the Macleans' keep. If not, he would travel back to London and try to find her. She was brave and smart, and she had a huge heart. Janet had come to love her as much as he. It had been an added bond between them.

For a moment he wondered whether Janet could have been involved in any way, but he dismissed it. She did not have Felicia's recklessness.

He would find Felicia. And he would start at the Macleans.

Chapter 11

❦

PAIN raged throughout his arm.

He was hot, so hot.

Maggie stood in front of him in a flowing blue gown, her lovely, long blond hair blowing in the wind, her soft brown eyes full of laughter.

"Catch me if you can," she said and ran toward the Sound of Mull.

He ran after her, laughing at first because he knew he could catch her. But the faster he ran, she ran even faster. It was as if she had wings rather than legs.

She turned and beckoned him, teasing him as she often did. He increased his pace until his heart beat so loudly it could surely be heard in Edinburgh. But still he could not close the distance between them, and she was nearing the cliff that overlooked the sound.

He tried to call out to her, to stop her, but his words were lost in the wind, and her form began to dissolve in front of him.

"Maggie!" He reached out in supplication. To bring her back. To stop her headlong flight into the sound. All he found was mist.

"Rory?"

A voice. Soft but insistent.

Maggie?

"Rory?" Louder.

Not Maggie's voice. Maggie was gone.

He moved again. His arm was aflame.

"My lord."

He forced his eyes open. His lids were heavy. Every movement required enormous effort.

Still he opened them, wishing instead to go back to the darkness, to the dream of Maggie standing in front of him.

He tried to focus. A lass. Red curls had escaped from her braid and framed her face . . . the woman calling him back to consciousness sat on the narrow bed next to him was Janet Cameron.

Another image flashed through his mind. Arms around him, holding him. He had relaxed in them, felt comforted by them.

"Rory?"

She should have been gone. But now he remembered that Lachlan had not followed his order. She had been here, caring for a child.

"The child?" he asked.

"Alina is better," she said. "Moira and Robina are looking after her. You kept pulling off the poultice. Someone had to stay here."

He remembered. He had felt a presence next to him. Warm. Gentle. He had thought . . .

He did not know what he thought.

Janet Cameron stood. Her gown was stained with blood and something else, probably the mixture used in the poultice. She went to the table and returned with a cup. "You must be thirsty."

He was. He tried to sit up, and it took every ounce of determination he had. He looked at his arm, but it was covered with a poultice.

"I wish to see it," he said.

She started to shake her head, then surrendered. She carefully untied the poultice and swabbed the discharge with the towel. The arm was swollen, the small wound ugly. The skin surrounding it was hot to the touch.

"A slingshot," he said with disgust.

"A small wound is often more dangerous than a large one if not attended. And it is far better now than it was yesterday," she said. "Moira's potions are wondrous. She said she would teach me."

"Yesterday?"

"You have been asleep more than a day," she said.

A day!

It could not be. He could not have slept so long. There was much to be done, and Janet . . . she was to be on her way home.

Yet he felt comfort in her presence, and now he realized she had stayed with him these past hours.

"I was to return you to your family." It seemed all the devils in hell were foiling him in that effort. Every day delayed, though, added risk to his clan. There was no way he could defend his Macleans against a combined campaign of Campbells and Camerons, especially since both of these clans had influence in the Scottish court.

He knew he probably could not travel yet, and though he tried not to recognize it, he felt a sense of belonging with the lass, as though she was somehow meant to be here.

The notion was part of the fever. A delusion.

She replaced the poultice carefully, her fingers sure, gentle. Even then, every touch sent streaks of pain up his arm.

"You must be hungry," she said when she completed her task.

He was not, but he knew he needed nourishment. "Has no one been here looking for you?"

"Nay," she said.

He closed his eyes at that. Something was very wrong, but he could not ken what it was. Not now. His head pounded as if a dozen men with hammers were striking inside his skull.

"My thanks, Lady Janet," he said.

Her cheeks flushed. But then the room was warm. Or was it just him?

"I will fetch some soup," she said.

"Tell Douglas I wish to see him," he demanded more forcefully than he'd intended. He was in no position to give orders.

She stood her ground.

"Aye," she said, "if you swear not to try to stand."

It was an easy thing to pledge. He was as weak as a newborn kitten and had no wish to demonstrate that truth in front of her.

He nodded.

She still hesitated, then turned and left the room.

He did exactly what he had pledged not to do, but he had to test himself. He swung his feet to the side of the bed and tried to sit again. *You can do it. You have to do it.*

He sat there a moment, using every reserve of strength he had.

He had to be strong for the Macleans.

A moment passed, or was it hours? His head ached, and his arm protested the slightest movement.

The door opened, and Douglas entered. "Thank God you are better," the steward said.

"I think it is more to do with Lady Janet and Moira than God," Rory said. "How are the others?"

"We have not lost another Maclean."

Rory closed his eyes in relief. Janet had said the lass was doing well, but . . .

He posed the question uppermost in his mind. Janet had

said no one had asked any questions, but he could barely fathom that. She had been here a week now. "Have there been any questions about Lady Janet?"

"Nay. It feels strange. I thought we would have had a visit from the Camerons by now. A search party."

It did not make sense, and Rory did not like things that did not make sense.

"We should send the lass home," he said.

Douglas was silent for a moment. "She has been here nearly a week now," he said. "If we return her now, there could be consequences. Her reputation will be ruined. And we cannot spare the loss of another man for an escort." The steward frowned. "It was a poor decision on my part," he said. "I should not have agreed to the scheme."

"I should have taken her back myself, fever or not," Rory said. "Do we have anyone who can make his way safely into the Cameron properties and try to get information?"

"Aye. Fergus is married to a Cameron. He has taken food to her family before."

"Send him today. Give him whatever he needs. I do not want him to be obvious. Just to listen and report back as soon as possible. Tell him there will be no rent due this year."

"Aye."

"Does he know that Lady Janet is here?"

"Aye. He was with us on the raid, but he will say nothing."

Rory had been away too long to know who could be trusted and who could not. But he trusted Douglas's assessment.

Still, it was only a matter of time before word leaked out, if it had not already.

"Send him now. What about the Campbells? Can anyone enter there?"

Douglas shook his head. "I know of no one, but Archibald may."

"Talk to him. In the meantime, keep an extra guard. No one is to go in or out unless I know about it."

"Aye, my lord." Respect had crept into those words this time. Rory noted it, but he did not care.

"And the lass?"

God's eyes, but his head ached. Nearly as much as his arm. And, he feared, his heart. He would never forget the look in her face as she tended Alina. The tenderness. The compassion.

Then the warmth and life she had transferred to him as she lay against him.

He was sickened by the thought that she might pay for that compassion. She could have been gone, but she chose to stay and help care for the wounded. And himself.

What if she were blamed for his actions? Until now he had thought mostly of the harm to his clan.

But now he was beginning to realize the great harm that might well come to her on her return.

"It should be up to her," he said finally.

"And if that decision is damaging to Macleans?"

What was the worst possibility? An innocent ruined because of an action by his clan, or his clan attacked and persecuted because of the good intentions of a few men.

Where did his loyalties lie?

The Macleans. The walls whispered the answer. He should be their protector. Was that not why he had returned?

Yet he could not abandon a lass because of his clan's misguided actions.

"I want our men to train harder," he said. "I want them to start storing grain and food within the walls. They need to be prepared for a siege." He paused. "But I will give myself to hostage first. I will allow no harm to come here."

Douglas stared at him for a long second. "We need you, Rory."

"You need peace more," Rory said. "How will the Macleans react?"

"They will know we have a lord back," Douglas said.

FELICIA returned to Rory's bedchamber with hot soup. She heard voices and hesitated before going in.

It should be up to her.

And if that decision is damaging to Macleans?

I want our men to train harder.

For the first time, she realized what she had done. In fleeing headlong and stubbornly staying here, she might well be responsible for their deaths. Moira. Lachlan. Rory. Robina. Alina.

She'd heard it said that the Campbells had been searching for a woman when they raided the village. They had been looking for her. Reason enough to destroy a village. At least for Campbells.

When Alina was first brought in, Felicia had been struck with guilt that her clansmen had committed such acts. But now she knew her own actions—her own blind thoughtlessness—could bring much worse upon the Macleans, as well as her own clan. Her desires—freedom from a wretched marriage—had cost other people far more than she'd ever expected.

Now she had to leave, not to escape to London, but to return and to try to put things right. It no longer mattered what happened to her. Alina's life mattered. Moira's life mattered. Rory's life mattered.

She heard the weakness in his voice, the pain not only of his wounds but of the decisions she had forced him to make. He had been willing to sacrifice his life for her.

For her.

No, not for her. For Janet Cameron, the daughter of a neighboring clan, which, while not completely an ally, was not an enemy, either.

How could she now tell him who she was?

She thought of the acceptance she'd had in the past days, the feeling of worth she'd gained by it. How could she now brave the hatred and disgust sure to come?

There was but one thing to do. She had to leave and return home before anyone discovered where she had been. She would tell William that she had been hiding in caves all this time and be there in time for her father's escort. She had three or four days. No more.

At least she'd had a taste of life, of passion. Regret warred with determination, despair with acknowledgment of what had to be done. She balanced the tray with the bowl of soup, a tankard of ale, and bread and knocked, then entered.

Rory was sitting up on the bed. As before he wore no shirt, only hose, and they molded his lower body well, too well. They clung to his muscled stomach. She dared not look lower.

Sweat dampened his face, which was rough with new beard. His jaw was clenched, as if it took every bit of his concentration to remain upright.

His mouth softened as he saw her, but there was a hard glint of resolve in his eyes.

"Douglas, leave us," he said. "And make sure our man leaves immediately."

"Aye, my lord," Douglas said. He bowed to Felicia. "My lady," he said. "We are all grateful."

She had not thought she could feel worse.

She placed the tray on the table and watched him struggle to rise. "Stay in bed," she ordered.

"Nay, there is much to do."

"More reason for you to rest. You cannot help anyone if you get worse."

He paid no attention to her but struggled to his feet. He swayed, and she moved to his side. He slipped his arm around her shoulders and stumbled rather than walked to the table. The reliance startled her. The laird was not a man to lean on anyone, even now. His touch sent now familiar frissons of heat steaming through her. He looked at her through pain-clouded eyes, but he could not hide the attraction any better than she could.

She wanted to hold on to him.

She closed her eyes for a moment, prayed for the strength she knew she needed. Not physical strength but the strength to leave him and go to another man.

They were still for a moment, as if caught in a painting.

Then he slid in the seat, nearly taking her down with him. She heard him mumbling. It sounded like an oath.

She felt like uttering one herself. Duty and need, truth and lies were tearing her apart.

Her gaze returned to his face. He was regarding her with frustrated need, combined with pain.

She felt his brow. It was not as hot as it had been earlier, though it was warmer than natural. Perhaps rest and Moira's magic were working. She prayed so.

"Eat, my lord," she said.

"Moira's soup?" he said.

"Aye, but I added a few herbs."

He tasted it, winced.

"I had hoped it would be improved," she said, though she had tasted it as well and found little improvement. Still, she had hoped.

"It is," he replied, but she saw the lie for what it was. She wished now that she had not allowed herself to be dismissed from the Dunstaffnage kitchen so easily. To be truthful, she had not tried overly hard. She would rather drive an arrow with a bow.

She should find a way to depart the keep before it was impossible. Yet she wanted these few moments with him. She wanted far more. She wanted to assure herself that he would defeat the fever. How could she leave without knowing that?

How could she not leave?

He stopped eating, and his gaze met hers.

"We need to talk, my lady," he said.

She had heard enough outside the door to know what he wanted to talk about. How could she sit there and allow him to agonize over choices that were necessary only because of her reckless adventure?

She did not say anything.

"Do you wish to marry James Campbell?" he said.

How could she say aye, when she had kissed him so passionately so recently?

"It does not matter what I want," she said. "I am only a woman. My . . . family makes that decision."

"Many women marry for love."

"Do they?" she asked skeptically. "I think they are few."

"Then you do not love the Campbell?"

She did, but not the way he meant. She did not know how to reply, but he apparently took her silence for agreement.

"Lachlan seems to think you may be reluctant. Or afraid."

"You have talked to him?"

"Only briefly, when I first returned."

She was silent again.

"Is Campbell a monster then?"

"Nay."

A muscle in his jaw worked. "Then do you fear returning because you have spent time here, without a chaperon?"

Her gaze met his, and she knew hers must be roiling with emotion. She did not want to lie to him. Not even by omission. He was not the kind of man who tolerated dishonesty. She had already seen and heard enough to know he had not wanted to return, but did so because of duty. She knew he had loved well and had given his heart.

She'd learned all that about Rory Maclean in a week's time.

She also realized he would never forgive her if lies brought death to his clan.

But she had to lie to save him. "Nay, I do not fear that," she said.

His gaze was unwavering, as he searched her face.

"And I do love James Campbell. We had an argument. I ran away because I wanted to think . . . and it was an adventure."

"You want to return then?"

"Aye." Her heart was breaking.

She was still standing, and he stood. Again she saw what the effort cost him. But he stepped closer to her and brushed his lips against hers. The unwounded arm went around her and pulled her closer.

She trembled from the resulting waves of sensation that swept over her, that raced through her body. She felt the rising and falling of his chest, his heart beat, the lingering heat from the fever.

She must have the fever as well. This was madness.

With a lump in her throat and sick emptiness in her stomach, she knew he was seeking the truth, and the truth was one thing she could not offer him.

His lips moved slowly, sensuously, across her face, awakening even more sensations both gentle and fierce. Then they turned questioning, asking questions she could not answer.

His lips pressed harder, this time demanding not asking. She knew suddenly that she had been waiting all her life for this warmth, this wanting.

She heard a soft groan, and his lips became seeking, as if he, too, were trying to find his way in an unknown thicket of tangled emotions. Anger was at the edge of them, but the core was pure, raw desire.

Fear squeezed her heart. She could not love this man. She could not.

Pull away!

She felt a sudden wetness on her cheeks, a growing tightness behind her eyes.

He stilled, then slowly released her lips. His eyes reflected a sorrow that stabbed to the core of her being. He lowered his arm, and he looked weary and defeated.

"You must sit, my lord."

He said nothing but went to the bed and sat down, his hand catching hers. "I am sorry, lass. I had no right. I wanted to know the truth of it. I wanted to know if you truly loved the Campbell."

"And you know now?" she said. Her voice sounded strange even to her. Husky. Hoarse with emotion and need and sadness.

"Aye. I do not think you love him."

"Because you kissed me?"

"Because of the way *you* kissed me, lass."

"And you had no feeling at all?"

His hand tightened around hers. "Aye, I did. But I have had no luck at marriage, and my wives have had less luck. I will no' be passing on death to another."

"Will you tell me about them? You kept calling for Maggie."

His mouth tightened, and a muscle twitched in his jaw. The dimple in his chin seemed to deepen. "She died in childbirth, as did the child. She loved life and laughter, and she did no' deserve her fate."

His face was a study in pain and guilt. Her heart broke. Did his pain come from the Campbell curse, or his belief in it?

He lifted the finger of his good hand and wiped away a tear from her face. "I should no' be burdening you with this," he said. "It is enough that I cannot marry again, and I want you to be safe. I wish I knew how to make it so."

The uncertainty of a certain man touched her to the core. She had never met anyone who cared as much as he did for his people. For his sense of honor. For her.

Except Jamie.

She touched his face. It was still warm. She knew he was still in pain.

Well, she would have her own honor as well. "I will go home," she said. "I wish to go alone. Now."

He looked at her for a long moment. "You cannot go alone. You are my responsibility. I want to know that you will not be hurt because of something we did. I have sent someone to the Camerons."

And he will know that Janet Cameron is at home.

"It is not your fault," she said. "And Archibald thought he was doing a fine thing."

He shook his head. "They think wives are like saddles. Lose one and gain another."

Most men did. At least, that had been her observation. It was her fortune—or misfortune—to find the one who did not. And he was forbidden to her for so many reasons.

She lifted her chin. If he would not let her leave, then she would have to find a way. It seemed more than a little ironic, that not long ago he had wanted her to leave and she had been plotting how to stay.

Chapter 12

❧

JAMIE first checked the caves he'd introduced to Felicia years ago. Finding nothing—not Felicia nor any sign of her presence—he rode to the Cameron property bordering Maclean territory. He carefully crossed a tiny swath of McDonald land, a clan hostile to the Campbells.

His horse was exhausted and dark with sweat when he reached the Cameron's keep. Immediately after identifying himself, he was admitted through the thick gates.

Janet's father was in Edinburgh along with Jamie's, involved in more court intrigue, no doubt. But Janet's mother, Lady Jane Cameron, greeted him effusively. "You have returned," she said. "We can plan the wedding then."

"Aye, Lady Jane," he said. "And I am most anxious to see your daughter."

Lady Jane nodded. "Of course. I am pleased that there is eagerness between you. I wished a love match for her."

"I will try to make her happy."

A frown marred Lady Jane's lovely face. "She has been unlike herself since her return."

"Has she said anything?"

"Nay. Only regret that she missed you at Dunstaffnage."

"I regretted it as well," he said. So she had said nothing about Felicia's disappearance. He wondered that the escort had apparently said naught about the escape of their charge, but then if they had retrieved their rightful lady, the men probably would not admit to being outfoxed by a woman or overtaken by brigands.

If Janet had said nothing, she must have had a reason. He decided to say naught about his cousin's disappearance until he talked to her.

I will have supper prepared for you," Lady Jane said. "And I will send her to you now."

"I cannot stay," he said. "I must leave in several hours. There is urgent business. But I wished to see Lady Janet first."

She beamed as if that were proof of his devotion, then sent a servant to the kitchen before ascending the stairs just inside the entrance.

He paced the hall with restless impatience. He would ask to borrow a fresh horse and be on his way as soon as he saw Janet. He wanted to know what she knew about Felicia, what part she had played in this.

Though he could not believe she would play any part.

She came down the steps. She wore a dark blue gown, and the colors deepened her blue eyes. She moved with an unconscious grace that had always entranced him.

Her face lit when she saw him, but he also saw little small signs of worry. She curtsied and held out her hand to him.

"I would like to talk to you," he said.

She met his gaze steadily, though he detected apprehension, even fear.

He looked at Lady Jane, who had followed her. She nodded her approval.

Janet led the way into a music chamber off the great hall. The room was large enough for a small audience. A harp stood at the front, and there were also several lutes and a vielle.

Hands folded in front of her, she sat in one of the chairs, while he paced. Finally he blurted out his question. "What do you know about Felicia's disappearance?"

She looked up at him. "I had hoped she had found you."

Shock jolted through him. He had not expected that answer. He had been told at Dunstaffnage that Janet had been drugged, that she knew nothing about the substitution, nor of Felicia's disappearance.

"You knew what she planned?"

"Aye," she said, her eyes challenging him.

She had never done that before.

"You helped her?"

"Aye," she admitted again.

"Why?"

"I could not stand by and see her marry the Earl of Morneith, not when I . . ." Her voice trailed off.

"When you?" he prompted.

"When I was so happy," she said in a soft, uncertain voice.

He held out a hand to her and urged her up from the chair. He folded her in his arms, something he had never done before. He had done what was expected. She had been an acceptable bride, a lovely bride, in truth, and he had always liked her. If he had ever had a reservation, it had been that she seemed to have little spirit. Next to Felicia, she had seemed colorless.

But now he saw in her what Felicia had apparently seen.

He did not know whether Felicia's actions had been the wisest thing, but he understood her desperation, and he appreciated Janet's loyalty to her.

"I thought . . . I was afraid you would be angry," Janet said after a prolonged silence.

"I only wish I had been there," he said.

"If you had, Felicia would have done nothing," Janet said. "She thought you might be able to help her secretly in London, but she was insistent she would do nothing that would bring blame to you."

A fist clasped and tightened around his heart.

He should have been her protector. He had always thought he was, but he realized he had not been in important things. Felicia's adoration had flattered him, her exploits amused him. He wished he had been more to her. In truth, he did not like himself very much at the moment. He had allowed himself to be manipulated by his own father. Now he discovered that his cousin was ready to sacrifice herself to save him. She had not waited for his return for fear that he might risk himself.

"Where did she plan to go if she could not find me?" he asked.

"You were the beginning and end of her plan," Janet said.

"Caves? A ship? What?"

Janet looked helpless. "She said it was a terrible plan, but she had no choice." Her eyes begged him to understand.

He did. He could not think of Felicia with all her intelligence and curiosity being paired with Morneith, a notorious womanizer in his sixth decade. She would wither and die.

"And no one knows what happened to her?"

"The escort returned to Dunstaffnage and found me there. I was their only concern, and the steward at Dunstaffnage did not wish word to get out until they had a chance to find her."

The Macleans would love to get their hands on a Campbell.

Jamie swore silently to himself. But if they did have his cousin, would they not have asked for a ransom by now?

"Does your father know?" she asked.

"Nay. Everyone, including William, is praying that she will be found before the escort arrives." He paused. "Do you know where she is?"

"She was going to hide in caves until she felt safe enough to try to reach you in London," she said.

"I checked the caves in the area," he said. "Nothing. Nor did I encounter her on the road from London."

"She planned to dress as a lad," Janet said, her eyes worried. "I should never have helped her. You would have returned and . . ."

"Once Felicia decides to do something, I doubt anyone could stop her," he said dryly.

"But if anything terrible has happened to her . . ."

"She could be in London now," he said. "I would never underestimate my cousin. She has your mare?"

"Aye."

He knew how important the mare was to her. It had taken immense generosity for her to loan the mare to Felicia. He touched her cheek, realizing how little he really knew her.

"I will find both of them," he swore.

She looked up at him with blue eyes full of trust. Yet she was not the shy, quiet lass he'd thought. He was finding depths that delighted him.

He leaned down and kissed her lightly. He called upon all his willpower not to deepen the kiss, not to explore those depths.

"I will have to borrow a fresh horse," he said.

She nodded. "And eat. My mother ordered some food."

He nodded.

"Where will you go?"

"There have been Maclean raiding parties," he said. "They raided one of our villages and stole cattle around the time Felicia disappeared. I am thinking they may have found her. If not, they might have heard something."

She frowned. "You are not going alone?"

"Aye. Their walls are impenetrable. A full force would accomplish little. A lone wayfarer would not be a threat, and they do not know me. I will say I am a Stewart."

"Better a Cameron," she said, surprising him yet again. "We are at peace with the Macleans. I can find you a crest and plaid with our dyes."

Her body trembled. Fear. For him. Humbled, he regretted how little time he had spent with her, how much he had taken for granted.

He held her tight. "Thank you."

"Please be careful."

"Aye," he said. "I have much to come home to." He straightened. "Will you get the garments while I eat? I must leave shortly."

"I will bring them to you at the stable. 'Tis better if my mother does not know."

"You have been with my cousin too long," he said, then touched her lips with his fingertips. "I canna wait until we are wed."

Her face flashed with pleasure. "I will find some clothing for you while you eat."

He leaned down and kissed her hard, bringing her body close to his, then reluctantly let go.

The sooner he found his cousin, the sooner he could return.

FELICIA stopped in to see Alina. Baron greeted her with a bark and a frantically waving tail.

Robina, along with Alina's mother, had been caring for the child while Felicia had been with Rory.

Robina stood when she came in. "Alina's mither went to the kitchen," she said. "She says she can cook and wanted to help."

That, Felicia thought, would be a godsend to everyone here.

She knelt down beside Alina. "How is the bravest lass in Scotland?"

The child flushed with pride. Pain was still etched in her face, but her color had returned to normal and she breathed easily.

"Is my lord better?" Alina asked. "Robina said you were caring for him."

It amazed Felicia that Alina worried about her laird, when she still suffered so from the burn and the wounds to her leg.

"Aye. Moira is a fine healer."

"Moira says my leg might heal." The words were said with such hope that Felicia's heart caught with sudden agony. Alina would bear the scars inflicted by Campbell clansmen throughout her life.

"Would you like me to sing a song?" she asked.

She would be trying to slip away tonight. The thought of seeing neither Rory nor Alina again only intensified the agony she felt. She wouldn't know if Alina would run, or if Rory would love once more. She wouldn't know whether Lachlan would finally find his place, or if Moira ever learned to cook.

It was startling to her that she could come to care so much in such a short period of time. She wondered whether it was because her heart had been waiting to open, to find a place. Why did God open it here?

She started to sing a song, a sad one about unrequited love.

"No," Alina said. "The one you sang before."

Felicia started to hum, then the words came. Tender and loving. Comforting. She wished it would wipe away the hurt inside. She suspected nothing could.

* * *

$\mathcal{L}$ACHLAN rode with a troop of Macleans. They were to patrol the border between their land and the Camerons. The Camerons had once been allies, but a marriage between the Cameron lass and a Campbell would create an alliance that bode no good for the Macleans. Archibald and Douglas had hoped to nullify that alliance with a marriage between Lady Janet and Rory.

Lachlan feared they may have made it worse.

The Campbells apparently had felt safe enough to pass over Cameron land to raid Maclean villages. The fact that Macleans had stolen the Cameron lass and must return her without marriage could well destroy any hope of an alliance.

He and his fellow clansmen had been sent by Rory to patrol for intruders, for a marauding Campbell or Cameron troop. Feeling totally inadequate for the task, he'd tried to demur. But Rory had threatened to go himself, and his brother was obviously not well enough yet. Lachlan would not be responsible for the death of yet another Maclean lord.

He was to patrol half of the border, Archibald the other half.

The night was cold but the sky was clear, the full moon lighting the gorse-covered hills.

Lachlan's troop visited the village that had been burned. They were already rebuilding. He left two men there to help, then left two more men to guard a road that wound between the hills.

There was only one more pass. He would leave two more men there.

The first slivers of dawn pierced the darkness as he looked down at the pass from a vantage point above. He was about to position two men to guard the pass when he saw movement.

He peered downward. A man on a dark horse rode through the pass. He seemed to cling to the shadows of the terrain.

Lachlan considered the possibilities. Most Scots were afoot. That meant the man below was of rank, or was a valued soldier.

A Campbell spy?

Or a Cameron?

Mayhap neither.

An image flitted through his head. Three years ago. An encounter with a group of armed men . . .

He was not going to allow that to happen again.

He gestured to two of the three men with him to circle around so that the man would be surrounded. Then he mounted and rode down to accost the man himself.

He put a hand on his sword. He, like his brothers, had undergone training. Unlike them, he'd never had the inclination to use it.

He rode the horse down the hill and reached the road just as the horseman appeared from behind a rocky edge.

Dawn had spread across the eastern part of the sky, and Lachlan saw the crest. A Cameron.

His gaze went to the face, and he froze.

He'd gone to Edinburgh with his father eight years ago. He had been but a lad. Rory had already gone to sea. Patrick had been left at Inverleith to guard the Maclean properties.

His father had pointed a young man out to him. "There is the spawn of the devil," he'd said.

It had been Jamie Campbell.

The same man who approached him now.

Chapter 13

❦

In the dawn's early rays, Jamie saw recognition—sudden awareness—on the face of the young man who faced him.

He swore as a second man appeared to his left and another to his right. He would be a good catch for the Macleans. A large ransom would be demanded if indeed his life wasn't forfeit.

It went against his training to submit meekly. His hand went to the hilt of his sword, and he saw the Maclean in front of him do the same. As did the two men with him.

None of the three looked to be particularly dangerous. Jamie had trained his entire life. He was expert with the sword, and his horse was skilled in war and recognizing even the slightest signal.

He was not going to go down without a fight.

As he drew his sword, so did the others.

He decided to go for the leader first. He looked the youngest and least skilled. And if the leader was eliminated, his men might well disappear into the hills.

He touched his heels to his mount, turning the gelding ever so slightly, then charged his opponent. To his surprise, the rider easily avoided his charge, skillfully moving his horse away just in time to avoid a blow.

Too late, he became aware of still a fourth man. He felt himself being dragged down from behind, and then three more men were on him. He fought back, frantically searching for the sword, but it was gone.

And then everything went black.

FELICIA stayed with Alina until the child went to sleep. She was tired beyond words, both in body and soul. She was aware that a tear trickled down her cheek, and she ignored it.

She did not want to go back to her room. She could not sleep. She knew she needed to stay away from Rory. Just before dawn, she would go to her room, don the lad's clothes, and slip down to a place she could hide until a party left the keep. She hoped she could meld in with them.

Until then, she wanted to stay with Alina, to feel needed and wanted a few hours longer.

Alina's mother entered the room with a bowl of soup.

"She is sleeping," Felicia said as softly as possible.

"The soup can wait then." The older woman paused, then added, "Ye have been so kind. I will no' forget ye. Nor will Alina."

"It is very easy to be kind to her. She has so much courage."

"Ye can leave now, my lady. I will sit by her."

Felicia looked at the woman's drawn face. She had spent the day trying to earn her way by taking over the cooking chores from Moira, who was still looking after the wounded.

"I would like to stay here with her," she said. "Why do you not get some rest?"

The woman nodded gratefully, but her expression was still unsure. "Ye are a great lady, and we . . ."

Felicia swallowed hard. How many times had she passed villages without really looking at the people? She had tried to be thoughtful to the servants at Dunstaffnage, and she had often tended wounded with the healer, but there had always been an invisible line she'd been expected to honor. Now she doubted that line. Why should an accident of birth make someone more or less than another?

"You need your rest, and everyone knows that Inverleith needs a cook," Felicia said. "You canna do it here, not with listening every second for every breath. Use my chamber. It is next to here, and I will call you if there is any change."

"I canna' do that."

"Aye, you can," Felicia said. "You would be doing me a boon."

The woman nodded, tears shimmering in too-old eyes. "No one knew whether to hope when Lord Rory returned home. I will tell them 'tis a good thing. I hope ye stay, Lady Janet."

She left, and the words lingered in the room.

Felicia went to the window. She had not gone down to the great hall for supper. She did not want to see the men who had such high hopes for a marriage for their laird. Nor did she wish to see the heightened activity as those in the keep made preparations for a possible siege.

She continued to stare down at the courtyard. Macleans were leaving with carts and returning with them filled with food and grain. But in addition to the regular sentries, there were two men at the gate, checking as each man left and returned.

Families had evidently been ordered to come into the keep from outlying villages.

Because of her? Because Rory had sensed her reluctance to return? Because she had led him to believe she did not wish to marry Jamie Campbell. Or was it because of recent Campbell raids? Her family's vendetta against the Macleans. Either way she felt responsible.

And soon he would discover who she was. She was amazed that as yet there seemed to be no outcry about her disappearance. She vowed to escape the keep tonight. Then all could get back to normal. And if she could not find a way, then it was time, well beyond the time, to reveal that she was a Campbell.

She had no idea what would happen then. No doubt, Rory Maclean would feel betrayed. Would he try to hold her hostage? If so, the long-lasting feud would explode into war. Her uncle had been waiting for an opportunity, held back only by King James's edict. He had allowed William the occasional raid but all-out war was not something James wanted, with a hostile English king across the border. It was understood that it was only a matter of time before the two countries went to war with each other, and James needed all the clans he could pull together.

Her supposed abduction would give her uncle all the reason he needed to attack.

But holding her hostage went against everything she had learned about the Macleans. About Rory and Lachlan, and even Archibald and Douglas. They were decent men.

But then she'd thought the Campbells were as well. And yet both clans over the years had inflicted murder and rape and misery on the other. She truly did not know what either would do now.

She went back to sit with Alina.

And finally her eyes closed.

* * *

*L*ACHLAN stared at their captive. He was still unconscious from the blow one of Lachlan's companions had leveled.

He thanked God that the man still breathed. He did not even want to think what might happen if Angus Campbell learned the Macleans had killed his only son and heir.

"Bind him," he ordered the others who were in much more of a mood to kill the Campbell.

Rory would know what to do.

At least, Lachlan hoped to God that Rory would know what to do.

He knew what *he* would do. He would find out why a Campbell had been so reckless as to venture onto Maclean land and then release him. Without ransom. A gesture of goodwill.

But a previous gesture of goodwill had led to his father's death.

Lachlan had lost confidence in his own judgment then. He had never regained it. He had always wanted to see the best in everyone. Unfortunately, he had learned that some had no best.

He sighed.

For now, he could only hope the capture of the Campbell would do more good than harm, but he feared that was false hope. Nor did he know how the capture would affect Janet Cameron. She was, after all, the man's betrothed.

He wished she had confided in him. Something other than the Macleans frightened her. Whether it was the man on the ground or no', he did not know. He did know he did not want to take the man back to Inverleith until he knew more.

"There is a deserted croft two miles east of the keep," he said. "Take him there. Keep him well bound. Rory will have your heads if he escapes."

"Aye," one man said with new respect.

Lachlan looked at the bound Campbell on the ground. It had taken four of them to take him.

Lachlan knew he did not deserve the respect.

* * *

FELICIA jolted awake and glanced at the window. Light flooded through. It was past dawn. Well past dawn. She could not believe she had slept.

She glanced down at Alina. Asleep. Which was a miracle. Felicia wished she could take on the child's pain and absorb it. But Alina had finally gone to sleep, and so, apparently, had she.

Had she lost her chance to escape?

"Moira said you were here," Rory said from the door where he leaned against the wall, watching her with brooding eyes. "Do you not believe in sleep?"

"I think I just was," she said with a croak. How long had he been there watching her? Had his entrance been what awakened her?

He gave her a half-smile. "You look as if you've had no sleep at all."

"That is not very gallant."

"You look appealing when you are tired," he said. The smile disappeared as if he had not meant to say those words.

But she clutched them to her heart. No one had ever called her appealing.

"You need rest and food," Rory said. "I am told you did not go to supper last night nor did you eat this morning."

"I wanted to stay with Alina," she said.

He had shaved, or someone had shaved him. He wore a clean linen shirt and was wearing a plaid rather than trews. His face was still flushed slightly, and he wore his arm in a sling. The shirt bulged over the bandage on his arm.

"Moira says it is better," he said, obviously noting the direction of her stare. "She is making me wear a poultice, though," he said. "It makes me smell like a moldy tree."

It was the first time she had heard him try to be amusing or anything but the stern, uncompromising leader of his clan. "You should be abed as well," she said.

"There is too much to do. Archibald and Lachlan are patrolling the borders, and others are warning the crofters."

"You really believe Inverleith will be attacked?"

He nodded wearily. "The Campbells raided one of our villages. We stole our cattle back. And they raided again. Something has been started that cannot be stopped." He paused, then said softly, "I had hoped . . ."

"Hoped what?"

"To bring peace, but now I think it was a foolish aim. How do you stop a century of hatred?" His eyes were full of pain, and failure.

"I want to go back," she said.

"Not until I know you will be safe," he said.

"I will be," she lied.

"I've sent someone to the Camerons," he said.

"Yes, you told me," she said, aware that he did not know that was one reason she had to flee.

She stood. She knew immediately it was a mistake. She had meant to avoid him these last few hours. She had meant not to think about Rory Maclean and what might have been.

Nothing might have been. If she hadn't run away, and if Archibald hadn't tried to take matters into his own hands, she would not have met him. She would never have known the way a heart could swell, and her body could tingle, and blood could run warm and sweet.

She might never have known the jolt that rocked her each time she was in his presence.

Was this love?

It could not be. People did not find themselves in love in a week. Yet he was everything she thought noble in a man. Strong. Courageous. Yet also concerned for the weak. Loyal to his people. Committed to peace.

How would he view a liar?

But the now familiar current passed between them, sweeping them up in its pull. She saw it in his eyes, even as she felt its intensity.

She reached out to touch his cheek. "You no longer look like an outlaw," she said.

He smiled crookedly, the dimple in his chin deepening. "Looks can be deceiving."

"Not always," she said.

Sorcery. Nothing else could account for the way her body moved toward him, into his, or the way she rested her head on his shoulder.

His hand caressed her face and moved to the back of her neck. Her mind cried no, but her body wouldn't heed the warning. It was too caught up in all the exquisite feelings he evoked in her.

"Janet," he whispered.

The softly spoken word, much like an endearment, brought her back to reality.

She jerked free with such force that she stumbled, and his hand steadied her. His face was filled with bafflement.

She knew he wanted an explanation, but she was saved by a knock on the door.

He stared at her for a moment, then strode to the door and opened it.

Lachlan stood there. His gaze went from his brother to Felicia, then back again.

"Rory," he said. "You are needed downstairs."

"What is it?"

Lachlan shrugged. "A decision must be made."

She watched the two brothers silently communicate, then Rory nodded.

"I must go," he told her.

Before she could ask a question, he left.

Something of import had happened. Had Lachlan discovered who she really was?

Her heart hammered in her chest. Whatever had happened, she had the very bad feeling that it bode no good for her.

* * *

*R*ORY looked at the prisoner.

Jamie Campbell sat on the dirt floor of a croft. His hands were tied behind him, and his legs bound in front of him.

Rory knew that he must be in pain from the position. But all he saw was anger.

"You are Jamie Campbell," he said. He had never seen Campbell, though he lived but thirty miles away. The two clans had nothing to do with each other, other than the raids they inflicted on one another. If Lachlan had not recognized him . . .

"Aye."

"What were you doing on Maclean land?"

Campbell was silent. The Macleans who stood on either side of him moved in a threatening gesture.

"No," Rory said.

Campbell looked surprised. He raised an eyebrow in question, and Rory found himself admiring the man.

"Leave us," he told the two men with him.

They hesitated, then filed out the door. Only Lachlan remained.

Rory stooped down and cut the ropes on his prisoner's ankles.

Jamie Campbell stretched them, then looked at his captor warily. "Whom do I have the . . . pleasure of addressing?"

Rory could not help but grin at the impudence.

"Rory Maclean."

"I did not know you had returned."

Rory shrugged. "You did not answer my question. Why are you on Maclean properties?" He looked at the Cameron crest, and the plaid with distinctive Cameron dyes. "And in Cameron plaid?"

He knew why. Campbell was looking for his betrothed. What he didn't know is why an emissary from the Camerons had not approached him.

But how much did Campbell know?

Campbell shifted. "Would you cut these ropes around my wrists? They are . . . annoying."

"Considering that several of my kinsmen were killed recently, I find it hard to sympathize."

"I had nothing to do with that."

"You can discuss that with the two outside. One lost a brother." Rory tilted his head, regarding his prisoner blandly. "You have the space of a breath to tell me why you are here."

The Campbell hesitated.

"I am not fond of spies," Rory said.

For the first time, uncertainty flashed across his prisoner's face. He was obviously weighing every word he said.

At last he shrugged as if finally making a decision. "My cousin is missing. I have been searching for her. Nothing more. Do you think I would attack Inverleith by myself?"

Rory tensed. Of all the answers, that was the one least expected. "Your cousin?"

"Felicia. She has been missing more than a week now." It was obvious that the man was not lying. There was no reason to do so. Why would anyone want a woman when they had taken the Campbell heir?

Rory struggled to keep his emotions concealed. Yet he felt as if he had just been struck by lightning.

Suddenly everything started to come clear. The lass had not wanted to be returned to the Camerons. He realized now that she had made one excuse after another not to be returned to them.

Because she was not one.

Felicia Campbell.

But why . . . ?

Perhaps she had thought the Macleans would do her harm if they discovered her true identity. It was the Macleans, after all, that had taken her, believing her to be Janet.

He recalled the lies. All of them. He also remembered the kisses. Had she tolerated them, waiting only to escape? *Had they been lies as well?*

White hot anger filled him.

He tried to reason with it. She had not asked to be abducted by Archibald. She'd had every reason to fear for her life.

But surely after the first few days she should have realized he would not harm a woman. Even a Campbell. The lack of trust was like a dagger thrust.

And now he had a second prisoner, one even more unwanted than the first.

"You know where she is," Jamie Campbell said suddenly.

"Aye, she is safe."

Campbell breathed audibly. Then he looked up again, as if having a sudden thought. "You did not know . . ."

"Who she was? Nay, not until now. I thought she was your betrothed, Janet Cameron."

Jamie Campbell closed his eyes, obviously aware of what he had said, that he had given the Macleans another weapon.

"Unlike the Campbells, I do not make war on women," Rory said.

"No? That is not what I have heard," Campbell said mockingly.

Rory's mind went back to the raid more than a decade ago. The screams. The madness.

"Your cousin will not be harmed," he said. "I cannot say the same about you."

He walked out then, into the mist that had returned, and turned to Lachlan, who followed him. "Say nothing about Janet Cameron or Felicia Campbell," he said.

Lachlan regarded him curiously. "Aye," he said and stood, waiting for the next order.

Rory hesitated as he tried to absorb what he had just been told, and the repercussions. He had known that something was wrong, that the lass should have been insistent about being returned to her family. He recalled every lie, every evasion.

He should have known earlier that all was not as it seemed. If the Cameron lass had been missing this long, the Camerons should have been at his gates, asking for his help in the search. Yet he had been mesmerized by the lass, intrigued by the mystery, and entranced by her efforts on behalf of his people.

But why had she been reluctant to let him take her to the Camerons? Once there, she would no longer have to fear him once he discovered who she really was. The Camerons would protect her.

So why had she not leaped at the opportunity?

Could the Campbell be lying?

Rory considered himself a good judge of character. He had to be that. When he selected a crew, he knew they would be together as long as nine months to a year and their lives would depend on the character and abilities of each one of them.

He'd measured the man in the croft. He instinctively believed him.

That, alone, startled him. Believe a Campbell?

He ran over his alternatives.

He kept going back to why Janet—no, Felicia—had not wanted to return home.

But that would come from the lass.

Then he would test the words of each against one another.

He would discover who was lying and why.

And then he would have decisions to make. Decisions that could mean the survival of his clan.

He fought the emptiness that suddenly overwhelmed him. He could not get beyond the lies. She had played on his loneliness like a master musician.

Lachlan and the two men were waiting for a decision.

"We will take him to Inverleith," he said. "We should be able to use him to good advantage."

He watched as they brought out the Campbell.

Janet—no, Felicia—would probably watch them ride in. She would realize that her . . . masquerade was over.

He forced his emotions into a box in the back of his mind, as Campbell, his hands still tied behind him, was assisted onto his horse.

Rory needed time to think. He needed time to temper the anger.

It went deeper than anger. He had actually thought he might be able to care again.

Now he knew it had been naught but an illusion.

Chapter 14

JAMIE suffered the furies of the damned as he sat astride a horse being led by a Maclean.

Their going was slow. Night clouds filled the sky yet again, making the trail difficult to follow. Jamie's horse had stumbled more than once on the narrow path that wound around the hills.

Time to think. Too much time to think. He might well have condemned Felicia. And himself. He could live with the latter, but not the former.

He knew he had made a terrible—perhaps fatal—mistake when he had identified the woman the Macleans held as his cousin.

If only he had known they *had* held a woman.

He'd thought if they had her, the Maclean would have said something. And he had been at a loss to explain why he'd been on Maclean property. Searching for a lost lass seemed as good as any explanation. He even thought for an instant he might be able to talk himself out of a problem. Most Scots would offer to join the search for an innocent lass.

He had ignored the fact he was dealing with Macleans.

He closed his eyes for a moment, wishing he could take that instant back. He would gladly give his own life to do that.

If the Maclean did not kill him, most assuredly his father would want to do the deed. His father did not tolerate failure, nor would he tolerate his son's walking into the arms of his greatest enemy.

God's blood, but his shoulders and wrists hurt. The ropes bit into his flesh, and they pulled his shoulders back. His legs were free to hug his mount, but the reins were held firmly by the man riding in front of him.

The physical discomfort paled in comparison to his concern over his cousin. He had watched the Maclean's face when the man realized he had Felicia rather than Janet. Emotion had flitted across his face. Disbelief. Anger. And something more.

How had his cousin ever convinced him she was Janet? The two looked nothing alike. Janet was a true beauty. Felicia . . .

He tried to think of her as a female, not a cousin who was as close as a sister. She was not beautiful, yet he had always enjoyed her company. She was intriguing and challenging. While he admired those characteristics in a friend, he was not sure he would be similarly enamored as a husband.

Or would he?

His interest in Janet had spiraled when he'd discovered she was not the obedient lady he had always thought. He'd always believed he wanted a complacent and pleasant wife. Now he knew how bored he might have become.

He might never have a chance to explore this adventurous side of Janet.

He looked at the rider ahead. The Maclean's back was stiff, as if he was keeping himself tightly in control.

Something was brewing here. Perhaps he could use it.

If he—and Felicia—lived long enough.

ELICIA was jolted awake by Alina's mother. The woman looked rested, though Felicia was exhausted.

She had stayed at Alina's side for hours, trying to convince herself that the wee lass would fare well without her. Her heart ached and cried for the child, as well as for herself. She would return to Dunstaffnage, for that was best for both Macleans and Campbells. She could suffer the proposed marriage, knowing that by doing so she would not be putting others at harm.

She held Alina's hand, reveled in the trust she saw in the child's eyes.

She did not want to leave. In a matter of days, she had found a place for herself. She had found what being a woman was about. She suspected she would never again feel the fevered desire she had felt—still felt—for the Maclean lord.

A place secured by a lie, she told herself. By a mountain of lies, both uttered and made through silence.

She left when Alina's mother returned before dawn, rested and ready for the kitchen. Felicia went to her chamber and located the lad's clothes under the mattress. She thanked the keep's careless housekeeping that they were still there.

She hurriedly changed, then tried to push her hair under a cap. The more she tried to tuck her hair up, the more it came tumbling out. She went to the window. Dawn was not far away, and she had to be gone with the first group of tenants to leave the gates. Some left for their fields. Others were charged with bringing in wood.

She looked in the small mirror and knew the truth. She would never get all her hair under the cap.

What would happen when she returned home, sheared like a sheep?

She had no choice. It was the only possible way of leaving. She had taken a dirk with her from home and had hidden it along with the lad's clothing. She touched the blade with her finger and drew a fine line of blood.

It was sharp enough.

Reluctantly, she took a handful of curls in one hand and began to cut. Red curls dropped around her feet. She cut more until she had only a cap of curls. She felt naked as well as much lighter, but she had no time for regret. She got down on her hands and knees and pushed the hair under the bed, suspecting it would not be found for another decade or so. Not unless a housekeeper appeared magically.

She took some ash from the fireplace and rubbed it in her hair until it became a dingy black, then she placed the cap on her head. She rubbed her hand across her cheek, trailing more ash across it.

She would not bear close scrutiny but perhaps she could pass in a crowd. In any event, it was the only chance she had.

She made a bundle in the bed. She hoped it looked like a sleeping person. She doubted anyone, especially shy Robina, would try to wake her. They had all been trying to convince her to get more rest.

With only a brief, regretful glance back, she left the chamber, keeping to the shadows. She said a small prayer. Surely God would be with her. She wanted only to rectify her mistakes, her misguided flight that had resulted in such unintended consequences.

She left her room and went down to the great hall where the Maclean clansmen slept this night.

They had been coming in all day—men, women, and

children. The hall was filled, particularly the area around the fireplace. She had helped find blankets for them all and assisted in the kitchen by adding more and more water, potatoes, and meat to great pots of stew.

But now the keep was still, except for the soft snoring of several hundred Macleans from small villages. Their cattle were just outside the walls. At the first sign of trouble, they would be brought inside.

Felicia planned on being one of those leaving at dawn to replace those tending the cattle. The tenants were on foot, not on horses, and she hoped she could get lost in their midst. She would then have a chance to separate from them and make her way back to the Camerons. She would have to travel on foot, avoiding the paths and roads, relying only on the stars to guide her. She had already prepared a story about getting lost and the Macleans' kindness in caring for her.

She could no longer try for London, nor to find Jamie. Too many people would discover she had been at Inverleith, and her disappearance would cast blame on the Macleans. She would not be responsible for more slaughter. Nor could she admit her true identity to the Macleans. She could not bear to see affection and respect turn to hatred, nor was she sure that she would not be used as a pawn. In any event, she would be returned to her uncle, probably with a demand for ransom.

She managed to leave the tower without being seen, and she went around to the back of the stables. Then she leaned against the wall and allowed herself to slide down to the ground. An hour or so of sleep before dawn, before the gates would open.

But she could not sleep. She thought of Rory Maclean, of his kisses and gentleness. A tear trickled down her cheek, and she wiped it away impatiently. She had to do this.

* * *

ORY pushed both men and horses. He wanted to get back to Inverleith. He wanted to confront Janet. No, not Janet. Felicia.

Felicia. He kept reminding himself.

He wanted to see the truth in her face. He wanted to see her reaction when she knew he'd learned the truth. What lies would she utter then?

The kisses had been nothing but more lies. Her tender caring a facade to keep from being unveiled.

She had no choice. She had been taken by his men.

But that truth couldn't fill the sudden void he felt, or the anger at being misled into caring about a Campbell.

He realized that part of his anger was directed at the situation he now was in. Through no intent of his own, he held both the son and niece of the second most important person in Scotland, just below the king.

He should be pleased. He had gone from being the unknown and unproven second son of a clan of diminishing strength and influence to someone who held the Campbells' future in his hands. The Campbells would not dare lay siege to Inverleith, not without risking the life of their only direct heir.

But unlike the Campbells, he had no wish to play with lives, not that of James Campbell and certainly not that of a woman. He did not mistreat or use women, no matter the last name. It mattered not that he had been deceived or, even more excruciating, that she had touched a part of him he thought well protected.

Why was she traveling as Janet Cameron?

And why had there not been a hue and cry for Felicia Campbell? Why had her cousin come alone rather than with an army of Campbells?

Rory did not like mysteries. He did not like lies. He did not like Campbells.

They approached Inverleith. He stopped and rode to Campbell's side. He took out his dirk and cut a piece of cloth from the man's mantle, then wrapped the cloth around his prisoner's eyes.

He did not want James Campbell to see how few men he had, how unprepared Inverleith was. Felicia Campbell would have seen much of Inverleith, but he hoped she did not have the understanding that a warrior would. He ached at the thought she might betray him, but then he knew how foolish that thought was. She had not come to spy.

He swore under his breath as he finished tying the knot. James Campbell was still. He asked no questions, nor did he try to avoid the blindfold. Yet Rory could see the muscles tense in his shoulders, the strain in his face.

He looked up at the sky. The first fingers of dawn touched the hills, lighting them with a soft glow. The castle would soon be stirring. Would Felicia go to the window when she heard the horn? Would she recognize the Campbell with the blindfold covering most of his face? Still, his hair was an unmistakable color of gold.

Would she try to flee?

He spurred his horse, and the men behind him did the same, leading the Campbell's horse at a trot.

The gates opened, and they entered, then he ordered that the gates be closed and no one allowed to leave.

No one without his personal permission.

He stopped near the entrance to the tower. He picked three men from those gathering about the courtyard.

"Take him to one of the cells below. The first level. He is to be given food and water and blankets, but no one is to see him other than myself," he said. "The blindfold stays on until he is inside a cell."

"Who is he, milord?" one of the men asked.

"James Campbell," he said shortly.

The name spread quickly. More and more of his men and villagers appeared in the courtyard, whispering loudly. Some swore, others wondered at the man's fate. It was obvious some would like to dispatch him immediately.

Campbell slid a leg over the saddle and slid down with surprising grace since his hands were tied behind him. He must have heard Rory's orders, the angry taunts of Macleans, but he gave no sign that any of it rattled the icy calm he maintained.

"Nothing is to happen to him," Rory added in a low voice. "If there is any punishment, I will be the one inflicting it."

One of the selected men—he knew all three, and, to the best of his admittedly short knowledge, they were to be trusted—looked disgruntled at the order.

"Is that clear?" he asked.

"Aye," one said reluctantly. "What about his bonds?"

"Cut them once he is locked in the cell."

He turned his attention back to Campbell. "Try to escape, and my blacksmith will fit you with irons."

He saw a muscle flex in the man's throat and realized he was not as relaxed as he tried to appear.

"Take him," he said.

He watched as two of the assigned men took Campbell's arms and led him around to the back of the keep, to the stairs that would take them to the dungeon below. The cells were cold and always damp from the moisture that seeped into the rocks. There was no light other than that furnished by the guards. It was a mean place, but at the moment Rory felt no regret.

Ordinarily, a prisoner—a hostage—was asked to give his parole and was housed in the residence area of the keep, but he could not stop thinking about the way Felicia Campbell had fooled the whole of Inverleith. If she had such talents, who was to say her cousin would not as well?

The Campbells were not known for either their civility or their honor. He had to admit that neither did his clan have a better past. His ancestor had cast a stain on the clan that would be forever etched in its history.

He watched until the Campbell disappeared, then he

went to look for Felicia Campbell/Janet Cameron. He would discover what he wanted to know, and then he had decisions to make.

"What are you going to do?" Lachlan suddenly appeared at his side. His brother had been to the rear of the party, but Rory had no doubt he had heard his orders.

"I am no' sure," he said, falling back into boyhood brogue.

"Remember, we took her. She did not come of her own free will."

Rory spun on him, his anger barely under control. 'Twas true that the lass had not come of her own free will, but she had certainly returned his kisses of her own free will.

Or had she? Had that been part of her masquerade as well?

Lachlan looked tired, but he had been on patrol for more than two days. Rory had left several men to guard important passes, but their possession of the Campbell heir gave them a weapon they'd not had before. He would still be careful, still maintain patrols, but he doubted there would be an all-out onslaught now.

His immediate objective was Jan . . . Felicia. He wondered whether he could ever stop thinking of her as Janet.

To blazes with the woman. She was just another lass, and a Campbell one at that.

He took the stone steps two at a time and went into her chamber without knocking, and he glanced around in the morning light. Several lumps in the bed drew his attention.

He breathed easier. She was here. He was startled at how relieved he was.

Because he wanted to vent his anger? His bewilderment?

Or because for a moment he feared he would not see her again?

He erased the last thought from his mind.

He leaned over and pulled back the heavy covering, only to see her gown and petticoat bunched up to look like a sleeping figure. His breath caught in his throat, and his chest constricted.

Until this very moment, part of him had disbelieved the prisoner. Part of him had hoped . . . he hadn't even realized it until this very moment, but the thought had been there.

Had she left the keep? If so was she on foot somewhere in the hills? Fear replaced outrage. There were wolves and wild hogs, along with other dangerous predators.

He went to the chamber next door. His entrance woke Alina. Sleepy eyes regarded him solemnly.

"How are you?" he asked.

"Much better," she said primly.

"Do you know where Lady Janet is?"

"Nay, but she was here last night. She is an angel."

An angel indeed.

"Was she here after dark?"

"Aye, my lord."

Then she would not have had a chance to leave. The gates were closed at nightfall, and he doubted whether anyone would have left before he arrived this morning.

He went back into her room. Where could a lass hide? And what would she be wearing?

He glanced around again and something on the floor caught his glance. He stooped down and ran his finger along the rug. Then he saw a red hair. Then another. He got down and looked under the bed. Piles of curling copper-colored hair had been shoved under the bed.

Rory knew now how she'd expected to leave. The only question was whether she had been able to get outside the keep. He doubted it, especially since he had just given orders that no one was to leave.

Had she watched him ride in with her cousin? Is that why she disappeared? Or had she planned it all along?

Had she planned it when she returned his kisses? When she had melted into his arms?

He picked up a metal cup from the table and threw it

against the fireplace. He stood, stunned by his own violence. He had never thrown anything before, not even in his worst moments. He believed in self-discipline.

But he had not practiced it these past days. He'd sworn not to love again, not to care in a way that sudden loss would rip the guts from him. He had been successful for nearly eight years, and now . . .

And now the devil was having his joke. He had lowered his guard, had allowed a copper-haired lass into his heart. And not any lass, but a member of the clan that had cursed his family.

No bride of a Maclean will live long or happily, and every Maclean will suffer for it.

Two women he'd loved had died. How could he possibly have forgotten that?

I do not believe in the curse.

Maybe not the curse, but he did believe in fate.

Let her go.

But he couldn't. Not until he knew why she hadn't wanted to go home. Not until he knew she would be safe.

Her cousin was a different matter.

He turned toward the door, and stopped.

A young lad stood there. His cheeks were smudged, but nothing could hide the great blue eyes.

They looked frightened.

Defiant.

Angry.

His heart beat faster.

She looked like a warrior. It was obvious she knew he held her cousin. An unexpected jab of agony struck him as he realized she had returned to protect James Campbell, not for him.

Chapter 15

❦

"*L*ADY Felicia Campbell?"

She saw no advantage in denying it. "Aye."

When she had first encountered Rory Maclean, Felicia thought he had the coldest eyes she'd ever seen. She could not imagine colder ones.

But she had been wrong. She saw them now.

She shivered inside, though she tried not to show it. She had been right to want to run. He hated her now that he knew she was a Campbell.

He knew! And he was looking at her as if she were a particularly unpleasant insect.

When she had heard Jamie's name mentioned in the bailey, she knew she could not leave, even if the gates had not been closed. She had no doubt that he had come to his enemy's land to save her, and now she could not leave him, even if it meant facing Rory.

But how could she rescue Jamie? She had precious little to bargain with.

Instinctively, she felt that both she and Jamie would fare far better with honesty than attempted bravado or foolish acts. And so she had steeled her nerve and decided to offer anything to save her cousin who had risked everything for her.

From the Maclean's expression, she had nothing he wanted.

"You cut your hair," he said, surprising her with his cool, indifferent scrutiny.

"Aye."

His gray gaze bored into her. "Why did you no' leave when you had a chance?"

She hesitated. "The Camerons would have sent me back to Dunstaffnage." She saw in his icy eyes that she, as a person, had ceased to exist for him. Because she had lied to him? Or solely because she was a Campbell? Either way, a gaping hole yawned inside her. How had he become so important to her? So quickly? Why did she care what he thought of her?

"Why were you with the Cameron escort?" he persisted.

"I thought I could travel with them as Janet until I could escape them."

"Why?" he asked again.

She lifted her head and met his gaze directly. "My uncle had sent for me. He had arranged a marriage." She did not add it was at the king's order.

Nothing flickered in his expression as he continued to study her, obviously for more lies. It was all she could do to keep her hands steady and stand tall and resolute.

"It was not to your liking?" he asked after a moment's silence.

"Nay." She could not still the shudder that took her body.

"The bridegroom?"

"The Earl of Morneith."

She saw the corners of his mouth turn downward as if he knew the name, or the man, and did not like it. She also noticed his body tensed. She looked down at his hands and saw the fingers of his right one clenched into a fist. His gaze followed hers. He straightened out his fingers and flexed them, as if he had just become aware of what he had been doing.

"You were going to the Camerons for help?"

"Nay, I hoped to lose them in the fog. And I did. But then your men . . ."

He frowned. "Where were you going?"

"I hoped to find my cousin in London. I thought he could help me."

"James Campbell?"

"Aye."

"He would disobey his father for you?" His voice was suddenly harsh, his eyes even colder, if that were indeed possible.

She was silent for a moment, surprised at the barely suppressed anger in his voice.

He turned away from her then and went to the window and stared out toward the Sound of Mull. Then he turned back to her. "You had already cut your hair when I returned, before you knew we had James Campbell."

She was silent.

"You were going to leave without telling me?"

"I thought—" She stopped suddenly.

"You thought what?"

"That it would be best for everyone, that when you discovered who I was, you would want me gone."

"Where were you going?"

"Back to Dunstaffnage. I thought I could reach it before an escort came for me." She was amazed that her voice sounded steady.

"Did you think I would misuse you if I discovered you were a Campbell?"

"At first, I did not know," she said. "I had only heard tales of the Macleans." She hesitated, then added, "They were not stories to inspire trust that you possessed a . . . sympathetic nature."

He raised an eyebrow. "At first?"

She wished she could take back that slip of her tongue. But she was not going to explain it. She was not going to tell him that fear had changed into something else altogether, and that it was not fear of physical safety that had prompted her to try to flee. It was fear of the very look that was on his face now.

"From the pot into the fire, my lady," he said. "Did you not consider the risks when you left Dunstaffnage?"

"Such as being abducted by the Macleans?" she said with a tart edge to her voice. "Nay, I must admit I did not."

The corner of his mouth turned up slightly. "A most unpleasant surprise, I assume."

"Aye," she said defiantly.

"You are a very good liar."

"You never asked if I was Janet Cameron," she countered. "You assumed so."

"What else did I assume wrongly?" he asked, a dangerous glint in his eyes.

A muscle throbbed in his cheek, and she felt a throbbing of her own deep in the most private part of herself, a throbbing that had become a part of her only in the past few days.

"I do not know what you mean." But she did. He meant the kisses they had exchanged, kisses she still held in her heart. She did not want to, but she knew it would take more than harsh words to dislodge them.

He touched her cheek. Her feelings were magnified, the longing intensified. There was a searching in the touch, a question she couldn't answer.

His head lowered, and his lips captured hers, hard and demanding. There was nothing gentle this time. No searching. No asking. He meant it as punishing.

Still, she responded in kind. Her body needed no urging as he pulled her into his arms. The embers that had glowed between them flared, enveloping them in a circle of fire and need.

For a moment, she lost herself in his arms, in the feel of his lips against hers. The yearning deepened as her body pressed into his.

Then he wrenched away from her, turning again to the window, leaving her to stand alone. Her body ached from wanting, from the burning sensations his nearness aroused in her.

"What would you do to save him?" he asked suddenly.

Her thoughts and body still occupied with what had just happened, it took her a moment to understand what he was saying. Then she understood, just as she remembered why she had returned to this chamber. To beg, to bargain for her cousin's life.

"Anything," she whispered, startled, then horrified at the change in conversation, at the sudden implication of what he was saying . . . of what she was admitting. How could she have forgotten Jamie even for a moment? Especially in the arms of the man who held his life in balance?

"Anything?" he repeated, and she did not quite understand the sudden bleakness in those gray eyes.

"Aye. He must have come to look for me. It is my fault he . . . that you . . ." She looked up at him. "Let him go. Keep me. I will do anything you wish."

"Such devotion," he said. "But not a very good bargain for me. Jamie Campbell is a valuable hostage."

"I am, as well," she said. "The king—"

She stopped suddenly.

"What about the king?"

"He arranged the marriage," she said in little more than a whisper. "So you see, I can be a valuable hostage."

"You would go back to Dunstaffnage, to a marriage you abhor for your cousin?"

"Aye," she said in a small voice.

"It would be a poor bargain for Macleans," he said curtly. "Campbells will not attack Inverleith as long as I hold the heir. "And why bargain with you, when I already have you?"

"You will not harm him?"

"Not as long as he is of use to me."

"I want to see him."

He gave her a long, level stare. "I think not." He went to the door and paused there. "You will not leave this room."

"I want to see Alina."

"You were ready to leave her easily enough," he said.

"Not easily," she whispered. "Not easily at all."

He hesitated, then nodded his head. "Just the two rooms. I want your word that you will not go beyond them. If you do, you will be confined to this one."

She swallowed hard. The heat she'd felt so recently had turned to ashes, cold and bitter. She shivered.

For a moment, his eyes seemed to warm, but then he turned away. "I will send Robina to you. And some water. It appears you need a bath."

And then he was gone.

She leaned against the wall, drained by all the emotions that had just rampaged through her. Her heart became a great yawning hole.

She didn't know the man who had just left. She had thought she had learned something about him, but she knew now it was not nearly enough.

She did not know what he would do.

GOD's blood but she was a mystery to him. Or was it sorcery? Why else had he kissed her?

She had stood so bravely in front of him, her face smudged and her shorn hair, dark with soot, clinging to her face. She looked like a sprite who had been hiding in the woods.

Her hair, the coppery curls, were gone, and he could not

even imagine what the loss had cost her. And she had obviously cut it before he had returned. To run away from Inverleith. From him.

She had not given him a chance to help her. It was astounding how much that realization hurt.

Neither had he been able to block the jealousy that had flooded him when he discovered she would risk all for her cousin, and that the young Campbell would risk all for her. Her eyes had softened when she talked of him, when she had said she would do anything to help him. *Anything.* Even, apparently, bed Rory.

She had not trusted him at all. She still did not trust him. He felt he still did not have the full story behind her escape. What woman would flee her home alone? Where had she planned to go after London? Had she hoped Campbell would flee with her?

The church frowned upon unions between first cousins, but still they occurred.

He had no right to jealousy. He had no hold on her, could never have one. Campbells and Macleans did not marry. The one time they did had ended in disaster.

Her family would never permit a union. Neither, he knew, would his. They were already aching for James Campbell's blood. It was complete irony—or the devil's doing—that the only woman who had even tempted him in nearly a decade belonged to the family that had cursed his.

More than tempted. God's blood, but he had found something in her that had restored at least part of his heart.

All he had, really, was a weapon he did not want, but, for the sake of his clan, would be forced to use. And if Felicia Campbell wasn't lying about the interest of the king—and why would she?—then he had two. If Morneith wanted her, he would pay handsomely for her return.

His gut rebelled at the thought. He knew Morneith. He was a corrupt man who owed his loyalty to no one king. If King James thought he could buy Morneith's loyalty with a young lass, he was mistaken.

The London court was filled with French spies, and Rory had done business with Paris officials. He knew that Morneith had pledged his support to Henry in London as well as to James of Scotland. The man was a traitor as well as one known for his excesses in women, drink, and other vices.

Knowing she'd risked her life to escape Morneith, how could he allow Felicia to wed him? If Morneith's treachery was ever proved, Felicia would be at risk as well.

Yet interfering with the king's business could endanger his entire clan.

That dilemma, and that damnable jealousy, had made him lash out at her. It was unfair. He'd known it. And he detested himself even as he'd said the words.

He'd hoped the anger would cool the passion she always aroused in him, the yearning to keep her at his side, the instinctive knowledge that she would fill the vast void within him.

It had not. He had watched the proud tilt of her head, thought of the courage it took to defy a king.

He heard his own groan, deep as an animal in pain.

He had returned to save his clan. He saw no way to do that without destroying an innocent. One innocent life against so many.

He went next door and entered after a brief knock. Alina was sitting up and eating soup from a spoon her mother held.

"My lord," her mother said. She was wreathed in smiles. "Alina is much improved."

"I can see," he said gently. "Is there anything else you need?"

"Nay. You and Lady Janet have been so kind."

Lady Janet. What would happen when she knew Lady Janet was really Lady Felicia Campbell, a member of the clan that had inflicted her daughter's wound? He considered telling her. Not to cause Felicia harm, but to prevent hurt, to take the brunt of any anger.

He thought of her bravery moments earlier when she had confronted him, tried to explain. She would want to tell Alina in her own way.

He left the room. He felt aimless. And empty. Lonely. He thought he had conquered that, but knew now he had not. There was no one with whom he could confide. Not Douglas or Archibald. Neither would understand.

Lachlan? But Lachlan lived in his own world, studiously avoiding responsibility.

He would have to depend on his own instincts.

Felicia Campbell had destroyed his instincts.

He went to his chamber. There was always wine there.

Once there, he took off his plaid and linen shirt. He looked at the bandage protecting his arm and took it off. It still ached, was a little warm but far better than it had been.

He needed to shave, but that could wait. He needed rest. Yet while his body was weary, his mind was far too active to rest. Images flickered through it. The golden-haired Campbell heir. The woman he'd thought was Janet Cameron smiling up at him with dazed eyes after his first kiss. Felicia Campbell with her cropped hair and defiant gaze.

Their fates were in his hands, and he damned well did not want them there.

He pulled on a fresh shirt and trews. After a moment's hesitation, he filled a tankard with wine from a cask he had brought from Paris. It was early morning, but he'd had no sleep. Neither had his prisoner.

He went down to the dungeon. He felt the increasing chill as he went down the steps. He saw the glow of two candles impaled on iron spikes. Two of his men sat at a table, playing a game of chance.

Both stood immediately.

He looked around. He had not been here since he was a lad, when he and Patrick had explored the place. He still remembered the chills that ran through him, though he had been determined not to show it as Patrick strutted around.

He shivered from the cold.

"Where is he?"

"At the end, milord. We gave him food and blankets as ye ordered."

He nodded. "I want to see him."

A guard took one of the lanterns and a large key and led the way down the corridor to the last door. An iron-grated window allowed him to look inside.

James Campbell was lying down on straw, but he quickly stood as the light penetrated the cell. He blinked for a moment, then his gaze met Rory's.

"Open it," Rory told the guard, "then you can return to your game."

The guard fitted the key in the lock. The door creaked and grated as it opened. Rory doubted whether it had been used in years.

"I will git ye a chair, milord."

Rory nodded and took the lantern. He did not worry about Campbell escaping. There was, quite simply, no place for him to go.

Blond bristles stubbled the man's face. His eyes were tired. But Rory didn't see fear. He saw the same defiance that had been in Felicia's eyes.

The guard returned with a chair, then disappeared again. Rory didn't sit but put a foot on the chair.

He saw a bowl on the floor. A cup. Several blankets.

Still, it was icy inside. And damp.

He held out the tankard to Campbell, who regarded it much as he would a vial of poison.

"It is good wine," Rory said, and took a taste himself before handing it to Campbell.

"To what do I owe the honor of your visit?" the Campbell asked, still not accepting it. "And your wine?"

Rory wondered the same thing. He shrugged. "I remember it being cold and damp."

"And you care?"

"A dead hostage does me little good."

"Then I will humor you," Campbell said. He finally took the tankard and took a sip, then another. His gaze went back to Rory. "My cousin?"

"She is unharmed."

"You have talked to her?"

"Aye."

"What are you going to do with her?"

"You should worry about yourself, Campbell."

"If you misuse her—"

"You are in no position to threaten," Rory said. He felt the unreasoning anger rising in him again. He tamped it down.

"Not at the moment," Campbell retorted.

They glared at each other.

"It was a fool's errand, coming here alone," Rory said after a moment's silence.

"I did not intend to come here, only to a village. I wanted to know if anyone had heard of a lost lass. I meant no harm here."

"You know why she fled Dunstaffnage?"

The Campbell took another gulp of wine, then said, "I wish to see her."

To make sure their tales matched?

"Why did she leave Dunstaffnage?" he asked again.

"What did she tell you?"

"I want your version."

They were circling around each other like two dogs ready to attack.

Campbell's jaw set. "You cannot think she is a spy."

"Nay."

"How did she come to be here?"

Rory did not like being on the receiving end of the questions, particularly when he knew he was in the wrong. Campbell had ventured on Maclean land after Campbell raids on Maclean villages. Rory felt no compunction about taking him prisoner. However, his men had gone on Cameron land to abduct a young woman who had done nothing to harm them. But would admitting that make his clan guilty of treason, since Felicia was meant for the king's choice?

He had no good choices. He just didn't know what the worst ones would be.

It wasn't like the sea. There he had responsibility for his men, but each of them knew the risks when they signed on. Too many innocents were at risk now. No matter what move he made, people would probably die.

His only chance was the man in front of him. But could he trust a Campbell?

That was the reason for his visit, to take measure of the man. Would he be of more value as a hostage or as an ally? Could he possibly become an ally?

If the Campbell truly cared about Felicia, perhaps.

But Rory had so many conflicting emotions inside, he did not know whether he could make the right decision. There was anger, jealousy, loss, fear for his people, even terror for Felicia if she was, indeed, to marry Morneith.

"You haven't said yet why Lady Felicia left Dunstaffnage."

The Campbell stared at him for a long time, then shrugged. "I was in London delivering a message from King James. She left in Janet Cameron's stead with the Cameron escort. An escapade gone bad. She was separated in the fog." His eyes did not flicker, but Rory sensed the tension in the man's body that belied the words.

He was protecting her.

And Rory knew why. If Felicia had openly defied the king, *she* could be charged with treason.

Rory made his decision. The Campbell appeared to have ethics that he had not believed Campbells possessed. James Campbell probably felt Rory had none. Yet they needed each other if James Campbell was to save Felicia, and Rory his clansmen.

"If I release you from here, do I have your word you will not try to escape?"

James Campbell stared at him. For a moment, Rory thought he would refuse.

"I can see Felicia?"

"At my pleasure," Rory granted reluctantly.

Campbell continued to hesitate, and Rory knew how difficult it must be for him to yield to a Maclean. He could see that the Campbell probably preferred the discomfort of the cell to accepting a favor from a Maclean.

"What do you want in return?"

"Your ear. We might have common purpose."

Campbell still hesitated. "And Felicia?"

"She is comfortable enough."

Campbell finally nodded.

"Say it."

"You have my word. As a Campbell."

Rory wished he had not added the latter. The Campbell word was suspect, even when it came from Felicia. Especially from Felicia.

He did not need to be reminded.

"You will stay in one chamber," he said, "albeit a far more comfortable one than this. We have clansmen here from villages recently raided by Campbells. Family and friends died. I would not like to find you with a dirk in your back."

James Campbell's stare drilled through him.

Rory took his foot off the chair. He had always considered himself a good judge of character. He certainly hoped that he was now. Never had it been so important.

It went against everything he was and had been to trust a Campbell. And he might well be dooming the Macleans.

Chapter 16

❧

ROBINA appeared at the door of Felicia's chamber just minutes after Rory left.

Had he ordered it, or had Robina been hovering around?

How long would it take before everyone in the keep knew that she was a Campbell? She had no fear for her safety, though she did fear seeing the stunned disappointment and accusation in their faces.

The same expressions she had seen on the face of the Laird of Inverleith.

She did not know what she should have done differently. She could have tried harder to escape the keep, or she could have allowed herself to be taken to the Cameron keep. She might have told him sooner. But she simply had not known what he would do. She wished she had explained.

She no longer had his trust. Jamie might pay for her silence. She could not bear it if he were killed because of her actions.

Robina took one look at her hair, and her eyes widened. "Oh, my lady, what have ye done?" Then she clapped her hand over her mouth as if horrified by her utterance.

"It is all right, Robina," Felicia said. "I know I look . . ."

Robina burst out in tears.

"I look that bad?" Felicia said.

"Yer hair, your bonny hair," Robina wailed.

Felicia had never thought it bonny. It was untamable and too bright a color. In truth, her head felt very good without it.

"The lord . . ." Robina wailed again. It was obvious that she was among those who had harbored the unlikely hope that their lord and Janet Cameron would wed.

"The lord wishes nothing to do with me," she said. "And I must tell you. I am not Janet Cameron."

"Not Lady Cameron . . . ?"

"My name is Felicia Campbell."

Robina's mouth fell open. Her eyes grew even larger. "Camp . . . Camp . . . bell," she stuttered.

"Aye, but it does not change what I am," Felicia said softly.

"But, but . . . how . . ."

"Archibald took me by mistake, and I feared telling anyone."

Robina's face filled with confusion. "The Campbell the lord just brought in—"

"He is my cousin. I suspect he was searching for me." She paused. "I will understand if you no longer wish to serve me."

Robina shook her head. "No, milady. Ye are a kind soul. I saw it with Alina. Ye canna pretend that kind of caring. I will heat some water for yer bath and wash yer hair. Ah, milady, yer hair," she wailed again. She started to cry, and

Felicia sensed it was more because of her shorn hair than the fact she was a Campbell.

Felicia wondered how many others would share that generous feeling.

And how could she bathe in comfort when Jamie was locked in some dungeon? If only she could see him. If only she could help him . . .

Instead, she took Robina's hand. "Thank you."

The girl bobbed, then hurried out the door.

Felicia went to the small, steel mirror and looked at herself. She had not had the heart to do it earlier. Truly she must be a terrible sight to make Robina react so.

And she was.

Jamie would be as horrified as Robina. Strange that Rory had not seemed to share that distaste. His horror came from the fact she was a Campbell. He had not seemed to care about her hair.

Felicia brushed it and ashes fell around her.

A bath first, then she would see Alina. She would scare the child to death if she appeared now.

She felt a little like death herself. The chill had not left her, nor had the great void left by Rory's rejection been filled by Robina's generosity.

Felicia took off the lad's clothing and wrapped herself in the nightrobe Moira had provided her days ago, then went to the window and looked out. A small group of horsemen were waiting for the gate to open. Each one was inspected by Archibald. Not so much as a mouse could leave without permission.

Robina returned, followed by several clansmen with buckets of water. They filled the wooden tub that was kept in the small room off the chamber. All of them cast quick glances at her, but she did not know whether it was because of her hair or because they knew who she truly was. She saw no antagonism, no hatred in their faces, only respect and curiosity. She decided it was her hair. They could not know.

When the men left, Felicia sank into the water, and Robina washed her hair, then, when Felicia left the tub and put on a chemise and gown. Robina brushed her hair dry.

Next she would see Alina and try to explain to the child and her mother. She did not wish them to hear from someone else if, indeed, they had not already.

Robina stepped back and looked at her critically. " 'Tis really not so bad now, milady."

Not so bad. Faint assurance. Mayhap Morneith would be so appalled he would refuse her.

She recalled the way Rory had touched her hair, even crusted with ash, almost as if . . . he cared about her. There had not been Robina's horror.

But there *had* been anger. Deep anger and betrayal.

Would he take it out on Jamie? She did not think so. She would not think that of a man who had spent a day hunting for a lad, then riding all night to get him to Inverleith.

But she was only too aware of the hatred between the clans.

Hate twisted people. Had it done that to Rory Maclean?

She turned back to Robina, who eyed her warily, obviously wondering again if she had said the wrong thing.

"Thank you, Robina." Felicia took the few steps to her and took her hand. "You have been a true friend."

"A friend, milady?"

"Aye."

Robina smiled slowly.

"I am going to Alina," Felicia said. "I must tell her."

Robina nodded. "Her mother is helping in the kitchen. Alina is alone."

Felicia steeled herself. She would talk to Alina, then try to find out something about Jamie. If she must, she would beg to be allowed to see him.

Perhaps Lachlan?

But then Lachlan had not been to see her. Perhaps he, too, felt betrayed.

Felicia steeled herself and opened the door. There was no guard, but she had no doubt that Macleans had been warned to watch out for her if she wandered away from the two rooms allowed her.

She opened the door to Alina's room. The child was alone, and sleeping. Felicia touched her forehead. It was cool to the touch. Her breathing was easier.

Hopefully the pain had subsided as well.

Not wanting to wake her from much-needed sleep, Felicia sat down in a chair, and waited.

RORY accompanied James Campbell up the steps to the kitchen. Ignoring her wide-eyed stare at the Campbell, Rory ordered a maidservant to bring food and goblets up to Patrick's old chamber. He led the way up the steps to the third level. He stopped at his chamber to fetch the jug of wine as the Campbell waited in the doorway, and then he opened the door of the chamber next to his.

It was as spartan as Rory's own. His father had believed that comfort would lead to softness. But it was certainly an improvement over the dungeon.

Once inside, Campbell looked around the room. There was a small window set deep in the stone walls, a narrow bed, wardrobe, and chest for clothes. A small, battered table with two uncomfortable-looking chairs completed the furnishings. Wall brackets with candles were set into the stone walls.

The fireplace looked as if it had been unattended for decades. Ashes still littered its floor. The smell of dust was heavy in the room.

Rory was in no mood to apologize. Instead, he lowered the jug of wine to the table. "Sit down," he said.

Campbell started to say something, a protest most likely, then apparently decided better of it. He sat.

"You will stay in the room for the time being," Rory said. "There will be a guard outside."

"I gave my word," the Campbell protested.

"Aye, but forgive me if I do not wish to rely entirely on it," Rory said wryly. "It's for your protection as well. Several of my clansmen would enjoy plunging their dirks into you."

"I fear no Maclean."

"No? Well, *I* fear the consequences if you were slain in Inverleith." Rory knew he probably should not have admitted the last, but if there was any solution to this devil's mess, it would be only with the Campbell's help. "Not only for Macleans," he added, "but for Campbells."

The Campbell raised an eyebrow as if in doubt.

"I have been away, but even so I know James is worried about Henry, and war looms between the two countries. James does not want the clans fighting amongst themselves. It would require a protracted siege to take Inverleith. You know it, and the king knows it. He would not want two armies poised against each other if Henry invades.

The Campbell was listening.

The next part would be more difficult. Much more difficult.

"And then there is your cousin."

The Campbell's mouth thinned.

"Did you know about her betrothal to the Earl of Morneith?"

"She told you?"

"Aye." He did not say that he had forced it from her just moments earlier. "Did you know about it?"

Anger jumped into the Campbell's eyes. Until that moment, any emotion had been held well in check.

"You did not object to sacrificing her?" Rory said contemptuously.

"I did not know. I think—" He stopped suddenly, as if realizing he was being baited into saying things he did not intend to say.

"And if you had known?" Rory bored. He had to know more about James Campbell before he ventured further.

"I would have found a way to prevent it."

"Even at the risk of committing treason?"

The silence was broken only by a knock on the door. Rory strode over to it and took a tray laden with fruit, cheese, bread, and a roasted chicken. It smelled far better than anything that had come from the kitchen since he'd arrived. There were also two goblets.

He ignored the frown on the face of the clansman delivering it.

He took the tray to the table, poured wine into both goblets, and handed one over to the Campbell. Perhaps spirits would loosen his tongue.

But this time Campbell did not take it. Neither did he touch the food.

"What do you want?" Campbell asked abruptly.

"Just as you claim not to have been involved in raids on our villages, I personally was not involved in Lady Felicia coming here. She was in the wrong place at the wrong time."

"Personally?"

"My kinsmen became a little too enthusiastic in finding a bride for me."

Light suddenly dawned in the Campbell's eyes, and he started to rise. "Janet?"

Rory had told James Campbell at the croft that he had thought Felicia was Janet Cameron, but he had not explained how she had come to Inverleith.

"Aye, they thought she was too good for a Campbell."

Campbell swore softly, too softly for Rory to cipher. He did hear the word *cur*.

"Far better a Campbell than a Maclean," James Campbell said in a more audible voice. "Their wives have a way of dying early."

It was a direct hit.

"At least they do not need to flee from their families."

Another hit.

"Be sure that you will be held responsible," Campbell said, ignoring the jab.

"Ah, you want to make me responsible for what my kinsmen do, when you refuse to take any for your clan raiding my people."

A muscle throbbed in the Campbell's throat, but he said nothing.

"I knew nothing about the interception until they appeared at my gates," Rory continued. "And then the lady was strangely reluctant to return when I volunteered to return her to the Cameron family. I had been gone ten years and had never seen her. She allowed me to believe she was Janet Cameron. And I could certainly understand her reluctance to avoid her marriage to the Campbell heir."

Campbell started up off the chair, then sat back down. He struggled to remain emotionless, but Rory could see the anger teeming inside him.

"And now we both seem to have a problem." Rory left the words hanging in the room as he took a sip of wine.

"Continue," Campbell said in a steady voice laced with steel.

"You do not want Felicia to marry Morneith. I feel responsible for her current predicament. If not for me, she might well have reached you. She might have had a chance then, but now too many people know a woman thought to be Lady Janet is here. Obviously she could not be in two places at one time. It will not take long before everyone knows the woman is really Felicia Campbell."

Campbell looked hopeful. "I can still take her away. To France."

Rory shook his head. "If she simply disappeared now, the Macleans would be blamed, possibly for murder, mayhap for treason. I cannot allow that to happen."

Campbell stared at him. "You have something in mind, or you would not be talking to me."

"I have a question first. Why has there not been an outcry about Lady Felicia's disappearance?"

Campbell hesitated again. It was obvious that he was reluctant to say anything, to give any information to an enemy.

Rory played his trump card. "I can always turn her over to the crown."

"Fear," Campbell said after a moment's pause. "The steward, William, knew that he would be held responsible. He was hoping to find her before my father discovered she was missing. They have been searching everywhere."

Including, Rory knew, Maclean villages they destroyed, but now was not the time for more accusations. "How long before he reports her disappearance?"

"An escort was due either today or tomorrow to take her to Edinburgh for the betrothal ceremony."

"What will your father do when he discovers she's not there?"

Campbell shook his head. "He does not like to be disobeyed. Neither does the king."

"What would he do if he learned Morneith was a traitor?"

Campbell's gaze speared him. "You have proof?"

"I know Morneith. More than that, I trade in Paris. I hear much. The French have numerous spies in the English court. Morneith is a traitor as well as a lecher."

Campbell sat straighter in his chair. "That is not proof."

"Nay, it is not. And I doubt that French spies are willing to risk their necks, and more, to help convict the man. But there may be a way to trap him."

Now Campbell did take a gulp of wine.

Rory sat in the chair opposite him, his gaze meeting the Campbell's directly. He wanted to see everything in that face. He had to decide whether the man was up to a dangerous game, whether he could be trusted. If not, he would be sent back to the dungeon until Rory could develop another plan. He could not risk the Campbell's escape.

"He is said to have killed his last wife," Campbell said.

"He most likely did. He likes boys. Young ones."

The Campbell leaned over the table, his hands clenching. "You know this?"

"That is the rumor. I always pay attention when the French discuss the English, and the Scots."

"She's a Campbell. Why do you care?"

"Unlike you, she did not ride onto Maclean land of her own free will. I would have little compunction about holding you hostage, but I do not make war on women. Even Campbell women." He kept his voice emotionless. He knew that she would never be *just* a Campbell woman. She had seized a part of his heart, and he had not realized it until he'd thought he would lose her.

But he had lost her, or lost what he thought she was.

Even if they found a way to destroy Morneith, her uncle would never permit a marriage to a Maclean, and he could never forget the terrible heritage of his family.

"How do I know I can trust you?" Campbell finally said.

Rory shrugged. "You do not. Just as I do not know I can trust you."

Campbell said nothing. He took a piece of fruit and ate it, then tore off a chicken breast. "It is better than my earlier meal."

"I told them to feed you. I did not specify what."

"Moldy bread and water."

"I believe they were reluctant to give you even that much."

"They indicated as much." His gaze met Rory's. "You propose a trap then? When did you come up with this, ah, scheme?"

"On the ride back from the croft. I had to learn a few things first."

"About me?"

"Aye."

"And have you?"

"I have not discarded the idea. Yet."

"I have not agreed."

But he had. Rory saw it in his face. And, despite what he had said, so had he made up his mind.

It was not so much out of choice as it was of necessity.

They ate the rest of the meal in silence, both weighing each other. Rory knew he was being judged as he was judging the other man. Neither obviously had certainty.

They both knew they were risking treason. They both knew they were doing it because of the same woman.

"Does Felicia know what you are planning?" Campbell asked after they had finished.

"Nay. And I do not think she should. I do not want to give her hope that could be dashed."

James Campbell raised an eyebrow. "You care about Campbells?"

"I feel responsible for *one* Campbell," Rory corrected.

"You said I could see her."

He had. And he always kept his word. He cared about honor. His personal honor. The Maclean honor. He had never forgotten the stain that long ago ancestor had placed on the family name.

"If she wants to see you," he said.

The Campbell did not say anything. Just waited.

Rory went to the door, leaving the remaining food and wine on the table. He turned. "A warning. Do not try to leave this room."

He opened the door. A Maclean was standing outside.

Rory nodded to him and strode down the hall. He wanted the Campbell to think about what he had said. He did not want a quick answer. He also needed to talk to Felicia before going further.

He prayed he was doing the wise thing.

If he wasn't, lives would be lost. If he misjudged the Campbell he could destroy the clan.

Either way, he would lose Felicia.

But then, he'd never had her.

ALINA woke up when she moved in her sleep. Baron, who had been lying next to her, rose and stretched lazily, then nuzzled his mistress. The dog was obviously puzzled that she was not playing with him.

Alina reached out to touch him, then glanced up at Felicia. Her eyes widened as she saw the change. "Lady Felicia?" she asked.

"Aye," Felicia said ruefully. She picked up a cup, filled it with water from a jug on the table, and offered it to Alina, who drank gratefully even as she kept darting glances at Felicia. Baron nuzzled his mistress again.

Just as Alina finished her water, her mother entered with a tray. She took a step back. Like her daughter, her eyes opened wide when she saw Felicia and her shorn hair.

"Milady," she said, obviously shocked but too mannered to express it in words. "Oh my lady," she said. "I did not expect you. I have been helping Moira with the cooking."

"To Inverleith's advantage," Felicia said. "It smells very good."

"Have mine, milady," Alina said shyly.

"Nay, I cannot do that," Felicia replied. "But I will have some later."

She waited until Alina had sipped all the soup. When the child finished, Felicia started to open her mouth . . .

The door opened, and Rory stood in the doorway. "My lady, I wish to speak to you."

"You said I could . . ."

"I did. It concerns another matter."

His eyes were cool, his manner curt.

"But . . ."

"Now, Lady Janet." He emphasized the last word.

Confused, she rose and accompanied him to the door. She turned around. "I am so pleased you are better," she said to Alina.

Once in her chambers, she turned to him. "I do not understand. I thought . . ."

"The longer no one knows Felicia Campbell is here, the better," he said gruffly.

"But Jamie . . . ?"

"Only Lachlan and a few men know that you are Felicia Campbell. I have warned them all not to say anything."

"I told Robina."

"I talked to her. She will say nothing."

"Why are you protecting me?"

He looked at her, and his gaze was searching. He touched her hair, and she flinched. Not from his touch but from how she knew she must look. "I am sorry you felt you had to cut your hair," he finally said, "but you look . . . enchanting." His hand fell, though, and his expression told her the observation came reluctantly.

Enchanting? Her?

His conscience must be saying the word. Still, his eyes had the same fire she had seen in them before.

The embers of the fierce attraction that always glowed between them flared, enveloping them in a circle of heat that was exquisitely seductive. She felt the gnawing need again, the ache for something unknown, yet compelling.

He hesitated. His eyes clouded, then as if drawn against his will, he slowly leaned down, his lips touching hers. His hands moved along the side of her neck as his mouth explored hers ever so slowly. She knew how foolish this was, yet a pulsating anticipation infused her body, and every part of her responded to him.

She had to return. She knew that. This had been a magnificent adventure but too many people were paying a price. She did not belong here, nor could she ever belong here.

But from the moment his lips had touched hers, she had been helpless to resist. He brought her to life. He made every nerve tingle and her heart beat faster and her blood heat.

She responded with a passionate desperation. This was a moment she could steal, could hold in her heart when . . .

His hand touched her face, and suddenly she realized tears were falling down her cheek. Not wanting him to see the weakness, she put her head against his chest.

Yet another mistake. She heard his heart's rapid beat. She felt connected to him in a way she had never felt connected to another person, not even Jamie. A sense of belonging, of rightness.

She forced herself to pull back. She took a deep breath and wiped the back of her hand against her cheek to remove any evidence of tears. It could never be right. Realization was on his face, as she knew it must be on her own.

"Jamie?" she asked, knowing her cousin was but one obstacle between them.

His body stiffened. "He is in a room next to mine. And well fed."

"Thank you," she said.

"It wasn't for you." His announcement was stiff, curt. Miles apart from the kiss, from his touch.

"What was it for?"

He took steps away from her, putting distance between them. It did nothing to lower the temperature. It was as if streaks of lightning flashed between them.

"Tell me about your cousin," he said.

She did not know whether he was asking because he really wanted to know or whether it was to ease the tension between them. She did not know how to answer him. What would help Jamie, and what might hurt him? "Jamie is smart and loyal."

"A good son?"

She saw the trap. "He thinks for himself."

"Can I trust him?"

The words hurt. He did not mean only Jamie. He was wondering whether he could trust her as well. "I am not sure what you are asking."

"I think you are."

"He will die before he breaks his word."

His eyes turned to gray ice, and she did not understand why. His anger seemed to grow deeper whenever Jamie's name was mentioned. It made her fear for him.

"You will let him go?" she asked.

"No," he said bluntly. "He is valuable to me."

It was obvious that though he had touched her, even kissed her, he had dismissed her in his mind and heart. But then what else could she have expected? Especially now that she had shorn her hair and looked more lad than lass.

"What can I do?" she finally asked.

He raised an eyebrow. "At the moment, nothing, my lady."

No more Janet. Not even Felicia. She had become "my lady" again.

She looked at him, searching for more. She saw nothing there. "What about me?"

"You can stay as long as you wish."

"It was my fault I ran into your men. I never should have tried—"

"What is done is done," he cut her off.

She looked for a hint of the passion and gentleness she had felt before. It was gone, lost in that expressionless face and cool gray eyes.

She thought she knew why. He felt honor bound to protect her, but that put him, and his clan, in jeopardy.

She knew the penalty for treason. She could not allow either Jamie or Rory to pay it for her.

Desolation filled her. Emptiness. Pain.

She had no choice now. But then she never had.

She would find a way to reach Morneith on her own. And she would wed him.

Chapter 17

⨋

WHY could he not control himself around Felicia? Rory fumed as he paced the floor of his chamber. The simple fact was he could not. She looked at him with her expressive blue eyes full of conflicting emotions. One of those emotions was always passion. A passion for life and a willingness to confront it.

She had renewed his own. He had not realized how much he had lost when Maggie, then Anne, died. He had been so afraid of caring again, of causing another woman's death, that he had walled himself off from everyone, including his family.

She had intruded into that walled fortress. He was intrigued by her recklessness, most recently evidenced by her shorn hair. Such hair suited her face far better than the long hair pulled back from her cheeks, but it would scandalize the court. The shorn curls framed her cheeks, softening her face. Her dark blue eyes appeared larger, the mouth more vulnerable. Even more inviting.

Forget about her.

She would be gone in the next few weeks. She was as much forbidden fruit as the apple was to Adam, and he had to remember the consequences of giving in to that temptation.

And now he had a great deal of planning to do.

He had no doubt as to the motivations of the players. King James, always fearing an English invasion, needed Morneith's large army. Rory surmised that Morneith, who would betray his king only if he thought the English would win, needed a powerful friend—and ear—at court. And Angus Campbell would do whatever King James requested to keep his favored place beside the monarch.

James Campbell had just returned from the English court. He had obviously heard none of the rumors Rory had, but that didn't matter. Rory could give him sufficient information to make Morneith think the Campbell knew far more than he did.

Morneith would believe a Campbell who just returned from the English court far more readily than he would a Maclean.

The question was how far would Felicia's cousin go for her? How deep was the connection between them?

As much as he tried to deny it, jealousy remained a prickling needle inside him. He wished he were a better man, but it was damned difficult to hear the two praising one another.

The devil take it. He could waste no more time mooning like a young lad. He did not believe anyone other than Alina, her mother, and Robina had seen Felicia since she had shorn her hair and dressed as a lad.

There was no way to keep Felicia's presence unknown much longer, but he would keep it quiet as long as he could.

Once it became general knowledge, the senior Campbell could be expected to come after his niece. King James would realize victory could come only after a long siege and suggest patience while diplomacy commenced.

But Rory wanted to bait the trap before them.

He would need Lachlan's assistance. No one else. Not even Douglas. The fewer involved the better.

Rory went down to the practice field. Douglas was training several of the young lads who had come in from outlying villages, but halted the session when he saw Rory.

"Where is Lachlan?" Rory asked.

"He took men out to relieve those guarding the passes and roads," Douglas said.

Rory thought about sending someone for him, but decided against it. The cold, crisp air and long ride was exactly what he needed. He went down to the stables and asked a groom to saddle the fastest horse in the Maclean stable.

LACHLAN had returned to patrolling Inverleith's borders after bringing in the Campbell heir. He took with him a new troop of men to replace those already guarding the passes and roads that led to Inverleith.

He had no idea how Rory truly felt after discovering that the lady he thought was Janet Cameron was Felicia Campbell. His brother kept his emotions in firm check, and only a small tick in his cheek had acknowledged the surprise given by their prisoner.

Lachlan had felt a boulder drop in his stomach. He had noticed the new lift to Rory's steps, and the glow in the lass's eyes. There had been little doubt the two had been attracted to each other.

He liked the lass as well and had even thought that perhaps Archibald's wild scheme might really come to fruition. It was time for some joy to come to Inverleith, and to his brother. ·

Now, it never could be. His brother could never wed a Campbell. He doubted that Rory would stay, which Lachlan had earnestly prayed would happen. As the youngest son, he had never sought the mantle or responsibility of laird. In truth, the clan would probably turn away from him and seek leadership elsewhere.

He would never overcome what happened three years ago. Had anyone whispered the details to Rory? As far as he knew, nothing had gone outside the clan, but enough inside knew the rumors to distrust him . . .

Lachlan replaced two sentries over a pass with new ones. 'Twas not impossible that the Campbells might approach from a northern point on the sea and ride south through the mountains. Two more stops and he could return. He worried about Rory. He had seen how his face had visibly grown harder after the Campbell's capture, but he did not know his half brother well enough to predict what he would do to the Campbell and Felicia.

Lachlan did not blame Felicia. She'd had little choice but to play a role when she had been abducted. Lachlan only wished that she had trusted someone enough to tell the truth before Rory discovered it.

Rory had a strong sense of honor, and honesty. He was also a man who saw things in absolutes. A man was honest, or he wasn't. He told the truth, or he didn't. He was brave, or he wasn't.

He expected everyone else to live up to his own stern standards.

To Lachlan, life presented more compromises.

He heard the approach of a rider and looked up.

'Twas as if he had summoned Rory in his mind. His half brother rode easily, but then Rory had always been good at everything he tried.

Lachlan walked his horse over to Rory.

"Rory?"

"Can you come back to Inverleith?"

"Aye. I think your men can find the way on their own."

Rory raised an eyebrow at the use of his "your men."

Lachlan went over and talked to the remaining Macleans, who nodded. He then mounted his horse.

He rode next to his brother, something he had never done before. Even last night, they had been separated. Rory had ridden in front and Lachlan in back. "Lady Felicia?" he asked.

Rory looked at him. "Do you think I would harm her?"

"Not physically."

"Then how?"

"She cares for you. 'Tis obvious to everyone."

"She lied to me."

"Have you never lied? Not once? Not even for a very good reason?"

Rory ignored the question.

"Not everyone has your sense of integrity," Lachlan said after a long silence.

Rory shrugged. "She cares for the Campbell."

"They are cousins."

"It runs deeper than that," Rory said, "but that is not why I am here."

"I was wondering about that," Lachlan said easily. "You do not often seek me out, or ask my advice."

" 'Tis not advice I need. Have you told anyone who Felicia really is?"

"Nay. You told me not to."

"I am pleased *someone* listens."

"Everyone listens," Lachlan replied wryly. "They simply may not agree. They have their own ideas."

"Like abducting a Campbell," Rory responded.

"That was a mistake."

Rory's gaze speared him. "There is no discipline here. No order. What in God's name have you been doing?"

"I did not ask you or Patrick to leave," Lachlan reminded him. "I have no authority while you and Patrick are still alive."

Rory was silent.

"Are you sending her back to Dunstaffnage?" Lachlan asked.

"Not immediately."

"Am I permitted to ask why?"

"She ran away because her uncle ordered her marriage to the Earl of Morneith."

Lachlan searched back in his mind for everything he knew about the man. They often had minstrels and storytellers stop at Inverleith. In exchange for a meal and a few coins, they would sing a song and carry the news.

Morneith had been the subject of those tales more than once. He had to be three times Felicia's age and was known for hanging tenants who poached on his land.

He waited to hear more.

"It was no escapade as the Campbell said. She was trying to get to London to find him. She thought he might help her."

"And she ran into us, instead."

"That is one way of putting it."

Lachlan phrased the next comment carefully. "It is one thing to hold a Cameron. Another to hold a Campbell."

"It is worse than that. The marriage was arranged by the king."

Lachlan's fingers tightened around the reins. A war with the Campbells would be disastrous, but with the king? The clan had no hope.

Rory had never confided in him until now. Before Rory had left for the sea so many years ago, Lachlan had been but a lad, one who had his mind in books rather than on the training field. Everyone had expected him to go into the church.

"What about the Campbell heir?"

"Campbell is opposed to the marriage as well, but there's bloody little he can do about it."

"And you?"

"There is something, but it could bring harm to Inverleith and our clan."

"I think the harm is already here," Lachlan said.

He saw the surprise in Rory's eyes, and he ached at how much he wanted his brother's approval. He'd never had it from his father.

"What do you mean?" Rory asked.

"You do not want to send her back."

"Not to Morneith."

"You are planning something?" Lachlan asked.

"Aye."

Lachlan remained silent. He knew Rory well enough now to realize he was thinking aloud, that the words would come without prompting.

"I would have to trust the Campbell," Rory said. "What did you think of him?"

Lachlan was startled that Rory asked his opinion. He considered an answer for a few moments. "He reminds me of you," he said finally.

Rory crooked an eyebrow. "Is that good or bad?"

"A little of both," Lachlan replied. "Neither of you betray much of what you are thinking. But he came after her alone. He obviously has a strong sense of loyalty, if he was willing to come on Maclean land to look for Felicia without escort."

"More foolhardy than loyal," Rory replied caustically.

Lachlan shrugged.

"You like Jan . . . Felicia," Rory continued.

"Aye."

"It does not bother you she is a Campbell?"

" 'Tis not her fault."

"Nay, it is not," Rory agreed.

Lachlan waited again. Rory was mulling something over and obviously wanted someone to listen.

"I have information about Morneith but no proof," his brother finally said. "I do not know the man, and I have to be here if we are to keep the Campbell lass. But someone might be able to tempt him into making a mistake."

Lachlan sat up in his seat. He had feared Rory might take his anger out on the woman. Instead, he wanted to help her. He had been wrong once again about motives.

"You want me—"

"I am thinking about the Campbell. 'Tis obvious he cares about his cousin. And who better to approach Morneith than a member of his future family? No one would suspect he would be in league with us."

"Will he agree?"

Rory shrugged. "He indicated he might, but I would want someone near him. Someone I do trust."

Lachlan's hope had come tumbling down seconds ago. He did not want to raise it only to have it smashed again. He wanted his self-respect back. He wanted trust returned.

He nodded.

Rory did not say anything else. Instead he spurred his horse into a trot, leaving Lachlan to follow.

JAMIE paced the room restlessly. True, it was better than the hole down below with its cold dank walls that had felt like a coffin. Still, the walls closed in on him here.

He loathed being at the mercy of the Macleans.

He had seen the results of their raids. He had also been responsible for raids on their lands, just not the most recent ones. They were the despised enemies. Barbarians.

They had taken his cousin.

He had been promised a visit, and yet there had been none.

He went to the window and looked out. The courtyard was busy. Men were bringing in animals or wheelbarrows full of belongings. Children were playing in one corner.

Inverleith was preparing for a siege.

He thought about the conversation he'd had earlier with the Maclean leader. He knew little about Rory Maclean except he was the second son of the old laird and that rumor had it he once led a raid in which women and children were killed. It did not bode well.

Yet he had not been left in the cold, wet hole where he'd first been imprisoned, and even there he had been allowed blankets and food. Here, he'd had a good meal along with a jug of reasonably good wine.

He'd also found himself almost liking the Maclean and his wry sense of humor, even when it was aimed at Campbells. He seemed protective of Felicia, even after discovering she was a Campbell. He wondered what had happened in the time his cousin had been here.

It really did not matter. There was no way a Maclean and a Campbell could ever wed after that despicable deed more than a hundred years ago. Nor would he want his cousin to wed one. He was not a superstitious man, but it was true that many Maclean brides had died early. The curse had taken on a life of its own.

In any event, his father would never allow such a union. Never. It would mean war, and his cousin would understand that.

His gaze searched the defenses of Inverleith. Walls were fifteen feet thick and sixty in height. It would be no easy matter to take the keep.

The only weakness appeared to be a lack of trained men. But then they might well be out patrolling Maclean boundaries.

He swore silently at his helplessness and started pacing again.

RORY entered through the gates into the courtyard. Douglas and Archibald appeared to be doing a good job preparing Inverleith. Herds of animals were grazing just outside, and some had been taken inside the gates. Training continued in the courtyard. The sentries on the wall had been doubled.

He and Lachlan dismounted, gave their reins to the young stable lad, and went into the tower.

The ride had relieved some of the tension that had built inside him. He had become increasingly confident that his plan could work.

They stopped by Felicia's room first. She was poring over a book, and with a start he recognized it. Caesar's *Gallic Wars* in the original Latin.

She glanced up as the door opened, and her lips spread into a smile when she saw Lachlan, then her brows knitted together as her gaze met Rory's. And held.

He was still charmed by the deep rich blue of those eyes, even as he knew he had not been included in the glance that flashed between his brother and the Campbell lass.

"You can see your cousin, Lady Felicia," he said. He kept his voice cool and emotionless, even though, as usual, the sight of her brought a flooding warmth through his body.

She stood, relief eloquent on her face. Had she thought he had lied to her earlier when he'd assured her that James Campbell was unharmed?

"Thank you," she said.

"How is Alina?"

"She is sleeping. It is the best thing for her."

She looked at Lachlan, her eyes questioning. Rory realized she had not seen him since her transformation from a Cameron to a Campbell.

Lachlan gave her an encouraging smile, then approached her. "My lady," he said.

Her tentative smile became a grateful one, and something tugged at Rory's heart. He recalled how difficult it had been to control his emotions, his mixture of anger and dismay even as he'd wanted to reach out and touch her with gentleness, not with that sudden angry kiss.

But it was just as well that he had. He had to keep away from her, even as she had to stay here until his plan worked.

Or failed.

He went back to the door and held it wide. "My lady," he said in a voice that sounded cold even to him.

She glanced toward Lachlan. He nodded.

He wanted that smile for himself. God's eyes, but he knew something was very wrong when he was bedeviled with jealousy of both his enemy and his brother.

He hurried his pace to the steps, then led the way up. The guard posted at the door stepped aside.

"Any trouble?" Rory asked.

"Nay, milord."

Rory opened the door.

The Campbell whirled around, saw Felicia, and his frown turned into a cautious smile.

Felicia was not as constrained. She ran over to him, looked at him for a moment, as if to make sure he had not been treated poorly, then hugged him. Then she stepped back and looked again. Rory saw her gaze go over the man's gashes and bruises.

The Campbell looked uncomfortable under her gaze. "They are nothing," he said dismissively. "Are you unharmed? If the Macleans did anything . . . ?"

"Nay. They have been kind."

Campbell's green eyes glittered. "They have been holding you against your will."

She shook her head. "I wanted to stay. It was . . . safe."

Campbell looked at her with worry and doubt carved in his face. It was clear that though he had seemed to accept some of what Rory had said earlier, he had not been convinced.

The knife turned inside Rory. The two Campbells were

looking at each other with an affection that he had known only too rarely.

"A nice reunion," he said. "Now that you both know the other is alive and basically unharmed, Lady Felicia will return to her room."

She whirled around and looked at him. "What are you going to do?"

"I want to talk with your cousin." He found himself stressing the word *cousin*."

"I want to stay."

"That is not possible."

"Why?"

Rory turned to Lachlan. "Take the lady back to her chamber."

Lachlan sighed. "Aye."

"Put someone at her door to make sure she does not leave the chamber. Then return."

"I won't go," she said.

"I can carry you," Rory said.

The Campbell took a step toward him.

Rory saw Felicia's gaze move from his face to her cousin's. She bit her lip, then surrendered. "I will go," she said. "But I want to see Jamie again."

Jamie. Not James. Not cousin.

"We will see," Rory said.

She glared at him. All the softness that he had once seen in her eyes was gone. Anger glittered in them. Then she seemed to cloak herself in that outrage. Her back stiffened, and she walked out.

Lachlan arched an eyebrow, then followed.

"Was that necessary?" the Campbell asked.

"Aye, unless you want to put her in even more danger than she is now."

"I do not ken your meaning."

"I have learned much about Lady Felicia in the past days. If you accept my proposal, it is far better she knows nothing about it, or she will want to play a part. That could be very dangerous."

Campbell's silence was answer enough.

"Sit down," Rory said.

"I do not care to."

"Then I will," Rory said, taking the one chair in the room.

"What is your proposal?" Campbell asked. He stood at the window and looked out.

"Inverleith is impregnable," Rory said, reading his thoughts.

"Aye, if you choose to assault from without," Campbell said. "But it can be a prison in itself."

"I am fully aware of that."

"You know my father will mount a siege if my cousin isn't returned. The king will give his approval. Every clan who had ever felt wronged by the Macleans would join us."

"They would not risk your life."

"If I were you, I would not wager the future of the Maclean clan on it. My father feels deeply about honor."

"Honor?" Rory asked, lifting one eyebrow. "Campbells?"

The Campbell glared at him. "We have never chained a woman to a rock to drown."

Rory felt the familiar wave of shame that such an incident had occurred in his family. Still, the Campbells had as long and horrific a list of infamies.

He shrugged. "We both have relatives we cannot defend. But we both have much to lose as well."

Campbell sat on the table. "What do you have to offer?"

"I know who in the English court has given Morneith money. If you dangle that in front of him, he will have to act."

"And why would I do that?"

"You do not want him to marry your cousin."

"Why would he believe I would defy the king and my father for Felicia?"

"Not only for Felicia. For money as well."

"You want me to play a traitor?"

"Aye. It is the only way. I thought you wanted to help your cousin, or is she just a poor relation?"

Anger flared in Campbell's face, but he controlled it. "She is far more than that."

Rory wanted to explore that now, but that would be naught but self-torture. He had what he needed. The Campbell did indeed care deeply about Felicia. He would have to rely on that.

"Why me?" Campbell asked.

"Because soon all of Scotland will know that Felicia Campbell is here. I cannot leave now. And the words coming from a Campbell would have far more weight than if they were to come from the person who was holding the man's intended bride as hostage."

"You plan to keep her here then."

"Unless you wish her to wed Morneith."

"How do I know I can trust you? You might be leading *me* into a trap."

"If you have not noticed, I have you. I do not particularly want you, but I will keep you if I must to save my people. Trapping Morneith solves both our problems. The king should be most grateful to you for revealing a traitor, and there would no longer be a question of a marriage to Morneith."

"And you? What do you get out of this?"

"Peace. That is what I came back to do.

"Peace?" Campbell's brows shot up as he regarded Rory with a penetrating gaze.

"This feud between our two clans benefits neither of us. It only hurts our tenants."

"How do you think we can trap Morneith?"

"Go to Edinburgh. Drop a name to one of his retainers. Wait until he tries to reach you. Then arrange a meeting place where a king's man can listen. Draw him out. Let him condemn himself."

"And you?"

"I will keep Lady Felicia here. She will be safe. If you need me at any time, send a messenger."

"Who?"

"One of my people. He will stay where you can reach him."

"You do not trust me?"

"As long as I have Felicia, yes. And you may need help."

"And you will give it?"

"I will do what I can."

"That is comforting," the Campbell said sarcastically.

"Make no mistake. I wish I could take your place. If I could find a way, I would leave you in the cell below. But as the son of Campbell, you have access to Morneith that I do not."

Campbell stood. "You are risking much in defying the king and keeping Felicia here."

Rory did not reply.

"Why?"

"I told you. I feel responsible for your cousin."

Campbell studied him for a long time. "I am not sure it is safe here for her."

"It is the only safe place in Scotland for her at the moment."

"You will pledge her safety?"

"Aye."

"I will destroy you if she is harmed," Campbell said, then emphasized, "in *any* way."

A knock came at the door. Rory opened it. Lachlan entered.

Rory ignored Campbell. "Join us, Lachlan. I have just explained everything to Campbell."

Lachlan looked at Campbell. "You have agreed?"

Campbell hesitated. He looked from Rory to Lachlan and finally nodded.

"Your word?"

"Aye."

Rory felt a fleeting moment of triumph, but with it came the knowledge that the plan, such as it was, was dependent on the deceptive skills of a Campbell. He wanted to be in the midst of it. He did not want to be the puppet master, looking on from afar. Nor did he wish to stay here in the close proximity of Felicia Campbell.

"It is done then."

"How do I leave here?"

That was a problem Rory had not quite figured out yet.

"I will help him escape," Lachlan said.

They both turned and stared at him.

"I will have two horses saddled. Campbell can wear a helmet and one of my plaids. I will tell the sentries that we have been sent on an urgent errand."

Rory narrowed his eyes. "You will look the traitor."

"Aye," Lachlan said. "But it is a way I can stay at his side." He smiled crookedly. "I have reason if discovered. You usurped my place and took our clan down a dangerous path by taking Lady Felicia. The Campbell promised me and the clan protection."

It would have been a lie if Rory said he had not thought of that. But he could not ask Lachlan to take on the mantle of traitor.

"It is the only way, Rory," Lachlan said quietly.

Rory glanced at Campbell who was listening intently. "Campbell?"

The man nodded.

"You made an oath to destroy me if anything happened to Lady Felicia," Rory said through clenched teeth. "Now I make one to you. If anything happens to my brother, you had better never venture away from Dunstaffnage again."

Campbell shrugged. "You have what I want. I will have what you want. A counterbalance for both of us."

Rory felt sick. Lachlan would not only risk his life, but his place as a Maclean.

"She means that much to you?" Rory asked.

"It seems so," Lachlan said lightly.

Rory looked at both men.

The Campbell nodded reluctantly.

Rory felt the sand slipping from beneath him.

He truly did not want this.

But he could see no other choice.

Chapter 18

⚬❊⚬

*F*ELICIA could not know.

Campbell readily agreed. "She would not want anyone put in danger on her behalf. She has a worrisome tendency of taking events into her own hands and getting into trouble." The words were said with a tenderness and understanding that rankled Rory.

But after she had masqueraded as a Cameron and attempted to escape as a lad, he could not disagree.

Still, he knew it would be one of the most difficult parts of the plan. He would have to tell her that her cousin escaped without her, and that Lachlan had gone with him.

He did not like lying. It was excruciating that he would have to do what he had so recently accused her of doing.

Would she believe Lachlan could be a traitor to his family?

He would worry about that later. He had other matters that needed attention.

Douglas, for one. He had not yet told either Douglas or Archibald about Felicia. It was time.

The bell rang for supper. The great hall filled with thrice the number usually fed. He would be expected.

Rory went down to the kitchen and ordered trays of food to be delivered to both Felicia and the Campbell. He also made sure that both had a guard at the door. He took care to choose a well-known slacker to watch James Campbell.

Then he went to supper.

Unlike past meals, the clansmen were subdued. They spoke in low tones rather than the usual boisterous ones. It was obvious the two recent raids had both angered and frightened them. They cast quick glances at their new lord, not concealing their uncertainty as to his mettle. He recognized that, and knew only time would create trust.

He had no time.

He asked Douglas to sit next to him. Archibald had taken Lachlan's place in checking on patrols.

"Are we ready?" Rory asked.

"For a siege? Aye. We have the food. We have water. We have training to do, but our men are learning fast. And we have Campbell. No one will storm the keep as long as we hold him."

They were holding on to that. How would they feel when he disappeared? When Lachlan disappeared?

He and Lachlan had debated about telling Douglas. He was as loyal and honest as any man could be. But if he let anything slip, Lachlan's life could be forfeit. Still, for Lachlan's sake, someone besides Rory had to know.

Rory turned to his food, which was considerably improved. He would try to hire Alina's mother as a permanent cook. Her husband could be employed in any number of positions.

That thought was just as disquieting. It meant that somewhere inside he was considering staying.

Where in the devil was Patrick?

Rory wished with all his being that Patrick would return. He was not good at subterfuge.

Now he was spinning a web that might entrap him and his clan as well as its intended prey.

He thought of Felicia. He was gradually becoming used to the name. Was she still worried about her cousin? About her own future? He knew he could not do anything—or say anything—to help her.

After supper, he went with Douglas to the armory.

Since he had not done that since he'd returned, Douglas stood and waited.

"A mistake was made when Archibald abducted the lady you know as Lady Janet Cameron," Rory said.

Douglas's brows knitted together. "Wha' do you mean?"

"You abducted Lady Felicia Campbell."

Douglas's mouth opened, then closed.

"The Campbells raided the village the other night because they were looking for her," Rory said. "She was trying to run away from a marriage planned for her. When she arrived here, she was afraid to tell us who she really was."

"A Campbell?" Douglas said in wonder. "But—"

"You liked her," Rory finished.

"Aye," Douglas said. "She would have made a fine—" He stopped again.

Rory shook his head. There apparently seemed no end of the desire to find him a bride.

"What are you going to do?" Douglas asked.

"She is our responsibility," Rory said. "She will stay here for the time being."

Douglas stilled.

"Speak up," Rory said.

"I would agree we should go to war for your bride. But . . . for a Campbell?"

"It is a matter of honor," Rory said, cutting him off.

"At least we have the Campbell heir."

Rory knew he would eventually have to tell Douglas his

plan. He was not sure now was the time. One careless word could condemn both James Campbell and Lachlan.

He did not like making such choices in loyalty, and honor. It had always been so simple before. So clear. One served his God, his king, his clan, his family.

Now he did not know the best way to serve any of them.

"Aye," he said, feeling like the worst of liars, "we have the Campbell heir."

"And the lady?"

"She is to be treated with the respect her rank deserves. And for what she has done for Alina and others as well."

Rory watched as the man struggled with his own emotions.

"Aye, she is well liked," Douglas said. "But that was before . . ."

"She is the same person. Her care for the wounded was not a subterfuge."

"She should have—" He stopped suddenly.

"Said what? You had brought our enemy into our gates. She knew nothing about us except that we abducted young women and were lifelong enemies of her clan."

Douglas flushed.

Rory continued. "I told you because it will not be long before the Campbells and the rest of Scotland knows that Janet Cameron is at home and Felicia Campbell is the one who is missing."

"She told you?"

"Nay, her cousin. The Campbell."

"We are returning her?"

"Nay. She may be of some use in negotiations."

Douglas nodded. "Should I tell the others?"

"Aye, but I want no disrespect or unkindness."

"I will see to it. That does not extend to the Campbell?"

"It does not," Rory said. "He was moved to where he is for political reasons, but I care not what happens to him." It was true, to some extent. He did not care after his task was completed. In truth, he did not care for the Campbell at all.

The man's self-assurance grated on him. If Rory was truly honest, he realized it wasn't his self-assurance—a quality he usually respected. It was the obvious bond between him and Felicia.

She is out of reach.

Even if she were not a Campbell and the curse were meaningless, he would always live in fear that another of his wives might die in childbirth, along with the child. He did not believe he could survive another agony like that. He still felt the sharp pain of memory. Of loss. Of guilt.

He did not wish to think of it multiplied.

He said a good eve to Douglas.

Everything was in place. The Campbell would escape tonight with Lachlan's assistance. He wondered whether Felicia would feel betrayed by her cousin. It was not satisfaction, but a gnawing pain at playing with lives that haunted every moment of this day.

He probably should not have cut short the visit between Felicia and the Campbell, but time was short. And Felicia could not know what was about to transpire. The smallest slip could mean disaster for all of them.

Was that really the reason? Or was he wanting to keep the lass from her cousin?

Tomorrow she would be left entirely alone.

Rory did not want that, yet he saw no alternative for it.

He had one last stop tonight.

JAMIE spent the afternoon pacing the room.

He was a prisoner, but worse, he feared he was being manipulated.

It had sounded right earlier. He did not doubt Morneith was a traitor. He had always despised the man.

But then he had always despised Macleans as well. How could he possibly trust Rory Maclean?

Still, he was far more comfortable, and Felicia seemed

to be well. Had he been wrong about the Macleans all these years? He did not want to think so. It would destroy the tapestry of all he believed.

Could he trust the new lord?

The man was not the raving predator he had expected when he was first captured. He had thought, in that moment, his life had ended.

He'd puzzled, though, over the Maclean's simmering hostility, even as his enemy provided a certain civilized imprisonment.

Civilized or not, it *was* imprisonment.

Jamie despised his feeling of helplessness. He could not see Felicia to assure himself that she truly was safe. He had had only those few moments to see her. Her eyes had been bright, her greeting warm. She had demonstrated no fear of her captors, but then he would have expected no less. She was a Campbell.

The door opened. Rory Maclean strode in.

"Another visit so soon? I am honored," Jamie said in a voice laced with sarcasm.

"We have details to discuss," the Maclean said, ignoring both his words and manner.

Jamie crossed his arms over his chest and leaned against a wall. He was not going to make it easy for his captor.

"You need information," the Maclean said curtly. "The rumors about Morneith came, as I said, from French spies as well as diplomats trying to negotiate a marriage between King Henry's sister, Mary, and the French King."

"There was talk of that in London," Jamie said.

"The French distrust King Henry and his ambitions in Europe, and particularly Wolsey, who is the power in England now. Louis feels the Scots are the only reason Henry does not attack them."

Jamie nodded. He had heard many of the same sentiments at the Scottish court. Both the Scots and the French felt King Henry had his eye on France but feared being attacked from his neighbor to the north if he struck. And King Henry had reason for such a belief. If the English attacked France, King James most certainly would seize the opportunity to move on northern England.

"The French do not want Scotland weakened," Rory continued. "Henry does. I was told by a diplomat that Wolsey swore Scotland would collapse from within. It was presented as a reason for a marriage between Louis and Princess Mary. The diplomat said France could not depend forever on Scotland to be a detriment to an English invasion of France, that some Scottish nobles hungry for land and titles had already promised loyalty to Henry in exchange for more lands.

"Another French spy identified one of those men as Morneith. He passed the information to me because we have done business together in the past. He had heard Maclean land might be among the reward. Others confirmed the story that emissaries from Henry were meeting with Scottish lairds."

"Morneith was the only man mentioned?" Jamie asked, intrigued despite himself. It made sense, all of it.

"Aye. Buckingham was said to be the intermediary with Morneith. The sum of twenty-five thousand pounds was mentioned as well as our lands. There could be other traitors as well, but Morneith was the only name specifically menioned."

The Maclean paused. "This news was one reason I returned when I did. I wanted to establish alliances. It would be necessary to be believed." The Maclean paused, then added, "I had hoped to end this feud between our two clans."

Jamie did not answer immediately. He thought he had been sent to London to remove him from making any protest about a marriage between Felicia and Morneith. His father knew he considered her a sister, and a loved one at that. Perhaps there had been more to it as well. Perhaps

King James had heard whispers of betrayal and had hoped Jamie might hear something at the court.

If the latter was true, he certainly had heard naught of interest other than continuing concerns about the intentions of France and Spain. He had delivered greetings from King James to King Henry, and sympathy on the death of Henry's newborn child. He had not lingered at a court where Scots were considered crude ruffians.

He was also bemused by the Maclean's statement that he'd intended to end the feud between the two clans. There was no doubt it was bleeding both families. But his father . . . he hated the Macleans and had given the Campbells' steward, William, permission to raid and harass them at every opportunity.

"How do I know this is true?" he finally responded.

"You do not. If I were you, I would be suspicious as well," the Maclean said.

"Then why should I believe you?"

"Because I hope you care about your king and country as well as Lady Felicia. If Morneith is a traitor and can recruit others, James will have a dagger in his back. If Scottish lands go to outsiders, Scotland will be divided and weakened."

Jamie nodded. *It was dangerous*. Morneith was a powerful man, and the Maclean had received his information from the French. It could well be a trap to divide the Scottish crown, or even drive more wedges between the English and the Scots. His head could well be at stake.

And yet if Maclean was right, it should be easy enough to prove by Morneith's response to several questions.

Still, he was not happy about leaving Felicia here in an enemy's camp. He instinctively believed the Maclean, but he had believed others before and turned out to be wrong. Neither did he like the way Maclean looked at Felicia. The man's face was difficult to read, but earlier there had been a brief flash of anger and desire when he and Felicia had greeted one another. It had lasted so briefly that he was not even sure he'd seen it. A flicker, nothing more, before the Maclean's expression had been controlled again.

"She is safer here," the Maclean added. He'd obviously seen the displeasure in his prisoner's eyes.

"I am not so sure of that."

"She disappeared once. Do you believe your father would give her another chance? He might well try to wed her immediately."

Jamie knew that was exactly what he would do. Still, it went against all he was to leave her here. "I want to talk to her first. Alone."

The Maclean frowned.

"I will not go otherwise," Jamie said.

"Aye, you can see her," Rory conceded reluctantly.

"And what do I tell my father?"

"That you were able to escape, but she was not."

"He will ask the king to demand her release."

"I am hoping that you can expose Morneith before he has a chance to act."

Jamie was beset by even more doubts. "Why would you risk so much for a Campbell lass?"

"I told you. I feel responsible for her plight. Honor demands that I set it right."

"And in doing so, perhaps solve another problem," Jamie said, cynicism lacing his words. "I would not depend on currying favor with my father, if I were you. Or the king. Both of us could end without our heads. Mine, though, would be in the most imminent peril."

The Maclean did not argue the point.

"When do I leave?" Jamie finally asked.

"Tonight."

"But I see my cousin alone first."

"She cannot know the plan."

"No," Jamie agreed. He did not enjoy the moment of understanding that flashed between them. Yet he could not fault the Maclean's reasoning.

"Your brother, Lachlan, is he to be trusted completely?"

The Maclean hesitated a second too long before saying, "Aye. I would not commit him if not."

It was a warning, intended or not, that gave Jamie pause. Still, he did not see a choice. Too much was at stake.

The Maclean studied him for a moment, then nodded. "I will take you to her now." The Maclean's voice hardened slightly, and again Jamie wondered what had transpired since Felicia entered this keep.

⌀HE supper gong rang, but no one had invited her to leave this chamber. Felicia had put on one of the dresses Moira had provided and had brushed her cropped hair until it fairly glowed.

Then she had sat and waited. Surely Lachlan would come for her, even if Rory did not.

The laird had been avoiding her since learning her identity. That much was clear. She ached inside that such was true. She missed him, missed the piercing gaze and gentle touch. A surge of warmth flowed through her as she remembered his lips on hers, the way her body responded to his.

An agonizing pain caught in her chest, even as she knew how foolish it was. Rory was her family's enemy, and they had known each other only briefly. How could she have such strong feelings? She tried to tell herself it was only that no one had paid her heed before. She was reacting to an admiration that was new to her. Her heart was not involved. Only her pride.

She kept telling herself that.

Then why did she feel such a devastating loss?

She tried to concentrate on Jamie. What did Rory plan to do with him?

She could not imagine anything terrible. He could be hard and cold, but there was also something tender and vulnerable in him.

Or did she only imagine it?

A knock came at the door, and her heart lurched.

Jamie entered. Alone. She felt a disgraceful disappointment that Rory was not with him.

Jamie regarded her for a long moment, his eyes searching hers. "Are you really unharmed?" he asked.

"I am," she said softly. "No one has been unkind, not even when they discovered I was a Campbell."

"And the Maclean?"

"He has ensured my comfort," she said.

"He has not . . . forced his attentions . . ."

"Nay," she said, and it was not a lie. She had invited his attentions, but she could not tell Jamie that.

He lifted her chin with a fisted hand to look into her eyes.

"You look sad."

"I was worried about you."

"What happened to your hair?"

"I cut it."

"I noticed," he said wryly. "The question then is why?"

She did not want to answer that.

"Felicia?"

She knew him well enough to understand he would wait for an answer. "I was going to dress as a boy and try to leave when the gates opened yesterday morning."

"And why did you not?"

"I saw them bring you in."

He gave her a crooked grin. "And you were going to try to save me?"

"I hoped, and then I decided—" She stopped.

"Decided what?" he urged gently.

"To plead with the Maclean to release you."

"And what did he say?"

"Nothing," she said miserably.

"You thought he might allow me to leave? Just because you asked. Why would that be?"

She did not reply. He would hate the fact that she had

pleaded for him. Yet he only looked at her with that quizzical expression.

"Be cautious about who you trust, Felicia," he said.

"What is he going to do with you?"

He shrugged. "Keep me as a hostage," he said.

"You have not been mistreated?"

"Nay."

"Have you given your parole?"

Something flickered in his eyes. "No. But I am well guarded, and he knows no one can leave Inverleith without his permission."

"Your father will be furious."

"He often is."

"With the Macleans, I mean."

"Does that worry you?"

"Aye. There are children here. And people who have done no wrong other than to live on Maclean land."

He raised an eyebrow at her defense. "The same might be said of Campbell tenants."

"I do not want anyone hurt because of my foolishness."

"I only wish I had been at Dunstaffnage," he said softly.

"You could not have done anything for me there. My only chance was to find you in London without anyone knowing."

"Ah, my little lioness. I can imagine no other woman attempting what you did."

"You are not angry with Janet?"

"For helping you? Nay. I think more of her."

"Oh Jamie, I am so glad. I was afraid . . ."

"Do you have so little faith in me, then?" he asked, his lips turned in a frown.

She threw her arms around him and hugged him tight. He was the only person who had loved her since her mother and father had died. He had been her knight as a child, and a dear friend and brother later.

"Oh no," she said. "I do have faith in you."

"Promise me something."

She looked up at him.

"Never forget what you just said. Always know that I love you. I will always protect you."

A shiver ran through her. She had the strangest feeling he was trying to tell her something he could not put into words.

"I trust you," she said simply.

It was then she noticed that the Maclean had entered the room and was staring at them with those inscrutable eyes.

Chapter 19

JAMIE gazed down at the lass who had come to mean so much to him. He remembered when she had first arrived at Dunstaffnage. She had but five years and was obviously frightened and bewildered.

But still she had marched up to him, stared at him for a long time, then announced quite solemnly that she expected him to be her champion. It had been pure bravado. He had smiled then, and she had made him smile many times since. Smiles had been rare before she appeared.

His life had been training and discipline. His mother and father were often at court, and his guidance came from a sour steward and a number of demanding tutors and instructors in arms. Not long after Felicia arrived, he found her outside the room where the tutoring sessions were held. Even though the material was advanced, she had a thirst for knowledge that always eluded him. He had been amused, though, and insisted that she be allowed to stay for the sessions.

As she grew older, she would watch him practice with the broadsword and other weapons and, at twelve, had asked him to show her how to do it.

The sword had been almost as long as she was tall, and yet she had worked at swinging it and using a shield. She continued until she could best at least a few of the worst Campbell soldiers. Her size helped. She could dart in and out while others were hampered by heavy armor.

She had a dogged determination that amused and endeared her to nearly every soldier. Her desire to help often ended in disaster. Once when she decided the food was too bland, she added huge amounts of mustard. Every man was sneezing and wheezing.

'Twas not so long after that that his father secured a good cook.

All those thoughts went through his head as he looked down at her and knew that on the morrow she would feel betrayed by him. He wondered, not for the first time, whether he should tell her of the plan, but he was only too aware of her impulsiveness.

So he returned her hug, feeling awkward as he did so. His family did not indulge in gestures of affection. Although she would often throw her arms around him, he never initiated such gestures. Nor had he with Janet.

Then he became aware of the man behind him.

He had discovered what he wanted to know. Felicia had no fear of Rory Maclean, nor any of the Macleans. Though he was loath to leave her here, he had no other solution. She should be safe enough.

"I think my warden has returned," Jamie said. "I must go."

She turned and looked at the Maclean. Her heart was in her eyes, and suddenly he realized that . . .

It could not be. *Not a Campbell and a Maclean.* Neither

family would tolerate it. Then there was the curse. No Maclean wife . . .

No!

He swore then he would return and take Felicia to live with Janet and himself.

*R*ORY had opened the door, not expecting to see Felicia in the Campbell's arms, nor to hear Jamie Campbell's softly spoken words, *"I love you,"* and her response, "I trust you." What had she said before he entered?

Words that he would have liked to hear, and never would. She would learn of what he had planned, putting her love in harm's way and keeping the secret from her.

She would never forgive him, even when she realized they had done it for her. Particularly then.

He controlled his reaction to the scene in front of him. Felicia made no attempt to step away from the Campbell. Instead, she seemed to move closer, as if for protection.

Trust. Well he neither deserved it nor did he need it. He had his own life to live, and she could be no part of it.

He turned his gaze to the Campbell. "It is time to return," he said shortly.

Campbell looked back down at Felicia. "Remember what I told you."

Felicia frowned as if she sensed all was not as it appeared. He'd noticed earlier that she missed little and was uncommonly sensitive to nuances. Now her gaze moved from man to man. Questions were in her eyes.

Campbell saw it as well. He turned to Rory. "My thanks for the visit," he said.

"I trust it put your mind to ease as to her treatment," Rory replied.

"As much as it could be, seeing that she is in the hands of Macleans," Campbell replied.

He turned then and left the room. Rory lingered a moment. "I have ordered supper sent up to you."

She looked up at him with the solemn blue eyes that always affected him in a ridiculously heady way. He ached to share supper with her, but he knew by now the way she affected him, the odd way his heart shifted whenever he looked into her face.

He also was not certain how she would be greeted as a Campbell, despite his warning to Douglas. He did not want her hurt any more than necessary. And he had few doubts that tonight—the escape of her cousin without her—would be wounding to her.

Yet it was the only way he knew to keep her safe.

"Good eve, my lady. You will let Robina know if you need anything?"

"I can see Alina?"

"Yes."

As he shut the door behind him, he knew he could not shut out the forlorn expression on her face.

$\mathcal{L}$ACHLAN sat next to his brother at the head of the table. Though supper was long over, everyone lingered, as they sought comfort in their numbers.

Drink flowed. Gloom turned to boasting. The Campbell's capture and the possibility of a siege was both heady and sobering. Laughter was louder than usual. War was an adventure, the rightful pastime of warriors, but this time they would be going against a king's favorite and mayhap the king himself.

The hall was far more crowded than usual. The women from the outlying villages sat quietly, their eyes worried and their voices silent.

In truth, Rory would have liked being anywhere else, but he knew it was important that he give the image of confidence, particularly when all the keep learned of the Campbell's escape and they would soon learn of Lachlan's betrayal in the morning.

Had he spun a web that could entrap even the spider?

Lachlan was quiet, no doubt thinking about the evening ahead.

Rory turned to him. "You are sure about this?"

"Aye."

"You will come to me if you need anything. I will be telling Douglas after you are gone, and swear him to secrecy. Someone other than myself should know."

Lachlan nodded.

Rory returned to his food but he could not eat. He was gambling with at least three lives, perhaps more.

"Visit the lass," he said finally. "Take her down to see the filly."

Lachlan looked surprised at the change of subject. "May I ask why?"

"I suspect she feels very much alone."

"You could take her," Lachlan said.

"I believe she would prefer you."

Lachlan shook his head. "I do not think so, brother, but I will do as you ask." His expression said he suspected the real reason, that Rory no longer trusted himself with their bonny guest.

"Then report to my chamber."

Lachlan took a sip of wine and gave Rory a wry grin. "Of course, my lord."

FELICIA nibbled at her meal, long grown cold. She did not really understand why she could not sup with her cousin, or with the Maclean clan in the great hall. Was it because she was a Campbell? Did everyone know her true identity now? She felt like a leper.

She finished, then opened the door. A Maclean stood outside.

"I would like to see Alina," she said.

The clansman nodded, and she walked to the next chamber. Alina looked up as she entered and struggled to sit. A smile spread across her pale face. "My lady."

The smile lit Felicia's gray mood. She sat down and reached for the girl's hand. "Can I get you anything?"

"Mum was just here with soup."

Felicia looked at the table next to the bed. A bowl of soup sat there with bread and water. "Can I help you eat it?"

"Ye, my lady?"

"I would very much like to."

Alina's shy smile stretched wider. "I was laying here thinking about it, but—"

Felicia picked up the bowl and spoon and brought it to Alina's lips. The lass swallowed it. Felicia continued until the soup was gone, and Alina had consumed the bread.

"I can tell you are better," Felicia said.

"Thanks to ye," Alina said. "Ye have been so kind."

"I like you. Very much," Felicia said. "Would you like a story?"

"Aye."

Felicia searched her memory. "There was once a young maiden who lived with her father in the woods," she said. "He hunted for food and found fuel for the fire.

"But she was very lonely. There were no children to play with, nor as she grew older, no young man to seek her out. One day, she took a walk and found the most beautiful waterfall she had ever seen, and she started to go there every day.

"She made friends of the forest animals who ventured to the waterfall, including a young fawn and its mother. There were hares, and squirrels who would eat from her fingers. And birds that would fly down and flutter around her. Even a wolf joined them. It seemed there was a truce around the magical waterfall.

"And she learned from them. They showed her how to find the choicest mushrooms and greens and onions. Yet she wondered who would come and share the magical kingdom with her.

"Then her father hurt himself with the axe, and she had

to stay and take care of him. There was little food, and she did not know how she could feed them.

"The animals waited for her to come to the waterfall, but after several days without her, the deer decided to find out why. She very cautiously ventured near the small croft, knowing that the girl had warned her many times that her father hunted animals and she must remain hidden during the day."

Alina's eyes had brightened as she listened intently. "What happened?"

"Sofia—her name was Sofia—went outside. A tear fell from one of her eyes as she told the deer what had happened. The other animals gathered around, wanting to help, but none knew what to do. They did not care for the hunter, but they had come to love Sofia, who was so kind, and they did not want to see her so sad.

"Then the deer turned and ran away. The hares, though, stayed, knowing they were safe. The birds took perches around the croft. The wolf joined them, ignoring the hares that ran back and forth in distress.

"They were all guarding Sofia . . ."

Felicia heard the door opening softly, and she saw Lachlan in the doorway. The flickering lights of the candle cast shadows across his face, giving the usually open face a dark, secretive look.

"I thought you might be here," he said, then cast a look at Alina. "And how's my favorite lass?" he asked.

Alina's eyes sparkled with pleasure. "I am much better, milord."

"I am not 'milord,'" he corrected, "I am Lachlan. And I am very pleased to see you looking so well."

"I want to have my hair cut like Lady—" she stopped herself, obviously not quite sure what to call her visitor.

"She does look charming," Lachlan said easily. "But for now I thought she might like to see the foal she named."

"She was telling me a story," Alina protested.

Felicia leaned over her. "You need some rest. I will tell you more tomorrow."

"Will you sing a song first?" Alina pleaded.

Felicia looked at Lachlan. "Mayhap Lachlan would play the lute for us as well."

"Oh, yes," Alina said, her face glowing. "Please."

Lachlan looked as if he were about to refuse, then he ruffled Alina's long, dark hair and leaned down. "Lady Felicia looks charming, but I truly like your long hair." He straightened up. "I will be back."

In minutes he returned with the lute in his hand. He started strumming a tune.

She meant to sing along with him, but something about him stopped her. He had always seemed alone, somehow apart from his clansmen. There was an impenetrable sadness about him, one he tried to hide behind a light-hearted facade.

He looked at her, and for a moment his eyes were bleak, but then they seemed to smile again. "You were going to sing," he reminded her.

She did, and wondered whether her own confused emotions were evident as well.

R ORY forced himself to stay away from the Campbells.

Instead he went to the box in his chamber where he kept the opium. Before he left again for the sea he would give more to Moira, making sure that she understood its power.

He broke away a very small piece. It would go in the wine of the man guarding the Campbell tonight.

He then went to the window and looked out. Night had replaced dusk, and the sky was dotted with stars and framed by a part-moon. No clouds tonight, no mist. Only clear, cold night.

Fires burned in the courtyard; small groups of soldiers

huddled together. Women and children were using the great hall to sleep.

The sound of pipes reached him, the plaintive wail matching his mood. The sound usually stirred him. It was as wild and untamed as the Highlands and its soldiers. Now it merely deepened the loneliness.

He was frightened for Lachlan. For his clan. And for Felicia, if his poor plan failed to work.

He wanted to go to Felicia's room, to push away the uncertainty that plagued him. It was one reason he asked Lachlan to do so.

Could Lachlan carry out the masquerade? Would the Campbell turn on them? Would Morneith be so foolish as to walk into their trap? Was his information true, or had it been a French attempt to sow even more distrust between the Scots and the English?

Beneath him, the fires revealed two figures leaving the tower and moving toward the stable. He recognized his brother's lanky form and Felicia's smaller, graceful one. He wished he could see the pleasure in Felicia's eyes as she watched the foal. It was a gangling animal already showing signs of beauty and breeding.

He found himself moving toward the door, then down the stairs, and toward the stable. Lachlan would be a buffer between them.

He greeted the clansmen he knew, realizing how many he did not know, how long he had been gone. But each looked at him with trust.

God help him keep it.

The door to the stable was cracked, and he slid inside and walked toward the stall holding the mare and her baby. He stayed back as he heard her talk softly to the foal.

"Bonny lass. All legs and eyes, but you will be such a fine filly. She is, isn't she, Lachlan? She is quite exceptional."

"Aye, she is. And do not forget she is yours. Rory gave her to you."

"But that was before he knew who I was."

"Rory never breaks promises," Lachlan said. "It is a fault as much as a virtue."

"Why?"

"Because life is never black and white, all one way or another. Circumstances change, and what seems so clear one moment may not be so clear another."

Rory sensed that Lachlan was speaking as much about himself as about Rory. But it was an arrow hitting its mark. He had lived in a self-imposed isolation because he had been helpless to save those he loved. And he had judged others by his own rigid standards.

"He is lonely, is he not?"

"Aye, I believe so."

A silence then, and he could see in his mind's eye her fingers stroking the foal. He hurt inside. More than hurt. He felt his soul bleeding. Loneliness was a writhing snake within him. His brother was leaving on what could be a fatal mission. Felicia was forbidden. His older brother was missing.

He stepped out of the shadows and approached them.

Lachlan looked surprised, then slightly amused.

Felicia looked startled, then wary.

Did he look so fearsome then? Rory looked at her. "I came to take a ride," he lied. "I could not but help hear part of the conversation. The foal is yours, my lady. There were no conditions."

"Thank you," she said, then, "May I go with you?"

"It is cold, my lady."

"I have been cold before. About ten days ago, in truth."

"But that was not your choice."

She looked up at him. "That is not entirely true," she parried. "But I would enjoy a ride."

"I intend to ride hard." Another fabrication. He would not risk his animal by riding fast at night, not without a need to do so.

"I am a good rider."

He did not doubt it. He knew he should say no, but she had been a prisoner here for too long. He also knew she would not try to escape as long as her cousin was here.

Which would not be very long at all.

Could he deny her a few hours of pleasure? Even at a cost of a few hours of agony for him? Rory glanced up at Lachlan for assistance. He found none.

"I will saddle the horses," Lachlan offered.

Rory could have hit him.

"My—Janet's mare is here," Felicia said eagerly. Her eyes were brighter than he'd seen them since he'd discovered who she was.

Rory tried one last time. "The wind will be fierce along the coast."

"Of course," she said, looking at him as if the comment was beneath him.

He shook his head. She was as unlike Maggie and Anne as anyone could be. Both of them had relished peace. Felicia Campbell relished challenges.

He knew it was a mistake, but at the same time it seemed safe enough. A short ride to the cliffs and back. A bit of freedom for both of them.

He needed to get away from the keep and the concerns that tortured him. She needed a release from what must seem a prison to her.

If there were second thoughts, they had no time to surface. The stable lad brought Rory's favorite gelding to him, and Lachlan saddled Felicia's mare.

He helped her mount, then mounted himself.

They walked the horses to the gate, and Rory ordered them opened.

Once outside the walls, he guided them toward the point that overlooked the sea. The moon was bright enough to see the joy on her face as the cold wind buffeted them. She was as at ease on a horse as he was, and that was rare for a woman. But the exhilaration, whether it came from the ride itself or the freedom she felt, was obvious.

He felt it, too. It was something all too rare, this wild, uncomplicated surge of pleasure, the sharing of it with another person. He turned on a path that led to the sea.

They stopped on a cliff, and he dismounted. He helped her down from the mare. The moment he did and felt a surge of excitement, he knew it was a mistake. Yet he had known from the moment they left the gates behind that this would happen.

The wind blew the hood of her cloak off her head, and the short hair curled tighter in the damp wind that swept off the sea. The sea below was frothing, dancing high against the land.

He had been here days ago. He had been alone then, and lonely beyond bearing, and for some reason he'd felt the need to bring her here and fill the great gaping wound that had been his heart.

Now warm blood surged through his body, and he felt alive for the first time in many years.

She was close, probably too close, and she moved into his arms just as they opened to her. Both moves, he knew, were instinctive rather than planned, an inevitable joining.

It was what he had feared, and what he had needed.

It was why he had tried to stay away from her, yet agreed to allow her to accompany her on this ride.

He'd told himself she needed it, deserved it, but it was as much his own need that had spurred his action.

But none of that mattered as he looked down at her and saw her upturned face. Her eyes reflected the stars above, and her hair was bathed in moonlight.

He touched her face with his fingers, tracing the stubborn jut of her jaw up to the thick lashes that framed her blue eyes. Her short hair curled around his small finger like fringes of silk. Tenderness flooded him, as he ran his fingers through her hair, then pulled her to him.

She melted into his body as if she belonged there.

He bent his head and rested it on her hair, drinking up

the scent of roses mixed with the tangy perfume of the sea. It was intoxicating.

She moved and looked up at him with wide eyes full of expectation and wonder and bewilderment. So many emotions. He understood all of them, for they battled for his newly found heart as well.

His lips touched her cheeks, caressed them, then moved down to her lips. They met his as eagerly has he sought hers.

A wave hit the cliff and sent mist spraying against them. His arms tightened around her, his heat igniting hers.

And on the cliff that overlooked the sea that had birthed a legend—and a curse—decades earlier, Rory sought to defeat it.

Some destiny had brought them together. If not destiny, then the devil. He was not sure which. At this moment he did not care. He only knew that she had become his lodestone.

Their lips joined with a fierceness that nothing could break, a natural joining of something right and destined.

She responded hungrily, opening her mouth to his, her hands embracing him with the same frenetic desperation as his. Need begat a passion so deep and strong, he felt as if fire were consuming him. Their mouths savaged each other with a wild need to touch and feel and taste. To claim something that was forbidden, to make the impossible possible.

Need burned all the way through him, until nothing mattered except Felicia Campbell and the way she made him feel. Whole and alive. So very alive.

Her body melded against his, and he could feel every curve though her cloak. His body tensed, reacted, and hers responded by moving even closer until he felt he would explode with need. He closed his eyes for a moment, allowing himself to be swept away. Electric tension vibrated around them, enclosing them in a private world of their own.

He did not want to let go. Instead he crushed her to him. His hands stroked down from her hair, along her back as his tongue entered her mouth, probing, seducing, and she met each exploration with an eagerness that surprised and delighted him. More than delighted. She touched a place in him that no one had ever reached before, the deep private part of him he'd always kept barricaded against invasion, even from Maggie.

He released her lips and moved his own along the contours of her face. He felt her breath, warm and quick. Lightning leaped between them, jagged and violent, blinding with intensity.

He wanted to take her. In the cold. On the cliff. He wanted to become a part of her and make her a part of him. The violence of that need rocked him.

Not here! Not now!

The voice of reason? Or the voice of conscience? Whatever it was intruded, made him step back before he hurled both of them into an abyss of betrayal and tragedy.

"No," she protested.

He tipped her chin up until their gazes met.

"We cannot," he said. "If it were just the two of us—"

But even then he knew he could not allow this. Two wives dead. His mother dead within a year of her marriage. Patrick's within three. Lachlan's mother died in childbirth. His father had become a bitter man, blaming the Campbells and having nothing in his heart but hatred. Certainly there had been no warmth. Only the one rule: Kill Campbells.

And he had followed that rule.

If she knew . . .

He took another step back. Why had he brought her here?

Because he was a fool. Perhaps part of him had believed that by bringing her to the place he had brought Maggie, to the place he had come as a boy, he might clear his head.

Or was he merely excusing inexcusable behavior.

"I am sorry, Felicia. We should not have come here."

"Why?"

He had to hurt her. He had to do it for both their sakes.

"I used to bring my wife here." He did not add that he used to laugh at the curse, despite the history of his family. He did not say that he and Maggie were going to prove it meant nothing . . .

She bit her lip. "Did you love her?"

"Aye. I did."

"I am sorry."

He dropped his fist from her chin and turned around. He could no longer meet those wide blue eyes. She was obviously willing to risk everything for him.

He could not do the same. Nor would she want that if she knew everything.

"We should go back," he said.

Neither moved, though. Instead the wind moaned, and the sea below them crashed against its barrier.

She reached out and touched the side of his face, an expression of yearning crossing her face.

Then she stepped away and turned toward the horses.

He followed her and helped her mount, feeling the warmth once more. The connection. The fire.

He released her quickly and strode to his own horse. He mounted and, without looking at her, walked the horse back to the main road. He sensed more than saw that she was following him.

But he knew that while he could avoid glancing her way now, he could never remove the image of her wistful expression as he turned away from her.

Chapter 20

❦

FELICIA rode back to the keep, her gaze fastened on the stiff, tense shoulders of the man riding beside her.

It was not hard to realize that he regretted the ride, and regretted the kiss even more.

She did not. It had been a moment she would always remember.

She knew nothing could come of it. The one thing she had discovered about Rory Maclean was his sense of honor. She saw him battling it. And it was hurting him. More than hurting him. She feared it was destroying him.

At the same time, she felt stronger. For most of her life, she'd felt like little more than a poor relation, and then more recently, like nothing more than a pawn. But now people valued her. Some even valued her after knowing she was a member of an enemy clan.

And she'd had moments of magic that would light the remainder of her life, even if she had nothing more. Even now she was still comforted by the warmth that had so briefly enveloped them, with the attraction that was a live, wonderful thing between them.

She still tasted him. She still felt him as she'd leaned into his body. She would always remember, and treasure, the fire and the passion, and a windswept eve by the Sound of Mull.

*L*ACHLAN sauntered to the Campbell's room, a flagon with him along with a blanket.

The guard was standing outside the room.

Lachlan stopped. "My brother sent me to ask him questions," he said.

The Maclean soldier nodded.

"I thought a little wine might loosen his tongue."

" 'Tis too good for the likes of a Campbell." The guard gazed at the blanket in Lachlan's hand. "He no' need no coddling. Should ha' left him in the dungeon."

"Aye, I agree. But my brother thinks otherwise."

The guard frowned but obviously struggled to hold his tongue. His life and livelihood depended on the goodwill of the laird.

Lachlan held out the flagon. "Would you like a dram or two?"

The man looked thirstily at the flagon. Lachlan could tell what he was thinking. He was being offered a taste by the brother of the laird. No harm done in taking a sip. Or two.

"Thank ye," he said and lifted the flagon. He took a long swallow, then another before handing it back.

Lachlan opened the door, stepped in, and closed the door behind him.

The Campbell was lying on the bed but sprang quickly to his feet. He'd obviously been waiting, and none too patiently.

He straightened. "What time is it?"

Lachlan placed the blanket on the table. "An hour or so before dawn. There is no way to open the gates before then."

"I saw two riders last night. One was my cousin."

"Aye. She wanted to go for a ride. My brother accompanied her."

"At night?" the Campbell growled.

Lachlan shrugged. "He was going for his usual ride. Lady Felicia wished to accompany him."

Lachlan saw the angry rise in the Campbell's face. "He should not think about playing with my cousin."

"My brother is not dishonorable," Lachlan said, praying with all his remaining soul that it was true. There was something between Rory and Felicia Campbell that was like dry tinder in a forest. The merest spark could create a conflagration that could destroy everything, and everyone, in its path. *It is not your concern. It is Rory's. And only Rory's.*

But was it?

Not now. Nothing was important now other than the immediate problem. Getting out of Inverleith.

"I gave the man outside some wine," Lachlan said, turning away concerns that both he and apparently the Campbell had. "He should be asleep soon."

"And then?"

"And then you will change clothes. Lachlan opened the blanket and took out a plaid of Maclean dyes. "You will wear this."

A momentary rebellion crossed the Campbell's face.

"It is the only way to leave Inverleith," Lachlan said.

Without another word, Jamie discarded what he was wearing down to his small clothes, then with some distaste, started the process of winding the long plaid around his body, finally clasping it around his waste with a belt. "I need my dirk returned," he said.

"Not until we leave the Inverleith gates," Lachlan said.

"Trust is a wondrous thing."

"So is caution."

The Campbell's gaze met his. "I asked for your brother's pledge that my cousin would not be harmed. I want yours as well, and not only her physical well-being." The words were a very clear warning.

"No one here would want an alliance with a Campbell," Lachlan replied in a soft voice. "Nor do they want a war with your clan."

"That is not want I mean. They are attracted to each other. I noticed that immediately. I also know my cousin. Forbid something, and she will stand first to do it."

"My brother has pledged not to marry again."

The Campbell looked startled at the word *marry*. "I did not mean marriage. It would be impossible."

Lachlan considered the statement. It was impossible at the moment. But if the Campbell and he succeeded . . .

"No," Jamie said, obviously reading his thoughts. "It will take decades to make any union between Campbells and Macleans acceptable to the clans."

Lachlan rose and walked over to the window. The black of night would soon turn to the soft gray of dawn. It would not be long before they would leave. He thought about the message he would carry with him. A message to the captain of Rory's ship. That he carried it at all represented Rory's uncertainty over the success of this mission.

He opened the door. The guard was on the floor, his back leaning against the wall.

Lachlan pulled the guard inside and laid him on the bed, then glanced at the Campbell. "Come with me."

He led the way to his chamber just several doors down.

"My hair?"

"Use ashes from the fireplace. And hurry. I do not want anyone to find the guard until we leave."

The Campbell picked up a pile of ashes from the fireplace. "Do you never clean a fireplace?" he asked, his disapproval obvious.

"Then what would we do for disguise?" Lachlan retorted with a shrug. "This was a lesson your cousin taught us."

"She would," the Campbell muttered.

But soon he was finished. His hands black with ash, as was his golden hair.

"Your boots are too fine," Lachlan said as he handed the Campbell a pair of brogues.

The Campbell looked rebellious. "I like those boots."

"Enough to stay here?"

The Campbell glared at him, then sat down and reluctantly pulled off his boots.

Lachlan packed the Campbell's garments and boots in a saddlebag.

He handed him a helmet, which covered most of the Campbell's hair. "You will keep your eyes lowered as you follow me. I have already ordered two horses made ready for us. You are to relieve one of the border guards.

"Will they not know everyone?"

"We have a number of men from outside the keep. For their safety and their families'."

Safety from Campbells.

Lachlan did not have to say the words. The understanding was in the Campbell's eyes. But there was no apology, either. No hint of regret.

They could never be friends.

"Why are you doing this?" the Campbell asked suddenly.

"Why not?" Lachlan said carelessly.

"You know that your clan will consider you a traitor?"

"You could be labeled that as well," Lachlan said. "You are working with Macleans. Or," he added quietly, "are you?"

The question hung in the air between them.

"You question my honor?" the Campbell said.

"I do not know your definition of honor."

"Or I yours."

"We can argue the question until next year, but now we must leave. We will go directly to the stable. The horses should be saddled. You will say nothing. Just follow me and try not to look comfortable on the horse."

The Campbell gave him a brief nod.

Lachlan looked outside. A streak of gold crossed the distant sky. The first glow of sunrise.

He gave the Campbell a set of saddlebags, then picked up another. He grabbed his lute that leaned against the wall. Then he headed for the door and opened it. No one was outside. He gestured for the Campbell to follow him.

He smelled the odor of food cooking. His stomach churned.

The Campbell had been only too accurate when he'd asked if Lachlan was aware of the consequences of his actions today. Lachlan was only too aware, and the knowledge was like a dead weight in his stomach. Yet he felt that this one act might atone for the past. If peace were possible . . .

They strode quickly past the great hall, ignoring the throngs of people making their way there. Some looked at them curiously, but they all cleared a path. Then they reached the stables. The horses were, as ordered, saddled. Lachlan took the swiftest horse, leaving the Campbell to a slower one. He had no intention of being left behind.

They walked their horses to the gate, and Lachlan raised his hand to the sentries. Lachlan just prayed they would open quickly. It would not be long before the guard would be found, before the alarm was raised.

The gates opened, and the two men rode through them and beyond. Lachlan turned only long enough to watch the gates close again.

The Campbell had escaped. And with him, Lachlan Maclean. Traitor.

* * *

ℛORY watched Lachlan and Campbell depart through the gates. He did not realize he'd held his breath until they were through.

He continued to watch as the sun crept upward. A hour passed, perhaps more. The bailey below filled with his clansmen.

Then someone pounded on the door.

He opened it. Douglas, his face white, stood there.

"The Campbell," he said. "He is gone."

"He cannot be gone," Rory replied. "There is no way to leave Inverleith without my knowing about it."

"A man was sent to relieve the guard at the Campbell's chamber. No one was there, and he went inside. The guard was asleep on the bed. We have searched the keep. He is not here."

"No one could have left."

"Lachlan went through the gates at daybreak. He had someone with him. We think it might have been Campbell."

"Not Lachlan," Rory said.

"The man was tall. He wore our plaid and a helmet, but no one can explain who he is. And the guard at the Campbell's room . . ."

"Continue," Rory said when Douglas faltered.

"He said Lachlan gave him a glass of wine last night and he became dizzy almost immediately. He believes there was something in the wine."

It was time to tell Douglas. "Come in," he said. He closed the door firmly behind Douglas.

Douglas turned a puzzled gaze on him.

"Lachlan did it on my orders," he said.

Douglas stared at him, anger stirring in his eyes.

"We do not need another Campbell as a hostage. We *do* need one to set a trap that could benefit all of us."

"I do not ken your meaning."

Rory explained the plan, then added, "Lachlan was willing to jeopardize his reputation, his position with the family, even his life."

Douglas did not say anything.

"I have not asked questions since I have been back," Rory said. "I know something happened while I was gone. I have been waiting for Lachlan or you to tell me, but now I think it will have to be you."

"'Tis a wee late, is it not?" Douglas said with obvious resentment that he was not informed earlier of what Rory intended to do.

"It had to appear real," Rory said. "I needed your anger."

"I do not know that you can completely trust Lachlan," Douglas said reluctantly.

"Why?" Rory demanded. "I realized that there was a hesitancy to follow Lachlan but I believed it was because he had not taken hold here."

"That is not all of it. After you and Patrick left, your father was determined to make a warrior of him. But Lachlan, well, he has always been more of a dreamer. You know he considered the priesthood?"

"I know. Father forbade it."

"Aye. Instead he tried to change Lachlan. He took him to raid Campbell cattle. Four of us went, but your father insisted that he and Lachlan ride ahead. They ran into armed men. One came at Lachlan and he hesitated to use his sword. Your father took a blow meant for him."

Douglas lowered his head. "Archibald and I were not far behind. We heard shouts and raced ahead. There was a battle. We killed two and two others got away.

"Lachlan was on the ground, holding your father's head. He told us what happened. He blamed himself. Your father died five days later.

"We did not tell any of the other clansmen. They would believe Lachlan a coward, and he was all we had. Patrick was gone. You were at sea. But Lachlan could never take his place. Guilt racked him. The clan saw it and felt they could not depend on him. I am ashamed to say I did nothing to counter it." He paused. "I was angry. I suppose I still am. I cared about your father."

Rory shook his head. He wished he had asked sooner. He wished he had known what Lachlan had been suffering. But he had been contemptuous of the condition of Inverleith, and he had resented being called away from the sea. Then Felicia appeared and turned his life upside down.

"Father tried to make him into something he was not, could not be," he said. "And Lachlan paid the price for Patrick's and my freedom." Regret pierced him. He had fled Inverleith and had never looked back.

Douglas looked skeptical. "I do not know what he will do now," he said.

"He captured James Campbell," Rory reminded him.

"Aye," Douglas said. But Rory heard the doubt lingering in his voice.

"He is a Maclean," Rory said. "He would not have offered to go had he not believed he could do whatever was necessary.

"In any event, it is done," Rory continued, "and I trust him." He paused, then added, "it is important, though, that everyone, including Archibald, believe he helped James Campbell escape. "I want you to do everything you would have done had Lachlan truly helped the Campbell escape."

Douglas nodded.

"Someone had to know in the event something happened to me," Rory said. "I have also written out an explanation that I wish you to keep."

"As you wish, my lord."

"It is still Rory."

"Nay," Douglas said. "No longer."

Despite Douglas's doubts about Lachlan, it was clear that he had now transferred his total loyalty to Rory.

Rory hadn't wanted it, still did not want it, but now he had no choice. His distraction in the past had nearly resulted in the destruction of the clan, and most certainly that of his brother.

"Patrick is the rightful laird."

"Nay, it is time that we admit Patrick will not return. You must take your place. Especially now. The clan needs to know they have a leader who will stay."

Rory knew Douglas was right. They would not fight for someone who appeared for a few weeks, then intended to leave. He needed their loyalty.

"I am not prepared to agree Patrick will not return," he said slowly. "But if he does not, I will stay."

Douglas nodded. "I will tell them."

"Search Inverleith again," he said, hardening his voice as he saw two clansmen approach. "Every room, every closet, every possible hiding place," he added. "And send out patrols to the passes and roads."

The men left with Douglas.

Rory closed the door and leaned against it, his stomach churning. It was done. But what in God's name might he have done to his brother?

FELICIA watched the activity beneath her. She had slept little this night, and the few moments she had she dreamt of Rory Maclean. He approached her, coming closer and closer, and she would open her arms to him. Then he simply disappeared like a puff of smoke.

She'd finally risen from the bed and lit a candle. She tried to shake the feeling that something terrible was about to happen. The more she recalled the time she had spent with Rory, the more she had been filled with a foreboding. She'd sensed the tension, even a certain desperation in him as he'd kissed and held her, then built a barrier between them, avoiding even a glance, on the return.

The door opened, and two large Macleans entered. She had seen them before at the table in the great hall. They had been jubilant then about her abduction. Now they frowned at her.

She knew instantly that something was very wrong. She pulled her night robe tight around her.

"Have you seen the Campbell?" one asked, his voice harsh.

"Nay, not since yesterday."

They searched her room. It did not take long. There was not that much to search.

She was bewildered. "Jamie? Where is my cousin?"

"He is missing," one of the men said curtly.

He would not have left her here alone. Not without some word. She knew it. Deep in her heart, she knew it.

Had Rory Maclean done something to him? Did the fact she rode out with Rory last night have something to do with it? Jamie might well have seen it. He would not have held his tongue. She felt cold. Cold and even more alone than she had felt before she came here.

Surely Jamie would have left a message if he'd escaped. Perhaps with Lachlan.

"I would like to see Lachlan," she said.

The Maclean's mouth thinned. "He left at dawn."

Anger was visible in his eyes. He left without another word, shutting the door firmly behind him.

She opened the door and was stopped by a guard who stood there.

"I would like to see the laird," she said.

"He is busy."

"Will you tell him I wish to see him?"

"Aye, when we can."

He shut the door, and she went to the window. The gates were closed, and men were hurrying throughout the bailey, looking everywhere.

"Where was Jamie? He had given his parole. He would not violate it. He had come for her. She could not believe he would leave without her, even if he thought she might prefer to stay. It had been apparent earlier that he did not trust the Macleans.

And now?

The door opened, and Robina entered. Distress was

written all over her face. "Milady," she said. "Lord Rory sent me to look after ye."

"What has happened?"

"It is terrible. They think . . . but it cannot be true. I do not believe it." Robina was stuttering.

"What does everyone think?"

"The Campbell is gone. They think he left with my lord Lachlan."

"Lachlan?"

"Some are calling him a traitor, but I know it canna' be true, milady."

"Tell me everything."

"They found the man who was guarding the Campbell asleep in the room. It is said he was drugged. Lachlan and one other man rode out at dawn this morning. They think it was the Campbell."

Lachlan and Jamie?

"Why would he?"

"Some say because milord has returned."

"That does not sound like Lachlan."

"Nay, many of us do not believe it, but the others . . . many have never liked him."

"Why not?"

"I dinna know. No one really talks about why."

"I do not believe he would betray his brother," Felicia said fiercely. It occurred to her that it was very odd to find herself defending a Maclean against other Macleans when she felt betrayed by her own cousin.

She thought about last night again, the feeling that Rory was not saying something, that it was something more than the fact that he was a Maclean and she a Campbell.

Had he been worried about Lachlan?

She thought about the times she had seen them together. They had not been close, she had noticed that, but she thought she had seen affection in Lachlan's eyes when he had mentioned Rory could play the lute. He had never in-

dicated any jealousy of his brother, but rather seemed relieved that he had returned home.

And he was the one who had captured Jamie.

Nothing made sense.

But the only other explanation was that Jamie had
forced him in some way. And if he had, why hadn't Jamie
taken her with him?

Because he was trying to protect her from a marriage
she did not want? But he had to know she could not stay
here, that her uncle would not accept it. Angus Campbell
would destroy the Macleans and all those who supported
them rather than see her a prisoner of his greatest enemy.

And why the hostility of the guard at the door now? Did
Rory Maclean fear she would try to escape as well? Was he
furious about Jamie? With her? Did he think she assisted
Jamie in some way? He had just lost a valuable hostage,
one that could bring thousands of pounds to the Macleans,
and perhaps even peace. She was not nearly as important.

He had sent Robina to her. It most likely meant he did
not intend to come himself.

Robina helped her dress. She selected a dark blue velvet
gown that had once belonged to Lachlan's mother and sat
restlessly as Robina brushed her short hair. She would have
preferred to do it herself, but she wanted Robina's company. She did not wish to be alone. Still her mind raced
ahead.

Why had Rory not come himself? Was he out looking
for her cousin? And what would he do if he found him?
And Lachlan?

All the questions ran through her mind. Pounded at it.

She shivered. She wanted to see Rory. She wanted to
feel his strength, his warmth. She wanted not to feel so
alone.

"Ye are cold, milady," Robina said. "I will send someone in to stoke the fire."

Felicia did not answer. She was not cold from lack of a

roaring fire. Fear froze her. Fear for Jamie and Lachlan. For Rory.

"When did Lord Rory ask you to come to me?" she asked.

"Just before he rode out," Robina said.

"He is gone then?"

"Aye."

She wondered whether he had left when the two Macleans searched her room. The gates had been closed when she looked out earlier. Were they looking for Jamie both inside and outside the walls?

She felt as if she would jump out of her skin. She would have to sit and wait as those she cared about were running and being chased by others she cared about.

Robina pinned a cap to Felicia's short hair. Felicia stood and went once more to the window. "How many men did Lord Rory take with him?"

"I am not sure. Many," Robina replied.

"What will he do if he finds them?"

"I do not know, milady. None of us here know him well. He has been gone so long. I have only heard—" She stopped suddenly.

"Heard what?"

Robina's face reddened. "I canna say, milady."

Felicia searched her face. Robina's jaw was stubbornly set, which was unlike the young maid who was so eager to please. Her gaze would not meet Felicia's.

Felicia suddenly stilled. She remembered the fright she had when she realized she had been abducted by Macleans. She'd remembered hearing of a raid in which a ruthless Maclean killed women and children. It would have been twelve years ago.

Rory would have lived here then.

But then so had his father and older brother. Lachlan as well, though he would have been young. Still . . .

Her blood suddenly ran cold.

Could it have been Rory? Or had he been with his father?

No. She had seen him with children. She had seen his concern, his kindness.

A nibble of doubt ate at her. And if he was that Maclean, could she ever look at him in the same way?

She could not. She knew that with every drop of Campbell blood in her.

Chapter 21

✦≈≈✦

"**H**ow long do you think your brother will give us?"
"An hour, perhaps, if that much," Lachlan
said. "Maclean pride will have taken a bitter hit this morning."

They had been riding hard for several hours, and slowed
only long enough to rest their horses.

"Why are you doing this?" Jamie asked.

Lachlan did not answer.

Jamie had learned in the past few days that Lachlan
Maclean kept his own counsel. But he wanted to know
more about this Maclean who was willing to feign treason
to his clan. He wanted to know whether he could depend
on him if the need came.

He still did not know.

Jamie knew the Macleans would pursue. The Maclean

would have to come after them or lose the confidence of his clan. He could not make obvious mistakes.

He hoped they would have an hour's lead. That should give them enough of a lead to reach the border and come under the protection of Janet's family.

He glanced again at his companion. Lachlan Maclean was a puzzle to him, and he did not like puzzles. Too much depended on the younger Maclean's wiliness. And courage.

And on the older one's honor.

He was none too confident of either.

There were too many tales of Maclean atrocities, and now they had abducted a helpless woman.

Jamie looked upward. The sun was climbing. Their horses were tired and needed rest despite their superb condition. Though the Maclean keep was not as well kept as Dunstaffnage, their horses were in excellent condition. Still, he and Lachlan had ridden hard.

Lachlan slowed, obviously recognizing the animals' need for rest as well.

He pointed toward a wooded mountain. They left the road and turned toward a heavily forested area. Once there, the Maclean dismounted and started to lead his horse. Jamie did the same and followed as his companion moved farther into the wood.

The trees and undergrowth were dense, but Lachlan moved with a sureness that impressed Jamie. They soon reached what looked like an overgrown path, and their pace quickened.

The day warmed. They rested briefly atop the hill where they could see the road they had left. Riders moved swiftly along it, but none turned in their direction.

Jamie surmised that this trail had been used years earlier for raids into Cameron and Campbell properties. Since it was overgrown and barely visible, Jamie could only guess it had not been used in years and was unknown to those following them.

Lachlan was probably the most reticent man he'd ever ridden with, but then he had reason. He probably trusted Jamie no more than Jamie trusted him.

The horses breathed easier when they started again.

It was midday when he realized they were on Cameron land.

They had successfully escaped Maclean land. But he knew the test—the real peril—lay ahead. And he was not at all sure that Morneith was the Maclean's only target.

$\mathcal{R}$ORY divided his men, sending a group to each pass and road being watched. Archibald led one of them, a man named Davie the other.

He knew they would ride hard. Each one knew the value of the Campbell heir as a hostage.

He also doubted they would find anyone. Lachlan had placed each of the patrols. He knew the areas to avoid.

After dark, he led his patrol back to Inverleith. The gates opened, and they entered. Douglas met them.

Rory dismounted and handed the reins to a stable lad who approached. "Have the horses watered and fed," he ordered.

Douglas waited until the lad walked the horse away, then asked, "No sign of them?"

"Nay. Archibald is still checking the passes and roads. He has seen nothing, and his men are looking hard, but I think they are long gone from Maclean land."

Douglas nodded. "Good," he said in little more than a whisper. He apparently had rid himself of the doubts he'd expressed earlier about the plan. He hesitated, then added, "Perhaps we should tell Archibald."

"Nay, he is not a man to keep secrets," Rory said. "It is not that he would not try, but the righteous anger would be gone. Our people and the Campbells must both be convinced."

Douglas did not look completely satisfied, and Rory understood why. The two men had kept the clan safe these past few years with little help from the lairds. Rory knew how difficult it must be for Douglas to keep this secret from his friend.

He walked with Douglas toward the keep. His wounded arm ached. He was beset with uncertainty about the events he had just put into motion. He could have simply sent Felicia back to Dunstaffnage, and all would go on as it had in recent years.

Had he risked his entire clan to save her from a horrific marriage?

Yet an alliance with the Campbell heir could have many more benefits to the Macleans. It could stop a century of warfare.

Was it worth the gamble?

Rory looked up at the tower. Lights blazed in the great hall and flickered in rooms above. He saw a glimmer from Felicia's room.

"What is the clan saying?" he asked Douglas.

"There's confusion, anger. Some believe that Lachlan helped the Campbell. Others believe he was forced in some way."

"What would you have thought?" he asked, curious.

Douglas was silent for several moments, then said thoughtfully, "I would think he had a reason. He has always been one to think too much."

A good description of his half brother.

Lachlan was probably the bravest and most gallant of the three of them. "And about Lady Felicia?"

"They all know she is a Campbell now. The ones who do not know her grumble. The others defend her."

It was the most he could have hoped for.

He went inside the tower and up the stairs. He hesitated, knowing he should just go to his own chamber.

Yet he could not do that. He felt intolerably alone. He knew she must feel the same.

He went to her room. A guard stood outside. "You may go," he said.

Rory knocked lightly after the man left, then opened the door.

Felicia stood in front of the fireplace, her arms crossed in front of her as if she were cold. The flames from the fire made her cropped hair glow like copper.

She did not turn and look at him, though by the tightening of her body, he realized she sensed his presence.

"Is it true?" she asked in a small, uncertain voice.

The uncertainty was so unlike her, the words pierced his heart.

"That your cousin has escaped? Aye, it is."

"You did not find him?"

"Nay."

"And Lachlan? Did Jamie take him by force?"

"I think not."

She turned then. "You are not certain?" Distrust was in her eyes. Distrust and despair.

"I am not certain of anything." Which was probably the first honest words he had spoken. He was startled at her question about Lachlan. She appeared nearly as dismayed about him as her cousin.

"Jamie gave you his parole," she said. "He would not have dishonored himself."

His silence was a condemnation of the honor of James Campbell. He knew the Campbell had understood that, but it was more than a little difficult to condemn a man who did not deserve it, even by omission.

"He would not violate it," she said. "Nor would Lachlan act dishonorably."

"Lachlan marches to his own beat," he said. "I do not know about your cousin."

"I do," she said. "I do not believe it. Not of either of them." It was a statement of fact.

He realized she had put trust in Lachlan, far more than she had placed in him.

She was wiser than she knew.

He wanted to tell her everything. He wanted to tell her that Jamie had not left her, nor had Lachlan betrayed his clan. But he did not trust what she might do.

So why was he here?

He told himself it was because he owed it to her. He and Lachlan and James Campbell. All of them had lied to her, at least by omission, and he knew she must feel abandoned and betrayed. Under her bravado, he detected the same uncertainty that deviled him. She so much wanted to believe in her cousin. In Lachlan. Yet there had to be painful doubt.

He thought he was doing the right thing but was not sure. Sending others into danger while he stayed safely behind stone walls went against everything he valued.

"You do not, either," she said suddenly.

"Do not what?"

"You do not believe it, either."

God's eyes, but she could see right through him. Although she didn't know the cause of his uncertainty, she saw something. He had to divert her thoughts before she sensed the truth.

"It does not matter. They are gone," he said shortly.

"Jamie would not have left me," she protested stubbornly.

"He is a Campbell," he said, wincing at the cruelty in his words and tone. But she had to be convinced so that others would be, and underneath that need lay that festering jealousy for a man who was both enemy and ally. And a self-hatred for what he was now doing, making her believe that someone she loved would leave her.

"And you are a Maclean. Your clan kills children. They chain women to rocks," she struck out in anger.

"Aye. Remember that."

Tension radiated between them, a tension born of need and betrayal, of trust lost. Of his poor attempt to create a wall that was altogether too flimsy, and he sensed she realized it. Their pure need for each other was like a noose relentlessly drawing them together, no matter how hard they struggled against it.

Then she was in his arms. He was not sure who made the first step, or whether they made it at the same time. He only knew they needed each other, and that need was explosive.

He closed his eyes as his arms folded around her. He wondered whether her need was for him, or to assuage her sense of abandonment by someone she trusted with her whole being.

He wanted it to be for him, even though he knew how unwise it was. Still she warmed his soul, and he only now realized how much he had needed that heat.

When he opened his eyes again, she was looking at him with surprised wonder, as if she were as confused as he at the fire that continued to rage between them, obliterating every obstacle.

He muttered an oath.

Her lips parted in an impish smile. She never ceased to surprise him. When she first arrived, she had displayed a courage that startled him. He was even more surprised now that he knew who she was and the fear she must have had upon entering the walls of Inverleith. Instead of turning away from them, she had nursed Macleans and endeared herself to his family.

She had brought life to a place that had lost it.

He traced the lines of her face with his right hand. He had done it before, but each time he found something new there. It was a mobile face, full of feelings.

She stood on tiptoes and looked up at him with an invitation.

She was not pledged to a Campbell, but to a man she did not know.

He knew he was justifying the unjustifiable, as his lips met hers hungrily.

He had known it when he had taken the steps. He'd known it when he knocked on the door.

Yet she was alone in an enemy keep. She thought she had been abandoned by those she trusted. She needed . . . reassurance. Comfort. Or at least that was what he told himself.

Now he knew it was something altogether different. He could no more stay away from her than he could stop breathing.

It was a humbling realization. He'd always considered himself an honorable man and, in the past few years, a disciplined one. He had loved and been loved, and thought he had experienced all there was to know.

He had known nothing.

When his lips touched Felicia Campbell's, his world exploded into sensations.

Rory was torn between tenderness and violence, between the warmth he craved and the bitter harvest he knew his actions would sow. His lips sought hers, invaded her mouth, seduced. Demanded.

Part of him wanted her to be outraged. Wanted her to pull away, as he could not.

Instead, her mouth welcomed his with fevered intensity, with a need that was as strong as his own.

And once that happened, there was no retreat.

His lips bore deep upon hers, their tongues playing a sensuous and frantic game, as if each sensation would be the last either would have with the other.

He drew her closer to him, and she fitted into his body until every nerve ached and yearned. The kiss turned fiery, fed by their mutual need. He fumbled with the ties at the back of her dress. It fell, leaving a chemise and yards of petticoats to shield her body.

In seconds, they were gone as well. He ran his fingers down the soft angles of her body, lingering at her breasts. His lips brushed her breasts, and he felt them respond to his touch.

His body was on fire. As if sensing that, or feeling the same irresistible need, Felicia's body melted into his. Her arms went around his neck and played with his hair at its nape.

He could resist the fire in his groin. He had done it before. What he could not resist was the radiance she brought into his life. He had not realized how dark and bleak it had been these past years.

Still, he tried. "I do not want to hurt you."

"I am already hurt," she said. "And not by you."

He knew that was not true. His lies had hurt her. He saw it in her eyes. "Felicia," he said. "I . . ."

She put a finger to his lips. "I want to know what it is like . . . to—"

He touched her lips before she could continue. Her eyes were wide, the sapphire blue deep and riveting. They were, he realized, searching his for a response. For a truth he could not give her.

Neither could he turn away, nor ignore the wistful, almost desperate plea. He touched his lips to hers again, lightly at first, relishing the tender sweetness of them, but it was she who demanded more. He deepened the kiss, searing them both with a brand he knew he would carry forever.

He did not know where this would go, could go, but he did know he needed her. And she needed him.

Could it be so wrong then?

His hands moved tenderly along her body, feeling it tremble slightly. His eyes feasted on the slender, firm body that glowed in the flickering light from the fireplace.

For the first time, he mourned the loss of so much of that glorious hair. In his mind's eyes, he saw it curling down her back, and he longed to tangle his fingers in it. But even without it, she was irresistible to him, the shorn hair curling around her face in ringlets, her eyes bright with the wonder of the sensations she was feeling.

He wanted her. "You are sure?" he asked again.

"Aye. It might be all I ever have."

He did not want that to be true. He wanted her to have everything. But he could never give it to her. He *could* see her to France. He could help her escape Morneith if his plan did not work. He would take care of her. He made himself a promise.

Her hands went to the large buckle at his waist, but they were too small and too unfamiliar with it. He quickly unbuckled the belt and let the plaid fall to the floor, leaving only the long linen shirt.

He wrapped her in his arms, holding her tightly, allowing her to grow familiar with his body as he kissed her forehead, her cheeks, and finally her lips with infinite tenderness and promise. He felt the sensations building in her, and his body grew taut as he sought to control his own needs.

Her body moved compulsively closer to his, seeking an even more intimate union. He marveled at her lack of coyness, or fear, or modesty. She was open and honest.

He was not!

God's eyes, but he would not, could not, think of that now.

His kiss became more violent, even desperate. Somewhere inside he hoped she would back away, that she would solve the moral battle raging inside him.

There was both innocence and instinctive knowledge in her every response. He realized she probably did not know how her touch aroused him, brought him almost to the point of madness. It took every bit of control he could summon not to throw her on the bed and take her.

Instead he caressed her breasts, playing against the sensitive flesh that changed, hardened under his fingers. He continued his seduction, moving his hands along the lengths of her body, bringing it to a readiness to take his. He knew he had gone past the point of stopping. But he wanted to give more than he wanted to take.

Felicia's legs nearly gave way. Sensations slammed her like winds in a highland storm. The need in her increased unbearably. As she touched and caressed him, and felt his arms tighten around her, she did not care about anything except satisfying the exquisite ache that had haunted her since she had met him.

He stepped back and pulled off his shirt, then sat in a chair and removed the soft leather boots. Then he stood.

She was stunned by the raw, rugged beauty of his tall hard body, by the muscles and dark hair curling on his chest. Shy and eager both, she reached out a hand to him in invitation.

He took it and led her to the bed. He guided her to a sitting position, and leaned over and kissed her lips, then moved downward, his lips lingering, inciting small blazes wherever they went. Then his mouth found her left breast and nuzzled it.

Any hesitation Felicia might have had vanished in the magic of his touch, the yearning she felt in him as much as in herself. Her heart thudded, the noise pounding in her ears. She felt his strength, and she relished it. She felt his need and responded to it. She felt his passion, and all her doubts and fears dissolved into a cavern of immense longing.

Her blood rushed like a storm-swollen river through her as he turned her body and again stroked her with hands that were pure sorcery. Though the room was cold, she felt the dampness of his skin and wondered whether it came from an inner boiling heat like her own.

All thoughts disappeared as his tongue roamed and stroked and seduced her body until every nerve in her body sang with life and expectation. When she thought she could bear no more he lowered himself. He did not enter her, but teased her body with his until it was her arms that pressed him into her. First there was an odd fullness, then an unexpected pain. She could not stop a small exclamation.

He stopped, withdrew. But through the pain, Felicia was consumed by need and the promise of some unknown pleasure. Her arms brought him back, and slowly, very slowly, he started to fill her again.

The pain receded, replaced by a yearning so over-whelming she could not comprehend it. There was pulsing eagerness and fierce expectation.

He hesitated, the warmth of his skin touching and brandishing, setting off even more sparks. Her body instinctively moved up to him, desperate to relieve the pressure inside, the terrible, driving craving that consumed her.

His kiss deepened as he probed deeper. The sensations were so new, so unbelievably delicious that her body responded, seeking more and more of him.

He moved in her, slowly, giving her time to get used to the feel of him, then the movements became a sensuous dance, a slow, hypnotic rhythm that her body joined. Her hips rotated in circular movements, even as she wondered at her own boldness, the new instinctive knowledge of what exactly to do.

He thrust deeper, and she felt he was almost at the core of her. An urgency seized her, and she pulled him even closer to her.

Then another thrust, and she felt an explosive ecstasy rock her, splintering into waves and waves of pleasure that surged through her. Her body shuddered uncontrollably, and she heard him mutter something. He collapsed on her, his breath coming quickly. She relished the gentle abrasion that continued to send tremors through her body.

He rolled over, carrying her with him, then clasped her tightly against him. She heard their hearts beat in tandem. Their breath intermingled.

Her body hummed and tingled and still sought to wrap itself around the part of him that had so awakened her. Every time she moved even slightly, rushes of sensations ran through her.

She had never thought that making love could be so . . . so shattering, like a shooting star flashing through the universe. She would never regret these moments. She would always treasure them.

She lay in his arms, wondering how anything could feel

so right, puzzling over how two members of warring clans could come together with such a sense of belonging. And rightness.

She snuggled in his arms. For the moment, nothing else mattered but his embrace.

Rory shifted slightly, gathering her even closer to him. "You are so bonny," he said.

She would have preferred words of love. But it was enough at the moment to know he thought her bonny.

He had given her a gift, and memories. He had given her part of himself.

It was so much more than she had ever thought she would have.

Chapter 22

JAMIE paused at the road into the Cameron keep.
Lachlan drew alongside him. "Why are we stopping?"

"Our horses need rest, and we can get some food here."

Lachlan raised an eyebrow. "You would not be wanting to see the Cameron lass?"

"That, too," Jamie said agreeably. He was not going to bypass a visit with Janet.

The gates opened when he identified himself, and Janet stood in the courtyard as he rode in. Her anxious expression faded into pure joy.

His heart soared, even as that reaction startled him.

He slid down from his saddle and walked over to her.

"I worried about you," she said softly.

He did not expect the thud of his heart when she said that.

She looked up at him. "Did you learn anything about Felicia?"

"Aye, but I will tell you more later." He turned toward Lachlan. "This is Lachlan Maclean. He assisted me, and I ask that you extend to him all the hospitality of your clan."

She turned and smiled at Lachlan. "Of course," she said as Lachlan dismounted.

Then she turned back to him. "How long can you stay?"

"No longer than a day. I must be off to Edinburgh." He paused, then added, "Have you had any questions from my father?"

"Some men from Dunstaffnage stopped, asking if we had any information about Felicia." Questions were in her eyes. He knew he would have to lie to her, just as he had lied to Felicia. He did not like being put in that position.

It's for Felicia's sake.

She turned to go inside, and her mother joined them, beaming as she saw him and Janet together. "It is good to have you visit again so soon. You will stay longer?"

"Nay, my lady, I cannot. I have urgent business in Edinburgh."

She looked toward Lachlan with curiosity. "Lachlan Maclean?"

"Aye, he did me a very great service."

"Then he is welcome, of course."

He probably would have been, anyway. The Camerons were caught between the Macleans, who bordered their property, and the Campbells, with whom they'd had a long alliance. It had been a delicate line to tread.

"Have you heard anything about Felicia?" the lady asked.

More lies that would need explanation in the future. "Aye, the Macleans are holding her hostage."

Janet's eyes widened. She glanced quickly at Lachlan, then back to him. "What do they want?"

"I cannot discuss that with anyone but my father," he said. "But she appears to be well treated."

"But that was not what she—" She stopped suddenly and looked at her mother.

So did Jamie.

Lady Jane stared at her daughter, realization dawning in her eyes. "You helped her?"

"Yes," Janet admitted reluctantly.

Lady Jane's glance went to Jamie. "You knew she assisted Lady Felicia?"

"Aye," he said.

"Your father would break the betrothal if he knew," Lady Jane said. "He is not a man to cross."

"He will not learn it from me, and there is no other except your daughter, Felicia, and now you who know," he said.

But Lady Jane was not listening. She turned back to her daughter. "How could you do such a reckless thing? Lord Campbell could destroy us all."

"He was going to marry her to the Earl of Morneith," Janet replied.

Distaste crossed Lady Jane's eyes. "A poor match, indeed, but he is still her guardian. And is she any better off in the hands of the Macleans?"

Jane looked back at Jamie. "You said she was well treated. Did she speak to you, and how?"

"I was captured by the Macleans," he said. "They were planning to hold me, as well, but Lachlan helped me escape."

Two pairs of blue eyes turned back to Lachlan, who was still standing next to his horse.

"That was the assistance you mentioned," Janet said. "But why?"

"He does not agree with what the new laird is doing."

"The new laird?"

"Rory Maclean," Jamie said.

"I did not know he had returned," Lady Jane said.

"I understand he just arrived. He assumed the position of laird, taking it from Lachlan."

Confusion cleared from Lady Jane's eyes, but her expression was less friendly. "I understand," she said.

She did not. She thought what Jamie and Lachlan wanted everyone to think, that he was betraying his clan, his own family. That he probably hoped to curry favor with the king and be placed in his brother's position."

Jamie did not know if he would have the courage to do the same. Physical courage was something he could understand. He had no fear of dying. He did have fear of what others thought and believed of him.

"That could mean war," Janet whispered. "And Felicia will be in the middle of it." She hesitated. "You could not bring her out with you?"

"Nay," he said, beginning to feel a little of what Lachlan felt. "But now I can bargain for her. I can convince my father to pay the ransom."

"You do not think he would?"

"The Macleans are asking for a small fortune. It would have been far more if I had not escaped."

Some of the glow in Janet's eyes had faded. He knew he sounded less than heroic. And he wanted to be heroic for her. He did not want to see doubt in her eyes. Yet they had all agreed the secret could not go farther than it already had. Success depended on everyone playing certain roles.

He knew now it would be more difficult than he thought.

"We have to go on. I just wanted to assure you about Felicia."

But she was not assured, and he realized it. Her friend was being held in a keep ruled by a man who had been away for many years. Jamie himself had known little about Rory Maclean. Yet oddly he trusted him.

Odd, indeed.

Kernels of doubt crept into his mind.

He had given his word, and he would see it through unless he discovered he was being used. God help the Macleans then.

The two of them ate a quick meal, then got back on their horses. Edinburgh was several days off, even riding hard.

ℛORY held Felicia, wondering what angel or what devil had placed her in his arms.

Felicia had made him forget, temporarily, the scene that had haunted him since he was a young man. It would never be completely gone, but now he thought he could accept it.

He could make changes that might well end a feud that had meant so much misery for so many unintended victims.

He had slept on and off during the night. Each time he woke, he thought it was a miracle she was sleeping so easily in his arms. He wished it could last forever.

He pushed away the warnings. It could not. He knew that. But he could and would protect her.

What if there was a child?

That terrified him. He had lost a wife in childbirth. There were means to prevent a child, but he had not expected his weakness last night. He should have, but he had not.

Still, he had heard that women rarely conceived on their first time.

Please God, let that be true with this woman.

He could not take the chance again. She needed an opportunity to make a life without him.

She moved slightly, then opened her eyes. The first rays of a rising sun streamed into the room.

She gave him a shy smile that wriggled into his heart. She usually was not shy. Challenging, certainly. Shy, nay.

She squirmed against him, and he felt his body start to react again.

He was not going to let it happen again. Reluctantly he moved away from her and stood. He could not, however, take his gaze from her.

Her hair was tousled, and her eyes were sleepy, but there was no mistaking the desire in them. And the wonder lingering from hours ago.

He leaned down and brushed her cheek with a kiss, and she stretched like a cat. God save him, but she was lovely. And seductive. He suspected she had no idea exactly how seductive she was.

He had to dress and go below before anyone discovered what had happened. He had enough problems without having his clan suspect of his motives.

Rory pulled on the linen shirt he'd discarded last night and then wrapped the plaid around him, finally belting it. He did it all without looking at her. He knew if he did, he would probably pull her back into his arms.

He took the steps toward the door. Once there, he looked back at her. Her eyes were huge, and yet there was no anger or sorrow in her face. Only resignation. She knew, as he did, the hopelessness of any liaison.

"I will take care of you," he said.

"I will take care of myself," she said in a haughty voice, and yet there was a vulnerable tone of defiance. "You owe me nothing."

"I owe you more than you will ever know," he said. The words had come pouring out before he could stop them. He had said too much, revealed too much, but he couldn't take them back now.

She stared at him from the bed. Every curve of her body was outlined under the cover. He remembered exactly how she had felt snuggled in the curves of his body. He would never, ever forget the trust it implied, the way his body reacted to hers. And hers to his.

Nor the way his heart skipped when he looked at her.

He opened the door and left.

$\mathcal{J}$AMIE rode like the furies were behind him. Lachlan kept pace.

Neither had voiced what Jamie thought was on both of their minds. The sooner this was over, the sooner they could reclaim their reputations.

They stopped only to rest their horses, and when they did, they did it in silence. Despite their common goal, trust was fragile thing between them.

Late in the second day they reached Edinburgh. They separated. Lachlan could not risk being seized by the crown or the Campbell in retaliation.

He had changed clothes, and Jamie noticed how well he fit into his new role of minstrel. He had a fine voice and a true ear for the lute.

Lachlan would disappear into Edinburgh. Jamie had suggested a tavern where he should stay. It was an establishment that Jamie could also visit without questions being asked.

As an adviser and confidant of the king, Jamie's father was staying at Edinburgh Castle, and Jamie would lodge there.

Jamie watched Lachlan take one road, then he took the other. He would lie to his father, and to his king. His stomach clenched. He was not at all sure he could do what was demanded of him. He had always been in awe of his father. He had never consciously lied to him.

Would the lie be reflected in his face?

He started up the steep road to the castle.

FELICIA found a dress that she could put on herself. Robina, she thought, had probably been pressed into service elsewhere, now that there were so many Macleans flooding into the keep. In any case, she could do this for herself.

She combed her hair, a much easier task now it was so short, then she opened the door. She was surprised to find there was no longer a guard.

She went next door. Alina was sitting up, Baron lying

down next to her. The dog barked, and Alina gave her a shy smile. All the fever was gone, and a pair of crutches were next to her bed.

Felicia pulled down the sheet covering her and looked at the wound. It was still ugly, but there were no red streaks.

"I think you are going to be just fine," she said.

Alina's smile broadened. "Moira said that, too."

"I see you have crutches."

"Aye. Lord Lachlan made them for me."

Felicia should have been surprised. Lachlan was said to have betrayed his clan. And yet he had found the time to design and make crutches for a child.

The puzzle deepened.

Lachlan cared about Alina. He cared about Inverleith. Though he tried to affect detachment, Felicia had always believed it came from a deep sadness that she had never totally understood.

And now someone wanted her to believe he was a traitor. She simply didn't believe it.

But neither had she believed Rory Maclean could just walk away after last night. For a moment, she had wanted to throw something at him after he'd said he would take care of her.

As if she was a thing. Not a person who thought and cared and loved. But as a debt.

She was not a debt. She had done what she'd wanted to do. She had made a conscious decision to seduce him. She had wanted a taste of a world she thought she might never have again.

"Will you tell me the end of your story?" Alina asked, jerking her from her disturbing musings.

The story! She had no ending for it. She had thought then there would be a prince on a white horse. Her prince, however, had apparently put a price on her and then walked off.

"Perhaps tonight," she said.

She knew she would be alone.

She knew he would not be back.

Yet she could not blame him. He had never promised anything. He had, in fact, been fighting himself. That much had been obvious. She had invited everything.

So why was her heart breaking?

JAMIE's father was in a towering rage.

"I will make them pay. By God, I will make them pay," Angus Campbell roared. "And you, lad, how could you leave her?"

"Would you rather pay ransom for both of us?"

His father glared at him. "Walking into a trap. Damn it lad, I thought I taught you better." Then he turned his ire on Felicia. "And how was she taken? Why did the chit not wait for my escort as she was told?"

"I imagine because she was not enthralled with your choice of a husband," Jamie retorted. "Is that why you sent me to London? You knew I would disapprove."

"It does not matter whether you approved or disapproved," his father said. "You do not make the decisions for this family. Or for Scotland."

"I do not ken your meaning."

"The match was not my making. It was the king's. He will be in rare fury." Then a sly smile crept over his face. "Mayhap it means the end of the Macleans. He will not like his will challenged."

"Then he will not like what I have to say," Jamie said.

His father narrowed his eyes. "What do you have to say?"

"James wants an alliance between the Campbells and Morneith to strengthen the clans against King Henry," Jamie started cautiously.

"Aye, we have information that Henry plans an invasion."

"Possibly with Morneith's assistance."

His father stared at him. "If this is to help your cousin . . ."

"Nay. I heard the information in London," Jamie lied. "Morneith has been promised land and title to turn on King James."

"I cannot believe it. His family has been a supporter of the Scottish crown since the Bruce."

Jamie shrugged. "Mayhap he feels his fortunes rest more with the English than his own king."

"What proof do you have?"

"Demned little," Jamie said. "But I have names of men he has contacted. I have terms I was told he wanted."

"You would not be telling me this to stop the wedding."

"Risk treason? Nay. I would not. I was riding back from London to tell you of what I heard, when I discovered Felicia was missing. And why."

For a second, his father averted his glance, then he went on attack. Jamie had known he would. Angus Campbell always did when he was in the wrong. He blustered. "If you have no proof, there is nothing but your word. And the word of a stripling next to Morneith's has little value."

Resentment filled Jamie at the description of him as a stripling. He struggled to control his temper. "And if it were true?"

"If it were true, I would hang the man myself," Angus said.

"Do you wish to know?"

Angus bristled. "I am loyal to King James. If there is someone who intends to betray him . . ."

His voice faded away as if he were still unsure what to believe.

"You know his reputation," Jamie said.

"I know he is a libertine, but I have never heard anyone question his loyalty," his father said. "Who told you this calumny?"

"A friend of Buckingham's at the English court. He despised Morneith," he lied. "He wants war no more than we do."

"It is to English benefit to turn Scot against Scot."

"Aye, I understand that. But the Macdonald's lands were mentioned, and Maclean's, as the reward."

His father's eyes gleamed at the mention of Macleans, but the glow soon died. If the tale was true, the only way Morneith would get the land would be the defeat of King James, and that would mean the defeat of Campbells as well. Still, Jamie realized that Rory Maclean had been right. His father would have never believed any words that came from the Macleans.

"It could be a scheme of the Macleans to divide us," he said.

"Aye, I considered that. I still do."

"How did you escape?"

"The youngest Maclean. He was not pleased about his brother's return or Rory Maclean holding Felicia as a hostage. I promised him protection."

"You had no right to make such a promise. It is not binding on me."

"Aye it is. It is the word of a Campbell."

His father ignored that. "I will go to James about the rumor."

"Nay," Jamie said.

His father looked startled.

"Morneith would simply deny it," Jamie said.

"Then what . . ."

"I will tell Morneith privately that I know of the agreement, that I heard it from one of the participants. I will tell him of the sum agreed upon as well as the lands he would be granted."

"If you are right, he will kill you." A hint of worry crept into his father's voice. Or was it skepticism?

"Not if I tell him one other person knows. I will ask for a sum of money not to tell you or the king. I will arrange to meet him someplace where a king's man can overhear."

"Morneith is not a stupid man," his father said.

"Nay, but he could not risk not knowing exactly how much a danger I am. His head is at stake."

"I do not like it," his father said.

"Do you have a better suggestion?"

"I can confront him."

"Then he will have time to get word to his English friends and find a way to bury all evidence of his bargain."

His father looked at him with a new awareness. Or wariness. "Does this have anything to do with your cousin?" he asked again.

"The betrothal makes me all the more determined to reveal the man as a traitor," Jamie admitted, "but it does not change the danger he presents to King James."

His father stared at him for a long time as if searching beneath the words. He was obviously weighing his own alternatives.

"How was she when you left her at Inverleith?"

There it was again, the small accusation. "She said she was being treated well. She looked well." He did not mention her shorn locks.

"And you? Did they hurt you?"

"A few bruises and cuts. A wet, cold cell."

His father's jaw clenched. "I will send soldiers tomorrow to fetch your cousin."

"Inverleith cannot be breached."

"Then I will starve them out. The king will assist me."

"You will be starving your niece as well," Jamie persisted. "Let us wait until we know about Morneith's motives."

"Their abduction of a Campbell is a challenge," his father said. "Our honor is at stake."

"You could pay the ransom."

His father's face reddened. "Not to Macleans. Have you lost your wits, lad? Do not let your affection for your cousin affect your head. I will send someone to William immediately and instruct him to prepare for a siege."

Jamie had expected the response, though he had hoped to delay any action. He knew, though, that any continued protests would only put his primary mission in danger. Once Morneith was revealed, then he could reveal the Maclean's part and perhaps bridge a century of fighting.

He merely nodded. Rory Maclean had expected the reaction and it would take time to mount a siege.

His father sat down heavily and stretched his right leg in front. It was painfully swollen, a condition that always made him irritable. "How are you going to approach Morneith?"

"He is here in Edinburgh?"

"Nay. He is with the king on a hunting trip," Angus Campbell said grumpily.

"I will try to speed his return, then."

"I wish to see his reaction with my own eyes."

"He would not say anything in front of you."

"Do ye consider me a fool?" Angus asked. "Of course not. But I know of a room with a spyhole."

Elation filled Jamie. He had won at least one battle. His father believed him or, at the very least, was listening.

Now if he could only bluff Morneith into an admission. Then he would have to somehow find a way to bring Felicia safely home and, finally, restore that glow in Janet's eyes.

Chapter 23

ᗪᗷ

ᖇORY rode out at first dawn with a small troop of men and extra mounts. He intended to bring in those clansmen who remained in the destroyed village, and any others who farmed or herded on Maclean lands and had not yet come into the keep.

Archibald could have accomplished the task as well, but they both thought some clansmen might be reluctant to leave, even with the possibility of an invading army. Rory, as laird, must be obeyed.

Rory also knew he had to leave the keep, and Felicia. Guilt ate at him for bedding her. Yet he doubted he could resist her if he remained at Inverleith. She was like water to a man thirsting to death.

In the course of three days, they had found twenty-eight

clansmen who had been reluctant to leave their crofts. His last stop was at the village destroyed by Campbells. He found Alex and his father and three other men rebuilding. They had already rebuilt two crofts.

"You have to come with us," he said.

"Why?" Alex's father asked.

"The danger has increased," Rory said. "We expect more raiding from the Campbells, perhaps even a siege. We will need every Maclean on the walls."

The man nodded. It was his duty to come when the laird summoned.

"We found a few cattle," Alex said.

We will take them with us," Rory said. "We are bringing them in from other areas as well." He knew livestock represented a better life. The ground was not good for farming.

The Macleans packed what remained after the raid and followed Rory on foot. It would be a day's march.

When they arrived at Inverleith, the area around the keep was thick with livestock. Rory worried about how long the land could continue to feed them.

The gates opened for them, and they passed another group of horsemen leaving the keep. He knew that Archibald had continued patrolling all the passes and roads to Inverleith, as well as the coast. Too many Scots had been surprised by raids from the sea. He wished for a moment that he was at Duart, across the Sound of Mull on the Isle of Mull. The sea protected the island from raids, and it was virtually unassailable.

But that was another branch of Macleans.

He rode to the stables, wearily stepped down from the horse, and gave the reins to a stable lad. He took a moment to look in on the new foal. She was nuzzling her mother, obviously in search of food. New life. New beginnings.

"Has Lady . . . Felicia been here?" He knew everyone should know her true identity by now.

"Every morn' and eve," the lad said. "Fer a Campbell, she ain't so bad," the lad added, then looked appalled that he would speak so.

"Does everyone else believe that as well?"

"Aye, milord."

"Do they think we should give her up?"

"Nay. We would be seen as weak then. And she is a real lady, she is." Pride was in the lad's voice.

Rory hoped it was the community feeling as well. There had been a woeful lack of pride when he had returned.

Rory meant to restore it to them, one way or another, even as he intended to protect Felicia. If Lachlan and James Campbell failed, or if Campbell betrayed them, he still had the means to spirit her away to safety. He left the stable and went to the armory where Douglas bent over the books.

He looked up as Rory stepped inside.

"'Tis good to have you back. Some villagers brought more cattle."

"How many are there?"

"We have over five hundred people inside. Of them, two hundred have borne arms. They are training the villagers. We have enough food for a prolonged siege, and our wells should be able to supply enough water, though we will have to ration."

"We will not ration," Rory said. "I will challenge Campbell to a personal fight first."

"You have not trained in years."

"It is true I have grown rusty. A sailor fights the sea, not usually men. But I plan to start today. First I need some rest."

Douglas nodded. "You look as if you haven't slept in days."

"I haven't."

"Should I keep them at watch?"

"It will take at least a month for the Campbells to call in their men and arm them for a siege. But they can send raiding parties our way. I do not want our cattle to disappear. I want every man in training. I want to know who are slackers and who are not."

"Aye," Douglas said, then changed the subject. "The lass has been helping in the kitchen as well as with the wounded."

Rory did not have to ask what lass. He ignored the remark. "I will be back about mid-afternoon."

"I will have our best fighters available." Douglas eyed Rory. "You look able. I remember you used to be very good."

"Ten years ago," Rory said wryly.

"It is something you do not forget."

"I pray not." With those words, Rory went up to his chamber. He was far too exhausted to have more than a yearning to see Felicia. It would grow, he knew, but now all he wanted was a bed and a meal that was not oatmeal. He took off his sweat-stained plaid and shirt and lay naked on the bed. The exhaustion was a blessing. It blocked thinking. Feeling. Wanting.

At least he hoped to hell it would.

Edinburgh

Jamie paid a visit to Morneith's home in Edinburgh. He discovered the man would not return for eight days.

Eight days was a lifetime. His father had already sent word to William at Dunstaffnage to prepare for a siege of Inverleith.

He left a letter and asked that it be sent to Morneith. Perhaps it would speed his return, or at least make the man worry.

He had thought about the words long and hard.

My dear Morneith. I have news of my cousin Felicia

Campbell as well as greetings from the Duke of Buckingham in London. I think we may have many common interests and would like to discuss them with you.

After leaving the note for Morneith, he decided to look for Lachlan.

Lachlan interested him. He appeared to have no ambition to be laird, nor did he seem to have any deep convictions at all. He was obviously well read, but he treated almost everything as mildly amusing, including his current role as traitor. Jamie realized now it was all a facade to keep any more intimate questions from surfacing.

It did not comfort him, though, to depend on a man who was a mystery.

Jamie found Lachlan in the tavern he'd suggested.

Lachlan was strumming a lute, but no one paid attention to him, nor to Jamie. Jamie made his way over to the table and sat across from him.

"You play well," he said as if he had never heard him before.

"A coin or two would not be remiss," Lachlan replied.

Jamie took one from a purse he carried and tossed it to him.

Lachlan returned to his lute. He had a fine, deep voice, but no one in the tavern seemed interested. When he finished his song, he asked in a low voice. "Have you talked to your father? Or to the Earl of Morneith?"

"My father, aye. He is doubtful but willing to be proven wrong. As for the earl, he is on a hunting trip with the king. He may not be back for eight days. But I sent a message. I thought it best to let him worry."

Lachlan strummed the lute. "Bad luck, that. I will be staying next door. I rented a room. 'Tis the second one above the butcher shop. You can find me either there or here. The owner here has employed me. I get food and whatever coins are given me."

"With what name?"

"Campbell seems to be a popular one in Edinburgh," Lachlan said with a slightly amused twist of his lips. It was not quite a smile but more a cynical observation.

"With good reason," Jamie said.

Lachlan shrugged even as he lowered his voice. "Your father? What does he plan to do?"

"March on Inverleith. But you already knew he would."

"Rory expected it. I'd hoped you had more influence."

"I am but a stripling in my father's eyes."

A customer lurched over and put a coin in front of Lachlan. "More," he said.

Lachlan started strumming again as Jamie left the tavern, chafing against the delays and hoping his missive to Morneith would end the waiting.

"*T*HE laird has returned," Moira said, a new excitement in her voice.

Felicia had noted a hum of anticipation in the keep. Perhaps it was all the people streaming in.

Everyone had a task. The women who had come for protection had found the conditions not to their liking and had taken it upon themselves to clean the many fireplaces, sweep the floors, and clean the great hall.

Felicia helped as well. She'd never been still. She could not be now. So the hours she did not spend with Alina, she assisted in the kitchen. An early awkwardness faded when she brushed aside protests and carried bowls of stew to families.

He was safe. Thank God for that. Would he seek her out? Her body warmed at the thought of seeing him, at memories of the last time.

She kept hoping he would stop and see her. Or Alina. Her heart pounded faster whenever she heard footsteps or voices. But none belonged to him. She heard gossip, however. First from Moira, then Robina. He had gone immediately to his room. He planned to train with several clansmen later.

Fear ran like a rain-swollen stream through her. She knew single combat was often used to settle disputes. Could he possibly be thinking of challenging a Campbell? Jamie would be the logical one to fight for the Campbells.

She finished serving the loaves of bread and bowls of stew for the midday meal.

No sign of the lord.

She returned to her chamber, then went to Alina's. Alina's mother would be down in the kitchen. Baron greeted her by jumping up against her gown and barking a welcome. She leaned down and picked him up, rubbed his ears, and listened to the dog's small groans of pleasure.

"Do you have an end to my story?" Alina asked.

Felicia did not. She wanted a prince who would fight for her heroine, but she had not yet found him. And Alina was smart enough not to accept a lesser being.

Why could she not be as smart?

She was certainly attracted to Rory Maclean. She would not admit any deeper emotion to herself. But he was certainly not her prince. He did not want her. Not enough to test the feud that had stretched between their families. So why did he remain in her every thought? Why did she look for him in every face she saw and in every figure that prowled the halls of Inverleith?

He was going to train this afternoon. Jamie had always said she was good with the sword. She had not his strength, but she had an agility that helped her nearly defeat him more than once.

"Nay, love," she answered Alina's question. "I do not have an end, yet. They are telling their own story in their own time. But I think you might help them if you could but go to the window at night and think about them."

Alina's face froze. "I canna walk."

"Ah but I see a pair of crutches."

Alina's face clouded.

"Lachlan made them."

"Does that make a difference?"

"Mither said he is a traitor."

"I do not believe that," she said.

"I dinna, either, but mither—"

"I think Lachlan is an honorable man, and he made those crutches just for you." *More honorable than his brother.*

Alina looked torn between belief and doubt.

"Things are not always as they seem," Felicia said. *Could that be true now with Lachlan? And why was she the only one to question his desertion?* "You know now that I am a Campbell. Does that change the way you feel about me?"

"Oh no, milady."

"Then should you not hear from Lachlan before judging him?"

Alina considered that and nodded, her eyes clearing.

"Now will you try your crutches?"

As an answer, Alina reached out for the crutches and stood, balancing herself slowly. Her face paled with the strain, but she held on and took several hops to the window. She rested against the edge and looked out.

Felicia joined her. Her gaze went to the men training below.

She directed Alina's attention toward the sea visible from their room. It looked so inviting to her. She understood Rory's fascination with it. The sea called to her as well.

Alina shivered. "It looks cold," she said.

"Ah, but think of all the places it takes you," Felicia said.

"Where would you go?" Alina said. "If you could go anyplace?"

"I think to India."

"I want to stay here," Alina said seriously.

"Why?"

"My mither and brother. And da."

"That is a very good reason."

"They came to see me today."

"They did?"

"Aye. The new laird brought them in," Alina said happily. "Da is guarding the walls," she added proudly.

Alina's father was a farmer and herder. He should not be guarding walls. But pride reflected in Alina's face. The pride of the Macleans.

Felicia had noted that the sentries had been doubled. "You must be very proud of him," Felicia said.

Alina nodded. "I am," she said. "And Alex . . . and John." She flushed.

"John?"

He came here a few days ago after I did. He confronted the Campbells when they tried to take our cattle." Adoration was in her voice.

How had that escaped her? But then she had been preoccupied lately. "Has he been to see you?"

"Aye," Alina said shyly. Felicia smiled inwardly. She had been besotted with her cousin when she was a child, but then he had become more like a brother. As she had grown older, a deep friendship had replaced any romantic notion.

"What will you do, milady, if your uncle comes?" Alina suddenly asked.

"I have little choice in the matter," she replied.

"If you did? Would you leave us?"

If she had a choice?

She did not. She had discovered that in the past few weeks. Her uncle had given her no choice. Rory had given her no choice. Even Jamie, whom she had trusted, had given her no choice.

"Would you like to learn to read?" she asked, trying to turn the conversation elsewhere.

"Oh, aye, milady. I have always wanted to learn, but the priest says there is no need to teach girls." She gazed up, her eyes lighting. "Ye know how?"

"My cousin made sure I learned."

"Is he—"

"He is the Campbell your laird captured."

Alina frowned as if uncertain how to respond to that.

Felicia understood. The Campbells had raided her village and killed several people. Felicia's cousin was the son of Angus Campbell. Alina had been able to exclude her from the taint of Campbell blood, probably because she was aware that women had few choices, but she wasn't sure that should cover Felicia's cousin as well.

"He was not among those who raided your village," Felicia said.

Alina nodded reluctantly. "Ye really will try to teach me to read?"

"We can start right now," Felicia said, eager to have her mind turned to something, and someone, other than the laird.

"How?"

"Right now you should learn letters. I will say them all, and you say them after me. Then I shall show you how they look."

Alina rose from the window seat and used the crutches to return to her bed. She sat on the side, her face tipped to one side, her expression full of anticipation.

"First, there is *A*," Felicia started.

"*A*," echoed Alina.

"Then *B* and *C*."

An hour later, Alina had memorized the first half of the letters. She was quick and eager.

"I will try to find something to write on, and a quill," Felicia said.

The only person she knew might have the materials was

Douglas. She knew from the kitchen gossip that he was spending most of his time in the armory now.

She left Alina repeating the letters and walked quickly down the steps to the armory. As she expected, Douglas was there. As she had not expected, so was Rory.

She stopped in mid-step. She had known he was back, of course, but she had not expected him here. Now she knew that she should have.

"My lord," she said with a slight curtsy, even as she tried to keep her face straight and her tone impersonal.

He looked magnificent. He was wearing a plaid and white linen shirt and soft leather boots. He also wore chain mail and held a helmet in his hand. A shield lay nearby.

He was every inch a warrior.

"My lady," he acknowledged. "I hope you are well."

"As well as a prisoner can be," she said, bitterly hurt by the coolness of his voice.

"You are our guest."

"I think not," she retorted, making an effort to keep her tone as indifferent as his. But her gaze could not leave his.

His eyes darkened, but his facial expression did not change. Then she saw a throbbing of a muscle in his throat. He was not as indifferent as he wanted her to believe.

She forced herself to turn away from him and look at Douglas instead. "I am teaching Alina to read and write. I need paper and a quill and ink."

Douglas glanced at Rory, who nodded.

"Aye, my lady," Douglas said. "I will send them to your chamber later. For now, I am due to work with the laird."

A devil danced in her head. "My thanks," she said and turned and left.

She went up to her room. She would show him that she could take care of herself, that she was not just a woman to be used, then abandoned.

She still had the lad's clothes she meant to use to escape. Would Rory remember them? She doubted it. They looked much like the clothes worn by many clansmen, though they were perhaps a bit richer. But then clothes were often handed down to be given by the church. She would try, anyway.

She put the trews on, then the brogans under her dress. The material was long enough to cover them as long as she did not move too quickly. She would have to glide, at least long enough to reach the armory. She stuffed the shirt inside the trews. Several petticoats covered the bulge.

She closed her door and tried to glide down the hall. She nodded at several servants as she passed them, then kept her head down as she passed the great hall.

Hopefully, there would be no one in the armory. If there was, she would have to give up the prospect of challenge. A moment she badly needed.

The armory was empty. She looked around the room. It was filled with helmets and shields, swords, and even mail. Some looked very old.

She closed the door and in minutes transformed herself from a lass into a youthful soldier. Though she was slight in stature, she was not all that different from a young lad. The mail gave her more bulk, and the helmet covered most of her face.

She looked among the swords and found one that balanced nicely in her hands. Though the broad sword looked thick and clumsy, it was remarkably maneuverable, even for someone of her size and weight.

Felicia left the armory and went out to the training area. She watched as Rory battled Douglas.

Douglas was older, but she knew immediately he was skilled. She studied Rory's movements, just as she had once studied Jamie when he trained.

She had almost bested Jamie only because he had not expected a contest. Rory would not expect a contest either.

Pride drove her now. She was not a possession to be used. She would not sit in a room waiting for men to make decisions for her.

She was only one of a number of clansmen waiting to train. Some held their shields and swords awkwardly. Others plunged against their opponent with more enthusiasm than skill.

Most were watching the duel between their laird and Douglas. Parry and thrust. Plunge forward against a shield, then move backward to avoid a counter blow. Find a weak spot. A moment of carelessness. A vulnerable body part unprotected.

She knew all the tricks. Jamie had been a good teacher.

Douglas found one of those spots, and thrust his sword toward Rory's shoulder. He spun, but Douglas suddenly changed tactics and hit Rory's knees, just below the shield. Rory went down.

In training, it was a defeat.

Rory stood and, as was common, invited another challenger.

She stepped forward.

A man laughed behind her.

Rory Maclean did not laugh. She could not see his eyes behind the helmet and knew hers were just as difficult to read. Before he could think, or consider who might be standing in front of him, she struck.

Surprised, he barely had time to lift his shield to counter the blow. But then he stepped backward, taking her off guard, and his sword went against a shield she barely had time to raise.

He advanced, and she was already off balance, but she took a step backward, moving just in time to avoid another blow.

Through the corner of her eye, she saw a crowd watching.

She was not going to lose.

She knew she had one advantage. He had been fighting Douglas. He was far more tired than she.

But then she had not practiced of late, either.

A sudden stroke almost took her to her knees. But she was able to turn and strike at his knees, which Douglas had hit earlier. She was so much shorter than him that it was easy.

But he wasn't going to go down again. She heard the grunt of pain, but he remained standing.

Then he struck hard against the shield. She felt the jolt through every muscle. Yet she realized it was not as hard as it could have been. If it had been, she would have gone down. He would not hold back in training.

He knew . . . he'd recognized her.

How?

She struck back with all her strength, hearing the clang of her sword against his shield. It echoed through her being, the power of the thrust placing her at a disadvantage. Her sudden desperation had caused her to make a mistake.

But instead of a blow, he stepped back and kneeled in a sign of respect.

She stood there.

Shouts rang throughout the courtyard. They were for a young lad who had taken on the laird and nearly defeated him.

But she had not!

She had not wanted to be indulged. She wanted to fight a battle. Anger churned inside her. Holding her dignity intact, she turned and went inside the tower, even as she heard the sound of questions: who was the lad?

But Rory Maclean knew. And instead of fighting her, he humiliated her by not doing his best, by holding back, by pretending.

As he had pretended from the beginning.

She went straight to her room, taking the armor, the mail, and sword with her. By all the saints, she would not mind plunging it into some sensitive part of Rory Maclean.

Chapter 24

ORY had recognized Felicia almost immediately
when she presented herself on the field. He had
been amused at first, and then his amusement faded as he
discovered she was very good, and he had to work hard not
to be defeated by a slip of a lass.

He was tired. Douglas, though aging, was a superb tac-
tician. And though Rory had the advantage of strength, he
knew he could not use it against her. She was quick, and
wily, and competent. She knew exactly where to land
blows. And he had to withhold some of his power. He had
not wanted to injure her.

How in the devil had she learned to fight with a sword?

His salute at the end did the opposite of what he intended. He had meant to honor her, but she obviously took

it as an insult. He saw it in her stiff shoulders as she marched away to the keep.

He tried not to listen to the speculation. Everyone was wondering who the young lad was. No one had recognized her but himself. And that was because he knew her better than anyone.

He knew those blue eyes, and the particular grace with which she moved. He also now knew the determination. She had meant to best him. And she almost had.

Another side of the intriguing Felicia Campbell. She continued to startle him. She sang with the voice of an angel. She had joined in serving food from the kitchen when no one required it. She had healing skills as well.

And now a warrior.

He took off his helmet and ran his fingers through the sweat-drenched hair. He needed to wash, then he would visit Felicia.

Not wise.

She was obviously angry with him, and he understood why. He had bedded her, then left with little more than a careless lover's worthless words. He had offered to take care of her, realizing too late that it was exactly the wrong thing to say.

Now he knew how wrong. She took pride in taking care of herself. He had treated her little better than a paid woman. He had not meant it. He had, instead, been too involved in accusing himself of being all kinds of a knave to consider her feelings. He had wanted to assure her he would help her. In truth he had already put a second plan into action in the event that Jamie and Lachlan failed. Trapping Morneith had always been risky, and Rory had no idea how good a conspirator James Campbell was.

But he'd used all the wrong words. And he had left hurriedly because he feared committing even more sins. But in trying to avoid more pain, he'd obviously committed the greatest hurt of all.

God's eyes but he was a fool.

He ignored questions as he strode toward the keep and took the steps two at a time. Once in his room, he took off the plaid and washed. He changed to a clean linen shirt, trews, and a leather jerkin.

He took a deep breath, wondering how this had happened. How a mere lass could turn him inside out? How she could make him question everything he said and did?

He trod down the stairs. She was not in her chamber. He went to the one next to hers and opened it. Alina looked up at him.

"I am looking for Lady Felicia."

"She was here earlier," Alina said. "She is teaching me letters."

The depth of his disappointment struck him. So did alarm. Where would she have gone?

He returned to her chamber. She had been here. A helmet was on a chair, as was the mail. The lad's clothing was in a pile at the end of the bed.

It looked a forlorn pile.

A lump in his throat made breathing difficult. He closed his eyes as he suddenly realized how she must have felt these last days. He thought he was being noble. Instead he had been cowardly. He had taken her, and left her. He had fought her, yet not given her the respect of being honest in the contest.

The room felt of desolation.

He was the reason.

He cared—no, he more than cared—about her. And he had hurt her, just as he had hurt every woman who had ever cared about him. Now he had to find her. He had to find some way of making amends.

And then what?

The curse still followed his family. His own personal devils made him a solitary, haunted man.

Leave her be.

His mind told him that. His heart had a different instruction.

He had to find her.

He went down to the stable and to the stall holding mother and foal. No sign of a young lass with short hair. The stable lad said she had not been there.

"Inform me if she does," he said curtly.

The lad look startled, then touched his forehead. "Aye, milord."

The kitchen!

He strode quickly to the kitchen. It was filled with newcomers. Moira looked up from huge pot several helpers were placing in the great fireplace.

"Milord?"

"Is Lady Felicia here?"

"Nay, I have no' seen her since she helped with the midday meal." Her brows knitted together. "She could be with Alina."

"She probably is," Rory said, not wishing to raise an alarm until he knew more. There was no way for her to leave Inverleith. The gates had been closed most of the day except for a small stream of men who went to guard the cattle outside.

Except . . .

He had left orders that every person entering or leaving be identified by another one.

He was learning exactly how devious and inventive she could be. He left the kitchen and strode to the gates. They were closed. The sentries seemed alert.

"Has anyone left here in the past hour?" he asked.

"Nay," said one. "We have not open the gates."

"You know my orders. No one is to leave unless he is identified by others."

"Aye," one said, then another.

He turned away. She had not left then. Where would she have gone?

She was not in the great hall. He started up to the stairs. Knowing something about Felicia now, he suspected she had explored the tower in the first few days. She would probably know all its many rooms.

He inspected all the rooms on her floor, coming at last to the nursery.

He hesitated outside. He had not been in it since Maggie's death. The two of them had often visited the room and talked of their coming child. The pain was still in him, the lingering sorrow for what had been lost. But the sharp edge of agony had faded.

He opened the door and was, oddly, not surprised when he saw her sitting next to the cradle.

She looked up at him. Dusk had fallen, and the room was full of shadows.

"How did you know where to find me?"

"I looked everywhere else," he admitted.

"You thought I had escaped."

He kneeled, his face level with hers. "I had hoped you would not wish to."

"Why would I not?"

Her eyes were in the shadows, and her gaze darted away from him, as if she did not want him to see what was in them.

"Why here?" he asked.

"I explored the keep the first night I was here. I knew this room was . . . no longer used."

"It is not. We have not had bairns here in a long time."

"That is sad." If it had been a mere comment on the obvious, he could have accepted it. But there was a longing and regret in her voice that reached out to him.

"Aye." He knew the emotion he'd tried to keep at bay was in the crack of his voice.

Their gazes met, and the anger in hers faded in the empathy he felt reaching out to him. She knew sadness, and regret. He realized he had never asked her how she had come to be the ward of Angus Campbell. He had, in fact, asked little. He had not wanted to know. To know was to care. And he was too afraid to care.

He had taken much.

He'd given nothing.

Yet something in her reached out to him, just as it had to Moira and Alina and others.

He stretched out a hand, taking her slender one in his. She tried to withdraw it, but he tightened his grasp.

"You are a good warrior," he said.

"You allowed me to win," she accused.

"I was tired."

"You knew who I was."

He knew lying would not help him now. "Aye, I did. I have come to know you."

She glared at him, and his heart contracted. She looked so fierce and yet moments earlier so vulnerable.

"But you certainly tested me," he added.

"You did not try."

"I tried to protect myself. You are a dangerous opponent."

Her gaze turned suspicious. "I do not need humoring."

"I do not think I would dare," he said.

Her eyes narrowed dangerously. He thought for a moment she might hit him.

Instead she stood with great dignity, this time successfully pulling her hand from his. "I have need of better company."

He stood as well.

He meant to leave, but as in so many other occasions with her, he could not quite remove himself. Her blue eyes were shimmering, glazing with just a hint of tears.

"I want to go back to Dunstaffnage," she said.

"And to the marriage?"

"It is better than being considered your—"

He stopped the words with his mouth. She tried to move away, but his arms caught her.

His lips caressed hers. She resisted but only for a fraction of a moment, and then her lips yielded, opened to his. Still, he felt a certain resistance.

He released her and stepped back. "You could still go to France," he said. "I have a ship. I know a family that would look after you."

"They would blame you," she said. "They would believe you—"

"Did what my ancestor did?" he asked. "There would be no proof," he finally said. Then he shrugged. "There could be something else, but . . ." He stopped before he blurted out a plan that, in all likelihood, would not even work.

Tears glazed her eyes, but she blinked them back.

He felt he was walking on white hot coals without boots. "God's eyes but I want you," he said.

"Do you?" she whispered. "You did not say that a few nights ago. I felt . . . bought."

He turned away, unable to bear the pain in her eyes. "I did not intend that," he finally said. "I wanted only to help you do what you had intended to do before we so abruptly interfered."

"And if I do not want that any longer?"

He turned back to her. "I am a Maclean. You are a Campbell. We cannot change that."

"Not that, perhaps, but that does not mean there could not be peace."

"You are still pledged to another," he said. "And your father would never permit a marriage with a Maclean. In truth, I cannot blame him, considering what happened years ago."

"That was a hundred years ago."

"That is nothing in the Highlands. We like our feuds," he said bitterly.

"But if we can leave—"

"I cannot leave Inverleith again, especially not with you. Your father would destroy the clan. I cannot do that.

Even if that were not true," he interrupted her, "I have vowed never to wed again."

"You do not believe the curse?"

He shrugged. "I married twice and buried both wives and one child. I will not see you follow the same path."

He heard her withdrawn breath. "Is that why you left me?"

"Aye." He looked at the cradle beside her. "The cradle was for my child. A son, as it turned out. But he died at birth and also killed my wife." Just moments earlier, he had thought he had accepted the pain. Now, hearing his own harsh, broken words, he knew he had not.

"I do not believe the curse," she said. "Women die in childbirth."

"Aye, but every woman who has married into the clan has died within a year or two. Curse or not, I cannot bear another loss. I will not."

"What if I am willing to take the risk? Do I have no say?"

His eyes met hers. He touched her face. "You are bonny and gallant, and God knows I want you." He tried to control the jolt that ran through him as he realized how much. "But I will not risk your life."

She seemed to weigh his words, then turned abruptly and went to the window.

He felt a sudden chill in the room as if spirits of the lost mothers and children lingered here.

Was that why he'd never returned after Maggie died?

Why had Felicia been drawn here of all places? Did she feel the chill as well? Did it touch Campbells?

The shadows had deepened as they talked. He looked for a candle and found none, but then there would be no way of lighting it. This floor was rarely used, and they did not keep the sconces in the hall lit. Before long, it would be pitch black.

"We should go, lass."

"Felicia," she said. "My name is Felicia. Felicia Campbell." The anger was back in her voice.

"We should go, Felicia," he corrected himself.

"You go," she said. "I wish to stay here. Unless you wish to keep me prisoner again." Her voice was stubborn, determined.

Rory did not know what to do. He had tried to explain, but his explanation had obviously failed. He wanted to touch her, but that he knew would be fatal.

By the saints, he wanted to taste her kiss again. He wanted to feel her passion. He wanted to plunge himself into her warmth. He wanted to wake up next to her and watch her sleep. He wanted to hold her and never let go.

"Felicia," he tried again. She turned then, and in the gloom, he saw tears glistening against her cheeks. It was the first time he had seen her cry. She wiped them away impatiently with her hand.

He wanted to kiss them away.

He held out his hand, and she took it. They were like lodestones, meant to come together. It had been obvious since they first met.

But even as they stood next to each other, Rory knew a chasm lay between them, one he did not know how to cross. "I meant no insult the other night," he said. "I want you safe. I want you to be happy. I can offer you neither safety nor happiness, nor even life."

"I know," she said, and there was resignation in her voice, even as her hand held tightly to his. "I did not before, but I do now."

Rory closed his eyes against the pain that radiated between them. They were both prisoners of hatred, and history, and duty. And there was no way of ever bridging them.

JAMIE waited to hear from Morneith.

He received a response the third day he was in

Edinburgh. Morneith had evidently interrupted his hunting trip. An encouraging sign.

He read the reply. *"I would be honored to meet the son of my very good friend and the brother of my future wife."* Jamie almost gagged at the sentence.

It suggested a meeting in Morneith's Edinburgh home tomorrow.

That did not suit Jamie at all.

He refused, citing previous engagements. He suggested meeting at supper in his father's rooms at Edinburgh Castle instead. He added that his father was ill, and they would not be disturbed.

He waited another day for a reply. Despite Morneith's warm words, he obviously was in no hurry.

That worried Jamie. So did the time being consumed.

He decided to take the next step. He needed help. Janet's father, Dugald Cameron, was in Edinburgh, and he invited the Cameron chief to supper. The Cameron readily accepted, anxious to hear every detail of Felicia's abduction and Jamie's own capture and imprisonment.

"I would not have suspected them to abduct a woman," he mused. "Since that first Lachlan Maclean tried to murder his wife, the Macleans have sought to recover their reputation."

"They believed her to be Janet," Jamie said. "She was under Cameron escort. I was told that the captain of the guard made the decision without telling Rory Maclean. They were hoping for a marriage between the two."

"Over my body," the Cameron said. "I would not allow a daughter of mine to wed a Maclean. I am not a superstitious man, but there have been far too many deaths."

"What do you know of them?" Jamie asked, interested in Cameron's opinion.

"I knew Patrick. He was a born warrior. No one could best him in a fight. And when there was not enough around here, he went to France to fight against Spain. With his father's approval. The old laird had numerous French contacts and relationships. He wanted to strengthen them. He always believed that Scotland's one hope was a firm alliance with France, and much of Maclean wealth was in trading with the French."

"What happened to him?"

"No one knows. He just disappeared. Most believe him dead. If he had been taken prisoner, there would be demands for a ransom. Some word."

"And Rory Maclean?"

The Cameron shrugged. "I know little about him. I saw him years ago, before he went to sea. I attended his wedding to Margaret McDonald, and I liked the lass. I hoped the curse had been broken," he said, glancing quickly at Jamie. "I was saddened to hear of her death a year later. I haven't seen Rory Maclean since. I know little about him, except his father said he was a good seaman and trader." Then his eyes sharpened. "You would not have left her there had you thought she would be harmed."

He was the first one to have reached that conclusion. Not Janet. Not his own father. Gratitude flooded him. "Nay, I would not."

"I have been caught in the middle," Cameron said slowly. "Rory's father was a friend, but after a Maclean raid on the Campbells, your father made it clear I had to make a choice. I could not be an ally to both, and we could not afford to alienate the Campbells." He sighed heavily. "I have not seen the Macleans since. I hear only gossip."

Cameron's gaze went back to his. "What did *you* think of the new laird?"

Jamie knew he had to be cautious. Despite his words, Cameron might well have more loyalty to his father than to his future son-in-law. Jamie knew his father was feared, especially by his neighbors.

"Do you know Morneith well?" he asked, ignoring the question about Rory Maclean.

The man's mouth thinned. "Aye. He is ambitious."

"You knew about the betrothal between the earl and my cousin."

"I heard. I could scarcely believe it. Felicia is no' a beauty but she could marry much better." Cameron's gaze found his. "I would not be surprised if she had run to the Macleans herself. With my daughter's help."

Jamie did not say anything.

"I know my daughter," Cameron said. "She is shy and even timid at times, but she would do anything for someone she cared about." He paused, then asked, "Would you?"

So he was not so sure after all about his future son-in-law's motives.

"Aye," Jamie replied. "I hope so."

"Then if you need assistance, come to me."

They finished the meal in silence, Jamie mulling over what had been said, the offer of assistance. He knew the Cameron chief and had always liked him, but the man usually faded away beside Angus Campbell. Now he wondered if he had underestimated him.

Jamie left and started for the tavern where Lachlan stayed. He had not gone far when unease crawled up his spine. He looked around. The road was nearly empty of both people and conveyances. He was sure, though, that some noise or movement awakened his senses.

He could not go to Lachlan's tavern now. Not if there was the slightest chance that he was being followed.

He turned down another street and walked briskly to another tavern and went inside. It was not crowded. He took a chair against a wall, where he could watch the door, and ordered a tankard of ale.

When it came, he took a sip and almost spat it out. It was the worst he had tasted.

Two men entered, their eyes sidling around the room. They were dressed roughly, and one had a scar above his eyes. Both were armed. They sat at a table and ordered ale.

Jamie finished his ale and ordered another, raising his voice slightly to fake drunkenness. He drank it quickly, tossed a coin at the man who owned the establishment, stood, and strode to the door. Once outside, he hurried down the road until he found an alley. He entered it and backed up to the building. The walls were dark with smoke from peat fires, and he wore a dark mantle. Even if someone peered in, they would have difficulty seeing him.

He waited.

In minutes, he heard loud, disgusted voices. "Wher' did 'e go?"

"The earl will 'ave our 'eads."

Jamie wanted to step out and smash their heads together. Instead, he slunk back into the blackness of the building. He had discovered what he wanted to know. He had apparently worried the Earl of Morneith. Whether the two footpads had been ordered to follow him to learn more about him, or whether they had been dispatched to kill him was the question.

The answer was not important enough to alert Morneith that he might not be the foolish, greedy man that Jamie planned to portray. Better to let the man's lackeys make excuses for their own incompetence.

But he had learned that he would have to be very, very cautious in the future.

Chapter 25

❦

Two days after the incident outside the tavern, Jamie dressed in one of the rooms allotted to his father at Edinburgh Castle. Frustrated that he had not received a reply from Morneith, he'd spent a restless night after returning from yet another tavern.

He was sick of spending each evening under the pretense of debauchery. He enjoyed lifting the cups with friends, but he had never liked excess. He'd been cautious about seeing Lachlan too often and had made a habit of going to several taverns.

He had not seen the two men who'd followed him that one night, but he had sensed eyes on him. Someone was obviously interested in his movements, and that someone had employed better spies. Had that person felt the two men had lost Jamie out of carelessness, or because Jamie was more than he appeared to be? He suspected Morneith had waited to meet with him until finding out as much as possible.

As if he had mentally summoned the earl, a servant knocked, entered, and handed Jamie a card.

It was from Morneith.

Jamie bade the man to enter and then allowed him to stand as he finished washing. Jamie looked at himself in the mirror. He had not yet shaved and decided not to, nor did he comb his hair. He wanted to look as if he'd had a long night of drink and perhaps worse.

He poured wine from a pitcher into a goblet that sat on the table. It was an ungodly hour to drink, but good theater. Then he condescended to look at Morneith's man, who did not quite conceal his anger.

The message was verbal.

"The Earl of Morneith would be honored to accept your invitation to sup. He suggested tonight, if that meets with your pleasure," the emissary said. He was unexpectedly well spoken, obviously more than a footman. Was he here to weigh Jamie?

"Tell your lord that I eagerly await his presence," Jamie said wryly. He named a late hour.

The messenger continued to hold his ground. "His lordship wanted to know if your father will be present."

"Nay, he is suffering from gout," Jamie replied.

"I will inform him. Thank you, my lord."

Jamie studied him. The two who'd followed him earlier had the mark of scoundrels about them. This man looked, and sounded, more presentable, and yet there was a feral gleam in his cold, dark eyes, which lingered far too long, and familiarly, on Jamie.

Jamie did not want to be obvious in his own perusal, although his mind was quickly memorizing the man's every feature, the clothes that proclaimed him a rank above servant. He turned his back and poured more wine into his goblet. He drank it in one long drought, then turned back as if he'd just then remembered the man.

"Are you still here?" he said carelessly. "You are dismissed."

Swift and ugly anger filled the man's eyes before he bowed slightly, then turned. His shoulders were rigid with insult.

Jamie smiled to himself. He had taken an intense dislike to the man, something he rarely did, particularly when he had no reason except for physical looks. There was something about his visitor, though, that raised hackles along his neck.

He placed the goblet down. The wine was thick and sweet in his throat. He was surprised to find it inferior to that which was offered him as a prisoner at Inverleith.

Jamie went to the narrow window and looked down over the courtyard. He watched as his visitor mounted a horse. No mere servant. He wished he could have asked the man's name, but that might have been revealing. The man he wanted Morneith to believe he was would not ask a servant's name.

He only hoped that his act was convincing. Morneith had to consider him a blackguard and reckless fool. He doubted whether he could secure an admission from him; if not, Jamie wanted to bait him into attacking him. It was risky. He knew that. And he hadn't told his father that part of his plan. But he wanted this done, and he wanted it done quickly. He wanted to stop the siege against Inverleith and see Felicia free and safe. He wanted to hold Janet in his arms and explain everything to her.

He shaved and combed his hair. He had to learn more about Morneith's "messenger." But that would have to wait. More urgent matters were at hand.

FELICIA walked alongside Alina, ready to steady her if she started to fall. The dog, Baron, had been left in the chamber. Felicia feared that he might trip Alina in his attempts to get as close as possible to his young mistress.

They reached the steps. Felicia suggested Alina wait there until she found someone to carry her down.

Felicia found a burly man in the great hall.

He looked at her curiously. "Ye are the Campbell wench."

She internally winced at the word but tried not to show it outwardly. "Aye."

"Alina is my cousin's lass. He said ye have been good to her."

"She is easy to be good to."

"Aye, she is a sweet lass." He did not say anything more but followed her up the stone steps to where Alina waited. "Want to go for a wee walk, do ye?" he said.

"Lady Felicia is taking me to see her foal."

The man's eyes turned to her again, then he simply nodded and picked Alina up and followed Felicia down the stairs. "I want to stop in the kitchen," Felicia said.

She collected two carrots, gave one to Alina, and the three of them went to the stables. Felicia could not help glancing around to see whether there was any sign of Rory, even though she knew there would not be. Days had passed since the night in the nursery, and she'd had only a few glimpses of him. He had been away most of the time.

Now she understood why. Her anger was gone, lost in the stark pain she had seen in him. He had not lightly dismissed her as she had believed. He truly thought that he was doing what was best for her. Best for his clan. He was mastering his own needs for those of others.

But he did not know what was best for *her.* She would run toward a few moments of happiness, even knowing they might be of short duration. After tasting the sweetness and passion of the moments with him, she did not think she could bear to live without them. It was one thing to live without knowing love. It was another to know and lose it out of cowardice. And live with regret.

She shook the thought from her head as she led the way to the stall where the mother and offspring were stabled. The Maclean clansman held Alina so she could see the foal inside. The baby was eagerly sucking her breakfast.

"Ohhhhhh," Alina said. "She is verrà bonny."

"Aye, she is." Felicia held out the carrot to the mother, who accepted it daintily, then started munching.

But Alina's eyes were drawn to the foal, which was still endearingly awkward with its long spindly legs. The foal stopped suckling and regarded the three of them with eyes that seemed too large for her head.

Alina held out her hand, and the foal took a cautious step forward, then another, until Alina could touch its velvet skin. The baby nuzzled her, pushing against the small hand.

Alina laughed. It was the first time Felicia had heard the sound. She wished with all her heart that she could tell Alina that she could ride the foal one day. She wanted to keep the family here and teach Alina to read and write, to ride. To laugh. To dance to the pipes.

She ached with the need.

She had always loved children, but she'd never felt this fierce maternal instinct before.

Alina is not mine. She has a mother and father and brother. And even perhaps a young lad to marry someday.

She closed her eyes for a moment. Wanting was such a fierce thing. And she wanted so much. Rory. A child. No, children. She wanted to excite Alina's natural curiosity and then nurture it in her own children.

Fiercely and with incredible pain, she realized that to stay would put Alina in harm's way again. Alina and her family, and other families like them. Felicia really had no more choice than Rory. She knew that, and realized now what he had been trying to tell her. You cannot buy happiness with someone else's pain.

She felt something soft nudge against her hand. She opened her eyes and looked down. The foal was nuzzling her now, as if she sensed Felicia's distress.

She stepped back out of the way and ran into something hard. She whirled around, anticipation and joy belying that resolve.

But it wasn't Rory. Her heart plunged as she recognized the helmet, the chain mail.

Douglas. The man who, with Archibald, had plotted to take her and bring her here.

She wondered how long he had been there.

"Milady," he acknowledged. He looked uncomfortable.

She waited for him to continue.

"The laird said you might like to go riding. I can accompany you."

"Where is he?"

"Patrolling, my lady." It was obvious he planned to say no more.

She hesitated. The sun was bright, the sky a rare blue. The temperature was warm for autumn in the Highlands. She would need no cloak. She was sorely tempted. But instead she asked a question. "You did not find Lachlan or my cousin?"

"Nay. They are gone. We heard that they reached the Cameron keep and left for Edinburgh."

"How do you know?" Relief flooded her, but uncertainty remained as well. She still could not imagine Lachlan being a traitor to the clan.

"One of our clansmen is married to a Cameron. He just returned."

She puzzled over the news. Why would Lachlan go to Edinburgh? And Jamie? Had he gone to his father? Would he help in raising an army against Inverleith? Against Rory?

The thought was another sharp thrust inside. She still could not believe he had abandoned her, even if he realized she was in little danger from the Macleans.

"I can take Alina back," the burly clansman next to her said.

"I do not know your name," she said.

"Brian, milady."

She turned to Alina. "I will see you later."

"Can I stay here longer?"

"As long as you and Brian like," she said.

She followed Douglas down to where the mare was already being saddled. She darted a quick glance toward him.

"Lord Rory said you would want to go," he said.

He assisted her into the saddle, then easily swung onto his own mount.

The gate opened as they neared it, and he rode in silence. His face under the helmet was nearly invisible. She did not know what he was thinking, but she did sense he was not happy with his orders.

Even while she enjoyed being outside Inverleith and on a horse, she felt something was wrong. They rode for nearly an hour, then he turned down a path, the path that Rory had taken her once. It led to a rise, then to the sea.

As they reached the crest of the hill, she saw a ship anchored just off shore. A long boat was pulled up on the beach, and several men sat nearby.

She halted her mare and looked at her companion.

"It is Rory's *Lady,*" he said. "He sent for it some days ago."

That was around the time Lachlan and Jamie left. "Why?"

"It sails for France," he said. "Rory said you wished to go there. I have a message for someone you can trust in France, as well as sufficient gold for you to take up residence."

"What if I do not wish to go?"

"He told me about Lord Morneith," he said. "He said you'd hope to go to France before Archibald—" He stopped abruptly, his mouth pursing into a grimace. " 'Tis my fault it all happened.' I should not have encouraged Archibald with his lunatic idea."

"Rory said nothing to me about this," she said, her heart dropping to her feet. She thought again about their conversation in the nursery, the sadness in him. Had he been saying good-bye?

Douglas was silent.

"If I just disappear . . ."

Again silence.

"He could not let anyone know, or someone would come for me," she said. "My uncle will believe the Macleans killed me, just as his ancestor tried to kill another Campbell. He will go after Rory, just as our family killed the Maclean who tried to kill his Campbell wife. Rory and the clan."

"I am beginning to learn something of our laird," Douglas said. "He has something in mind. He would not allow the clan to be hurt."

Perhaps not the clan but himself?

She continued to turn thoughts over in her mind, to find a thread to follow.

Jamie. Lachlan. Another scene flashed in her mind. Rory fighting in the courtyard. It was the first time she had seen him train. She knew from others that he had eschewed fighting some time in the past and had turned sailor and merchant. She also knew sieges often ended with personal combat between two champions, with little consequence for the people of the losing side other than a new laird.

He would never allow his clan to suffer for a decision he had made. *A decision to help her.* Did he fear he might lose and she would be sent to Morneith? Was that why he wanted her aboard a ship?

She closed her eyes. She could bear the latter, but not the former.

Neither could she risk even the possibility of the clan being destroyed because she did not wish to marry the man chosen for her. She thought of Alina. Moira. Robina.

Would the clan blame Rory for letting her go?

She could not let him fight her battles. "I will not go."

"Then I was told to put you aboard."

"I will find a way to return."

He was silent for a long time, then he sighed deeply. "Archibald was right about one thing. You are a good match for my lord."

"Even though I am a Campbell?" she said.

He smiled for the first time since she had met him. "There are always exceptions." But then his face sobered. "Come, my lady, I must get you aboard."

She thought about turning the horse and running, but his gelding looked far swifter than her mare. And once they went down to the beach, there would be more men waiting.

There was but one way.

He started to turn toward the path down to the beach. She suddenly kicked the mare and pulled tightly upward against the reins. The mare, unused to such treatment, reared, and Felicia kicked her feet loose from the stirrups and slid from the horse.

In a second, Douglas had dismounted and knelt by her side. "My lady, are you all right?"

She moved slightly, then moaned as if agony had just struck her.

She heard him mutter what sounded like a curse.

She knew he could not risk moving her, not without help. He went to the crest of the hill that sloped down toward the shore. His back was turned to her, and then he started down, apparently to seek help.

His horse was closer to her than to him.

Do not turn!

She moved quickly, mounting his horse, then leaned down and grabbed her mare's reins as well. He turned then, but it was too late. She dug her heels into his mount's side and, leading the mare, she rode away, ignoring his shouts.

He would have miles to walk to get back to Inverleith.

She would have a fine head start.

She was not sure where she would go. She only knew she had to reach her uncle and convince him that the abduction had been purely her doing. She would tell her uncle there was no blame to be found with the Macleans and that she would marry as he wished.

It was, she thought numbly, the only way to save Rory Maclean and his clan.

Still, her heart was broken, and she thought it could never heal. She realized that her prison had turned into a home, and her jailers into family. She would probably never return, never see them again.

But he had been ready to risk everything for her, even his life, and she could do no less for him.

JAMIE had seen Morneith before, but he had been a young man intent more on the pleasures of the court than sizing up its courtiers. He had never had a conversation with him, and all he knew came from rumors.

Rumors could be unreliable.

He prepared carefully for supper. He found a source outside the castle where he obtained a good wine. A small keg, in truth. He talked to the cook inside the castle and gave her a gold piece to provide special delicacies.

And then he talked to his father about who should use the small spyhole.

It had to be someone trusted by King James. A member of the Campbell family would be suspect. It came down to his future father-in-law who offered to help. Though he was allied with the Campbell clan, Dugald Cameron was well known for his independence and loyalty to the crown. He had fought with James when he invaded Northumberland years earlier in behalf of Perkin Warbeck, pretender to the English throne.

To Jamie's surprise, his father agreed to talk to Dugald. The Cameron had been outraged by the prospect of a traitor at court, and also by the fact that his future son-in-law had been followed and possibly was in jeopardy.

Once all was set, Jamie waited. The spyhole was in the anteroom of the space allotted for his father when he was at court. Only a few other confidants to the king rated such privileges.

The king himself had shown the spyhole to Angus Campbell. The castle was a hotbed of intrigue, and it behooved one to know his enemies, he'd said, hinting that there were others elsewhere.

There was a small room behind the one where he awaited Morneith. It was entered from the room next to this one through the wardrobe and was large enough for one person. The hole was nearly invisible. If someone did not know it was there, it would be almost impossible to detect.

Dugald was there now, his large body cramped into a small chair.

The appointed time came. And went.

Morneith arrived late, as if he, too, were making a point.

The man who had called on Jamie with Morneith's card was with him. His expression was not cordial.

"I am sorry I was not clear," Jamie said. "The invitation was for the earl only."

"No misunderstanding, young Campbell. Cleve will wait outside."

The man nodded cordially at Jamie, but his eyes were as cold as any Jamie had seen. Without speaking, he stepped outside and closed the door.

Jamie raised an eyebrow.

"I am an important man and as such have enemies. I take precautions. You might consider that as well, young Campbell."

"It is Lord James," Jamie corrected him with a bland smile.

"Lord James, then," he said. "I am honored, and may I add, a little surprised."

"We have friends in common," Jamie said, "but we will

talk of that later. Try this wine. I was told it is excellent." He poured from a pitcher into goblets, and took a sip from his own.

So did Morneith. Appreciation spread across his face. "It *is* excellent. From the king?"

Jamie allowed the earl to think so. It raised his level of influence.

They supped and exchanged pleasantries. Jamie was weighing the earl and knew that, in turn, he was being weighed.

Unlike Jamie's father, Morneith was a lean man in build and had a hungry—and cruel—look about him. He wore a mantle of rich, green velvet, and his belt was adorned with jewels.

"I have just returned from London," Jamie said, leading the conversation where he wanted it to go.

Morneith raised an eyebrow as if to ask why that information might be of importance to him.

"I overheard a conversation about Maclean lands," Jamie continued. "And a sum of twenty-five thousand pounds." He prayed that Rory Maclean's information was factual.

"And why would I have interest in this?" Morneith asked.

"Campbells have an intense interest in what happens to Maclean lands."

"You still have not explained why I should care."

"Because the conversation I overheard was between Woolsey and Buckingham. I do not think it is a conversation that would please King James.

Morneith showed no emotion. He just waited.

"It seems that the English Crown might have some interest in obtaining supporters in the Scottish court."

"I am sure that would be the English hope," Morneith said.

Jamie decided to go to the heart of the matter before

Dugald Cameron became bored. "Your name was mentioned as well, my lord."

Morneith sat up. "That is a calumny."

"Mayhap, though I think not and doubt King James would see it as such. He does not like traitors. I understand he will return in three days from his hunting trip."

"You have no proof."

"I do not think King James will need much more."

"You have concocted this fairy tale to get my lands," Morneith said. " 'Tis no secret the Campbells have coveted them." He laughed. "James will see through your small plot." He started to rise.

"There are others who know as well," Jamie said with a slight smile. "I think they are people the king will trust."

"Not your father, or he would have called off my betrothal to his niece," Morneith blustered.

"You do not see her here," Jamie said with a small shrug.

"I heard she was hostage of the Macleans."

Jamie just smiled.

For the first time, doubt—and fear—entered Morneith's eyes. "What do you want?"

"I have not yet told my father," Jamie said, "but I have urged him to reconsider the betrothal." He took a leisurely sip of wine. "I find myself in need of a loan. A substantial one. Perhaps one-half of the twenty-five thousand pounds you received from the English."

Morneith glanced around the room. It was small, and they were alone. His own man stood guard outside.

"Blackmail, young Campbell?"

"An ugly word. I prefer to call it a partnership between future in-laws.

"And what will keep you from exploiting this partnership in the future?"

"We will be relatives, my lord."

"If you say anything," Morneith said, "I will deny all. I

will have witnesses that you came to me with a plot to join the English, and I refused. After all, you were just at the English court. I have not been there."

"Aye, but you *have* been on the border."

A twitch in Morneith's cheek indicated Jamie had struck a blow. The questions the earl apparently still had were whether Jamie had any other proof and who else knew. And who in London had talked to him? It was information he would have to have to keep his head.

Treason could result in terrible penalties.

So far, Morneith had avoided any direct admission. He could claim he was simply trying to trap Jamie. But then he could have no idea a third person was listening.

Jamie hoped that Cameron could hear everything. But he knew he had to lead Morneith into more damaging information.

"I want the promise of Maclean lands," he said. "I understand other lands were promised to you as well as gold."

Morneith merely nodded. An easy promise to make with no paper involved, and the earl knew there could be no paper. It would damn Jamie as much as himself.

And a promise was easy when one of the parties intended to kill the other. Jamie was quite sure that was what was intended.

"It is a bargain then?" he asked.

"As you said, a partnership. But it will take me several days to get the funds together."

"I await your pleasure," Jamie said.

Looking into Morneith's coal black eyes, he knew pleasure was not what Morneith had in mind, unless it was the pleasure of killing him.

Minutes after Morneith left, Cameron knocked and entered. He did not ask, but poured himself a tankard of wine.

"My God," he said.

"Is it sufficient to go to the king?"

"Nay. It is enough for me, but the king? Or for a conviction of treason? I think not. Morneith was cautious, and as he said, he could always claim he was testing *you*."

"We need money to exchange hands," Jamie said.

"Aye. But I will report what I heard to your father. He may believe differently."

"I will go with you," James said.

Moments later, they were in his father's luxurious furnished room. Cameron spoke first. Then Jamie.

Angus Campbell's face flushed with anger, then darkened. "The blackguard," he said. "But Dugald is right. The king will require more proof. He has set Morneith high and will not want to look the fool for doing so."

"I will arrange another meeting," Jamie said. "Mayhap with someone the king trusts above all men."

Both James and Cameron looked at Angus. He had demurred earlier, because his son was involved and his loyalty might be suspect. But now Cameron was involved, he might feel differently.

"Aye, boy, I will do it."

Chapter 26

⚜

"G OD's eyes, you allowed a lass to outwit you?"

   Douglas winced. He did not do that often. In truth, Rory had never seen him flinch before.

"I did not think—" Douglas snapped his mouth shut. He looked miserable. He had walked miles back to Inverleith and had, no doubt, berated himself all the way back.

"I want every horseman out looking for her. She will head for either Dunstaffnage or the Cameron keep," Rory said, though he had a very bad feeling that they would not find her. She was uncommonly resourceful.

Douglas looked even more miserable as he hurried off to dispatch search parties.

Guilt, an altogether too familiar feeling lately, rushed through him. Felicia's escape was not Douglas's fault. It was his own.

He should have confided in her about the plan to trap Morneith. At least then she would know what she was walking into. Her conversation with Douglas made it clear she felt at fault for the coming siege.

Why had he not told her what they had planned?

It did not matter that her cousin agreed with him. He had learned how reckless she could be, how determined.

But that had not been the only reason. He'd been reluctant to share any part of himself or to trust anyone other than himself. He had lost too much. And that raid years ago had made him feel unworthy. He'd often felt that the death of his child and wives were retribution for his past deeds and not a result of the curse at all. He felt he deserved to be alone. He did not want responsibility for anyone but himself.

Indifference, he'd told himself, was better than pain. Loneliness better than loss. He'd had to trust—at least to some extent—James Campbell and Douglas, because he needed their assistance, but he had readily decided not to tell her. Not only, he realized, because he feared she might do something hasty, but because he had kept his own counsel these past ten years, and it was a habit he found difficult, if not impossible, to break.

He should have told her, given her some hope that she could avoid both marriage and any harm to his clan. He should have trusted her judgment.

In trying to protect her, he had put her in even more peril.

She was willing to sacrifice herself to avoid any harm or blame coming to his clan. He was humbled by it.

And terrified. If Morneith thought himself in peril, particularly from James Campbell, there was no telling what he might do.

He wished he knew what was happening with Campbell and his brother. It had been nearly a fortnight since they had left. He had expected a message, something. He knew, of course, that Lachlan had arrived in Edinburgh and had reached his first mate. Lachlan had sent a note with the ship, saying he and James Campbell had arrived. Then nothing.

He had welcomed the arrival of the ship. It meant he could send Felicia to safety while her cousin convinced her uncle that the marriage was an extremely poor idea, that he might be giving his niece to a traitor. And if anything went wrong, she would be safe. If Inverleith was besieged, he would offer personal combat or give up himself for trial.

He had not thought she would refuse to go. It was yet another condemnation of him. He tried now to imagine where she would go. Dunstaffnage was the most logical destination.

But her uncle was in Edinburgh, as was Morneith, or they had been. Would she possibly head there?

His gut told him she would. He did not know why. He certainly had not foreseen her reaction to a passage to France. Douglas and Archibald would search the ground between Inverleith and Dunstaffnage. He would go to Edinburgh.

He quickly mounted the stairs to his chamber and packed a few articles of clothing in his saddlebags. It would be at least several weeks, perhaps a month or more, before a major attack could be mounted by the Campbells. Raids, yes, but all his clansmen were inside Inverleith.

He would travel to Edinburgh. He had to let James Campbell and Lachlan know what had happened. He could send a messenger, but he wearied of letting others do what he felt he should do himself. He did not like the idea of others risking their lives for his decisions. He hated not knowing what was happening. He felt like a blind man in a maze.

And now he was faced with all bad choices. He was trying to protect Felicia. Felicia was trying to protect him. Lachlan was trying to protect all of them. And James Campbell? Who knew what he was doing, or even on what side he was playing?

They might all end in disaster because of poor choices on his part.

Could he live with the knowledge that he was responsible for even more deaths? More hardships for the clan he had come to help?

He had stopped praying when Anne died.

He started again now.

FELICIA felt numb as she rode away from the place she wanted to be.

The numbness kept despair at bay. She would not allow herself to think of what she was doing, or where she was going.

She only knew she wanted to remain at Inverleith. For the first time since her parents had died, she felt as if she had found a real home. And it was where she had fallen in love.

And now she knew that Rory Maclean loved her as well. He had not wanted it. He had denied it. But he had been willing to risk his life for her. She could do no less.

She knew someone would be coming after her. Mayhap not him, but certainly his men. He would feel responsible. She did not want him to feel responsible. She made her own decisions.

She would simply have to outwit them.

Knowing the gelding was the sturdier mount, she released the mare, then rode hard, stopping only long enough to rest the gelding and decide how to continue.

Taking stock of both her knowledge and belongings, she considered her choices.

Jamie had been captured on the road leading here, but he had been on the road. She knew from hearing talk that Macleans had often slipped over the border without being detected.

She knew all the roads and passes were being watched by Macleans. She had gone through the forests, avoiding the roads. She had come close to sentries but avoided them by going through the woods. Branches cut her arms and brushed the sides of her gelding. But the small cuts seemed not to bother him, and were only a small irritation to her.

Her grief was of far greater matter. It was smothering and made bearable only by the knowledge that she was finally doing the right thing for everyone. Her future meant little compared to Rory's and that of those who had befriended her, even after learning of her deception and her heritage.

She had debated over whether she should go by the Cameron keep, but she feared they might attempt to keep her there. Or that Rory might believe she would go there. Instead, she would go to Edinburgh. She would marry as her uncle wished, and Rory and the Macleans would be safe.

But she had so little to help her on the journey. Everything had happened so suddenly, and she'd seen only an opportunity to escape, to save the people she cared about, both Macleans and Campbells.

She had no coin. She had only the clothes she was wearing and her mount. A stolen one, at that.

Her heart clinched as she thought of Jamie. She could not help but feel betrayed by him. Or had he gone to Dunstaffnage to raise an army to rescue her? Or pay a ransom? Why had he said nothing to her? Left a message?

What would he do if she went to Dunstaffnage? Would he take vengeance on the clan who had captured him and held her? She did not think so, but then she would never have believed him capable of violating his word, his parole.

She finally decided her best opportunity to end what could be renewed hostilities—and more deaths—between the clans was to reach her uncle. She would go to Edinburgh. She would plead with her uncle not to take any action. She would insist that all the blame for what had happened was hers and agree to the marriage he'd planned for her.

But getting to Edinburgh presented problems. She knew a lady alone on a fine horse would be an invitation to brigands. And she would need food, and warmth at night.

Her assets? Her short hair. Her slender build. Her rich clothes. The stolen horse.

She could barter her garments and horse for a lad's clothes and a less fine mount. She would see that the Macleans were reimbursed. She had a few jewels still at Inverleith.

Settled on a plan now, she started again. Using the position of the sun to guide her, she plunged on into the woods and toward the hills that bordered Maclean land. She wished she could wait until night to pass the sentries, but she knew Rory would not be far behind, and she had no wish to tarry after dark, without fire, in a forest that had wild boars and wolves. She would just have to be careful. Very, very careful.

LACHLAN sat back and watched as Jamie Campbell entered the tavern. As he had on his few appearances, Jamie took a bench backing the wall where he could see all who entered.

The barmaid immediately took a tankard of ale to him and hovered around him suggestively. Lachlan doubted any coin was necessary for a tumble.

Jamie gave her a good-natured grin and a pat on the backside, but then dismissed her and drank from his tankard, his gaze still on the door. Only a flicker in his eyes acknowledged Lachlan.

Lachlan picked up his lute and started singing, but there was no appreciative audience tonight. The few patrons glared at him, instead. He shrugged and went outside. He knew Jamie would follow in several minutes. The last time they'd met they planned a way to detect whether or not Jamie was being followed.

Lachlan went up to his room above the butcher shop. It was small and held little more than a narrow, hard bed and some hooks for his clothes. He looked out the sooty window, and waited.

He watched Jamie finally leave and go down the street. One man who had loitered down the street straightened and started to follow him. Another man joined him.

Lachlan left his room, leaving the lute behind. He was wearing trews and a leather jerkin over a shirt. A dirk was inside his jerkin. He knew how to use it. He was not sure whether he could or not. There would be no need if the two men did not attack the Campbell.

Yet he did not like the looks of the two. Jamie had told him he thought he was being followed and had taken precautions several nights earlier to lose whoever it might be. They had planned then that Lachlan would linger behind to see whether the watchers remained before meeting with him.

Jamie's presence meant he had news. The looks of those following Campbell worried Lachlan. One held something resembling a club.

Jamie walked rapidly, and the two men increased their pace as well. Two men staggered out in front of Jamie, but Lachlan knew instantly they were not drunk. Jamie was now hemmed in by two men in front and two in back.

Lachlan sidled into the shadows as one of the men who had just materialized looked around.

He heard a curse. Then a scuffle. He took out his dirk and approached. Jamie was encircled, but he had his own dirk out. The Campbell ducked a blow from the club, but the attackers surrounded him.

Lachlan shouted to distract them. The four turned toward him, and Jamie took the opportunity to slice open the arm of one, then turn and kick a second man in the groin, sending him down to the ground in agony. One of the attackers turned back to Jamie, and the man with the club moved toward Lachlan.

He did not hesitate this time. Jamie Campbell's life was at stake, as well as Felicia's.

As his opponent raised the club, Lachlan moved quickly aside and thrust the dirk into the man's chest. He felt it go into bone, and the man jerked, then fell, the dirk still in his chest.

He turned around. The attacker Jamie had kneed was getting up painfully, taking a dirk from a sheath under trousers. Jamie was turned away, trading blows with the third man. He could not see the weapon the man was preparing to throw.

Lachlan threw himself at the man, deflecting the throw. The edge of the dirk caught his arm, and Lachlan was aware he'd been sliced. His arm went numb, but he knew the pain would surface. Blood spewed out. The attacker raised the knife again. Lachlan could not raise his left arm. He said a quick prayer, but then the man dropped the knife and fell, Jamie's dirk stuck in his back.

Jamie knelt beside Lachlan, tore off a piece of his shirt, and tied it above the long, bleeding cut.

"I have to get you to a physician," he said. Then he paused. "My thanks," he said simply.

Lachlan felt light-headed. He tried to stand but could not.

Jamie caught him under his right shoulder. "I am taking you to the castle. There is a physician there."

Pain broke through the shock. Waves of agony ran through Lachlan, and they deepened with every movement. "Your father?"

"You just saved his heir, my friend. I do not think he will turn you away."

Lachlan hesitated. "You . . . had something to tell me?"

"Not now," Jamie said. "Just lean on me."

Lachlan took a step, then another. It was as if lead had been added to his feet. Each foot became heavier and heavier.

Then his legs stopped working altogether, and the world went black.

FELICIA feared she might fall off the horse. She caught herself napping, which was not a good thing. Her mount was a spirited gelding, not a gentle mare, and it had a habit of taking small sidesteps when startled. The last thing she needed was to fall and lose her mount.

She had ridden through the day and part of the night. Once she had heard hoofbeats and moved deeper into the forest, dismounting and holding her hand over the horse's mouth to keep him from neighing. Then dark fell and she feared moving around.

She had meant to be away from the forest before nightfall, but the journey had been far more difficult and slower than she'd thought. The forest turned completely black. Clouds eclipsed the stars and moon, and she had no idea which direction to take. She knew only too well that she might well just go in circles, endangering both of them.

And so she sat on a log, unwilling to lie down or let go of the horse's rein.

It was a fearful few hours. She flinched at every sound, and there were far too many for comfort. The hoot of an owl, the scurrying of a night creature, the frightened neigh of her horse. It seemed every few minutes, there was a new rustling nearby. She imagined all kinds of beasts waiting to devour her and her horse.

She had never been cowardly, but that was when she could face the danger. And now she was haunted by a sense of helplessness and grief for what had been and what would never be again.

As the blackness gradually lightened and turned gray, she ran her hand down her horse's neck, then used the log to mount. She looked to the east where the first glimmers of the sunrise showed her the direction she wanted to take.

Her gown and cloak were damp from last night's fog, and her arms were marked with red welts. A shiver ran through her. It was going to be a very long day after an even longer night.   .

ᴿᴼᴿʸ had ridden through most of the night. He knew the paths, and he used a torch to show the way. He passed several groups of searchers. None had found anything.

He rested the horse and himself at a sentry post near the clan border. He shared the fire with the sentries along with oatmeal and hard bread. Then he started again at first light.

Felicia would have had to rest as well, for her mount's sake as much as her own. He knew her determination now. She would keep going until she dropped, but she would take care of her horse.

He tried to think as she did.

Impossible. No one thought as she did. That provoked an internal smile. He even felt a peculiar twitch in his heart.

It crossed his mind that it was rather frightening that he was starting to think like Felicia. At least he hoped he was.

She was making him daft. She confused him, intrigued him, delighted him. She was imaginative and bold, and the unexpected became the expected with her.

She would have to change clothes. Even Felicia would not risk traveling public roads alone. That meant stopping somewhere. Douglas had told him the ride had caught her by surprise, as intended, and so she'd had no time to prepare. She would have only what she wore, and the horse.

The horse.

She would try to sell the animal, or trade it. He was certain of it. And then what? She would probably try to obtain a lad's clothing. With her short hair, she could certainly pass as one. She already had at least twice before.

That meant stopping in a village or at a croft. There could not be that many between here and the road to Edinburgh.

He wondered how best to use what little time he had. He could watch the road to Edinburgh, or he could stop at nearby crofts. The problem with watching the road was he might have already missed her.

His heart pounded at accelerated speed. If he chose wrongly . . . ?

If he did not know her as well as he thought he did, she could be killed by thieves or footpads. Even worse, she might make Edinburgh and be given to Morneith.

The thought froze his soul.

He decided to leave the road and search for crofts where she might trade for what she needed.

He only prayed that he was right.

Chapter 27

⊗∾

ANGUS Campbell was abed when Jamie returned with Lachlan.

Jamie had carried the Maclean until he reached the castle, then a servant helped him to his rooms. Angus had a large room down the hall, next to the receiving room with the spyhole. Jamie's was several doors down the corridor.

They were all part of a suite of rooms made available to the king's adviser. The rooms were small, though, cold and not very comfortable. Jamie disliked Edinburgh Castle and rarely stayed there.

"Summon the physician," Jamie ordered the servant.

"Aye, my lord."

"Has the king returned?"

"They say on the morrow," the servant said. "A messenger arrived to tell the kitchen to expect the royal party."

Was that why he was attacked?

He had not thought Morneith would dare. The man was obviously more desperate than he'd believed. He had not so much as blinked during their meeting.

Jamie knew he should be dead now. Probably would have been without Lachlan's interference. He could take down three, but the fourth presented a problem. Unfortunately he had but two eyes, and none in the back.

He looked down at the still-unconscious Lachlan. Despite the cloth cutting off the bleeding, blood still seeped from the wound. Maclean had lost altogether too much.

Lachlan Maclean had been a puzzle. But there was no doubt now as to his courage.

He would not die for it. Not if Jamie could prevent it.

He looked at the wound. The knife had split his arm open. Nearly the length would require stitches.

He got some water from a pitcher on the table and used a towel to wipe away some of the blood. He released the cloth he'd tied tightly above the wound, and blood ran heavy. He quickly tightened it again.

Where in the blazes was the surgeon?

As if summoned by Jamie's thoughts, a knock came at the door, and a lean, cadaverous-looking man entered and went directly to the bed where Lachlan lay. He regarded the wound, then shook his head. "I should cut the arm off."

"Nay," Jamie said.

"A wound that extensive will surely become putrefied."

"We will wait."

"It could kill him."

"We will still wait," Jamie said. The least he could do was to give Lachlan the chance to make the decision on his own.

The physician shrugged. "I will have to cauterize it then."

"Do it while he is still unconscious."

The physician took a scalpel from his case and went to the fireplace and placed the knife in the flames.

He returned. "Who is he?"

"A man who has just saved my life," Jamie said shortly.

"I will do what I can, but I can promise nothing."

Jamie nodded, a sick feeling deep in his gut. He had underestimated Morneith, and Lachlan Maclean was paying the price. He vowed to make Morneith pay.

The physician returned to the fire and retrieved the knife, then pressed it down on the open wound. Lachlan's body jerked, though his eyes remained closed. A sweet, sickening smell of burned flesh filled the room.

The physician put an ointment on the burned flesh, then took out a small bottle. "When he wakes give him a drop of this."

"What is it?"

"Cannabis and saffron. The cannabis comes from India. It helps with pain."

Jamie nodded. Of course King James would have the most modern of treatments.

"I will be back in the morning to see him."

"Thank you."

The physician closed his case. "My name is McCarty if you need me again tonight."

Jamie closed the door behind him and sat next to Lachlan. Tomorrow, he would send another note to Morneith. This one would be more harshly worded. If he did not receive a substantial amount of funds, he would go to the king and mention the penalty for attempted murder of a Campbell.

FELICIA found the croft she wanted. It was on Cameron lands but a distance away from the keep. The fields were neat, fat sheep grazed in the fields alongside two milk cows. Industrious people, she thought.

She rode to the front of the croft. It was mid-morning, and she was famished. The smell of food came from inside.

Her stomach growled.

She probably looked like what she was: a fugitive on a stolen horse.

A girl of five years or so poked her head out, and her mouth formed a perfect O. She scurried inside, and then a man appeared. His eyes narrowed as he saw her. His gaze wandered over her rich but torn gown, then her cropped hair. Finally, his gaze went to the horse.

"Milady?" he said, a question in his voice.

"Sir," she said, "my father is very ill in Edinburgh. One of our retainers was accompanying me, and we were beset by brigands. My companion was killed, but I was able to get away."

The farmer listened without comment.

"I could go back home but then I might not get to my father before . . . before . . ." Her voice broke off. "I must go on."

"Someone from the Camerons will aid ye," he said. "I will send one of my lads with ye."

"Nay, I cannot wait. But I cannot travel like this, either." Tears started rolling down her face. They were not that difficult. She had been on the edge of them all night.

"What can we do, milady?"

"A lad's clothes, if you have them. My hair . . . I had a fever and lost most of it. 'Tis a blessing now. No one would look twice at a lad. You can have the horse in return for the clothes and some food."

"Ye do not plan to walk?" Suspicion had turned into sympathy.

"Aye," she said.

"My lad will take you to the next village in our cart," he said. "Ye might find someone going to Edinburgh from there."

"Thank you," she said with heartfelt gratitude.

"We canna take the horse. It is too grand."

"Then keep him until someone comes for him. They will repay you for your kindness."

"We will pray for your fa."

While a strapping young lad hitched the cart to a pony, she quickly changed into what must have been his clothes a few years earlier. She gobbled down a bowl of oatmeal and fresh bread and gratefully took a large hunk of cheese. Her gown was neatly wrapped beside her. The crofter refused to keep it.

Before long, she was bouncing up and down on the cart. The sun was shining. Her stomach was full. Her heart was dark, though. She had succeeded. But the success led to Edinburgh, an angry uncle, and Morneith.

She folded her hands in her lap, forcing herself not to clench them into a fist. Her eyes closed.

ᴸACHLAN woke to agony. When he moved, the fire in his arm spread throughout his body.

"Do not move," a voice told him.

He opened his eyes.

Jamie Campbell loomed above him. He put a cup to his lips.

"Drink," Campbell said.

Lachlan obeyed. His throat was thick and dry. The liquid was bitter. He coughed.

"The physician said it would help with the pain."

"My arm?"

"Badly cut. The physician wanted to remove it. I said that decision belonged to you."

Lachlan nodded. His eyes went to his arm. It had not been wrapped, and it was black and ugly. "Where am I?"

"Edinburgh Castle. In Campbell rooms."

Lachlan tried to grin. He feared it was more a grimace. "Your father?"

"He has not wakened yet, and thus does not know. But he already believes you helped me escape from Inverleith. He will be grateful for last night."

"The attackers?"

"Two were dead. The others badly injured. Morneith will have to find new villains."

"You wanted to see me tonight?"

"Aye. To tell you about the meeting with Morneith. He was careful, but there was no doubt he has taken money from the English. Dugald Cameron listened in through a spyhole, but there is not yet enough to convince the king."

"Then what?"

"I sent a note to Morneith this morning. He knows I know he tried to have me killed. He will be more worried now. And careless, I hope."

Lachlan tried to move, and pain savaged him.

"The physician will return this morning," Jamie said.

"I do not want to lose my arm."

"I will make sure you do not."

Lachlan nodded, then closed his eyes again. A heavy drowsiness was moving through him. He welcomed it.

FRUSTRATION drove Rory. The crofts directly along the way to the Edinburgh road had seen nothing of a young lady on a large bay horse. He finally found the gelding at midday. He recognized the large horse hobbled and grazing alongside a pair of sheep.

The farmer was reticent. 'Twas obvious he had little love of the Macleans and was skeptical of his concern.

"That is a Maclean horse," Rory said.

"How do I know that?" the farmer said stubbornly.

"The lady had short, cropped hair," he said. "She was staying with us."

"She said her fa was sick."

"Aye. We were going to send an escort with her, but she became impatient."

The farmer shrugged. "She said someone would be along to claim the horse and would leave something for the clothes we gave her. And the ride."

"What ride?"

"My son took her to the next village."

"Is he back yet?"

"Nay."

He was not too far behind. He took several coins from the purse hanging from his belt. "Here," he said. "My thanks. I will take the horse and leave this one here. Someone will come for it. There will be more gold."

Then with a fresh horse, he started toward the village.

FELICIA thanked the lad and watched as he turned the cart and started home. She still had no money, but in the village she could barter her locket for a few coins.

It was still a long way to Edinburgh. A very long way.

She went by a bakery and asked if anyone would be going to Edinburgh or a village on the way. She offered the locket for a few coins.

"'Twas my puir mother's," she said, hoping she sounded like a country lad. "Jest buried her, I did, and I am going to Edinburgh fer a job."

But her story did not work this time. She was regarded with suspicion. "Did you steal that?" a woman asked with a frown.

"Nay."

"It looks too fine for the likes of you."

She drew herself up straight. "It is mine."

"Indeed it is," came a voice from behind her.

Her heart lurched. Her legs started to give way.

"Oh, my lord," the woman said, fumbling with her hands.

Felicia started to turn and bumped into him. She took a step back. Rory Maclean looked every inch the lord in his plaid and jeweled leather belt with the crest.

His gaze on her was amused rather than angry. He grasped her arm in a firm hold. "My nephew," he explained. "He keeps running away. His mother died a few months ago, and he misses her."

The woman's face creased in sympathy, all suspicion gone.

"And he will keep the locket," Rory said.

He purchased two meat pies, then steered her out the door. She went obediently enough. At least for the moment.

They reached the horse she had left at the Cameron croft. He mounted, then offered her a hand and helped her swing up behind him. Without another word, he guided the horse out of the village.

RORY was awed by Felicia's creativity. She'd had nothing when she had left Inverleith. Nothing but the horse she had taken. She had made her way through Maclean land, past guards, had managed to obtain food and clothes and a ride.

He silently vowed that he would strengthen the guards along the border.

He felt her arms around him as he walked the horse through the village and out into the wooded countryside. They had tightened more than necessary for balance. The warmth of her body spread through his.

Rory looked for a private place to stop. He left the road and rode up a hill cloaked with heather. He had taken this road before, and he remembered a glen, and waterfall.

Several minutes later, he found it. A waterfall tumbled down a craggy mountain into a pool below.

He stopped, slipped his right leg over the saddle, and dismounted, then he offered his hand to Felicia and caught her as she slid down. He held her for a moment, relishing the feel of her, tightening his embrace in thanks that he had found her unharmed. Thankful that the brigands who roamed the countryside had not found her. He had not realized how much he'd feared for her until this moment. He had not understood how deeply he cared.

She clung to him, her body still, her weariness apparent

in the sag of her body against his. He could almost believe she was relieved that he had found her.

Knowing that he could stand like this forever, he gently disengaged her hold and stepped back. He tied the reins of his horse to a branch and took the sack holding the meat pies from the saddle, along with a cup.

He put the pies down on a rock and studied her. Her eyes looked huge under the lad's cap. Her face was smudged, and her clothes were too large.

She looked beautiful.

He touched her face, his fingers caressing her cheekbone. "You are a woman with altogether too many talents," he said.

"Too many?"

"You are a very good liar," he said. "A wizard at disguise. A competent swordsman. An adept horse thief. All of which worry me."

Her startled gaze met his. Despite his words, even he heard the love in them.

"No honest talents?" she asked with a breathless catch in her voice.

She had an abundance of those as well. She had a huge, courageous heart. She had a way with children.

God's eyes, but she had a way with him. He would have to tell her that . . . soon.

He leaned down and kissed the dusting of freckles on the tip of her nose, then drew back quickly. For now he would have to tell her exactly what he, Lachlan, and her cousin had planned, and he knew she would hate him for it. But he knew now he must. She would keep running away, trying to save him and his people. And the next time she might not encounter people as decent as the crofters.

First he wanted these few moments. He wanted to see himself reflected in eyes that now brightened with trust, and hope.

He shook his head in dismay. How could one slender

woman have wrapped herself so intimately around his heart?

"How did you find me?" she asked.

"I tried to think like you think."

She grinned at that. "It must have worked."

"Aye. It is frightening."

She laughed, a happy bell-like sound. He could not recall her laughing before. He loved the sound of it, even though he knew that in the next few moments she would probably hit him.

He delayed an explanation a few moments longer.

Instead, he offered his hand and led her to the pool. He scooped up crystal clean water for them to drink, then offered her a meat pie.

She scooped up a bite with her fingers and ate. His own hunger was forgotten as he watched her enjoyment. He had never thought eating a particularly sensual activity before, but she made it one. She ate with relish, and little crumbs of pastry sprinkled her lips. He couldn't help himself. He leaned over and tasted them.

His lips played on hers with a slow sensuality as he licked every vestige of crumbs before indulging an appetite of an entirely different nature. Her mouth opened to his, and her hand went up to his neck, coaxing him nearer.

Rory knew he would regret this. Worse, he knew she would regret it, once he told her everything.

It did not matter at the moment. A bright sun bathed them with rare warmth. Birds sang in nearby trees. The laughing sound of the waterfall was a lullaby.

She filled his senses.

He felt the immediate reaction of his body to her, the swirling eddies of desire that overruled every warning. He felt her quickened breath, and his heart raced. His hand loosened the leather ties of the plain woolen doublet she wore. A rough shirt lay underneath, and he undid the ties to reveal her breasts.

His lips nuzzled one, then the other until her nipples hardened and thrust outward. He felt the same hunger in her as that tormented him.

"Felicia." His voice was a groan that echoed throughout his being. It was part protest, part surrender. And all need.

He wanted to touch and be touched. He wanted the reality of her, not another ghost that would haunt him.

His mouth pressed harder, his tongue urging hers to open to him. As she readily acquiesced, he explored and teased. He recognized her urgency as well. It was in the growing pressure of her hands, in the glow of her eyes. His body tensed with desire too long held in check.

He pulled off her doublet with his hands and then the rough trews she wore. Only her shirt remained. He felt himself harden under his plaid, and he undid the belt and unwound the long piece of cloth until he, too, wore only the long flowing linen shirt.

His hands went under her last remaining garment and caressed her body until he felt her tremble.

He hesitated then. He should tell her first. He should confess that he had lied, that he had allowed her to believe her cousin had deserted her. He had allowed her to fear for him.

"No," she protested, her hand pulling him to her with a plea that broke his will.

His lips returned to hers.

$\mathcal{S}$HE felt his hesitation.

His eyes looked tormented, and everything in Felicia melted at the sight. He had never been a man to show emotions. He had guarded them as if his life depended on it.

But then his lips pressed back on hers again, and all was right with the world.

Her blood had felt like warm honey when he first touched her, as his lips had explored and tested. But as they pressed down, and her body fitted into his, it turned to hot lava. She knew what to expect now, the magic of desire and love and satisfaction. She had dreamed about it since that first time. She had dreamed and yearned and felt the heat in her body and worried that she would never know it again.

Her arms went around his neck, her finger catching and fondling a thick lock of slightly curling hair. His mouth pressed harder, his tongue urging hers to open to him. As she complied, his tongue probed, igniting sensations in every sensitive part of her body.

All the loneliness and despair she had felt earlier exploded in raw need. She wanted his soul. She wanted his heart. And she wanted him deep inside until they merged into one. Her hands tightened around his shoulders, urging him closer. His shirt rode up, and so did hers. His body melded against hers, and he entered her slowly, creating an aching, agonizing need. She moved against him with instinctive circular motions, drawing him farther and farther inside. His strokes increased in rhythm and power until the two were riding the crest of an incredible wave, a giant force that swept them along with unthinking madness, drowning them in waves of pleasure.

He gave one last stroke, and she felt rocked by bursting sensations. His warmth flooded her, and she knew a completeness that she had never felt before. He collapsed on her, his breath coming in ragged gasps, as their bodies quivered in exquisite reaction.

They lay next to each other, silent, for several moments. She treasured the quiet intimacy, the shared wonder and quiet profound happiness she felt. "I love you," she said.

It was a difficult admission for her. She'd so seldom felt loved or loveable, and now she was holding out love and fearing it might be rejected.

He turned to her, and her heart thumped, and her blood turned cold. His eyes did not answer as she'd hoped. She'd known a match between them was impossible. She'd known yet . . .

But something in his face frightened her, and when he reached out his hand to her, she refused it.

"Something is wrong," she said. She should have seen it earlier, but she had been so happy to see him. She had run from him but had felt such unexpected joy when she saw him that she had not asked questions.

He sat up, and she did the same. Her eyes did not leave his.

A muscle in his throat jerked. She had seen it before, and she knew it meant something she would not like.

"There is something I must tell you," he said.

She did not answer. Her body was still singing its own song, but her mind was warning her.

"What?" she said in a low voice.

"We wanted to protect you," he said.

She felt a sudden tightness in her heart, and it was not from lovemaking. She knew from his expression she was not going to like what he had to say.

He touched her face. "I should have told you, and you would not have endangered yourself."

Her body tensed. The warm sensations seeped away, leaving only a chill.

She waited.

"Lachlan and your cousin did not escape. It was planned."

She tried to put pieces together. "I do not understand."

"I had heard that the Earl of Morneith was a traitor, that he had sold his loyalty to the English king. We . . ."

"We?"

"Lachlan, James, and myself . . . thought we might be able to trap him into an admission. You would be free."

She stared at him. The words echoed in her head. She had thought Jamie had abandoned her. That Lachlan was not whom she thought he was. That Rory had been betrayed.

She had felt an emptiness that drained her soul.

"Why did you not tell me?" Her voice was impersonal.

"I feared you would do what you just did. Try to help."

"And be foolish enough to ruin everything?" The betrayal she had felt days ago was nothing like the one she felt now. She had been lied to. Repeatedly. She had not been trusted. She had worried about Rory and Jamie meeting in combat. She had . . .

She swung her hand back and hit him with every ounce of strength she had.

Chapter 28

HE blow was stronger that Rory expected. His head snapped back, and his face stung with the power of it.

But just as punishing was the stricken, wounded look on Felicia's face.

"I am sorry, lass. We were trying . . . we wanted to protect you."

"You and Jamie lied to me. You did not trust me."

She wore only the too-large shirt that fell to her knees, yet she looked every bit the warrior. She radiated defiance. Anger. And worst of all, betrayal.

He wanted to take her back into his arms, wanted to feel her body against his once more, but he knew that was the worst thing he could do. He had betrayed her trust, and he knew he would have to work to get it back.

She was not ready for any overtures, though. "You did not trust me," she stated again.

"You would have wanted to help."

"And I am so helpless and foolish that you have to lie to me for fear I would endanger Jamie and your people on a whim?"

"No one is less helpless than you, lass," he replied wryly. "That is the problem. You have too much courage. And it was important that Morneith and Campbell thought you were being held for ransom. That meant Macleans had to believe it as well."

" 'Tis my life, not yours," she said. "I may be given few choices, but I choose for myself what I can."

He was silent. She was right. He should have told her. He had no right to make decisions for her. He was as bad as Angus Campbell.

"I am sorry, lass. I thought . . ."

A tear glimmered in one eye. It seemed to be caught there, glistening, and then it started to roll down her face. It shattered his heart far more than harsh words or a torrent of tears. He lifted a finger to wipe it away, but she stepped back.

She took another step, then spun around and found her discarded clothes. Without comment, she pulled them on.

Sensing it was best to leave her be for the moment, he went to his saddle bags. It was time to change clothes. He did not want to wear the plaid where he was going. Instead he pulled on a pair of fine wool hose and a serviceable leather doublet. He added a flat-brimmed hat with a feather. It was the costume of a merchant, clothes he often wore when visiting foreign cities.

She stood and watched, her face closed, her mouth drawn in a tight line. There were no more tears.

"Come," he said.

"I will not go back to Inverleith."

"We are going to Edinburgh," he said.

"Why?"

"I have to know what is happening with your cousin and Lachlan. They might need help."

Her eyes widened. "You are taking me?"

"I am certainly not sending you back to Inverleith alone," he said with a small smile. "I would have no idea where to find you next."

Her solemn blue eyes searched his. "Would you want to?"

"Aye, lass. I would have you safe."

A curtain dropped over her face. It was not the answer she wanted. It was not the answer he wanted to give. He wanted to tell her he loved her. That he had been terrified for her. That he wanted her beside him always.

God's truth, but he loved her.

He could do none of those things. There was still the bloody curse. The stain that lingered on his soul. And Campbell would never approve a match.

So why had he just damned himself by taking her?

He put a finger under her chin and lifted it up to meet his gaze. "You must do as I tell you," he said. "Do you promise?"

"I will tell you when I cannot," she replied.

It was not a satisfactory answer but he suspected it was as good a one as he was likely to get.

"I am a merchant, and you are my apprentice," he said.

She nodded.

He went over to the horse, untied the reins, and mounted. Then he offered her a hand, and she swung up easily behind him. He felt her hands around his waist. They were not as tight as they had been during the short ride from the village.

Yet after an hour or so, he felt her head rest against his shoulder.

Good. It was a long journey.

* * *

"A Maclean in my rooms?" Angus Campbell stared at his son with displeasure. "The king's physician called to heal my enemy? You must be daft."

"That enemy saved my life," Jamie said calmly. He was accustomed to his father's rages. Unfortunately it was time to tell him more. And that would probably invoke even more anger. He readied himself for a storm of invective.

"Only because you involved yourself with kidnappers and brigands."

"The Macleans did not kidnap Felicia."

Angus glared at him. "You said they did."

"I did not. I said Felicia was at Inverleith. She was there because she was fleeing a marriage *you* arranged. Is not that the reason you had the king send me to London? You knew I would not approve."

"Your approval means nothing to me. She is but a lass. She does what she is told."

"Are we talking about the same Felicia?"

Angus frowned. "Bring me proof about Morneith, and I will undo the marriage contract. But I will have no Macleans under my roof."

"Is it not proof that Morneith tried to have me killed after I accused him of treason?"

"You do not know . . ." Angus tried to bluster, but the flame of anger was in his eyes. "It could have been Macleans. They might have wanted both of you." It was obvious he was still reluctant to believe the Macleans had any redeeming qualities.

"You do not want to see what is in front of you because the Macleans are involved," Jamie said coldly. It was the only time he had ever openly defied his father, and the sudden reddening of his father's face told him the thrust had hit home.

"Be careful, James," his father warned him. "You cannot underestimate the Macleans. They have been killing and raiding Campbells for years."

"As Campbells have raided and killed them. The new laird, Rory Campbell, wants an end to it. He wants peace."

"By kidnapping my niece and imprisoning my son?"

It was time to explain everything. Jamie honestly did not know what his father would do, or say. He might well be disowned for plotting with Macleans.

"The Maclean had nothing to do with kidnapping Felicia. His men took her, thinking she was Janet Cameron, to bring him a bride. He wanted to return her immediately, but Felicia did not wish to go. I understand she feigned an illness."

Angus stared at him in horror. "She preferred the Macleans to Dunstaffnage?"

"To Morneith, aye."

"They took you," Angus blustered.

"I trespassed on their land looking for her. What would you do if you found a Maclean on Campbell land?" His gaze riveted on his father's face. "I did not escape only with the help of Lachlan Maclean. Rory Maclean planned it."

"In God's name, to what end?"

"To reveal Morneith as a traitor. And to protect Felicia. We needed time. If Felicia was held for ransom at Inverleith, Morneith could not claim her." He hesitated because he did not know how his next words would be taken.

He would have to trust that Angus Campbell could stifle his hatred of the Macleans long enough to discover where his own best interest lay.

"I told you I heard news of Morneith's treason in London. I did not. Rory Maclean learned of it in France. It came from French spies in the London court. But the Maclean knew you would not believe him. Nor would he have the access to Morneith that I do."

His father stared at him in disbelief. "You plotted with

the Macleans against one of the king's favorites? You lied to me?"

"How long will he be a favorite if he is proved a traitor?" Jamie asked. "And how grateful would the king be if you revealed the plot? As for the lie, it was necessary. You would not have believed a Maclean. But now you've heard Cameron. You know someone tried to kill me."

He watched his father struggle with decades of hate for Macleans and his loyalty to King James.

His father sat down heavily and leaned on the cane he now used to offset the gout. His eyes were lined with red streaks from lack of sleep because of the pain. Jamie remembered another man, a robust soldier and rider, and he was struck by the change. He had not noticed how stark it was until now.

"You risk your heritage by allying yourself with the Macleans." Angus Campbell still was not quite able to wrap his mind around Jamie's revelations. "And by lying to me. There is always Neil." Neil was his father's nephew, the nearest male relative next to Jamie.

"Aye, you could," Jamie said. "But you taught me to honor courage and loyalty. Lachlan Maclean saved my life twice. He will probably lose his arm. He might lose his life. Rory Maclean has risked the wrath of his king, and yourself, to reveal a traitor."

His father sighed wearily. "I have a debt then."

"Aye, and so do I. To the Macleans and to Felicia. I cannot believe you would sacrifice her to a monster to further your aims. You must have known his last wife died suspiciously."

"The king—"

"You are the closest man to the king. He would have listened to you if you had fought him on this."

"One does not fight with his king. He serves him."

"Do you serve him by letting a traitor remain in his midst?"

The fight seemed to fade from his father's face. Jamie

realized again how old he looked, and ill. Fear struck him. Had that been why his father had approved the marriage? He had been too ill to fight?

Jamie had not seen his father often in the past several years. He had stayed mostly at Dunstaffnage, while his father had taken up residence in Edinburgh, and what few visits Jamie made had been brief. He had been surprised when he had been sent to London to deliver a message of congratulations to King Henry. It had not made sense to him. Now it did. His father had been preparing him to assume a place next to the king in the event he could not. It had not been Felicia at all, though his absence would also have been a convenience.

"You trust the Macleans?" his father finally said, surrendering.

"Aye."

"You believe you can trap Morneith?"

"He is frightened, or he would not have tried to have me killed last night. I think he will be even more frightened—and desperate—to learn his villains failed."

"What do you plan?" his father said wearily.

"Another invitation. A threat."

"From now on you will be guarded by Campbells," his father said.

"The king returns tomorrow. Is there someone you and he trust completely? Someone totally loyal to him. In addition to Cameron? We will need more than one witness, and one unrelated to me."

His father thought for several moments. "A Stewart cousin. He is nonpolitical and has few ambitions. He is hunting with him."

"He will return with King James?"

"He is usually at his side."

"Will you talk to him?"

"Aye. I will want you with me."

Jamie agreed. He wanted to take his own measure of the man. The penalty for treason was too harsh for him to risk failure. "I think it would be best that no one knows that the man in my rooms is a Maclean."

"The men who attacked you?"

"Dead or badly injured."

"Good," his father said. He hesitated, a muscle in his cheek twitching. "I will see this man . . . this Maclean." He struggled to his feet, pain crossing his face with each movement.

Jamie felt a twinge again. It cut into the victory he'd just won. His father had treated him as an equal. It was the first time in his memory.

"I will take you to him."

"No, I wish to see him alone."

Jamie hesitated. He did not think his father would harm a wounded man, particularly one who had just saved his only son. But he also knew how ruthless Angus Campbell could be, and how many times in Scottish history that hospitality laws had been violated, and atrocities committed. Considering the history between the Campbells and Macleans, Jamie truly did not know what to expect of his father.

"I will not harm him," his father said, reading his expression.

"And the other Macleans? You sent word to mount a siege."

"Aye, on your words."

"It was important that everyone believe—"

His father glared at him. "Preparations for the siege will continue until my niece is returned."

Jamie's gut tightened. He had won one battle, but he realized the flimsy structure of their plan could tumble down.

$\mathcal{J}$AMIE supped with the king when he returned the next day. He was one of nearly seventy guests. He was seated near the high table, next to Ian Stewart. His father, he suspected, had something to do with that.

Morneith was present as well. He was seated at the high

table on the left side of the king and queen. Angus Campbell was on the other side.

As he entered the room, Morneith's eyes went to him, widened, and he turned to the queen, who sat next to him, and said something. The queen smiled, but Jamie noted it was more polite than spontaneous.

Queen Margaret was a renowned beauty, and it was said that her marriage was a love match. King James was known for merriment and high living, and his banquets and homecomings were always elaborate affairs. Tonight was no exception. Course after course was brought to the tables, and good wine continually replenished by a host of servants.

Stewart looked at the bruises on Jamie's face and hands and raised an eyebrow.

"Thieves in the street," Jamie said.

"How did they fare?"

"Not well."

"Good."

Jamie asked Ian Stewart about the hunt, then listened as the Stewart recounted tales of the king's bravery in a confrontation with a wild boar. He occasionally glanced up, his eyes meeting Morneith's. Although the earl quickly turned his gaze away, there was no missing the threat in them.

He liked Stewart. The man had no pretensions, and he told jokes on himself. Yet there was also a solemnity about him, and his devotion to King James was obvious.

The meal continued for nearly four hours. As the banquet drew to a close, Jamie asked the Stewart to join him for a glass of wine in his rooms.

"Be delighted," Ian said.

"I have to see someone quickly, then we'll go," Jamie said. He approached Morneith. "Ah, my lord, I am pleased to see you in good health. The evenings are dangerous these days, are they not?"

"I do not find them so," Morneith said coldly.

"The city is plagued with thieves and blackguards. I am surprised you have not yet been attacked. I will have a word with King James about it. My father has arranged a meeting with the high sheriff. You and I might trade tales about such lawlessness before then."

Morneith's mouth thinned. A muscle twitched in his throat. "I would be happy to accommodate the son of Angus Campbell."

"Tomorrow. Perhaps you would honor me by supping with me at the Rose and Spur. As you've probably heard, I was accosted last night by ruffians, and I think a public place would be more suitable than a private one."

"I have another engagement."

"Break it," Jamie said quietly. He added, "I left some papers in my room. You would not like it if anything happened to me."

Morneith looked startled.

"And I would suggest that you show good faith in our new business arrangement. The price for my participation has gone up."

He turned away before Morneith could reply, and met Stewart who looked at him curiously. Then he fell in at Jamie's side, and they walked from the great hall. Jamie saw Morneith's man, Cleve, outside. He stood there, his eyes cold and secretive.

Jamie met his gaze, smiled slightly, then led the way to his chamber.

"That man gives me cold shivers," Ian Stewart said. "I do not care for his master much more."

"Why does the king tolerate him?"

"He controls two large armies. James is convinced the English will invade. He needs him."

"What do you know of him?" Jamie asked.

"Just rumors."

Jamie said little until they reached the anteroom of the Campbell rooms. Lachlan was in the chamber next to this one. His father would probably stay with the king, especially as long as Morneith remained.

Jamie had some of the very good wine he had served Morneith. He poured a full measure in Ian Stewart's goblet, then one for himself.

"My father thinks highly of you," he said.

"I am honored."

"He said you are extremely loyal to the king."

Ian placed the goblet on a table and gave him a piercing stare. "Of course."

In for a pence, in for a pound. "I have reason to believe Morneith has been paid by the English to betray King James."

Ian's hand jerked, knocking the wine over. "That is a dangerous charge."

"But not as dangerous as a traitor in court, or on the field. What if part of an army suddenly turned in the midst of battle?"

Ian paled.

"I am not making charges easily. The information came from France, which has spics in the English court. I wanted to make sure before I said anything. I engaged him in conversation, told him that we had friends in common in the English court, and mentioned Buckingham's name. I also told him I wished the same arrangement he had, as well as some of the gold he'd received. The next night, four men ambushed and tried to kill me."

Stewart's face was grim. "If this is true, I will kill him myself."

"I need your help. Dugald Cameron overheard the conversation. He will testify to it. But it is not enough. The words could be interpreted in different ways. My father also believes it, but the three of us are linked together. I am betrothed to Cameron's daughter. We need a witness who is not connected to us. I heard you have the king's ear."

"I try not to take advantage of it."

"Which is why my father suggested you."

"I will do what I can," Stewart said, "but we must be

careful. There can be no question as to his guilt, or his armies might rise against James."

Jamie outlined his plan.

$\mathcal{F}$ELICIA turned and looked at Rory as they reached Edinburgh.

His face was tired and drawn, and she knew hers was probably the same. It was usually a four-day hard ride from Inverleith to Edinburgh.

They had made it in three by changing horses frequently. Rory had enough coin to purchase a horse for Felicia. They had traded for fresh mounts along the way.

When they stopped for a few hours to sleep, they were both exhausted. The first time they slept apart, but the second time the wind was cold and wet, and she fitted into his arms. He had wrapped them both in the plaid he had brought along, and despite his betrayal she had felt she belonged there.

Yet he said nothing about love. He worried about her. He felt responsible for her. He lusted after her. She had come to believe, though, that he did not, could not, love her because of his past. He had mourned two wives. He'd made it clear he did not want another.

She was angry. Angry and hurt and disappointed. And yet she was still drawn to him. Every time he helped her mount or dismount, she felt that raw longing and burning heat he always ignited in her. She found herself glancing at him far too often.

But now they had reached Edinburgh. Her uncle was here. Lachlan and Jamie were here.

All she could think of, though, was losing the man next to her. Thoughts of how empty her life would be overrode the anger, the resentment.

He turned his face toward hers. "You will not marry Morneith," he pledged.

But even that did not matter now. She knew she could never have Rory, Laird of the Macleans.

Chapter 29

ᐇ

RORY had never been at court, nor did he know many who had. His shipping offices were in Leith, not Edinburgh.

He could not move openly as the Maclean laird. As far as he knew, King James and Angus Campbell thought he held Felicia. He was very aware of the fate of the first Maclean who had harmed a Campbell lass, the one who had chained his wife to a rock. He had been stabbed to death in his bed.

It was growing dark when he found an inn near Edinburgh Castle. He engaged but one room, knowing it would seem odd to request a room for an apprentice. He also did not want to let her out of sight, not out of distrust, but out of worry for her. The fear of her coming to harm during her flight was still too vivid for comfort.

The room was small and dark. A smoky fireplace filled one side of the room, a narrow bed and a table another. He would be sleeping on the floor this night.

"What do we do now?" Felicia asked.

He had to find Lachlan. He had the name of the tavern Lachlan mentioned in the message that was sent through the acting captain of the *Lady*. He hesitated to take Felicia to a tavern, but he hesitated even more to leave her alone. Only God knew what she would do, and perhaps not Him.

"We are going to a tavern," he said.

Her eyes lit. "I have never been to one."

"I would hope not," he said, and she grinned at him, her anticipation at doing the forbidden overcoming her earlier anger.

He tried to scowl at the anticipation in her eyes, but the truth was she only endeared herself to him even more. She had an appetite for life and a curiosity about all things that never ceased to delight him. He thought how much he would love to show her foreign cities. In his mind's eye, he would see the wonder in her face as she saw Paris, India, Gibraltar.

He wondered if she would enjoy the sea as well. He suspected she would love it as he did, and he pictured her aboard his three master, her hair blowing in the wind, and her cheeks rosy from the wind and sheer sensual pleasure of the sea. He never would have entertained that thought about Maggie or Anne.

But Felicia was made for adventure.

It astonished him that he had such thoughts, that he saw her in his future at all, much less at his side in his voyages . . .

The innkeeper gave them directions to the tavern. The night was cold again. A fine mist filled the air. Felicia shivered at his side, and he wrapped an arm around her, pulling her closer. He tried to ignore the reaction of his body. He could not afford distraction. Not now.

At the tavern, he asked the barmaid about a troubadour,

while Felicia waited in the shadows, her gaze darting all around the large common ground.

"I have not seen him in several days," the proprietor said with a shrug.

Rory felt a tightening in his chest. If Lachlan had succeeded, the news of Morneith's treason would be everywhere. Something had happened to him.

He should never have trusted Jamie Campbell. Nor should he have thrust such a mission on Lachlan. He damned himself, and he damned the Campbell.

He nodded to Felicia, and she followed him out the door and into the street. The fine mist was still falling.

"He will be all right," she said.

"God help your cousin if he is not."

She was silent as they returned to the inn. He was bedeviled by possibilities. What had happened?

He could not seek out James Campbell. The Maclean laird would make a fine prize if he had misjudged the Campbell heir, and his clan would pay dearly if he were taken for ransom. Was Lachlan already a prisoner?

"He would not betray you," Felicia said, obviously reading his thoughts.

"You thought he had betrayed *you*," he shot back, once more inexplicably jealous at her defense of the Campbell.

She frowned at him. "*You* tried to make me think that."

He ignored that observation. When they arrived back at the inn, he asked the proprietor for a quill, ink, and paper to pen a missive. He wrote quickly, then asked for wax to seal it.

Now to deliver it.

"Will you promise to stay here?" he asked Felicia.

"Nay. I want to go with you."

She had the cap on, and she looked up at him with those expressive blue eyes and defiant chin. He was not going to win this particular battle. He had, in truth, won few battles with her.

They walked from the inn toward the castle. As he

neared it, he noticed the large numbers of soldiers guarding it. The king must be in residence. He stopped one and asked if he could send a message to one of the guests inside. He offered a pence as payment.

The guard accepted both note and payment and disappeared into the castle.

Rory turned Felicia around and walked away. He could only hope that the message would be delivered. And that he was not walking into a trap. He would watch from a distance and make sure Jamie was alone before joining him at the chapel.

AMIE was with Lachlan when the message arrived. He took it from the messenger and broke the wax. He read it hurriedly. *I am in Edinburgh and must meet you. St. Margaret's Chapel tonight. Your cousin is with me.*

It was a demand and a warning.

What in God's name was Rory Maclean doing here?

He looked up from the parchment and met Lachlan's gaze. "What is it?" Lachlan asked.

"Your brother is here."

"I knew he would grow impatient," Lachlan said. "But I thought we would have more time."

"Felicia is with him."

Lachlan winced.

"He wants me to meet him, and I will have to do it. I am meeting with Morneith tomorrow night. I do not want interference."

"You cannot go out alone. Morneith will be waiting for you."

Jamie swore. "If I do not, your brother might well show up here. He or Felicia. And I cannot take Campbell men with me. If they realized the Maclean was here . . .

He looked at the message again. Blazes take the man. He could ruin everything. And how could he even think of bringing Felicia? His blood ran cold. If Morneith knew . . .

"I must go."

Lachlan struggled to a sitting position. "I will—"

"Nay. I know this castle. I can find a way out."

He left before Lachlan could utter another protest.

He called in a Campbell servant, changed clothes with him, and stepped outside the room. No one in the corridors. He stayed to the shadows, walked down to the servants' area, and waited until several were ready to leave. He joked that he was trying to avoid a certain, persistent lady. They leered at him, obviously enjoying the discomfort of a lord, but they surrounded him and in minutes they reached the courtyard and left through the gates. Once well through the gates, they separated, but not before Jamie gave each a coin. He knew if they were paid, they would be more than agreeable to participate in such a ruse again if needed.

He nodded at the soldiers guarding the gate and continued down the steep road. With the King in residence, the streets were crowded, making it easy to blend in. He did not think he was being followed.

He reached the church and stepped inside. No one was about, so he selected a pew and sat down.

He did not know how long he waited before he was aware of a presence behind him. He leaned back on the bench.

"Where is Lachlan?" came the Maclean's voice at his ear.

He turned and looked around. Rory knelt behind him, his head bent as if in prayer.

"I was attacked by four men," Jamie replied in a low voice. "Morneith, undoubtedly. I had contacted him and suggested that I knew a great deal about his meeting with the English. I was going to tell Lachlan about the meeting but he noticed men following me, and he followed them. When they attacked me, he joined in the fight and was wounded. He is in my rooms at Edinburgh Castle."

Rory absorbed the information, fear for Lachlan settling in his gut. "How is he?"

"He may lose an arm. He has the best of care. One of the king's physicians."

Jamie heard an intake of breath, then a curse. He waited a moment, then asked, "Where is Felicia?"

Rory was silent.

"It is time we trust one another," Jamie said.

"She's safe," Rory said simply.

"Why did you bring her to Edinburgh?"

"She escaped from the castle, stole a horse, and planned to return to your father to prevent any more bloodshed. I found her on the road to Edinburgh. I knew that if I returned her to Inverleith, she would try to escape again, and I have little doubt that she would succeed." He sighed heavily. "I told her everything, and even then I realized she would try to get here, this time to help you.

"Bringing her with me was the only way to keep her from doing something reckless. At least now I can keep an eye on her." He paused. "And I had not heard anything from you."

"Morneith was with the king on a hunting trip," Jamie said. "He just returned. There was nothing to report."

Rory turned around. His gaze traveled around the chapel. "What can I do?"

"Return to Inverleith."

"That I cannot do. I am not good at letting others fight my battles."

"I do not want another Maclean on my conscience."

"How does your father feel about having a Maclean in residence?"

"He is getting used to the idea. Lachlan saved my life. He took a dagger thrust meant for me."

"What can I do?" Rory asked again.

"Have you ever met Morneith?"

"Nay. I have only heard rumors."

"Then be at the Rose and Spur tomorrow night. I am to sup with Morneith and explain he has few choices other than giving me a very substantial amount of money to keep silent. There is a private room upstairs, but it is not as private as most people would believe. It shares a fireplace with another room and often the proprietor declares the fireplaces in need of a chimney sweep. Words are then easily distinguishable between the two rooms. The king's cousin, Ian Stewart, will be in the second room. But another witness or two would be welcome.

Rory raised an eyebrow.

Jamie shrugged. "I hear a little blackmail sometimes flows from that room."

"Could Morneith be aware as well?"

"I doubt it. It's known only to a few people. One of my friends was blackmailed when he bedded someone else's wife there. There is a hefty price on those rooms and part of it is silence. Those victimized can not speak of it, either, since their . . . failings would become known."

Jamie stood. "I would like to see Felicia."

Rory hesitated, then nodded his head toward the back where a young lad sat on the last bench.

Jamie turned his head and looked. He had seen her cropped hair at Inverleith, but he had never seen her look so entirely like a lad.

"I will watch outside," Rory said.

As the Maclean left the chapel, Jamie approached the lad whose head was bent in prayer.

The lad looked up, and Jamie saw those bright blue eyes of the Campbell family.

"Ah, Felicia. I should have known we could not leave you back at Inverleith."

"I will never forgive you," she said, even as her hand reached out and clutched his.

"And the Maclean? Are you as angry at him?"

"He is not my cousin and my friend."

"Is he not the latter?" he asked. "Or something more?"

Her cheeks blushed. "He has no interest in me."

He held her for a moment, then she took a step back. "You have been hurt," she said.

"Morneith set his lackeys on me. Lachlan was following and joined in the battle. I have bruises. He was hurt far worse."

"How badly?" she asked, her face drawing up in worry.

"He will live," he said, wishing not to distress her. He wanted to wait until he knew more about how well the wound would heal.

"I would like to see him."

"He is staying in my father's rooms at the castle. I do not think you want to see him at the moment."

"Soon then. He was very kind to me."

He nodded, and her gaze went back to the bruise on his face.

"It is nothing," he said.

"It does not look like nothing, but now I cannot hit you. Not like I did Rory."

He raised an eyebrow. "You hit the Maclean?"

"Aye, and very well," she admitted with great satisfaction.

Several minutes later, he departed. Before he did, though, he caught glances exchanged between Rory and Felicia.

God help them both.

$\mathcal{I}$T was pure agony sitting across from Rory at the Rose and Spur and feigning indifference.

Indifference was the last thing she felt.

She had tried to seduce him last night after they returned from the chapel. She had needed him after hearing that Jamie and Lachlan had almost been killed on her behalf.

"It was not your doing," Rory tried to comfort her. "They are after a traitor."

"But if not for me . . ."

"If not for you, Scotland could be at peril."

But it had not comforted her. And while she knew he wanted her as badly as she wanted him, he had merely held her through the night. Part of him had withdrawn from her, and it hurt to the core. She wondered whether he could ever tear down that wall he'd constructed around his heart.

Still in the guise of an apprentice, she sipped the bad wine and kept her gaze on his face as he continued to glance toward the door.

Everything depended on whether Morneith was desperate enough to meet her cousin again. She knew about the first meeting. She also realized there had to be more witnesses.

Rory had assured her Jamie would be protected, that there would be others around. Jamie had assured both of them that he would be safe, and she wondered who among the diners might be there on Jamie's behalf.

Rory had not wanted to bring her. She knew that. She knew the only reason he had was that he feared she would find some way to join them anyway. And she would have. She was involved. She, too, could be a witness against Morneith. She had been left out too long.

The establishment was nearly filled with a mixture of young lords and prosperous merchants. Three men came in, talking in loud voices. One was a fine-looking young man with red hair and a red beard. The other two were less distinctive, though their voices were blurred with wine.

"There will be others joining us in our little game," he told the proprietor in a voice loud enough for the room to hear. They were led by the proprietor up the stairs to one of two private rooms Felicia had been told about.

Jamie entered and sat at a bench near the one window.

Minutes went by. Then an hour. She was beginning to think no one would come, when she saw a flicker in Rory's eyes.

She heard Jamie's booming voice. "Morneith, my dear man. How good of you to join me."

A grunt was the only answer.

Felicia was turned partially away from him, but she saw him glance around the room. His eyes rested on her, and she saw something malignant in the glance. His gaze lingered too long on her, and she remembered the dark rumors that had swirled around him.

She shivered as his gaze turned from her and studied the others in the room.

Morneith was a tall man, though not fat. His beard was neatly trimmed, and he was dressed in somber but obviously expensive clothes. His shirt had a fashionable high collar, and he wore a black velvet coat and silk hose. His face was lined, and his nose crooked, but the most startling feature were piercing dark brown eyes. It was the cold calculation in them that made them striking.

"I have engaged a room upstairs," she heard Jamie say. "We will have privacy. Now I hope you have brought what you promised."

"Lower your voice," Morneith said with obvious disgust, but he followed Jamie up the stairs.

Rory waited several moments, then he and Felicia mounted the stairs as well, knocking lightly on the door to the left. It was opened by the redheaded man.

He acknowledged Rory and gave her a searching glance, then turned back to his companions. "The show was in the event someone was watching below," he explained in a whisper.

Then he went over to the fireplace and stooped. Felicia and Rory did the same. Voices were audible. Barely, but audible. She wondered how Jamie had found such a place.

"It is not enough. 'Tis only a fraction of what you received from—" Jamie continued, his speech slurred as if he'd had too much to drink.

"You fool, be quiet. You will have us both in the castle dungeon."

"I want what you promised."

"I cannot bring it here. You will have to go to my residence."

"I prefer public places after the other night."

"I heard about that. I had nothing to do with it."

"A coincidence then," Jamie said in a louder, wine-slurred voice.

She heard the sound of a metal hitting the table. "You sotted young fool," Morneith said. "You spilled wine on me."

"I want you to talk to Buckingham, as well," Jamie said, ignoring him. "He should ha' even more gold for another friendly Scotsman."

"Your father has more gold than any of us."

"Aye, but he is tightfisted and refuses to pay my debts. Says I am unworthy. I will show him by gaining even more land than he has."

"You think Buckingham will offer a drunken . . ." He shut his mouth immediately.

"He promised land to you. He gave you money. My name is far more respected than yours, and more clans will follow the Campbells. When my father dies I will have three times the number of soldiers."

Jamie was arrogant, boasting, throwing his name in Morneith's face. Felicia tensed at the danger he was courting.

"Buckingham would have naught to do with a drunken lout," he said, his fury obvious even through the barrier of the fireplace grates. "He trusts me . . ."

He stopped suddenly. "If you want any more money, you will have to come to my residence," he said in a voice dripping with ice.

"I know Buckingham gave you—"

One of the men in the room with them suddenly dropped a tankard. Just as they had heard the one in the next room, Felicia realized Morneith could hear this one.

Silence. Then she heard Morneith say in a more moderate tone, "You can go with me to my residence now, and get your . . . money for the investment. Either way, I am leaving."

She, Rory, and Ian Stewart exchanged glances. Did Morneith suspect anything? Would he charge into the room? Or would he try to get rid of Jamie quickly? Surely, he would have had men watching the tavern. He was too cautious a man not to.

The door next to them opened and closed. She heard Jamie's complaining voice. "Another glass of wine first?"

"Nay!" Morneith replied. "There is much at my residence."

As soon as Felicia thought the two men had gone down the stairs, she turned to Rory. "We have to go after them."

"There are Campbells in the streets," Ian Stewart said. "They will not allow anything to happen to the son of the Campbell. But now if Jamie does get the money, then there can be no doubt." Fury turned his pleasant voice into a grating whisper.

"Is there any now?" she asked.

"It was Jamie's plan," the red-haired Stewart said. "He wanted no doubt."

She did not like Jamie's plan. He was taking too big a risk. They should have enough proof now.

"I am going after him," she said, opening the door and going down the steps. Rory was right behind her. But as she ran through the public area, she was aware of a commotion behind her. She turned. Rory was on the floor, and a rough-looking man loomed over him, blaming him for a collision.

She could not wait. Urgency filled her. She opened the door. Fear ripped through Felicia. She knew Jamie had just signed his death warrant. Morneith could no longer let a drunken young man wander about making charges, even if he had not heard the tankard fall. If he had . . . he would have to rid himself of the most immediate danger.

She darted out the door.

She reached the street in time to see two men holding Jamie, half carrying him down the street to a cart waiting there. She saw three men who had just left the tavern stumbling in that direction.

Suddenly the darkened street was lit by several torches.

Men surrounded those carrying Jamie. She recognized some of them from Dunstaffnage.

Hands, seemingly out of nowhere, grabbed her. An arm went around her neck, and she felt a dagger prick her throat. "Make a sound, and I will slit it," her captor said.

She recognized Morneith's voice. Everyone's attention was directed toward Jamie and the two men who had taken him. Apparently Morneith had waited in the shadow to see who else might emerge.

One of his hands sought a better grasp on her and found her breast. He cursed, then he dragged her farther into the alley. She knew she could not move, or scream. He had meant what he said.

"You were far too interested in me," he whispered. "Who are you?"

"Felicia!"

She heard Rory's voice, and her captor's arm tightened around her.

"Felicia," he whispered. "An uncommon name." The point of his dagger touched and cut her skin. "You would not be Felicia Campbell."

She started to say something, and the dagger cut deeper. "Do not speak," he said in a whisper. "Nod."

She did not move. She felt blood running down her neck. A burning pain.

More shouts. Sounds of men running.

He pushed her behind a pile of refuse and forced her down, planting his body on top of her. His dark clothes faded into the darkness.

The smell was suffocating, a combination of the garbage and the rich perfume he wore. His weight crushed her, and she felt him becoming aroused.

Light shone down the alley, but she doubted anyone could see them. She could not yell. Not with the knife at her throat. Morneith had committed treason. He would not hesitate to kill her to protect himself.

Her name was called again, but the sound was fainter. The search party was moving away from her.

Morneith rolled off of her, but the dagger point did not leave her neck.

"You *are* Felicia Campbell. My intended wife. How kind of you to come to me." He pulled her to her feet, the dagger still at her throat.

"You are a traitor," she said. "They will find you."

"Ah, but now I have a hostage."

"I am nothing compared to treason. Do you think my life would keep the king from taking you?"

"The king will have to find me first. And I do think young Campbell cares for your life. If I can leave Edinburgh, I have armies . . ."

She could not let that happen. "My cousin cares about his king above all."

"We will see, will we not. Tell me, Felicia," he said. "How did you happen to be dressed as a guttersnipe?"

"To trap you," she said viciously.

"Ah, you like a fight. I enjoy women who fight. I like breaking them. Not as much as a lad, but—you would make it easy to pretend."

She opened her mouth to scream, and his hand clasped over it. He had to move the dagger as he did, and she saw her chance. He was slightly off balance, and too confident. She twisted suddenly and kneed him in the crotch with all her strength. He groaned and let go so suddenly she fell, and she screamed as he did. The dagger fell with her.

She rolled away from him as he tried to straighten.

She saw the dagger at the same time he did, but she was faster. She reached for it just as he lunged for her, a spate of curses tumbling from his mouth. She felt his large body pin her down again.

Feet running. Her name echoed in the alley.

Morneith tried to grab her around the neck, but suddenly his body rolled off her, and she was able to grasp the dagger.

She turned. Rory was on Morneith, his hands beating his face, pummeling his chest.

She screamed again, and more men came running.

Rory stood up. Morneith lay bleeding, a sob coming from his mouth.

Rory turned and looked toward the newcomers.

And then she saw Morneith take a second dagger from inside his coat and start to rise. Rory's back was to him.

"Rory?"

He turned. It would be too late. A dagger was in her hand. She thrust it into Morneith's back.

He turned, looked at her with astonishment, then fell.

And Rory's arms closed around her.

*R*ORY'S heart beat frantically as he held her. Dear Mother in Heaven, but he had come close to losing her.

He had rushed after Felicia but had been delayed when a lout—probably someone with Morneith—tripped him, then started a loud argument, which drew more people. He had finally been able to break free and rush after Felicia.

Several men had rushed to a cart down the street, and he started in that direction, when he'd heard a scuffle and a scream in the ally that ran alongside the tavern. He'd turned and peered into the darkened alley. With eyes trained to see in the dark, he'd seen the two forms against the wall and the dagger at Felicia's throat. He saw the threat, but he could not attack Morneith as long as he had the dagger to Felicia's throat. And then, unbelievably she had managed to unman him, which gave Rory the opportunity he needed . . .

He felt the the blood running down from her neck. He released her and tore off a piece of his shirt and wrapped it gently around the wound, then he held her tight. He never wanted to let her go.

But he knew he had to. She had almost died. Because of

him. Because he had brought her with him. It had not all been, as he had claimed, to keep her safe. Part of it had been his need for her, his desire to have her with him.

And it had almost cost her life.

He released her. "Thank God you are alive," he said. "It is my—"

"Nay," she said.

He was startled at her vehemence. "Nay?"

"You will not blame yourself."

He was silent, not quite sure what she meant.

"It was my decision to come to Edinburgh, to the tavern tonight. It was my decision to go after Jamie. You cannot take responsibility for the entire world. You were not responsible for your wife's death in childbirth, or Anne's illness."

"You cannot—" he started to say, but then they were suddenly surrounded by armed men, one holding a torch.

Two of them grabbed Rory. He did not fight them.

"Nay!" she said.

"Lady Felicia," said the apparent leader. "Are ye . . . ?"

"I am not badly hurt. And let him go. He just saved my life from that . . ." She looked down at Morneith's body. Her voice sounded stricken.

The two men held on to Rory, and he did not try to get loose. She had nearly died, and then she had killed a man. Even if he had been a monster, Rory knew she must have some guilt, regret. Regardless of what she had said, he felt responsible for it all.

"I am sorry, my lady. We have orders," the leader of the men said. "I will have to take him to your uncle."

He saw her tense. "Nay," she said again.

But he knew it was useless. A favorite of the king had been killed. Rory had kidnapped the Campbell's niece and had held his son. They were not going to let him go.

And Felicia's wounds needed attention. "Go with them," he said in a harsh voice.

She got that stubborn look again.

"Please," he added, unable to mask the desperation in his voice.

She stared at him in the light of the torch. Then she nodded in recognition of her own helplessness. "I will talk to Jamie."

Rory thought it would do little good, but he wanted her away. He nodded as if he thought it would make everything right.

Before any of the Campbell men could react, she took the few steps separating them and stood on tiptoes. She kissed him, making a public announcement to everyone there.

Then he was hustled off.

Chapter 30

✤

*B*ANDAGED and dressed in a gown her uncle had somehow found, Felicia was summoned to her uncle's room. Had she not been, she had planned to confront him on her own terms. She had to know what was happening to Rory.

She had mentally prepared a heated defense of him. He had exposed a traitor. He had saved her life. The king and her uncle should reward him, not imprison him.

Her uncle regarded her as if she were a strange being from a faraway country, as if he could not believe she was a Campbell.

"You are a disobedient child."

She thrust her chin up. "I am not a child, Uncle." She knew she probably had looked like one when, hours earlier, she had first entered the Campbell rooms with her shorn hair and lad's clothes. He had taken one look at her and demanded that she dress as befitted her station.

She had started to argue, demanding to know what he was going to do with Rory, when Jamie entered. He looked unsteady, and blood covered the left side of his blond hair.

She ran over to him. "They have taken Rory."

"I know," he said, sitting down wearily next to his father.

The interruption did not halt her uncle's tirade.

"Nay. You are not a child, and that is the problem." He shook his head as if he were at a complete loss as to what to do with her. "You have been compromised," he finally said. "You have traveled with the Maclean with no chaperons. You have stayed alone with him."

Then he had ordered her from the room. She had obediently changed clothes and waited, praying that Jamie could weave a certain magic.

Now she was back, and her uncle was no less fierce. James, standing at her side, winked at her.

Her uncle glared at her. "Jamie tells me there is naught to do but marry him."

She was stunned. Her uncle advocating a marriage with a Maclean. She looked over at Jamie.

"He does not want me," she said.

Her uncle roared with displeasure. "Of course he wants you. Jamie says he loves you. He was ready to defy the king for you. I will have the scamp's head if he does not wed you after destroying your good name."

Jamie *had* woven magic.

And yet he would have to weave more in order to convince Rory to wed her.

Her silence obviously annoyed Campbell. "I will speak with him myself," he said, his voice terse with annoyance. "A Maclean, my God. Could you not find anyone else to foist yourself upon?" Jamie had obviously told him that her abduction was really no abduction at all.

"No," she said. "And I will not force him into an unwanted marriage. Just," she added defiantly, "as I would not be forced into one."

Baffled, Angus Campbell stared at her. She knew he was not used to being defied. And now both she and Jamie, his son, had done exactly that. He obviously did not know how to proceed.

He blustered. "Whether you like it or not, I will have a word with the Maclean. You are dismissed."

His face was red, and she feared he might have an attack.

"I will not," she said. "Do as you like, Uncle, and so will I. You can never force me to agree to something he does not want." She left, her small triumph overshadowed by a great hole in her heart. She wanted Rory more than life itself, but she would not force him into something he felt was wrong. And she knew how deeply he felt that he might have in some way been responsible for the deaths of two women he loved, and how he feared, above all, to be responsible for yet another.

RORY paced the small cold cell in Edinburgh Castle. Now he knew how Jamie had felt, and he suffered regret at having held him in a cell. He prayed that Jamie had survived this night's disaster, and that Felicia's wounds were slight. Even slight, though, there was danger of infection.

Since meeting Felicia, he had found himself praying quite often.

He saw a light approaching through the window in the iron door and stood. He had no idea as to what might come. All he knew was that he had made a terrible mess of everything. Lachlan was wounded, as was Jamie, and Felicia . . . God only knew what her fate would be.

The door creaked open.

Jamie stood in the flickering light.

There was something quite ironic about the situation. Jamie stepped inside with a torch and placed it in a sconce. He regarded Rory for a long moment. He looked wan, and Rory saw the large bump on the back of his head.

"Do you love my cousin?" he asked bluntly.

No comment could have surprised Rory more. "Aye," he said, refusing to lie to Jamie.

"She does not think so. My father says you must marry her, that she has been so compromised that no other man will have her. But she refuses. She says she will not force you into a marriage you do not want."

Agony sliced through him. "It is not a matter of what I do or do not want," he said.

"I should hate to have to defend my cousin's honor," Jamie pressed.

"I have lost two wives," Rory said, "and a child. I do not want Felicia to be a third."

"You surely do not believe in the curse?"

Mayhap he did. It was easier to believe that than to believe that his acts of nearly fifteen years ago had brought an ugly retribution.

"She loves you," Jamie said. "She has fought for you, and now she is ready to give up her life for you. I would say you are thinking of yourself rather than her."

The observation hit Rory like a lance in the heart. Perhaps he was doing exactly that.

"She is waiting outside," Jamie said and stepped out, leaving the door open for Felicia.

She was back in a gown, her cropped hair hid by a head covering. She did not rush into his arms, but stood in front of him, her face part hope and part fear.

That he had caused her so much uncertainty made him wince. He had brought her little but heartbreak and danger.

The last time he had seen her, she had thrust caution away and whispered words that had carved a place in his soul: "I love you."

But she had to know something else first. Then she would turn away from him.

He sat down on the hard stone ledge that served as a bed and drew her down next to him. "It is not only the curse," he said. "Years ago, I led a raid on Campbell property. I was young. I did not know how to lead. Women were killed, along with a child.

"I know not whether the curse has affected Maclean wives, but I cannot help but believe my own actions that day might have doomed mine."

He waited for disgust to fill her eyes.

"Did you kill any of them?" she asked.

"Nay, but I should have been able to stop it."

Compassion filled her face, and she took his hand. "You believe that is why your Maggie died? And Anne?"

He said nothing, the silence an admission.

"I thought it was the curse, and I have had my own share of guilt for that," she said. "It is time for all the hatred to end. I think my uncle is ready. He truly loves Jamie, and Lachlan saved his life. And despite his bluster, he knows he almost married me to a traitor because of his own ambition."

Rory touched her face. She was so earnest, and bonny, and enchanting. She thought she could change the world.

A spark of hope ignited in him. Perhaps she could.

But she was not finished. "And if it was the curse," she said, "a marriage, a love, between the Macleans and Campbells could end it for all time. It is our duty to our country, she added solemnly. But there was a sparkle in her eye, and a grin beginning on her lips."

He looked down at the sudden mischief in her eyes. Then it fled. "I've had few choices," she said. "Do you not know that I would prefer years with you, even months, than a lifetime without you? Do you not understand enough to let me make that choice?"

Jamie's words echoed in his mind. *You are thinking of yourself*.

He was right! Rory realized he had been thinking of his own pain, his guilt, and never considered her own. He wrapped his arms around her, felt the warmth of her body, and feasted on the love in her eyes.

"The king," he warned, "might not feel so benevolent."

"If my uncle is considering a marriage, then he must know the king will approve as well," she said wryly.

He pulled her tighter against him. Perhaps she was wrong. Perhaps he would still be tried by the king, but Felicia was worth fighting for.

She clutched at him as if her life depended on him. He suddenly realized that he felt the same way. Felicia had brought warmth and love and laughter into his life. He kissed her long and hard.

When they finally separated, she looked up at him. "Will you take me on your ship with you?"

He was going to say no. It was too dangerous. And then he looked at her face again and saw the hope and eagerness, the curiosity and intelligence. "Aye," he said, knowing he could do no less, and he felt an exhilaration at the thought of having her beside him, of sharing all that he loved with the woman he loved.

Her smile was brilliant. It lit his heart.

He was learning to trust again. Trust Felicia. But most of all trust himself.

The door opened again. Jamie stood there, and he looked at both of them solemnly, then smiled.

"The king wants to see you. Both of you."

THE audience was short.

Angus Campbell sat next to the king. The king's wife, Margaret, sat on the other side.

Rory and Felicia entered, hands locked together. Felicia glanced around at the faces, trying to read the verdict. What if her actions had hurt the Maclean clan?

Then the doors opened again, and Lachlan entered as well. His arm was bound against his chest, but his eyes were bright. She saw Rory glance at him, nod his approval.

King James studied the three of them for several moments. She sensed that he enjoyed their suspense.

Then he rose and approached them. "Ian Stewart and Dugald Cameron have informed me of everything they heard, and we have evidence from Jamie Campbell as well. In addition, one of Lord Morneith's men was discovered searching James Campbell's room while Morneith was meeting young Jamie at the inn. He has confessed to meetings with the English. A large amount of gold was found in Lord Morneith's residence, along with a document from the Duke of Buckingham, promising him certain lands in exchange for special services.

He waited a moment to let the words settle. "We owe you a debt of gratitude, and it would pleasure us if you accepted something in return."

"A marriage," grumbled Angus Campbell. "The blackguard has tarnished my nieces's name."

King James looked toward Rory in question.

Felicia froze. Rory had not actually asked her to marry him. What if he resented being forced into something he was not quite ready for?

But he did not. Instead, he turned to her. His tense lips gave way to a wondrous smile, one she had never seen before. He held out his hand to her. "Felicia, will you be my wife? Will you join with me in love to end the curse of fear and hatred and revenge that have divided our people?"

She was stunned at the words, at the heartfelt intensity of them. It was the first time he'd mentioned love. Her heart started to swell. She saw his smile begin to fade at her apparent hesitancy.

"Oh, yes," she cried, and in front of uncle, cousin, future brother-in-law, king and queen, lifted on tiptoes and kissed him.

Someone clapped, but he was returning her kiss, and she cared not who it was.

"The lass has no decorum," she heard her uncle mutter.

Rory finally drew away, and she turned. The queen's

hands were clasped together, and Felicia knew she had been the one who had clapped.

"The Campbells and Macleans," the king said. "If only we could end every feud in Scotland in such a way," he said. "I expect to be invited to the wedding." He stood and held out his hand to his queen, his eyes warmly intent on hers. They left the room, hand in hand.

Her uncle was left. He scowled as he approached them. He stared at them for a long time. "Cannot say I envy you, Maclean," he said. "She will drive a man mad."

It was as much approval as Felicia thought he would ever get from the old laird.

Rory only grinned. "I suspect you are right."

He took her hand in his and offered the other to the Campbell. To Felicia's surprise, the man seized it. Jamie grinned, and Lachlan nodded his approval.

Her heart sang. She reached up and kissed her uncle for the first time in her memory. He turned red, muttered, and looked flustered.

Then she and Rory left, hands —and lives—entwined.

They had a wedding to plan.

Epilogue

ℛ ORY heard the cry of a newborn babe.

He did not wait a second longer. He burst into his wife's room.

The midwife he'd had in residence these last two weeks was cleaning the babe with a linen cloth. Alina stood beside her, beaming as if she herself was a mother. And she would be, if young John had anything to do with it.

The midwife stood, cooing over the wriggling babe. "A lass," she said. "A foine, healthy lassie."

Rory's breath came back. Slowly.

Felicia smiled wearily. She looked wan.

Rory tenderly took his daughter in his arms, then sat on Fecilia's bed and displayed the bairn to her mother. Felicia investigated every inch, down to the smallest toe. Her smile would light the darkest night.

"What shall we name her?" he asked. It was too bad Felicia was already taken. Felicia meant happiness and that was what she had given him in full measure. He wanted the same for his daughter.

"I like Margaret," she said. "You told me your Maggie loved to laugh. And smile."

His heart moved inside his chest. He had told her about Margaret—Maggie—and she had listened without the jealousy he had felt when he thought she cared about Jamie in ways more deep than friendship. Her heart was huge, and she harbored an empathy and compassion that never ceased to humble him.

He nodded, unable to speak.

She smiled wanly. "You have a daughter as well as a son. Two healthy bairns."

"And my wife?"

"Content. And ever so happy." Her eyes glistened with tears, but he knew they were happy ones.

He felt the tension within him fade. Despite the fact that first birth had gone easily and young Jamie was thriving, he felt fear when she'd told him she was with child again.

Their first years together had been beyond his dreams. Lachlan had earned the respect of the Macleans and had stayed at Inverleith while Rory had returned to the sea, his wife beside him. His crew had been dismayed at first, afraid she would bring bad luck, but the voyage had been successful beyond their expectations. Each member had come to respect Felicia, who never complained and tended even the lowest member with great care and gentleness.

They had traveled to France, then Venice, and he would always remember the pure joy in her face as the wind caressed her face on board and the wonder in her eyes as she saw new lands.

Now she glowed with love, and the wonder was for her children. Their children. She reveled in motherhood, and every time he saw her with his son, he melted inside.

For her sake, he had tried to smother his fear when she

announced she was with child again. He had declined to go to sea and, instead, sent Lachlan in his place. The castle he'd once hated had become a haven. He and Jamie had found a deep friendship, and Jamie's father had gradually, though sullenly, accepted the marriage and the end of the feud. It had bought a new peace to Maclean lands, and both crops and livestock were flourishing. For the first time in his memory, fear among the Macleans had seeped away, and marriages, once rare, were becoming commonplace.

Although his arm would always be stiff, Lachlan had readily taken to the sea. It suited his personality far better than Rory had ever hoped, and his half brother continued the seagoing tradition that had brought Macleans wealth.

None of that mattered now, though.

Alina leaned down and picked up the baby. Felicia knew it was only a matter of time before Alina and young John wed. John had a crippled arm and Alina a crippled leg but their love, youthful as it was, made everyone else seem crippled instead.

"Now you know the end of the tale," Felicia said to her. "The prince came from the woods. He did not want to be a prince but he could not avoid what he was."

Rory now knew the tale she had started long ago. The whimsy that had a delayed ending.

Felicia reached out a hand to him, and he took it, clasping it tightly. "It is gone," she whispered. "The curse is gone forever."

Lachlan entered after a small knock. Just returned from a voyage to be by his brother's side during this event, he had been hovering outside. He held young Jamie, who, at eighteen months, was scrambling to be put down.

"See your sister," Lachlan said, leaning over so the lad could get a better look.

Jamie grabbed his sister's tiny hand, and wee Margaret's fist went around one of his fingers. Jamie grinned happily.

His heart brimming over, Rory watched as his wife put

her hand around both her children's hands. She would protect them as fiercely as she protected all that was dear in her life.

He knew then the curse was gone, destroyed by her great spirit.

And a love that he knew now could conquer anything.

In 1988, **Patricia Potter** won the Maggie Award and a Reviewer's Choice Award from *Romantic Times* for her first novel. She has been named Storyteller of the Year by *Romantic Times* and has received the magazine's Career Achievement Award for Western Historical Romance along with numerous Reviewer's Choice nominations and awards.

She has won three Maggie awards, is a three-time RITA finalist, and has been on the *USA Today* bestseller list. Her books have been alternate choices for the Doubleday Book Club.

Prior to writing fiction, she was a newspaper reporter with the *Atlanta Journal* and president of a public relations firm in Atlanta. She has served as president of Georgia Romance Writers and board member of River City Romance Writers, and is currently a member of the national board of Romance Writers of America.

Penguin Group (USA)
is proud to present
GREAT READS—GUARANTEED!

**We are so confident that you will love
this book that we are offering a
100% money-back guarantee!**

If you are not 100% satisfied with this
publication, Penguin Group (USA) will refund
your money—no questions asked!
Simply return the book before
April 1, 2005 for a full refund.

**With a guarantee like this one,
you have nothing to lose!**